THE DECEIVERS

THE
DECEIVERS

KRISTEN SIMMONS

**TOR
TEEN**

A TOM DOHERTY ASSOCIATES BOOK
NEW YORK

THE DECEIVERS

Copyright © 2019 by Kristen Simmons

A Tor Teen Book
Published by Tom Doherty Associates
175 Fifth Avenue
New York, NY 10010

www.tor-forge.com

Tor® is a registered trademark of Macmillan Publishing Group, LLC.

The Library of Congress Cataloging-in-Publication Data is available upon request.

ISBN 978-1-250-17579-3 (hardcover)
ISBN 978-1-250-17581-6 (ebook)

Our books may be purchased in bulk for promotional, educational, or business use. Please contact your local bookseller or the Macmillan Corporate and Premium Sales Department at 1-800-221-7945, extension 5442, or by email at MacmillanSpecialMarkets@macmillan.com.

First Edition: February 2019

Printed in the United States of America

0 9 8 7 6 5 4 3 2 1

For anyone who's ever clawed their way out of a hole,
Scraped by to get what they need,
Or had a dream they were told would never come true.

Don't give up.
I didn't.

THE DECEIVERS

CHAPTER 1

Some parents tell their kids they can be anything. Mine did not. I was not told that if I worked hard, my dreams would come true. Or that life was fair. Or that wishes were made of stardust, or candy canes, or were delivered by unicorns.

I was told the truth: that some people get lucky, and some people don't, which is why I'm skipping fifth period to ride an elevator in one of swanky Uptown's old arts buildings.

"What do you mean it's this weekend?"

Holding my cell tightly against my ear, I drill my opposite thumb into my temple, careful not to let the four girls entering the elevator on the fifth floor see the phone's blank screen.

They're late. According to the Copeland Ballet Academy's online schedule, Dance II—a requirement for all third-year students—gets out at ten to four on Mondays. Now I've only got twenty minutes to book it down Lake Street and catch the red line to Devon Park. If I miss it, I'm late for work at Pete's, and that's the last thing I need.

I've got five minutes to work some magic.

"No." I sigh heavily, catching the nearest girl's attention. She's got to be around my age. Sixteen, maybe a year older. Everything on her copper-brown face seems stretched by the tight bun she's wearing on the back of her head. Even her eyes seem a little too wide, like blinking takes effort. But she's pretty. Graceful, like a ballerina.

I stand a little straighter. I can be graceful. Kind of.

From the corner of my eye, I study their outfits. Two are wearing athletic shorts over pastel tights. All have on loose cover-ups made from the kind of fabric you can't wash in a machine. Soft, like cotton candy.

My black, shredded leggings, are reflected in every walled mirror in this tiny car, and I fight the sudden urge to glare at Wide Eyes, who looks like she's trying to decide if my lace-up boots and camo tank top are some designer brand.

Sorry, but not everyone's got Daddy's credit card in their back pocket.

"No, it's not your fault." I hoist my messenger bag up my shoulder and speak a little louder, just over the girls' conversation. "We knew it was coming." I make the Life is Hard Face. Wipe away a pretend tear with the side of my thumb.

Third floor.

Second.

A familiar rush fills my veins, but it's chased by a sharp prickling right beneath my collarbones, and a voice in my ear that says they don't deserve this.

I shove it aside.

"I'll see if I can sell the tickets," I continue. "Don't worry about that. Someone's going to want them. I mean, it's not every day the Joffrey Ballet does a recital."

One girl elbows another. I catch the tilt of her head in the reflection of the mirrored wall. They're all silent now, pretending to check their own phones or staring at the floor. Politely listening in on a conversation I'm only pretending to have.

"Mom, don't worry about it. I'm not missing the funeral. I'll . . . have another shot to meet David. It's no big deal. This is more important."

Ding. The elevator reaches the bottom floor with a gentle bounce. The gleaming metal doors part, revealing a lobby vastly different from the shiny upper levels filled by the Copeland Academy. Darkly stained wooden floors meet murals of dancers and musicians. Marble angel statues guard the upper corners. An old glass chandelier hangs from the ceiling. The building is a hundred and something years old, a historical landmark refurbished by the Sterling Foundation. At least, that's what the sign beside the front door says.

I step out of the elevator, nearly bumping into a guy with inky-black hair. He doesn't look up as he moves past, and I fight the urge to glare at him, instead saying a quick, "I love you," and "I'll see you soon," into the powerless phone before stuffing it into my bag. Pausing for effect, I drop my head and smooth back a mess of short, dark waves, still unused to how the blunt ends feel between my fingertips. I tried to comb it down for today's performance, but it sticks out in every direction anyhow.

"Oh, hi. Sorry. Are you all right?" It's Wide Eyes's friend, one of the elevator eavesdroppers. She's got a rich, unexpected accent, which reminds me a little of this mobster movie our neighbor used to watch on full blast every night. Standing beside me, she grips the strap of the duffel bag crossed over her chest. Her dark hair is back like the others', though it hangs in a long braid between her shoulders, the way mine used to.

I jerk my head in her direction, as if she's caught me by surprise, and give a little sniffle.

"Yeah," I say quickly. "Yes. I'm fine." My short, embarrassed laugh relaxes their rigid postures as I turn to face the semicircle they've formed. "It's just . . . my grandfather passed away, and I need to go to the funeral this weekend."

People always go for dead grandparents. It's one of the most universally relatable hardships.

"That's so sad." Wide Eyes pouts, one hand flattening over her heart. She's faking sympathy while I'm faking the reason behind it.

There's a nice symmetry to that.

"Thanks." I check the gold-framed clock above the elevators.

Two minutes to close the deal. My pulse begins to beat in time with the second hand.

"My mom really needs me. We were supposed to go see this recital together this weekend."

"The Joffrey recital," says Accent, with enough hitch to let me know I've got her, I just need to reel her in. The other girls look at me like I'm solid gold, and I'd be lying if I said I didn't want this minute to stretch a little longer. Sometimes it's nice to have something other people want.

"That's right. And get this." I lean in, and they lean in, too, ready for the secret. "I had tickets right behind David Aranoff."

"David Aranoff? Like the *director*, David Aranoff?" asks Wide Eyes.

I sigh again, relieved that they recognized the name. I'd never heard of the guy before two days ago, when I'd searched *Important Ballet Directors*. His name was the first to come up. "Bummer, right?"

"What's he doing in town? I thought he never left New York!" Another of the four gapes at me.

"He's got friends here," I say. "Maybe a lover. I don't know."

I giggle. *She* giggles.

One minute and counting.

They all look to the girl with the accent, waiting for her to take the lead.

Come on, I will her. But she doesn't move.

She needs a little push.

"You guys wouldn't want to buy them, would you?"

I open the messenger bag and take out two paper tickets I printed from the library last week. They may be in the top row of the balcony, but the price I paid—seventy bucks apiece—is absent, as it always is when you purchase from my favorite secondary ticket broker, Tix.com.

Or rather, when you print, and reprint, and reprint again. No one knows there's a problem until they show up at the event and find their ticket's already been scanned. By that time, I've already sold them three times over.

"How much?" asks Accent.

"I don't know. I bought them for three hundred. Maybe two fifty?"

Wide Eyes sees the row letter YY and makes a choking sound.

"Why would David Aranoff sit way back there?" Accent asks, skeptical.

"Don't ask me," I say. "My uncle knows his assistant. That's who booked the tickets."

The best lies are simple, that way you can't screw them up.

"Maybe he's scouting for an opening in New York and doesn't want to be recognized," says Giggles, now very serious.

"That's exactly what I was thinking." Sort of.

The door outside opens, letting in a wave of oppressive heat off the street. My time is almost up, but they hesitate.

I carefully tuck the tickets back into my bag. "Never mind. I'll see if one of the girls in my tap class wants them. Good talking to you." That seems like a polite, Uptown thing to say.

"Wait."

Accent's voice rebounds off the low, plaster ceiling.

"I'll give you one eighty," she says.

I stop, hiding my smirk, swallowing the cheer rising in my chest. My toes tap in my boots. I want to dance. Ballet, tap, I don't even care. One eighty is sixty bucks more than I got when I pulled this same hustle yesterday outside Frasier Music Hall.

"Two hundred," I say. *"Cash."*

Another beat, and then she nods.

CHAPTER 2

I run down Lake Street, fueled by adrenaline and desperation and the two hundred dollars in the messenger bag bouncing against my hip. The June air is hot and heavy, and I feel like a sponge, soaking it all in, but it doesn't slow me down. Nothing could right now.

A siren rises over the breath whooshing in my ears. The patchy grass and green leaves of the park on my right are only a blur as I skirt around businessmen and -women in their black suits, tourists with their shopping bags, street musicians with their upside-down bucket drums and cardboard signs. Someone nearby is selling popcorn; the smell of it makes my stomach grumble. Someone's singing, too, though maybe they shouldn't be.

The Lake Street SCTA station is above ground, the tracks traveling over the city streets, and by the time I get there the silver train is pulling in overhead. I don't need to see the red streak down the side to know it's mine. Lungs burning, I give a final push, lunging up the dirty cement stairs past a man playing a saxophone to the open-air platform.

"Wait!" I call, as if this might actually help. Shoving my prepaid card into the metal box, I hoist my bag up to shoulder level, turn sideways, and wedge through the turnstile before it's clear for me to pass. From overhead comes a loud clang, followed by an automated operator's voice: *Stand clear of the doors.*

In my mind, I can see Pete's ruddy, scrunched-up face asking what took me so long, and my stomach tightens. Feet slapping across the concrete, I reach for the closing doors. It's fifty minutes until the next red line comes through. None of the other trains go that far south.

Victory begins to crumble in my chest.

With a clap, the doors bounce open. The only way that happens is if someone was blocking one of them, and as I look, I see a guy in a gray T-shirt and jeans slipping inside the train further down the platform.

Stand clear of the doors, comes the voice from above.

I jump into the cool compartment, silently thanking the guy in the next car, and breathe a huge sigh of relief.

"Lucky you," says a woman in the seat nearest the door, tucking earbuds beneath her frizzy hair. I wipe the sweat off my forehead with the back of my hand. She has no idea.

The seats are all filled, so I hook my arm around a pole as the red line shudders, and then pulls out of the station.

Next stop City Center, says the automated voice as I fix the blunt, wavy ponytail that only holds three-quarters of my hair. I've ridden this train a hundred times since I was a kid, but still my gaze finds a map hanging at the front of the compartment. Under the bold black letters *Sikawa City Transit Authority* is a web of colored lines. Blue and green twist north. Yellow heads west to the suburbs and the airport. Red drops straight down. Someone's scratched out the last stop—White Bank—and drawn a head tilted back, mouth open, as if swallowing any train that ventures that low.

People say Sikawa City's a nice place, but those people obviously haven't been south of the river. It stretches out from Lake Michigan, forking at the old newspaper factory to divide the city in half. The seven neighborhoods north of Uptown are filled with private schools, coffee shops, and gated communities. The nine below they call the Circles of Hell for a reason. Devon Park, where I live, is near the bottom.

Rocking on its track, the train crosses the river and cuts through downtown, giant stone buildings rising outside the windows, stretching into the hazy sky. The money's burning a hole in my bag. I keep reaching my hand inside just to make sure it's there.

Most of the people in my car get off at City Center, leaving only a handful of stragglers and the lingering scent of fast-food burgers. As soon as they're gone, I claim one of the stained yellow seats facing the front of the train and open my bag. Careful to keep the bills hidden in the little cave of worn leather, I count them slowly, savoring the crisp feel between my fingertips.

Those girls didn't need this. If they had this much cash to shell out for back row show tickets, they have a lot more where that came from. Thanks to their poor judgment of character, I'm now two hundred dollars closer to college.

One day I'm getting out of Devon Park, and when I do, I'm not looking back.

That thought alone is enough to unknot the worry inside me, and I glance over my shoulder, just to make sure no one saw the money. Earbuds is still facing the other way, oblivious. In the seat behind me, a man in a stained undershirt is snoring, chin on his chest.

My gaze stops on a guy on the back of the train, lanky and slouched in his seat, staring through cool, black-rimmed glasses in my direction.

Held by his gaze, I grow still. Not because he's just taken my breath away or anything, but because he's clearly caught, and he's clearly comfortable *being* caught. Most people can't even really look like this at people they know, much less a stranger.

I've never seen him before. His face is all bold lines and tan skin. Dark eyes and glossy black hair. His lips pull into a small, one-sided smirk, drawing my focus. He's the kind of guy you remember, and though I balk, it might actually be my lucky day, because he's definitely not ugly.

Then, as if it didn't happen, he removes a pen from his pocket, lowers his gaze, and begins to write something inside the book on his lap.

And that stupid grin that's somehow crept onto my face fades, because I realize he probably wasn't checking me out, but my money.

On his charcoal-gray shirt is the silhouette of a bird—a raven, maybe—with a sharp beak and pointed talons. Now that I'm looking, I'm sure it's the same shirt I saw on the guy who blocked the doors at the Lake Street Station. I thought he was in the car behind mine; if he switched he must have done it at the last station when people were getting on and off. I would have noticed otherwise.

Wariness prickles down my spine. There was a guy with a similar build and black hair in the arts building, too. I didn't get a good look at his face, but this could have been him.

How long has he been following me?

I stuff the folded money into the very bottom of the bag. Playing it cool, I glance again over my shoulder. He isn't looking anymore. In fact, he's angled himself the other way, hiding his face from my view.

Next stop, Fullbright, calls the automated voice. I jolt up, gripping the back of the seat to steady myself as the train slows. There are still six stops to Devon Park, but I'll ride in another car, thank you very much.

And if he follows, well, we'll just have to have a conversation about that.

But as I step toward the glass I realize I've got bigger problems. Three guys have spotted me through the windows and are stalking toward my doors. Two of them I know well enough from school. The third, Marcus Kilroy, I know a lot better than I wish I did. The five and a half months we dated in sophomore year will forever go down under Brynn Hilder's Poor Life Choices.

He's standing right in front of me as the doors slide back, all big, saggy clothes and bright blue eyes. He holds his arms wide, as if he's St. Peter and he just opened the gates.

"Bloody Brynn," he says. "Where you going, girl?"

"Nowhere," I mutter, which from the look on Marcus's face is exactly what he expected to hear.

CHAPTER 3

During the first week of my freshman year at Robert Jarvis High, the counselor brought in a motivational speaker—a Jarvis dropout with track marks on his arms and prison tats on his knuckles, who'd gotten clean and found the Lord and now managed some noodle place in Mercer Township. Sweat ringing his collar and the armpits of his shirt, he stormed across the squeaky gym floor, bellowing like a corner preacher, the cord of the microphone tethering him to a worn-out speaker on the free throw line.

If you want something bad enough, he told us, *find a way to make it happen.*

Approximately three seconds later, he tripped on the mic cord and crashed straight into the front row, where the underclassmen were seated cross-legged on the floor like a bunch of preschoolers. We were packed in so tightly, I had nowhere to go. He broke his nose on my forehead, painting my face red like some slasher movie, and earning me a nickname that would prove unshakable: Bloody Brynn.

After school, I passed that guy buying drugs from Max O'Malley behind the bus stop shelter. Apparently if you want something bad enough, you really do find a way to make it happen.

I slide into a seat and Marcus takes the one next to me, trapping me against the window. As the train lurches forward, his arm comes over my shoulders. I shrug him off with a glare as his boys—Jesse and Terrance—take the double seat behind us.

"What were you doing in the city?" Marcus's bare arm skims mine, shades darker than my tan skin. His dad was in the Irish mob, which is where he got his blue eyes, but his pretty complexion comes from his mom, who spends all her time working doubles at the Walgreens in Amelia. Somehow, despite my father's brown skin, I still show my mom's pink blush.

"None of your business." I grip the bag a little closer against my chest.

"Come on. You missed last period. It's got to be good for Bloody Brynn to miss school."

It won't help to tell him not to call me that. The only time he ever stopped was when we were dating.

"Why were you at Jarvis anyway?" He's never there. I'm pretty sure he'd be an eighth-year senior if he ever tried to graduate.

"Met up with some friends at St. Agnes," he says, which means selling off Pete's stash to the after-school crowd at the Catholic school, a few blocks away from the Fullbright train station. I look out the window with a snort.

Pete, my mom's model citizen boyfriend, sells pharmacy-grade narcotics, which he roped Marcus into dealing sometime around the expiration date of our doomed relationship.

As it turned out, Marcus liked making money more than he liked me.

Now he's Pete's lapdog, and the only reason I'm sitting next to him on this train is because if I don't, he'll probably tell his boss I was acting weird and avoiding him. Then Pete'll get paranoid, and do something stupid, like accuse me of going to the cops, and bring the house down on my mom and me.

It's not worth it.

So I play nice—or at least nice for me, anyway—because it's better than the alternative.

"I had to turn in my time card at the library," I say. "I left after fourth period to make sure my supervisor got it before she did paychecks."

Marcus should go for this. I've been cleaning at the Sycamore branch four nights a week since before he and I broke up.

"Well, after you get off tonight you should swing by the old soap factory. There's a bunch of bands playing tonight and a spot on the couch with your name on it."

Because that's the royal treatment. A flea-ridden couch at the back of a dirty warehouse, where you can't get a cup of water, but you can buy a pill in every color of the rainbow.

"Thanks but no thanks," I say. "Math final tomorrow."

He groans, kicking one foot up onto the chair in front of him. "When are you ever going to use that stuff anyway?" I hate when he acts like he's stupid. He and I both know he could ace that final if he actually bothered to take it. He's always been good with numbers.

"One ounce for twenty bucks, two ounces for forty," says Jesse behind us.

"There you go," I say. "Math at its finest."

"Come with us." Marcus bumps my shoulder, and for a second I'm reminded what drew me to him in the first place. Not his confidence or the way he looks, but that softness right beneath the surface.

It's deeper, and harder to find these days.

"I'll pass," I say. "Some of us actually want to do something with our lives, you know."

He looks away, and I sort of feel bad for him. I don't know why. He's the one who signed up to work for Pete. He's the one who's missing school to sell drugs. No one made him do anything.

"Fancy Ms. Hilder's getting too good for us lowlifes," Marcus tells the others, his voice harder. "Maybe she's forgetting where she came from."

I steel myself against his words, and the simmering threat beneath them.

"How," I say through my teeth, "could I ever forget that?"

Of anyone, he knows the battle I fight. That I work late cleaning at the library, then wake up at five to make the bus to school. That every decision I make is weighted by the kind of consequences that spell a black eye, or jail, or worse.

Not like he's got it so much better.

At the Amelia Station, I glance back over my shoulder. The guy I saw earlier is still there, though he's now fully engrossed in his book. I shove down a little lower in my seat, hating that the wall Marcus and his friends put between us is actually offering a kind of protection. People from my neighborhood might tear each other apart, but they don't let anybody from the outside do it.

For the next forty minutes, Marcus and his friends talk about music while I get to work on my math study guide. Most colleges want to see algebra and trigonometry on your transcripts, but Jarvis only offers the basics. Math I-IV. Half of the students still fail.

I tune the others out, focusing on the future. I won't be distracted. One test at a time is how I get out of this place.

When we reach the Devon Park station, I put my math homework away and follow the other three out, sparing one last glance for the boy and his book.

He doesn't even look up. It makes me wonder if I imagined the whole thing.

18 MIDGARD DRIVE marks the end of a row of townhouses, divided into the upper and lower floors by a set of concrete steps leading to a raised doorway. Like all the other buildings in Devon Park, it's got a redbrick face, a result of some fire that started a hundred-something years ago by a cow that kicked over a lantern in a barn. The flames leveled the factories that Devon Park was known for, and as a result, everything was rebuilt in nonflammable material.

It's a shame it can't all burn again.

Our place, #18, is upstairs. Mom bought it flat-out when I was six, in the lawsuit that came after my father was shot and killed in a holdup at the convenience store around the corner. You'd think that would have given her a reason to get as far away from this hellhole as possible, but it didn't.

Pete used to live in #17, beneath our place, but he moved upstairs after my mom's second divorce, when I was ten. Now he runs his little pharmaceutical business out of the sub-level floor.

I sneak past the lower door, now barred by a black gate, and head up the steps. The bus from the SCTA station was late, as usual, which means I've got two hours to cram before I have to catch another bus to Sycamore for work.

My key jams in the lock, like always, then gives, and with a squeak the screen door pulls open. I slip inside quickly, bypassing the narrow living room with its blue velvet furniture and haze of cigarette smoke, to jog up the stairs.

"Brynn? Is that you?" my mom calls over the overenthusiastic hosts of *Pop Store*, her favorite celebrity gossip TV show.

"Nope! Intruder. Call the cops."

There are three rooms upstairs. My bedroom, the Devil's Chambers where Pete crashes with my mom, and a bathroom split between them. The Easter-egg-yellow walls are lined with an almost straight wallpaper border of little cartoon angels Mom picked up when she found The Church, aka married Reverend Willis, the preacher who did my dad's funeral.

It took him about four months to run for the hills. Can't say I totally blame him.

Hurrying into my bedroom, I close and lock the door behind me. Sweat beads on my forehead. In the summer it's always a sauna upstairs. Opening a window just makes it worse.

I flip on a fan that creaks as it rotates from right to left to stir the soupy air, and kneel beside my twin bed. With the strap of my bag still crossed over my shoulder, I push aside the white sheets and slide my hands between the worn-out box spring and mattress. My fingers reach the ragged edges of a hole, then feel inside, to where a plastic pencil box should be hiding between the springs. I've already mentally added up my earnings. With today's two hundred combined with what I already have, I've got just over four thousand total. That's three classes at Sikawa CC, plus the application fees.

One more year at Jarvis, and I'm a college girl.

But my fingers don't feel the smooth plastic of the box. I pull the mattress toward me, ducking beneath it to look up at the hole, but it's not there.

A cold hand of panic closes around my chest.

It has to be here. It's *always* here.

I push the mattress off the side of the bed, searching the box spring for anywhere it may have fallen. My hand digs deeper into the mattress itself, shaking it to hear the plastic bounce against the springs.

Nothing.

Ripping off my bag, I drop to my knees, ear pressed to the carpet as my hand stretches beneath the bed. Could I have moved it somewhere? Fallen asleep counting it last night, and left it on my nightstand? I look there now, but there's no box.

The money is gone.

It can't be gone, though. It must be here somewhere. I go through every drawer, look beneath every piece of furniture, toss the clothes out of my closet, but nothing. The fear inside me is growing, icy tendrils snaking around my lungs. I need that money. I *earned* that money—not just running cons, but working at the library. Mom doesn't know where I keep it. Pete never comes in here.

I don't think.

Racing out the door, I jog down the stairs, throwing myself in front of the TV in the living room. Mom's already wearing her work clothes—a snug black T-shirt that says *Gridiron Sports Bar* across the left boob, and tight white shorts over tan nylons. Her eye make-up's smoky—it accents the dark-brown irises we share—and her mouth is pulled to the side in annoyance as she leans around me.

"Watch out. They were just about to show—"

"Did you or Pete go in my room?"

"What?" She blinks up at me, then stands, mirroring my straight back and folded arms. I look like her, only tanner, seventeen years younger, and considerably less hair-sprayed.

"Did you go into my room?" I say slowly.

"No. I mean, I got some socks this morning, but I'm pretty sure they were mine anyway. Why? What's the big deal?"

Pete. It has to be him; no one else comes over. Somehow he found out about my money and decided to take it. Maybe he was playing a little joke. Maybe he thought he could take whatever he wanted, and I would just shut up and smile like everyone else in Devon Park.

Well, I won't. That was mine, and I intend to get it back.

CHAPTER 4

Thirty seconds later, I'm standing in front of the entrance to number seventeen, facing a guy twice my size in a white undershirt and stained khaki pants.

Eddie is one of Pete's bouncers. He's partial to gold things. Teeth, chains, etc. Also, bad tattoos. There's one on his bicep that haunts my dreams. It's supposed to be his daughter when she was a baby, but the giant eyes clearly belong to a swaddled goblin.

"What's the password?"

He likes to play this game where he pretends he doesn't know me. It got old after the first month. We've known each for three years.

"Let me in. I need to talk to Pete."

Mom's flip-flop footsteps clap down the stairs behind me. She keeps calling my name like she needs me, like I forgot something upstairs.

It's the same thing I do for her when she and Pete get into it.

But even if it's stupid to call Pete out, I can't let this go. This is my money. This is my future he's messed with.

When Eddie gives a low chuckle, I slip between his huge arm and the door, immediately on guard. Entering Pete's place is like stepping into a mine shaft that might cave in at any second. The dark hallway leads past a bathroom, into a kitchenette that's been converted into a bar. Pete keeps his money and pills in "the cage," the single bedroom on the left, reinforced by an iron grate and a sheet of Plexiglas. I once heard him tell Eddie it's bulletproof, but I know for a fact it's off an old camper shell he dragged in from the dumpster.

"Well if it isn't the little bookworm," Pete says as I step into the kitchen, shielding my eyes from the harsh overhead bulb. My internal temperature rises another ten degrees. Even from here I can smell his terrible cologne.

"You go through my room?" My voice is shaking. I exhale hard, trying to steady it. With Pete, there is no room for weakness.

Behind me, I can hear Mom talking with Eddie. She calls my name again.

Pete comes around the island to stand before me. He sticks his thumbs in the waistband of his jeans, rocking his hips forward. His short, thin hair is receding up the sides of his forehead. He's so close I can see every faded pock mark on his flat face.

"You're in a mood, aren't you? What's got Bloody Brynn all worked up?"

A hot flush sears my cheeks.

"I'm kidding," he says, squeezing my shoulder. "Isn't that what your friends call you?"

I shake off his grip. "Did you go through my room?"

"Why would I do a thing like that?" When he shifts, the bulb in the kitchen behind him lights him up, makes him seem like a giant, even though he's only a few inches taller than I am.

A breath lodges in my throat, hard as a stone. I won't back down like everyone else in the neighborhood. I will not be scared of him.

"I want my money back," I say.

Clear-eyed amusement fills his gaze, and brings a chill up my spine. Drunk Pete I can manage. Drunk Pete I can work around. But sober, he's smart, and twice as mean.

Mom appears beside me. Her hand closes around my elbow. "Brynn, honey, let's go upstairs. Pete's working."

"Are you accusing me of stealing?" he asks evenly.

Mom stills.

"If it's in my room, it's mine. You have no right to go in there."

"No right?" He laughs. "Do you own the house?"

"Do you?" I shoot back.

Mom tugs on my arm again. "That's enough, let's go."

Pete's humor vanishes as quickly as it comes.

"You'll be grown soon," he says, like he has no idea that my seventeenth birthday's tomorrow. "When I was your age, I was taking care of my three sisters. The bills. The food. That was all on my back. Must be nice breezing in and out, not a care in the world."

"I put in for utilities last month," I say. "And I did half the groceries."

"I told you that, honey." Mom's voice is too soft. Too soothing. Is this what I sound like when she's the one bringing the storm?

"Utilities. Groceries." He scoffs. "With the cash she's bringing in, you and me could take a little break, Allie. Head down to the beach for a couple weeks."

I want to kick him. I want to scream at him.

But mostly, I just want my money back.

"What are you talking about?" Mom says, still playful. "She gets a hundred bucks every couple weeks."

"I'm not talking about that job scrubbing toilets," says Pete. "I'm talking about the cash she's taking out of my pocket."

The air in the room shifts, blows cold on the base of my neck. A warning pounds in my temples. *Trouble,* it says. *Dangerous ground.* Pete's been toying with me since I came downstairs, but he's not anymore. He's had an agenda, and I walked right into it.

I ease back, aware of Mom's pinching grip around my elbow.

"I didn't take anything from you." Of course he would spin it that way. Say that *I'm* the one stealing from *him*. That has to be the only explanation for me getting ahead in life.

"Please," he says flatly. "Don't treat me like a stupid pigeon. I'm the one who taught you these tricks."

I cringe, but it's true. It's the most worthwhile thing he's ever given me. Personal lessons on how to cheat people out of their money.

He reaches into his back pocket, and pulls out the pencil case. The air seems to vacate from the room. I can't look away from that narrow blue box. It's like he's holding my life in the palm of his hand and can crush it with the flex of his fingers.

He pops the box open. The cash is stacked neatly inside. All three thousand, eight hundred, and twenty-five dollars.

"Oh Brynn," Mom whispers.

In a burst, I reach for it, but he snaps the case closed on my fingers. Pain zings up my hand. A cry rips from my throat as I jerk my shaking fist back against my chest.

"Where'd you get this?" he asks. "And don't say mopping floors at the library. You go through my wallet when I was sleeping? Figure out a way to get into the cage and snag yourself some pills when I was out?"

He steps closer. I step back.

He thinks I'm stealing his pills and selling them. His paranoia's reaching all new heights.

"That money has nothing to do with you," I say. "I earned it."

"Selling my product in Uptown? You know that's Wolves territory. You have any idea what they'll do to you? What they'll do to *me* if they think I crossed thirty-eighth street?"

I shiver. The Wolves of Hellsgate are a motorcycle club that runs the east side of the city. They move drugs, and shoot up rival gangs, and make Pete and Eddie look like rent-a-clowns at a county fair. A few months ago, I heard they hung one of their own upside down from a bridge. People found him with all his Wolf tattoos burned off by a blowtorch.

Who knows what they'd do to a competing dealer that crossed territory lines.

"I wouldn't touch those pills with a ten-foot pole," I say.

"Brynn's a good girl. She stays out of the business." Mom's reminder is weak.

"Then what were you doing in Uptown?" Another step, and Pete has me against the hallway wall. "You're supposed to be in school during the day, aren't you?"

Cold fear settles in the base of my stomach. Marcus must have called Pete and said he saw me on the train. In the span of a second, I try to imagine how that conversation went down. If Pete told him to tail me, or if Marcus volunteered the information. I knew they talked about me, but having it brought up like this reaches a new level of betrayal.

Mom turns to me, eyes wide. *I told you to leave it alone,* that look says. *I told you not to get involved with the drugs.*

"I . . . I wasn't selling your stuff." I manage through chattering teeth, pointing at the box. "I earned that money."

It's my only way away from him. Away from *this.*

"You ripped me off is what you did."

"I earned it," I say again. "Some of it's from the library, some of it's from cons I've run in Uptown." There's no use lying about it now.

Yes, I work a job mopping floors. Yes, it makes minimum wage.

Yes, I'm smart enough to know that isn't going to give me enough to break out of Devon Park.

But I keep it going, because Mom needs help with the bills, and the money's got to come from somewhere, and if Pete knew I was pulling in cash from cons, he'd take it, like he has now.

"What?" says Mom, and then quickly settles her voice. "See, Pete?" With shaking hands, she flattens her shirt over her stomach, over and over, though it's already flat. "This was all a mistake."

"Shut up," Pete snaps. I bite the inside of my cheek.

"Pete, honey," Mom slides in front of him. Reaches for his shoulder. "Let's talk about . . ."

His arm swings back, throwing her sideways into the kitchen island. She stays upright, but knocks a bottle off the table. The crash it makes as it hits the tile floor is loud enough to shake me to the bones.

The door closes as Eddie steps outside.

"Leave her alone." My voice is thin with fear.

Mom's at my side again. "Upstairs. Now, Brynn."

Pete glares at me, gaze narrowed. An unhinged anger, warped by desperation, takes ahold of all reason. As much as I want to leave, I want him to try to take a swing. Then I'll have permission to tear him up.

"What's it for?" He still hasn't even bothered to put the case back in his pocket, and it's killing me not to try to take it again.

"None of your business," I tell him.

"College," he says, and my skin turns blistering hot. Maybe he heard me say it earlier. If not, I know who told him. I regret every single thing I've ever said to Marcus. Every time I kissed him. Every night we snuck into my room.

"That's silly," Mom says. "Brynn's only a junior. What's she need money for college for?"

I hold still, perfectly straight. I know she's just trying to get Pete to back down, but I hate that she's not on my side.

"I don't get it." Pete's voice is lower now. "If you're so much better than the rest of us, why don't you just leave?"

I waver, like the ground is shaking beneath my feet. He can't kick me out. He doesn't own our house, Mom does.

"I can't just leave."

He leans closer. My back is pressed so hard against the wall I might knock it down.

"Sure you can. Walk out. That's all it takes."

I want to. I feel the urge to, bubbling like acid in my chest. But

I can't leave Mom here. Not like this. Even if I go to college, I'll be close enough to check on her. Close enough that she can come with me when she finally gets her act together.

I always told myself that leaving was inevitable—that this money was just part of the plan. But now that I'm facing the reality of it, I falter.

I am weak.

Weak.

The acid turns to a sob in my chest, but I don't set it free. I grit my teeth together and stare Pete straight in the face.

"You can't make me go."

"No one's leaving." Mom's voice wobbles.

Pete shakes his head at me. A high and mighty move that makes me want to scream. He takes the money from the pencil case and puts it in his pocket, then tosses the empty pencil case into the empty trash can at the corner of the kitchen. It clatters, plastic on plastic.

"You know what I do to people who steal from me?"

My hands fist, nails digging into palms. I'm strong. I'm going to be strong.

"Pete, please," Mom begs.

The longest minute of my life passes, and in his stare, I see contempt. Then he sighs, like I'm not worth the effort.

"I thought you were better than this." His voice is soft now.

I'm shaking so hard inside I don't think I could walk out of this house even if I wanted to.

"You're grounded. I don't want to see you out of your room for a month."

Somehow I find my voice. "You can't ground me." He's never attempted to punish me before.

He snorts and turns back toward the kitchen. Mom motions for me to back down, not to argue.

"What about my job?" I say. "What about *school*? I've got finals."

"It's not like you were really going to school anyway." He grabs a beer from the mini fridge on the counter. "Get in your room before I change my mind."

The last string holding me up snaps, and I grab Mom's outstretched hand. My knees are quaking as she leads me out, and up the stairs. Up we go again, all the way to my bedroom. Once there, I lower onto the box spring, my mattress still flipped on its side. I feel like I'm going to explode. Or implode. Like everything inside me is turning inward, swallowed by a black hole in my stomach.

"I'll talk to him," Mom says. Then she closes the door behind her.

CHAPTER 5

For an hour, I stay in bed, staring at the popcorn ceiling. Thinking about my lost money. Thinking about Mom bouncing off the kitchen island, and how much worse it's been before. Thinking about how heavily weighted finals are at Jarvis since so many students skip out on the last days of school, and how if I miss tomorrow's test, I'm going to fail my first class.

Mostly, I think about how much I hate Pete.

I hate him. More than I've hated anybody. More than I thought it was possible to hate somebody. But what's even worse than that poison inside is that I'm also to blame. I wasn't careful enough. I never should have left the money at home. I never should have trusted Marcus.

You can't trust anyone.

Fueled by that hate, I rise, and pace around my room. There's not much to my little sanctuary. My makeup, a few belts, and a framed picture of her and me two Christmases ago sit on a white and gold dresser. The closet is only big enough to fit my winter coat and a couple shirts. Beside my bed is a stack of Goodwill books that serve as a nightstand. Sitting on top is the same lamp I've had all my life; the shade has a cow jumping over the moon. I should probably get rid of it one of these days, but my mom likes to tell me how my dad picked it up at a flea market when she was pregnant with me, and I don't have much else from him. Seems wrong to chuck it.

Wonder Woman stares her challenge down at me from my only poster on the wall.

I can't stay here—not just for this grounding sentence. At all. I need to leave, like Pete said. But where would I go? As terrible as it is here, the streets are worse. I'm not an idiot; I don't have any other family, and anyone I'm remotely friendly with isn't stupid enough to take me in without telling Pete. I leave here with nothing, and it's just a matter of time before I'm back, head hung in shame.

But I don't have nothing. I have two hundred dollars.

Dropping to my knees, I dig through my messenger bag, pushing aside my eyeliner and lip gloss to snag the cash from the ballerinas I stuffed at the bottom. It's enough to get a roof over my head and some food in my belly for a couple days, but that's it. I need more.

There's still three more days until the Joffrey Ballet Recital.

I check my alarm clock beside the lamp. 9:07 PM. My shift at the library started an hour ago. If I leave now, I can catch the bus and get there just after ten. Jules, my supervisor, isn't on site tonight, but Matt, the night security guard, will let me in.

I don't plan on working, just using the services.

Someone working tonight will take the cash and let me put the new tickets on their credit card. I'll print some extras, then catch the train to Uptown, and sell them as people are leaving their shows in the theater district.

The idea takes root and spreads a desperate kind of hope through me. I need to make up my losses. I need to get out of here. Mom's already left for Gridiron, and Pete will be collecting money from his dealers with Eddie all night. I can leave and be back before either of them notice.

Once I've saved enough, I'll be out of here. On my own for good. I'll worry about school later.

Doubt has me crinkling the bills in my hand. What if Pete finds out I left? What if, in my absence, he takes it out on Mom? What if I can't sell the tickets, and I miss my finals, and I'm stuck here, under Pete's rule, with even less money than before?

I can't let that happen.

Tucking a knife in the back pocket of my jeans, I pack a few essentials in my messenger bag, just in case Pete finds out I'm gone and it isn't safe to come back. My prepaid phone and the charging cord. A couple shirts. Another pair of jeans. Socks and underwear. Some makeup.

I leave the rest; I don't want it looking like I ran away.

In the dark, I open my door and nearly trip over the bowl of chicken soup left on a tray outside. When Mom brought it up earlier, I ignored her, and maybe that was childish of me, but I couldn't face her after what happened downstairs. It's not that she didn't defend me. It's not even that she lets Pete talk to her the way he does, and push her around. It's because she doesn't leave, and when given the opportunity, I didn't, either.

I'm fixing that now.

Tiptoeing down the steps to the kitchen, I head to the counter beside the toaster oven, where Mom keeps a jar of quarters for the Laundromat. I shove a handful of coins into my pocket, and then, without looking back, make for the kitchen door—in case Pete is still downstairs, I don't want him seeing me leave.

Our backyard is only a small patch of dirt with an old barbeque, and I climb the chain link fence behind it, following the alley toward Shield Avenue. The city bus will take me to the Sycamore train yard, but the nearest stop is still three blocks away.

A barking dog makes me jump, and I swear under my breath as I begin to jog for the corner. Visions of Pete stomping upstairs drive me faster, and soon I'm in an all-out run toward the bus stop outside Jay's, the mini-mart where my dad worked. The windows come into view first—bright and barred like the other shops in the neighborhood. A neon sign blinks, advertising beer, and through the front door you can see rows of cigarette cartons behind the counter.

There's a shotgun behind that counter, too. I know, because my dad was reaching for it when the guy holding up the store put a bullet in his chest.

I'm going to find a way out of Devon Park. I'm going to replace that money, and find someplace steady, then earn my way into night school. I don't care if it takes me ten years. One day this place is going to be in my rearview mirror.

NO BUS TRANSFERS are needed to get to the Sycamore Library, and thirty minutes later, I'm down the steps, and jogging toward the employee entrance on the side of the gray stone building. As I approach, something at the front of the building catches my eye, and I automatically pause behind a hedge, ready to grab the knife in my boot.

A shadowed figure is passing in front of the glass doors. For a moment, I think he means to break in, and I consider running the rest of the way to the employee entrance to alert Matt the security guard. But the guy doesn't stop. He keeps walking right into the yellow wash of the parking lot lights, and it's then that I see his gray T-shirt and black hair.

My spine goes rigid.

The boy from the train.

As he turns, I can see his dark-framed glasses, and the outline of a black raven on his shirt. I duck behind the bushes, fearful he's already seen me—he would have had a clear view from the bus stop on the street, but he keeps walking toward the corner.

What is he doing here? First the arts building in Uptown, then the train, now in front of my job in Sycamore Township, at almost ten o'clock at night? This is no longer coincidence.

This guy is following me, but for what reason, I don't know.

I've never seen him before today. He could work for Pete like Marcus, but most of Pete's guys have been around downstairs. This guy doesn't look like he belongs in our neighborhood. His clothes are too nice. His back is too straight. Something tells me those jeans cost as much as I picked up from the ballerinas, so it can't just be money he's after.

What does he want?

As he rounds the corner, I abandon my plan to buy and sell more recital tickets, and instead follow him, keeping a careful distance so he doesn't catch on. I'm not stupid enough to confront him without backup—if he is some kind of stalker, I'll deal with him in a crowded place, where I'm sure he can't take me out. But I need the upper hand—I need to see where this guy's coming from—and I don't want him catching me off guard again.

Without slowing, he pulls his cell phone from his back pocket and lifts it to his ear. I'm too far away to hear who he's calling, but just in case he's on to me, I check over my shoulder to make sure he's not calling a friend to come around behind.

We're not in the nicest area of Sycamore; the tire store we pass has bars on the windows, and I can hear people fighting outside the gas station across the street. A desperate energy pushes me onward, beneath the looming stone warehouses, around the bums laid out on the sidewalk. The smell of garbage is heavy on the night breeze, and it's not until I reach the decrepit chain-link fence around the old train yard, that it finally gives way to a more metallic, rusty scent.

The boy slips through a hole in the fence, and walks toward a light in the back. As I pause, I can hear voices coming from that direction—not just one or two, but many—all raised over the steady thump of a bass.

Is he going to a party?

Before me stretches ten or more layers of track, surrounded by a sea of gravel, and lit by a high half-moon. Train cars sit dormant in small groups of two or three, covered by a graffiti I can only half make out in the shadows. Everything about this is dead wrong, but I don't stop.

I want to know why this guy has tracked me all over Sikawa City today.

Quietly as I can, I slip through a hole in the fence and jog after the guy, wincing as the rocks crunch beneath my feet.

As I get closer, I slow down, ducking behind the giant steel clasps between two cars. The voices are louder now, coming from down the row. I peek around the corner and see a lantern set on the edge of an open boxcar. Flashlight beams cut through the night, revealing a group of five people. A few more arrive from around the corner a moment later.

They're young, my age. A mix of skin colors and dress. Some of them gather around a central figure, some tan, muscular guy with blond, spikey hair who looks vaguely familiar. He says something that must be hilarious, because they all laugh. The others go get drinks from a series of bottles sitting on an overturned crate.

The guy in the raven shirt joins a separate group beside the boxcar—a boy with strawberry-blond hair who looks like a back-to-school ad in his white button-up and plaid shorts, and a guy with dark skin in a classy newsboy cap who's tucked his shirt in a little too tight. A pretty girl sits on the edge of the car, kicking her legs. Her hair is long, curly, and red as fire.

I can't lurk in the shadows without looking like I'm the creeper, so I head toward the drinks, keeping one ear turned toward the boy in the raven shirt and his friends.

"Did you finally finish the essay for Shrew?" the redhead asks him, as if this is the reason for his tardiness. I don't know who this Shrew is, but it reminds me of tomorrow's finals, which I'll be missing thanks to Pete.

"Are you just asking us because you turned it in early?" says the boy in the plaid shorts. "Because if so, I finished it last week and turned it in and she already gave me an A and told me I was the best student at Vale Hall. Fifty times better than one Charlotte Murphy."

By the way the redhead snickers, I'm guessing she's Charlotte.

The guy in the newsboy cap takes a swig from a green bottle, turning a little so that I can see the letters *NYU* on his tucked-in shirt. "It wasn't even assigned last week, Henry."

"I went back in time, *Sam*," says Plaid Shorts—Henry. "That's right. I made a time machine, and went back in time, which caused Shrew to add four thousand bonus points for ingenuity onto my original essay score."

"Then what's your Faustian Bargain?" Charlotte presses, lips curled in a smile. "What would you sell your immortal soul for?"

"A lifetime supply of hot chocolate," he answers, and when they laugh, he asks, "Is that too shallow?"

"Shallow is relative to depth of character," the boy in the raven shirt says. It's the first time I've heard him speak, and I find myself tilting forward, trying to read his expression in the shadows.

"Are you flirting with me?" asks Henry. "He is, isn't he, Sam?"

"Definitely," chuckles Sam.

Henry rests his head on the shoulder of the boy who followed me, bringing grins to both their faces.

I'm not sure what to make of this. This isn't the jerk I expected, tailing me around the city. This guy seems to have genuine friends, and the easy affection they all share pulls at me.

"So how'd *you* get an invite?"

I turn to find a girl on the opposite side of the crate, toying nervously with the bottles. I'm not sure how she snuck up on me in her wedge heels, but here she is, dressed like she belongs at a job interview rather than a train yard in her black dress and dark lipstick. Her dark hair frames her perfect-heart-shaped face, and she twists the ends around one finger.

"To this party?" I glance around again, swallowing as I take in the small size of the gathering. Do they all know each other? So much for blending in until I can figure out what my stalker wants.

"Oh right. *Party.*" She gives me a knowing look, but I have no idea what she's talking about.

I'm still watching Raven Shirt and his friends out of the corner of my eye. They've huddled closer, and it sends a warning across my senses. Are they talking about me? Do they know he's been following me around, or do they think I've crashed their party just for kicks?

Whispers of Bloody Brynn fill the back of my mind. I've been cornered by kids looking for a target more than once.

I pick up a bottle of beer just to keep my hands busy, but don't twist off the lid.

"Can you believe Damien Fontego's here?" she asks. "I had no idea he was one of the alumni."

My gaze flicks to the blond boy with the spiky hair currently making half the party laugh. Damien Fontego. The *actor*. Of course. He's in that show, *Kings of Rochester.* Mom watches it all the time.

She would die if she knew I was within ten feet of an actual famous person.

Did he go to school with the others, is that what this girl meant by alumni? I didn't even know he was from Sikawa. Either way, what's someone like Damien Fontego doing in an abandoned train yard in the middle of the night? Shouldn't he be in New York or Hollywood?

Maybe this girl is kidding—he could be a lookalike. My gaze roams around the rest of the group as I try again to figure out what exactly I walked in on, and lands on Raven Shirt.

Who is already looking right back at me.

A warm breeze blows across my skin. There's more than recognition in his stare, there's a hint of amusement, as if he's impressed I followed him.

It occurs to me that he might think *I'm* the one stalking *him*.

"Do you think it would be weird if I said hi?" The girl, still gawking at Damien, stops mid-sentence when I lift my hand.

"Sorry," I say. "Got to talk to someone."

She balks.

"*Okay,*" she says, in a way that sounds very not okay.

Adrenaline buzzes inside me as I head toward Raven Shirt, the tapered bottle now gripped in my hand. Maybe he's here with his friends talking about homework from whatever fancy school he goes to, but he's not getting out of this without explaining himself.

He meets me halfway between the drink crate and his friends. I can see them watching us around his shoulder as he stops, his mouth quirked in a half-smile.

"I know you, don't I?"

"You tell me."

"Sorry?" The smile drops away. He's taller than me by a full head, with broad shoulders and lean-muscled arms. I grip the bottle harder. I'm sure he won't try anything in front of all these people, but just in case, I'll be ready.

"You've been following me around all day," I tell him. "What do you want?"

He glances down at the bottle I'm now holding awkwardly between us.

"Not beer," he says. "My liver lacks the enzyme that helps me-
tabolize alcohol. It's common in Japanese people."

"Thank you for this More You Know moment." I drop the bottle
to my side. "Just answer the question. I saw you in Uptown, then
on the train, then at my job. What do you want from me?"

"Unless you work here, I didn't mean to show up at your job."
He glances down the long, dark row between the abandoned cars.
"As for the train, I had somewhere to go, like most people riding,
I assume."

"Uh huh, and where was that?"

"White Bank. Is that off limits?" He's amused again. I can hear
it in his tone and it makes my eyes narrow.

White Bank is the last stop on the line. If possible, it's even scar-
ier than my neighborhood. There's no reason for a guy who looks
like this to be wandering around White Bank, especially not with
that much cash. He might as well wear a shirt that says *I Make Bad
Decisions.*

"*I'm* off limits," I tell him. "So whatever you think you're doing—"

"Whoa." Taking a step closer, he blocks out his friends, still staring behind him. His chin lowers, until he can look me right in the
eye.

"We were just going the same way today. I'm sorry if I scared
you."

"You didn't," I say too quickly, then look away. I'm good at reading
people—I make good money doing it—and right now that regret
in his eyes and his tone, and the slope of his shoulders, is one hundred percent true.

"It's a big city," I say, the fire that pushed me here dwindling
down to embers. "You don't see strangers more than once in a day,
especially not in three different places."

He nods, mouth drawn in a serious line. "Then maybe it's fate."

"Fate."

"Clearly we're not supposed to be strangers."

I scoff. Cross my arms. Frown down at the stupid bottle I wish I'd just left on the crate behind me.

"Caleb." He holds out a hand.

After a moment, I shake it. His palm is big and warm, and I can feel each one of his long fingers as they curl around the back of my hand. The firmness of his grasp, and the steadiness of his gaze, take away some of the stupidity I feel for following him.

"Brynn," I tell him.

"Hilder. I heard your friend say it on the train."

Great. If he overheard Marcus call me "Fancy Ms. Hilder," what else did he hear?

"Good luck," he adds.

I pull my hand away.

"Good luck with what?"

He gives a confused smile and my stomach goes tight, like I just missed the punchline of a joke.

"Good evening, friends!"

At the announcement, we turn toward the open car, where the redhead—Charlotte—is now standing beside the lantern. A yellow glow casts over her long pale legs and short jumper, making her look like the star of a play.

"I'm glad to see no one was murdered on the trip over. What a buzzkill that would have been." She laughs, and I'm the only one who doesn't join her.

I'm warmed by a wave of self-consciousness. This isn't just any party. These people are here for a reason. I'm reminded of what the girl in the black dress said over by the drinks. *How'd you get the invite?*

What have I walked into?

I start to back away, hoping I can make a quiet escape.

"I'm sure you're all wondering why you're here," Charlotte continues. "Well, wait no longer. For the first time in three years we have an opening at Vale Hall, and if you've made it this far you might just be smart enough to get in."

CHAPTER 6

Whatever retreat I've started to make is stopped by Charlotte's words.

An opening at Vale Hall.

Smart enough to get in.

I may not have heard of Vale Hall before, but it doesn't take a genius to put it all together. They go to some rich prep school—I gathered as much from the fit of their clothes, and their casual conversation about essays on *Faustian Bargains,* whatever that is. My last essay for English was on why Hester Prynne sewed an A on her dress.

Certain people here tonight have been invited for some kind of initiation ceremony. It's clearly off the books—the location doesn't exactly scream school approved, and neither does the drink selection.

I glance back toward the crates where I met the girl in the black dress, finding she's moved closer to the open train car. *Alumni,* she called Damien Fontego. Pretty impressive that a fancy actor would come all the way out here for something like this. This place must be a big deal.

Big deal means money.

I'm really wishing I'd had a chance to print more ballet recital tickets now.

"Vale Hall's wait list is a thousand miles long," says a Latina girl with shampoo commercial hair. "They never open up enrollment. Why now?"

"Because the planets have aligned. Because Mercury is in the seventh house." Charlotte folds her arms over her chest. "Why do you think? Someone graduated and freed up a room at the estate."

My skin tingles at the word—*estate*. I wonder what these recruits have done to get an invitation. It can't just be the wait list— Charlotte alluded that they had to be smart to make it this far.

Probably some kind of special testing. I doubt the guidance counselors at Jarvis have even heard of it.

Charlotte strides across her boxcar stage. "You're here because someone's handpicked you to be considered for our opening. You know what this means, right? Forget whatever boring high school you came from. You go to Vale Hall, you're set for life. I'm talking scholarship money for every student. Room and board included. You want to be an astronaut? Our director knows people at NASA. If fashion's your thing, you'll get an internship in Paris. How's all this sound so far?"

Too good to be true.

With a snort, I look around, but everyone's actually buying this.

"The only thing we really can't help you with is acting," she says. "Absolutely zero contacts in the biz."

"Hey!" Damien calls out from the crowd, making Charlotte grin. Nervous laughter breaks out around me.

"Oh look," she says. "Try not to swoon, boys and girls. It's Damien Fontego. What was that little prize you just won, Damien?"

"I think they call it an Emmy," says Damien.

Everyone laughs.

Charlotte taps her nose. "That's it. *Emmy*. Damien graduated two years ago and landed a starring role on *Kings of Rochester*."

"Thank you, Vale Hall," he says.

Okay, impossible or not, Charlotte's got my attention now.

Caleb glances my way, offering an encouraging smile. He obviously doesn't know I haven't been invited.

"I'm a sophomore," says the girl in the black dress. "Are you taking transfers? Because I've been on the wait list since I was five, and if you tell me I missed the cutoff because I'm not a freshman, I might actually die."

Henry, standing to her left, makes a very worried face, though from the other nodding heads around her, I gather this is a common story.

"If you get chosen, we don't care if you're midway through your senior year," says Charlotte.

"Yeah right," I mutter. No school takes transfers that late. Especially one that sounds this good.

"It's true," Caleb says. "We take good people. Doesn't matter where they are in school, as long as they prove they can hack it."

I balk.

Charlotte's gone on to talk about room and board, and now I'm grasping onto her words with a raw, tentative interest. From what I can gather students live on campus, and there's some kind of dining hall with an ice cream machine that works even at two in the morning.

"This place must cost a fortune," I say.

"You can work off enrollment costs," says Caleb. "That's what I do."

I look at him again. Nice clothes. Straight back. Clean haircut. Nothing about him says poor.

But maybe it did once, before he went to Vale Hall.

I blink, screwing a thumb into my temple. Ten minutes ago, I didn't even know this school existed, now I'm picturing myself on some fancy *estate*, applying for internships in different countries. I need to come back down to earth before reality pops my balloon, and I crash.

But I don't walk away.

Because if this school really exists, and if, by some mistake, I randomly get in, I could live there. I could get out of Devon Park, away from Pete, and work my way into the kind of college I thought wasn't possible—the kind that means never looking back.

On the edge of the train car, Charlotte's red lips have curled into a smile.

"There's a reason we're meeting here tonight—why someone didn't bring you to the estate or call you on the phone. At Vale Hall we have a little initiation test. Just to see how much you really want this."

The reason for the invite is becoming clearer. The students weed out the kids they don't want, then must make some kind of recommendation to the admissions department. I've seen hazing in movies. They're probably going to make us streak down Sycamore Avenue or sing the National Anthem in the mall.

Call me desperate, but I might just do it.

"We're a family, and we don't let just anyone into our house. Consider it us looking out for each other."

Charlotte looks at Sam as she says this, and there's something intensely private that passes between them. A shared thought, that leads to him pressing his fingertips to his lips and blowing her a kiss.

I don't know why, but it reminds me of Devon Park—how the people stand up for their own, even while they knock each other down.

"So here's the deal," says Charlotte. "We're going to play a little game, and the winner gets an interview with our director. No waiting lists. No letters of recommendation. You do this one teensy tiny thing, we'll bump you to the front of the line."

The doubt inside me spreads—there's no way the students have this much sway. Still, I wait, eager and ready.

"Who in the class can tell me who Matthew Sterling is? Anyone?" She looks around the group. "Yes, in the front row."

"He's an actor?" tries a guy in a tight T-shirt with arms made for *Muscle Magazine*. He glances back at Damien as he says this, but Damien only hangs his head and laughs.

"You're cute," Charlotte says, "but not very smart. Next."

I bite my lip. The name's familiar, but I can't pinpoint exactly who he is.

"He's a senator," calls Henry. "He's probably going to be the next vice president. He's forty-eight years old and has steel-blue eyes. What?" He looks at Sam. "Anyone who's ever seen *Pop Store* knows that. They're always talking about how his navy suits bring out his eyes."

A few chuckles break the strained quiet.

Henry's right. I have seen Matthew Sterling, and he does have blue-gray eyes. He's been on that crappy local celebrity gossip show Mom's always watching after her soaps—*Pop Store*. There was something on about him the other day. His Sterling Foundation—the one responsible for fixing up a bunch of historic buildings in Uptown—was opening a new restaurant.

My stomach sinks. Matthew Sterling is a big deal. Wherever Charlotte's going with this, it can't be good.

"Ten points to Henry." When he cheers, Charlotte adds, "Don't get too excited, you're already in."

He cheers again.

"Today Senator Sterling and his lovely wife left for a benefit in Washington, DC, and while the cat's away, the mice will play. Their two kids, Grayson and Gabrielle, are throwing a little party at their house in Heatherwood tonight. Just a little get-together of a hundred or so of their closest friends."

Heatherwood is north of Uptown somewhere. The way it's laid out on the SCTA map, it might as well be a place in the sky.

"Your mission, should you choose to accept it, is to get a date with Grayson Sterling."

There's a beat of silence, then a girl with a face like a porcelain doll says, "Tonight?"

"Tonight," says Charlotte.

"You want some guy to ask me out?" The girl with the shampoo commercial hair scoffs. "This is a joke, right?" I guess she doesn't have all that hard a time getting dates.

"Am I laughing?" Charlotte's eyes sure are, even if her mouth isn't.

"That's not fair," Muscles complains. "Some of us are at a disadvantage here."

"Amateur," coughs Henry.

"Guess you'll have to be ultra-creative," says Charlotte.

"How are you going to know if we pull it off?" I adjust the strap of my bag over my shoulder as every set of eyes turns my way. I shouldn't have said anything—it's not like I'm going, I wasn't even on the invite list. By the way Charlotte's looking at me now, I'm sure she's wondering who I am and why I'm here at all.

"We'll know," Charlotte answers vaguely, in a way that makes me wonder if this is rigged—if they know Grayson Sterling, and he's in on it somehow.

"Do we actually have to go out with him, or just get the date?" asks Muscles.

"If you get the date, I'll be impressed enough," says Charlotte.

"This is crazy," says Dollface. "Even if we can pull this off, it doesn't guarantee anything. We still have to pass the interview with the director."

"I'm sorry," says Charlotte, as if she's offended. "Were you hoping for an acceptance letter tonight?"

I hadn't been—I didn't expect any of this when I came here—but now that she mentions it, that would have been nice.

She rattles off the address, and I pull a pen from my bag to write it on the palm of my hand. Then she says, "Good luck. I'd say I'll see you soon, but most of you I probably won't. So goodbye forever."

In dramatic fashion, she steps off the edge of the car into Sam's waiting arms. As she slides down his body, he holds her close, and whatever he whispers in her ear makes her giggle and shove him playfully away.

"So you're going?" Caleb asks as I put the pen away. Around me, the crowd is already dispersing. The girl in the black dress is hobbling through the gravel down the tracks in the opposite direction. Dollface and Muscles jog by her.

"I don't think so." I try to read Caleb's face, to see if there's any indication of a prank brewing, but I don't find it.

"Come on," he says. "Why not? What else are you doing?"

Besides breaking a grounding sentence, which will likely get me in a lot of trouble, not much. It wasn't like I hadn't snuck out of the house already anyway.

I glance to the twisted tag job on the boxcar behind him, illuminated by the glow of his phone. Maybe I should just stay here at the train yard. Make one of the boxcars into a little house. Of course, a major fumigation job would be required, but it might be worth it.

"Is it real?" I ask.

"What?"

"The whole thing. Your school opening up a spot. This game with Grayson Sterling."

He runs his hand through his hair, the corded muscles of his forearm flexing.

"Everything Charlotte said is real." When he talks, it feels like he's telling the truth, but Marcus used to feel that way, too.

"Even the ice cream at 2:00 AM?"

His lips quirk into a smile, and it's so genuine I'm taken off guard. "Even the ice cream. Even the pool. We're learning Kung Fu in PE."

I narrow my gaze. "You're kidding about that part."

He shakes his head.

"And anyone can get in?"

"Anyone who can pull off a date with the senator's son."

A sudden urge arises in me to tell him that I need this. That I can't go home. That I can do big important things if I can just catch a break. For some reason, I think he'd get it.

"Why him?" I ask.

"Why not? It's supposed to be a challenge."

"I get that, but why him specifically? He a friend of yours or something?"

Caleb laughs. "Definitely not."

"So he's an enemy. This is a prank on him."

He grins. "If I told you, that would be cheating."

"Come on." I grin back. "What's the catch? I won't tell."

"Neither will I."

Jerk. Cute jerk, but still a jerk.

"Caleb!" Damien Fontego strides up to us and slaps Caleb on the back. "We've got somewhere to be, my friend." He grins at me, a dimple digging into his right cheek, and yeah, okay, I kind of get what all the fuss is about, even if he is really short in real life.

"What's your name?" Damien asks.

"Brynn," I say.

He lifts my hand to his lips and kisses my knuckles.

It must be a thousand degrees outside.

"Enough already." Caleb elbows Damien aside. "See you around, Brynn."

"Sure," I tell him.

I back away, and then turn, feeling like I'm ripping off a

Band-Aid as I head toward the break in the fence. Beneath my feet, the gravel crunches. The moon is high over my head.

It's too late to print the tickets and go to Uptown—the shows where I would have sold them are already getting out. I either go home, sneak back in, and try again tomorrow, or find a cheap place to crash for tonight.

Or go to this party and try to get a date with the senator's son.

It's a joke—it has to be. Even if it wasn't, how am I supposed to pull this off? I don't know what Grayson looks like or how to get to his house. I don't have the kind of clothes I'm sure everyone else is wearing. I'm sure I could get a date—I can talk my way into just about anything—but why? Just to entertain some prep school kids?

I don't realize I'm almost jogging until I'm outside the fence and standing in front of the tire store. The breath scores my throat, echoing my pounding heart. To my left is the library, and the bus stop that will take me home. To my right is the SCTA station, and the yellow line that heads north to Heatherwood.

I think of Damien Fontego, kissing my hand. An estate where I can go to school and make my way toward college. I think of the easy way Caleb and his friends were with each other, and something squeezes in my chest. *We're a family,* Charlotte said. That's why they planned this whole thing. They wanted to make sure the person that got in was worthy.

What else are you doing? Caleb's smirk embeds itself in my memory.

Gripping my bag, I run for the train station.

CHAPTER 7

Two transfers, and one "Can you please give me directions, my phone died," later, and I'm camped out over the double seat on the yellow line to Heatherwood. My shirt—a ripped black tank top held together down the sides by safety pins—is a recent purchase. I paid a girl twenty bucks on the last train to trade with me. My jeans are shredded enough to be cool, and my old Chuck Taylors are always classic. The complete look is a little more metal than I usually go for, but edgy is better than thrift store for a north end party.

In the reflection of the bus window, I carefully outline my eyes with black pencil and apply my lip gloss. The conversation Caleb had with his friends when I followed him to the train yard comes back to mind—Charlotte's question ringing in my head.

What would you sell your soul for?

A different life, one where Pete doesn't exist.

A billion dollars, so I could go to a real school, one that could get me into a good college, and out of Devon Park forever.

My gaze drops from my own face in the window. I won't need to sell my soul if I can pull off a date with the senator's son.

A cool rush breaks through my shield, and I have to press my teeth together to keep from laughing out loud. A place like Vale Hall changes everything. It moves me out. Moves me *up*. It means a future where I won't have to put on short shorts and pray my cleavage is enough for a good tip at Gridiron Sports Bar. Where I won't have to work a nightshift at the library, or a convenience store and chance getting shot like my dad.

With a steadying breath, I force down my expectations. This could be nothing but a joke. A prank put on by these rich north end kids.

But if it's not . . .

If it's not, it's worth the risk.

My pulse flies faster with every stop. I bet the recruits who were invited all have cars. I bet they're already at the party. Over an hour has passed since I left the train yard. For all I know, the competition could have secured a date with Grayson by now.

I won't know until I get there.

The end of the yellow line is still over a mile from Grayson's house, and nerves fizzle in my chest as I make the hike up a twisted hill past the ivy-draped privacy walls and the giant metal gates. The houses beyond aren't marked by broken gutters or graffiti or barred windows; they look like castles. The cars that pass are all either black or white, and not one of them has a radio blasting, or a single bubble in the tint on the windows. It may be the same city, but this looks nothing like home, and it's got me on full alert. I bet my right arm Dorothy didn't feel half this intimidated when that tornado spat her out in Oz.

Finally, I reach the Sterlings' house, and find the gates open. There are two men standing at the entryway in gray suits, but they seem to be there more for intimidation than anything else, because a black Mercedes and a guy on a motorcycle pull in without pause.

There's no turning back now.

I walk faster. I don't want to give anyone reason to suspect that I don't belong here. Still, worry tightens the muscles at the base of my neck, reminding me this isn't my scene, and that if Pete finds out I'm not actually at home, I'm in serious trouble.

Get in and get out.

This is just another con. Flirting may not be my forte, but reading people is. I need to figure out what Grayson likes, and be that, just long enough to get him to ask me out. Then I'm gone, and if this was nothing more than a diversion it doesn't matter, because I'd already made the decision to sneak out tonight.

"Here we go," I mutter.

Jaw set, gaze roaming, I latch onto a group outside finishing their smoke break and pretend to be part of their conversation as we pass the guards and cut through the ten or so sports cars crammed in the driveway. The house is different than the others in this neighborhood. Harsh and angular. Metal and glass. I bet it's worth a million dollars, if not more.

A spark lights my blood, bringing a little smile to my lips. I'm about to walk into a party at the house of a US senator. Despite how much I tell myself I do this kind of thing for my survival, I'd be lying if I said I didn't like that first initial rush, that chance to be someone else, even for a little while.

There are people standing outside talking or smoking. Some of them my age, some of them a little older, though not by much. Are any of them Grayson? None of the other recruits from the train yard are here, so I'm guessing not.

I head down the stone path toward the entrance.

As I fix the messenger bag strap crossed over my chest, the door swings open, and I'm thrown back a step by the blaring music within. This house must have some serious soundproofing, because I barely heard it outside. As a couple topples out, all handsy and drunk, I set my expression to Unimpressed and slip inside.

The lights in the main room are dimmed, though there's a brightness coming from the open kitchen to my left. I navigate through the white leather couches and chairs, surveying the scene. Twenty plus people fill the room. Boys in jeans that are too tight. Girls in dresses that are too short. At parties in Devon Park, there are forties, red Solo cups, and more than one shade of skin, but here, everyone seems to have a glass or a full wine-sized bottle, and I'm the darkest tan in the place.

I make my way toward the large, open kitchen, finding the island's been converted to a bar, and the counter beside the sink into a buffet of pills and dime bags. No one looks like they're hosting, or drawing a crowd. The kitchen gives way to a dining room, and I cut through to where a framed family picture hangs on the wall.

There they are. The entire Sterling Family. Matthew and his wife sit in the center of the photo, gleaming like movie stars, all perfect skin and flawless hair and clothes that could easily pay first and last month's rent on a luxury condo. On either side stand their children. A girl who looks like a Miss America candidate with her golden updo and perfectly straight teeth, and a boy, about my age, who could be a high profile drug dealer. I lean closer to the picture, taking in his dark hair and sharp angles. Even his smile dares you to question him.

This must be Grayson Sterling.

Going back into the main room, I spot a stairway on the opposite side and cut through the crowd toward it. One hand on the clear glass bannister, I descend into a game room with a couch and a pool table, keeping my eyes roaming for the face I saw in the picture upstairs.

A couple guys in fancy headgear are playing video games on the giant TV plastered to the far wall. A bunch of people are dancing to the music in the middle of the room. A warning tingles in my spine as I step away from the only discernable exit. None of these yuppies are going to hurt me, but I'm careful all the same. I'm outnumbered, and don't belong.

I look for Grayson, but there are so many people, and it's too dark to make out anyone's face. Stepping into the room, I start to make my way toward the crowd, but a guy bumps into me, knocking me off balance.

"Watch it," I snap automatically.

"My bad." He grips my elbow to hold me upright.

My breath catches as my gaze lands on his. From behind his thick-rimmed glasses, Caleb's dark eyes smile at me. His fingertips brush the back of my arm, leaving heat where he touched as he pulls his hand away.

"Hi," I say brilliantly.

Caleb is here to see if I can pull this off.

Caleb is *here*.

Any doubt I felt since the train yard is carried away by a different kind of rush, this one warmer, and faster, flooding my whole body. I don't know if I'm happy to see him, or petrified he'll witness my epic failure, but either way his presence makes me feel not so alone.

Without another word, he gives the briefest smile, and releases me. He heads toward the people playing video games, leaving me staring at his T-shirt-clad shoulders, and lower, down the long lines of his legs.

"Now that is a show I could watch all day."

I turn to see a girl beside me, wearing a miniskirt and an even more mini shirt. Her dark eyeliner makes her look tough, but something tells me each strand of her messy bun is placed on purpose.

The girl in the photo. Grayson's sister. She looks different than in the picture upstairs. Older. Hotter, for sure.

She's watching Caleb.

"You know who he is? He looks familiar." She doesn't bother asking who *I* am.

"Never seen him before." Her gaze switches to me, and I can tell she's sizing me up, right down to my shoes. "Hey, have you seen your brother around? He told me to meet him down here, and—"

"Gabrielle!"

I'm cut off by a girl in a cream-colored dress, who comes stomping down the hallway, shoving people out of her way. She pauses in front of us, cheeks flaming.

"Your brother's a real sweetheart, Gabby. Next time he wants to throw a party, maybe he should try not insulting his guests."

Without waiting for a response, Mad Barbie hauls up the stairs. Gabrielle rolls her eyes and follows, and when I turn back toward the hall, a boy stands before me. He's wearing all black, right down to his fancy slip-on shoes, and is looking over the room with a pinched gaze, like the sight of all these people disgusts him.

Grayson Sterling, ladies and gentlemen.

With a quick shake of his dark, messy hair, he heads to a couch on the far wall behind a coffee table lined with snacks. Falling into the cushions, he hikes his feet up against the table, hands stuffed in his pockets, nudging someone's drink aside with the toe of his shoe. His head tilts back and he stares at the ceiling.

No one approaches him. I'm not sure I blame them. The guy doesn't exactly scream *I'm a good time.*

As I spy, a girl approaches and practically sits on Grayson's lap. It's Shampoo Commercial, now wearing a form-fitting red dress to match her painted lips. Competition lights inside me as she leans in and plays with the hair on the back of his neck. She's got the upper hand. I need to intervene.

But I don't, because he's ignoring her.

As I watch, he shifts away, putting six more inches between them. For a second, she only blinks at him, then, taking the hint, she rises, and makes her retreat.

One down, I'm not sure how many left to go.

Quietly, I slip through the crowd, watching him check his phone and then his watch. Dollface is here, now chatting up Gabrielle by the stairs. That must be her in. I spot Muscles, too. He approaches Grayson with a couple other guys, and grabs some licorice from an open canister on the coffee table. Grayson contributes no more than a few words when they talk, and doesn't stand up.

Muscles is making no headway. I don't see the girl in the black dress at all, so maybe she's already struck out. And unless Dollface thinks Grayson's sister's going to hook her up, she's no closer to the goal than Shampoo Hair.

My gaze turns again to Grayson. This is his party—at least some of these must be his friends. I don't know why they'd show up if he's always such a grouch, though. Surely they must see something in him. The question of what exactly is shoved to the back of my mind as Muscles pulls out his wallet, removes a bill, and passes it Grayson's way.

Slowly, Grayson leans forward to take it, but instead of tucking it into his pocket, he folds the crisp green paper into an airplane against his knee.

My own laugh surprises me. This guy is ridiculous. He's not socially awkward, but bored—he's literally playing with his own money.

It hits me then: he's like a little kid. If you don't give him something to do, he'll get in trouble.

A plan forms in my mind. If I'm going to get his attention, I need to be different than his other friends. I need to pull him out of this slump.

I need to get him to play.

As he sends his money airplane soaring, I slide through a gap in the wall of friends and snag it out of the air. Grayson's eyes land on me, mildly impressed, and as I unfold the bill and see that it's a hundred, I'm sure I look impressed, too.

Making sure he's watching, I tuck it into my pocket.

"That's mine," he says. The first words I've heard him speak over the music.

"Finders keepers."

Muscles laughs awkwardly, maybe surprised at my nerve. Leaning down, I grab a piece of licorice from the round plastic canister beside Grayson's crossed ankles. His eyes narrow as I bite off the end.

"My sister invite you?"

"Nope." *You don't impress me.* Everything about my body language exudes this, and that's not part of the act. Throwing around money when people are starving or trying to get into college pisses me right off.

His lips curve. Slowly, he lowers his feet to the floor and leans forward. "I didn't invite you."

"Nope."

His friends are watching now, trading whispers and trying to figure out who I am.

"Are you crashing my party?"

"Sure am." I take another bite of licorice. Chew slowly. I don't break his gaze, and I can tell this unsettles him. His mouth twitches a little.

"Drinks are upstairs if that's what you came for."

"It's not. But thanks."

"Then why are you here?"

His abrasive tone might intimidate some people, but not me.

"Maybe I was bored."

Ending the stand-off, he rises, his fine brows arched. I take another piece of licorice and pass it to him. He takes a bite. Everyone may be staring, but I don't falter.

"Who are you?" Grayson asks.

"I could tell you, but what fun is that?" I tap the licorice against my red-painted lips. "You want my name, you have to earn it."

This entire side of the room is watching now. I hope Caleb's looking, too.

His gaze tightens around the edges. "And how does one do that?"

"Let's play a game. If you win, I'll tell you."

I hold my breath, waiting.

The guy standing beside Muscles eggs Grayson on. Muscles scoffs, like this is a stupid idea.

But Grayson doesn't think so.

He steps around the table, and up close I see that he's only a few inches taller than me. He seems bigger farther away. He's not even quite as good looking as he was from a distance; all the hard lines of his face are almost too severe, like he's gone a lifetime being angry.

"What's the game?" he asks.

I turn and scan the room, finding Caleb talking to a girl by the video game station. His gaze slides over mine with only a hint of recognition.

"If you can put five pieces of licorice on someone without them noticing, you win."

Grayson snorts. Then he laughs. "That's the best you can come up with? I can think of better games." His gaze lowers over me, equal parts suspicion and intrigue. His finger flicks one of the safety pins resting against my side, a casual touch that says he's used to getting whatever he wants. It takes effort not to slap his hand away.

"If it's too difficult, that's okay. Have fun with your friends." With a wave, I start to walk away.

This fearless girl who's taken over isn't half bad.

"Wait."

I turn. His mouth has flattened. His black, collared shirt stretches as he crosses his arms over his chest.

"How am I supposed to put something on someone without them noticing?"

"You'll have to figure it out," I say.

He balks. "This is stupid."

"Something tells me you do a lot of stupid things, Grayson."

The insult, small as it is, is a risk, but I'm rewarded by a twitch of his lips. An almost smile.

"All right," he says. "You first."

"That's not how the game works."

Now he's smirking. "If it's too difficult, that's okay."

His patronizing tone flicks a switch inside me.

I slip behind him and grab a handful of licorice. "Watch and learn."

With that, I toss my bag on the ground beside the table, tuck the licorice in my back pocket, and saunter toward the crowd dancing in the middle of the room. Tapping my chin with one finger, I make a show of picking my victim, and then bypass the group completely to head straight toward Caleb.

CHAPTER 8

A scowl passes over Caleb's face as I approach. He looks away, the video game reflecting red and white lights on his glasses. The screams and shots fired on the screen are barely audible over the thump of the bass, a track of violence layered over bad pop music.

I stop before him, rising to my tiptoes to say, "Dance with me."

He tilts his head. The girl with the razor sharp bangs beside him takes a drink from her fancy wineglass like she's twenty-seven, not seventeen, and awaits his response.

I wait, too, genuinely nervous, because this may be pretend, but Caleb is not. This entire party feels like a scene from a movie—these people, strange props with their money and drinks and fancy clothes. Caleb and the other recruits from the train yard feel like the only things that are real.

Caleb's purpose—to watch me—hangs delicately between us.

"Excuse me," he tells the girl with the bangs. She smiles and turns away, and though Grayson is my mark, I start to taste my victory.

I walk toward the middle of the floor, feeling Caleb follow. Feeling Grayson, and half a dozen people around them, watching. Their gazes fuel me, put a little more swagger in my step. I become who they think I am, and in this moment, I love it.

On the outskirts of the crowd, where I'm sure Grayson can see, I turn back toward Caleb.

"What are you doing?" His tone is low and uncertain.

"Dancing. I told you." I slide close and wrap my arms around his neck. This is part of the show, of course, but I'd be lying if I said I didn't notice the warmth of his skin against my open palms, or the way the ends of his hair tickle the sides of my fingers. He's taller than me, and when he shifts his weight his belt brushes against my stomach.

From the corner of my eye, I catch Dollface, now standing on the third step, arms crossed, glaring in my direction.

Caleb leans closer. "I can't help you, you know."

My skin grows tight below my ear where his warm breath touches. My heart is keeping time with the thump of the bass.

"You don't have to do anything," I say. "Just stand there and look pretty."

Frowning, he pulls back.

"No. Like this." I flash him an enthusiastic grin.

The lines between his brows ease. He shakes his head and gives a small smile.

"That's better." My hips slide from side to side. With the lightest pressure of my fingers against the side of his neck, I have him following my lead. Automatically, his hands come to rest on my waist, and for a moment I forget all about Grayson and the others. I forget why I'm here. I only know that I've never danced with a boy before, and that it's not nearly as pathetic as I thought it would be.

In fact, it's sort of nice.

Even if this music sucks. Even if my right knee keeps bumping his.

I mean, don't expect me to line up for prom tickets or anything, but I kind of see why people do this now. Caleb's T-shirt is thin and soft, and his skin is warm beneath my forearms. The smell of soap and boy invades my senses, and the darkness around us presses in, drawing us closer.

"If you're trying to make him jealous, it's working," Caleb says, reminding me that this is just a game, and we're both just acting.

I stiffen for a fraction of a second, then slip back into my role.

"Is he looking?"

Caleb glances to the side, then back at me. "He's trying to burn me with his laser eyes."

I slide my hand down Caleb's chest, wondering if the way he flexes beneath my touch is because of me or because he doesn't like being pulled into this. Over the side of his belt I go, reaching behind me as I swing my hips a little wider. At the change in my movement, his lips part, and his gaze dips to my mouth.

He is close enough to kiss.

I swallow. This is a game. We are putting on a show.

He is one hell of an actor. Maybe he'll be the next from Vale Hall to get an Emmy, follow in Damien's footsteps.

I pull a handful of licorice from my back pocket and slowly ease my arm around his side to his back. He doesn't seem to notice. It probably wouldn't matter if he did, but I want Grayson to think this is authentic, and for Grayson to think that, I need Caleb focused entirely on me.

Very carefully, I slide my knuckles down Caleb's back, and tuck the red licorice into his back left pocket.

He makes a small choking sound.

"You seem to be confused about this test," he says. "I'm not your assignment, you know that, right?"

I bite my lip so I don't laugh. He thinks I just copped a feel.

"Oh man," I say. "I'm *all* mixed up."

I step back then, detaching one hand from the back of his neck and the other from just above his back pocket. Then I turn, practically giddy, and strut past Muscles and Shampoo back to Grayson.

"Ta-da."

He's shaking his head. "You told him what you were doing."

I shrug. "Go ask him if you don't believe me."

He does. Passing me, Grayson heads toward Caleb, and though I can't hear what's said, I get a pretty good idea when Caleb twists to look at the seat of his pants and pulls out a handful of licorice.

He sends me an incredulous look, then separates one of the vines and takes a bite.

I blow him a kiss. For the show, of course.

Grayson is already coming back my way, rolling up his sleeves like he's about to work.

"All right." He goes to the plastic bucket and counts out five pieces of licorice. He's all in now.

Even if he can't pull this off, which I'm betting he can't, he's determined not to lose. I've caught his attention now, and he's not going to let me beat him.

"These little dresses are working against me." He motions to the crowd in front of us.

He's not wrong. If he wants to do the same thing I did but with a girl, he's at a disadvantage. None of them are wearing baggy enough clothing to pull this off—they'd feel what he was doing right away.

"So sorry to hear that," I tell him.

He goes still, then gives me a sly smirk. There's a guy sitting on a recliner at the bottom of the stairs who appears to be sleeping, though I'd bet he's actually passed out based on the bottle cradled in the crook of his arm.

Grayson goes to him, and unceremoniously tosses the licorice into his lap. The guy doesn't so much as flinch.

Then he turns to me and gives a small bow.

Inside, I'm cheering with the other handful of bystanders who've watched this unfold. On the outside, I'm only mildly impressed, giving him my best slow clap as he saunters toward me.

"Easy," he says. "Give me a challenge next time."

"Who says there's going to be a next time?" I look at my invisible watch. "Oh, look at that. Time for me to go."

His humor fades in stages. First, it pulls his mouth in a thin line. Then it brings a stain to his cheeks.

It seems as if not many people tell Grayson Sterling no.

Still, there's determination in his eyes. He likes the challenge, and once again, I've given him a game.

"Stay," he says, like I'm a dog. "The party's just getting started."

It would be easy to say yes, and maybe that would be enough. But Grayson's already shown me how easily he gets bored, and I don't want to risk that with my possible future in the balance.

"Not really my scene," I say.

Chase me, Grayson. Play.

"Then let's go somewhere else," he says.

He's ready to ditch his party. Ditch his friends to go out with me.

What a standup guy.

I glance around for Caleb and find him just behind me, facing the video game screen again as if watching. I know he's listening to every word, though. He's too still, and his head is tipped our direction.

"Maybe another time." I walk toward the stairs.

"You at least owe me your name," he calls. "I won it."

I owe him nothing, nor do I appreciate the tone that says he won *me,* not just my name. But when I turn, my smile is one hundred percent real.

With a curl of my finger I beckon him over, feeling the glares of my competition hot on my back.

"Sarah," I say.

He repeats it, too quietly for me to hear over the music. His lips curve around the word. "What's your number?"

"That's another game for another day," I say, not willing to give him the power. Not willing to show him my drugstore model phone, either.

"That's not fair, is what it is."

"Life's not fair," I tell him. But just in case I need proof of this little interaction later, I offer, "Give me your number, and I'll call you if I'm bored again."

"If you're . . ." He scoffs. Still, he disappears into the hallway, returning a moment later with a pen.

Reaching for my hand, he writes the numbers on the back of my wrist, like a bracelet. His fingers skim over the palm of my hand as he does this, but it doesn't give me butterflies the way Caleb's touch did, and it's hard to hold still.

When Grayson's done, I give him one last killer smile and climb the steps, light as a feather. If I don't hold onto this bannister, I might just fly away.

"Hold up."

I turn, but it's not Grayson calling me, it's Caleb. My messenger bag is in his hands. I take it with a relieved sigh.

"Thanks."

His answer is an amused smirk, and then he returns to the floor.

I continue climbing the stairs to keep up appearances for Grayson, but I hope Caleb will follow. I even hang out a little while near the front door, waiting for him to come after me. He doesn't, though, not even when I go outside and slowly pass the smokers and rows of cars.

I don't understand what's supposed to happen next. Does he find me again? Am I to meet him and the others back at the train yard? Or am I actually supposed to go out with Grayson? Even after such a stellar performance, I feel a crash coming.

I get to the train, and make my connections, my heart sinking more with every minute that passes. Maybe someone else got a date first. Maybe this whole thing was an elaborate prank after all.

Caleb didn't get my number, so there's no way he can call and tell me I won.

But he knows my first and last name. Maybe he'll look me up and find my address. Any thought of staying away from home disappears from my mind. I need to get back. Sneak in before Pete finds out I left. If Vale Hall sends me a letter, I'll need to make sure I intercept the mail before anyone else picks it up.

It's after 2:00 AM when I get off the connecting bus, and hurry down the familiar streets toward Midgard. Reaching into my messenger bag, I check for my keys, but my fingers close around a folded piece of paper, hidden in the side pocket. Stopping beneath a streetlight, I pull it out and unfold the white stationery with a scripted *STERLING* centered at the top.

Thanks for the dance, it says. *See you soon, C.*

I hug the note to my chest and give a whoop into the night. I don't care if half of Devon Park hears me. Then I run the rest of the way home, unsure what happens next, just knowing I'm one step closer to getting out.

I'm so happy, I don't see Pete sitting on the front steps until I'm right in front of him.

CHAPTER 9

I was supposed to go through the back door. Sneak down the alley, go over the fence, avoid the front. I knew Pete might have returned downstairs to work by now. I knew it, and I didn't think.

The note from Caleb crumples in my tightening fist.

"Where you been?" Pete asks. "Awfully late for a kid to be out on her own."

I brace, unable to read his mood through the exhaustion in his voice. Automatically I glance over my shoulder, just in case I need to make a run for it.

Pete takes a long, slow draw off his cigarette, the end glowing red in the darkness.

"I was . . ." *Think.* "At work."

My shift only goes until midnight, but there's a chance he doesn't know that. He doesn't usually keep tabs on me.

My palms grow damp, even as a cool breeze rustles the weeds on the opposite side of the street.

"Come sit with me, Brynn," Pete says.

No, I want to say, along with a string of curse words and a kick to the chin. *You stole my money. You pushed my mom around. You threatened me, and you'll* never *do it again.*

I don't say any of it.

It's only now that the terrors of the neighborhood catch up with me. A man's soft crying in the abandoned building across the street. The wail of far off sirens; the slap of a screen door against the frame. The smell of cigarette smoke and trash, too long baked in the sun.

Pete's spicy cologne.

I sit an arm's length away from him, hate and fear boiling inside my stomach. He snorts, and rests his elbows on the step behind, leaning back. The collar of his shirt is open, revealing the undershirt beneath, and the thick gold cross he wears on a chain around his neck

"We need to talk," he says, staring blankly in the distance. "We never talk anymore."

"Yeah," I say, when it appears he's waiting for my answer. I'm in trouble, I'm sure of it, and the muscles in my legs flex, ready to stand and run should he turn on me.

"Things got heated earlier."

Get on with it. I can't stand waiting for him to yell at me, or do whatever else he's going to try. My heels are drumming into the cement step.

"I just worry about you. I don't want you going down the wrong path."

Another slow drag from his cigarette.

I don't believe he's worried—not for a second. The only path he wants me to avoid is the one that loses him money.

"You're a smart girl," he continues, and now my stomach's churning.

I hate that this person has so much power over me. That he says *sit,* and I sit. That he talks, and I listen. That even now I'm scared of what he'll do if I get up and walk away.

"I haven't appreciated that as much as I should."

When he smashes the end of his cigarette and tosses it into the street, I slide a little farther away.

"You want a cut," he says.

The contents of a small box beside him rattle as he picks it up and gives it a slow examination. I recognize the WPS insignia on the back, and know it's from Wednesday Pharmaceutical Supplies, where he steals the pills he later sells. Most of the name of this particular item is hidden by his rosy knuckles, but on the street, no one cares about the medical title. They go by color, and price, and effect.

"I need someone on the ground in the western neighborhoods," he says.

I hide a scoff in my fist. He wants me to sell drugs for him.

"What about Marcus?" I don't like throwing his name in for things that could give him more trouble, but he chose this life. I want to stay clear.

"Marcus has his hands full." The pills inside the box shift as he turns his wrist. "Anyways, I like the idea of you doing it. Pretty girl like you could move, I don't know, a thousand a week maybe, before my cut."

I perk up at this. A thousand dollars in a week is a quarter what it took me to scam in an entire *year*. In a month, I'd have made up my losses.

"Course, I'd have to trust you. This is a big responsibility."

I don't want this. I don't. I have a new plan, and it's called Vale Hall.

But if Vale Hall doesn't come through . . .

Pete's taken almost four thousand dollars of mine, and now he's offering me a way to get it back.

"I . . ." It's an easy answer. No. *No.* Why can't I say it?

Sweat drips down my temples. I swipe it away with the back of my hand.

Internships. Scholarships. *College.*

A house without Pete.

A home without Mom.

Vale Hall seems more like a dream every second that passes. But if I work for Pete, even just for a little while, I'd make up my losses—losses I only have because of him. I'd be able to go to Sikawa CC, and then transfer into a state school, like the counselor at Jarvis said. It's a solid plan. The best someone like me can do.

And now the thought of it is dusty, and dim, shadowed by Vale Hall.

"What did Mom say about it?" I ask.

"She'll come around."

Which means he hasn't told her. She won't like this. She's always told me not to mess around with this kind of stuff. I'm supposed to finish school—like she couldn't after she had me—and stay out of jail.

He stands, and I quickly rise beside him. He steps closer, and the backs of my legs hit the stone edging to the stairs. Panic flutters in my chest.

His arms open, and he hugs me.

I want to scream, and cry, and fight. I want to go back to when I was at the party and it didn't feel like I was being held underwater.

I don't move.

He pets my hair, and inhales. This isn't fatherly; it's slick, and wrong, but before I can jerk away, he lets me go.

"Good. You can start tomorrow." He climbs the stairs heavily, as if he's the one with the burden, and walks into the house.

I sit on the steps for a long time, waiting until the house is quiet and I'm sure he's asleep. When I finally go in, I sneak up the stairs to my room, and scream, silently, into my pillow.

I WAKE TO a soft knock, and before I answer, Mom slips inside my bedroom. She's in her red polka-dot pajamas, and when she slides into bed with me, her arm is warm against mine.

"Mother," I say, voice crackly with sleep.

"Daughter," she answers. "You shouldn't sleep in safety pins. You'll poke out an eye. Or a kidney."

I roll over, not sure what she's talking about until the cool metal on my side presses against my waist.

I'm still wearing my clothes from the party last night.

Last night.

I'm up in a flash. Images of Grayson and Caleb, of the train yard gathering, of Damien Fontego *kissing my hand,* fly through my head, excitement mingling with worry in my stomach.

Was all that a dream?

Reaching to my nightstand for the note Caleb left, I read it again, beaming like an idiot. He doesn't know my number, but I check my phone just in case he magically figured it out.

He didn't, of course.

But it's only seven in the morning.

"Worried about your finals?" she asks, jarring me out of the rush. I'd forgotten my math final in light of everything else. "Pete's got a meeting at the warehouse in a couple hours. You should go before he gets up. I'll cover for you."

I swing my legs over the side of the bed, thinking of the offer he gave me last night. The warehouse she's talking about is Wednesday Pharmaceuticals' distribution center, where Pete steals his drugs while security looks the other way. Is he already getting more product, assuming I'm going to help him?

Mom sits beside me. Judging by the determined look on her face, he hasn't told her yet, and I don't want to, either—not just because it will upset her, but because even if it does, she won't do anything. She won't tear into Pete like a hurricane, the way she did when Jollee Carter's dad called me "jailbait" in the sixth grade, or the way she does when customers at the Gridiron get too handsy. She can't, because she's scared, and she should be.

And that's the worst part of it all.

She will help me sneak out of the house to go to *school*, just so we don't upset the monster in the other room.

Her fingers scratch lightly between my shoulders and I sigh, then lean into her. My head finds the crook of her neck, more shoulder-length waves falling free from my ponytail, and for a second, I want to tell her about all of it. The train yard. The party. Damien Fontego, and even Caleb and Grayson. I want to tell her about the money, and college, and that we should get out of here together.

But I don't, because it won't change anything.

"Thanks," I tell her.

She pulls me closer, squeezing my bicep. I look up at her, seeing the perfect layers of hair she gets cut for free at Stylz on account of Pete's pull in Devon Park, and the lines of worry around her eyes and mouth that are so much more evident without her makeup.

"I love you more than pancakes," she says.

"I love you more than buttered popcorn."

A knock comes from the door downstairs.

In an instant, we're both up. The only people knocking on a door in this neighborhood at 7:15 in the morning are bill collectors and people serving court summons. While she dodges downstairs, I tear off the safety-pinned shirt and change into a baggy black T hanging off my dresser. Tucking Caleb's note and my phone into my pocket, just in case, I tiptoe out of my room, past Mom's closed bedroom door where Pete is still sleeping, and down the stairs.

There are two voices—my mom's, and a man I don't recognize. They're speaking quietly, standing just inside the front door. I catch a glimpse of a dark suit and sunglasses and freeze in my tracks.

Not a bill collector. A cop.

"You're taking her now?" my mom says disbelievingly. "Just like that?"

I freeze.

Scenes from the party come back in vivid colors. Was this

guy called from someone in Heatherwood? Am I in trouble for something that's happened? I feel for the hundred bucks folded in an airplane that is still in my hip pocket. Did someone accuse me of stealing?

I should have known one of those rich kids would have blamed me for something.

This could be about Pete, and that worries me even more. If I get questioned for my affiliation with a west end drug dealer, what happened at the party won't even matter. I'll have a lot bigger problems.

I creep out a little farther to get a better look at the man speaking to my mom.

He's as smooth as a bank teller, with dark skin, a short, neat haircut, and a square jaw. Though he's standing inside the house, he has yet to take off his sunglasses, so it's hard to place how old he is. Thirty-something, maybe. In his right hand is a black folder.

I'm torn between running and further investigation.

Because if I'm not in trouble . . .

If he's here because of something I did right . . .

"There she is."

He sees me before I think he can, while I'm still just peeking out from around the wall in the stairway. Guy must have X-ray vision.

"Quiet," Mom says in a low, sharp tone. "I told you, my boyfriend's sleeping. He works late."

"Of course," says Bank Teller. "I'm sorry."

I must not be in trouble—if I was, Mom wouldn't be motioning me down the stairs. With each step toward the door the capacity of my lungs grows smaller.

"You know this guy?" she asks.

I look at him again. Shake my head.

"We haven't met," says Bank Teller. "But she's been in touch with some of the other students. I'm Hugh Moore. I'm in charge of security and student outreach."

It takes a second for this to process, and when it does, it feels as if the floor has been ripped from beneath my feet. The other students. *Vale Hall* students. He's here because Caleb must have told the others what happened last night.

"Hi." Pulling at the hem of my shirt, I nod vigorously. "Yeah. Yes." I clear my throat. "I've talked to the other students."

Mom is staring at me as if trying to read my mind. After a moment she looks back toward Bank Teller.

"So that's it?" she asks. "I don't need to go?"

"Not unless you'd like to," says Moore. With a face as serious as his, he doesn't seem like the kind of guy who goes by his first name. "I'm happy to bring you back after you see the estate."

The estate.

Mom's face is absolutely blank. She glances upstairs. "I'd . . . better stay."

She's still planning on covering for me. Even though I wish she didn't have to, my heart still swells with gratitude.

With a curt nod, Moore faces me. "Vale Hall's director wants to meet you."

This is actually happening.

"Right now?" I should change clothes. Shower. Eat a healthy breakfast. Do push-ups or something.

I don't even have socks on.

"No time like the present," says Moore.

When it appears as though he's not going to elaborate, Mom turns and pulls me into a hug.

It leaves me hollow, and dizzy.

"You could've told me," she whispers. "A head's-up would have been nice."

"I . . ."

"It's okay," she says, as if she's trying to convince herself. "It's okay. This is big. He filled me in."

"He did?" I'm not exactly sure what that entails—if he covered the hazing challenge, or the train yard, or just this interview with the director.

"You're sure?" she asks.

I pull back, and she looks like I'm about to pull the plug on a beloved family member. She's giving me a chance to back out, but I can't. She has to realize that whatever happens, this is the biggest shot of making something of myself that I've ever had.

"Yeah, Mom. I'm sure."

She releases me, and crosses her arms, holding on to herself when she was just holding on to me.

"Well you'd better go then." She gives me a nervous smile. "You'll call me, right? Check in after you meet with the director?"

I nod. She never asks me to check in. Then again, no one in a fancy suit has ever picked me up for a private school interview before.

I turn to Moore. "Can I change clothes?"

But just as Moore dips his head there's a creak from upstairs. We all look in that direction, expecting her bedroom door to push open, but Pete does not emerge.

"Go," Mom says quickly. My shoes are on the tile beside the door, and she shoves them toward me with her foot while simultaneously snatching my messenger bag off the coatrack. My phone and Grayson's hundred-dollar bill are in my back pocket. Along with the hundred and eighty I have left from the ballerinas, I have enough cash to survive the city for a couple days if I have to, but this feels too fast. Too sudden.

"I haven't even brushed my teeth," I say.

She reaches for her purse, also on the coatrack, and pulls out a pack of spearmint gum. Pressing it into my hand, she says, "Good luck."

Then she looks back to her bedroom.

I have to leave before Pete sees me go.

I grab my shoes, and if Moore notices our strange, sudden rush, he doesn't say anything. He steps outside to wait, and as soon as I'm beside him, he descends the steps and begins walking toward the car.

"Bye," I say to Mom.

I should go, but it's like I'm waiting for something. I don't know what. I remind myself this is just an interview. I'll probably be back in a couple hours. We can talk about it then.

"Bye, sweetie." Her voice pinches with emotion. "Good luck."

And then the door is closed, and I feel like the cord holding me to her has been severed and I'm falling, or maybe flying, away. There is nothing to do but follow Moore to the black sedan parked on the curb across the street, and when I get there he opens the passenger door and closes it behind me.

The interior of the car is silent, but alarm bells ring loud and clear in my head.

Even though my mom's always given me a fair amount of freedom, it now seems insane that she let me go with this guy. I half wish she would come outside and stop me. This isn't how I imagined this moment would be. There is no golden chariot. No magic stallions to trample Pete into the asphalt as I make my grand exit. Caleb's note said he'd see me soon, but I'm too on edge to be excited.

"Where are we going?" I ask when he gets in. I hug my bag against my chest. I'm reminded of every elementary school assembly preaching stranger danger. This guy could be a serial killer for all I know.

"Vale Hall," he says.

Then he presses a button that starts the car, and drives.

HUGH MOORE IS not one for small talk. I try to ask him about the interview, or the folder he's set in the back seat, I even drop Caleb's name, but he gives only one-word responses. As we get on the freeway and begin the long loop around the outskirts of the city, he flips to a local talk radio show, and turns it up as they begin to discuss some scandal involving the mayor taking bribes from gang members affiliated with the Wolves of Hellsgate.

I cringe, remembering how when Pete stole my money, he told me I couldn't sell his pills in Uptown—that was Wolves' territory. I wish I'd actually done it. We'd see what a big man he is when a motorcycle club comes after him.

"Traffic," grumbles Moore, glaring at the five clogged lanes traveling our direction.

Shaking Pete and the Wolves free from my mind, I stare out the window. The city looks different from the highway than it does from the train, running right through its heart. The skyscrapers come together to make a jagged skyline rather than a stone and steel jungle, and you can't see the mucky river at all.

"When will we get there?" I ask.

"Maybe never," Moore answers, the car slowing to a crawl.

Forty-seven minutes later, as we wind through the upper-class neighborhoods with their fancy organic food markets and yoga studios, the nerves begin to eat me alive. My heels hammer against the floorboards. I'm still half convinced that is all the start of some elaborate horror story, and this guy's about to gut me and leave me for the vultures.

Finally, the neighborhoods give way to larger properties, and he turns at a twisted copper gate. When he types a code into the keypad on a stone column beside the driveway, it slowly, steadily, swings open.

In we go, down a long gravel lane lined by old oak trees. Giant and green, they stretch overhead, connecting at the very top to create a canopy for sunbeams to filter through. The grass beyond looks recently mowed; the flowers and bushes are all perfectly landscaped. If I'm not as nervous, it's only because I'm too busy being shocked to feel anything else.

This is the kind of place they show in helicopter views on *Pop Store*, where only the richest celebrities live.

The trees open to reveal a mansion, with windows the size of my bedroom and white steps leading to double front doors covered by twisted wrought iron. At least three stories tall, the sandstone siding is topped with a gray roof that comes to spired points at the edges, like a fortress. Before it, in the center of the circular drive, sits a fountain, and from it comes a spray of water that catches the breeze and mists the windshield.

"Here we are," Moore says.

I swallow.

We may be here, but this test isn't over.

I'm led into the mansion through the front doors, and find myself in a cylinder-shaped entryway, encircled by a spiral staircase that leads to a catwalk over the ground floor, and disappears down a hallway to the left. Just beneath it is a door, bracketed by two stone columns. They're topped with black marble statues of birds, ravens maybe, each with long hooked beaks and razor-sharp claws, that stare down from their high perches. They don't exactly give a warm and cuddly vibe.

Following Moore beneath them, I find myself in a large, lavish office. Apart from the slim black computer on the desk, it looks like something from another time. Fancy oil paintings of horses and battles and pale, soft women surround me. The words *Vincit Omnia Veritas* appear on a stone tablet set atop a wooden stand in the corner. It's like a museum. I can almost hear Mom's voice telling me not to touch anything.

"Wait here," says Moore, motioning to a plush velvet chair facing the desk. He disappears out the door.

Though the temperature is cool, the room feels warm, maybe

because of the brick hearth occupying most of the right wall, or the couches and chairs and drapes, all in shades of brown and gold. As the minutes tick by I grow impatient. I don't know what's coming next—what the director is going to say. Despite everything that's happened, it seems entirely possible that he'll roll his eyes and punish his students for jumping protocol.

I wander toward a large painting on the wall of a woman in a white gown, looking over her shoulder. Her pale back is exposed. I'm not much for art, but it gives me a weird vibe, like she's too thin, and too vulnerable.

"Beautiful, isn't it? It's a portrait of my sister."

I turn sharply to face a man in his fifties, with neatly combed gray hair and a suit like the guys wear at Marcel's Funeral Home near the Devon Park SCTA station. He's even got a deep-red hand-kerchief making a triangle in his breast pocket.

"I . . . Yes," I recover, wiping my hands on my pant legs. I try to stand tall, to look distinguished, but the man's piercing blue gaze knocks me down a peg. There's an authority to him that comes not from acting tough, but knowing you'll never have to.

In one hand is the folder Moore brought to the house earlier. He extends the other.

"Dr. David Odin."

I take his hand and find his grip firm and professional.

"You're Brynn Hilder."

"Yes, sir," I say. Mom always tells me you're supposed to say sir or ma'am when you meet someone for the first time, and though I've never really put much stock into social niceties before, this seems like the right time to start.

"Welcome to Vale Hall," he says.

CHAPTER 10

I did a school report on a place like this once," I say as Dr. Odin releases my hand. "Versailles. It's a palace in France. Louis the fourteenth lived there."

I'm babbling.

"I've seen it," he says with a pleased smile. "Would you like to?"

I can't tell if he's serious.

I become aware of how I must look. Half my hair sticks straight out the back of my ponytail. My clothes aren't fit to be worn in a place like this. Even the almost three hundred bucks in my bag feels like chump change.

Everything about me screams that I'm not good enough.

Swallowing the lump in my throat, I follow the director to the large desk in front of the windows. He sits behind it, and motions for me to take the chair across from him. Behind him on a wall is a fancy framed certificate from Yale that says *David R. Odin, Doctor of Philosophy in Psychology*.

He's probably going to try to get in my head. I shield my thoughts behind a curious but not too eager expression. Interview or not, I don't want him poking around in there.

"I'm certain you must have questions," he says. "I can begin, but I'd rather hear your thoughts. Why don't you have a seat?"

He doesn't look at me or talk to me like I'm a teenager. He treats me like an adult. I can't help but appreciate that, even if I can't figure out what he wants me to say.

The chair is soft and plush, and it takes an effort to sit up straight without being sucked into it.

"This is the school?" It feels like a stupid way to start, but this isn't like any other school I've seen.

"It is. Vale Hall is a small private academy, hosted on my property."

"This is your house." It's impossible to hide the awe in my tone.

He smiles. "My grandfather invested in various businesses during his time. My father, before he died, worked as a congressman. The Odin family has lived on this property since the eighteen hundreds. I keep a private residence at the back of the property now, but yes. This is my house."

Old money, my mom would call it.

"So you're the principal."

"We don't really have a principal. Vale Hall uses an alternative structure. There are four professors; they report to me. There's also Ms. Maddox, who's in charge of the residential staff, and Min Belk and Hugh Moore, who oversee security and student affairs, and manage our work-study programs."

I wonder where Moore disappeared to—I haven't seen him since he left me in this office.

"How many students go here?" I should let him interview me, but now that the floodgates are open, I can't stop asking questions.

"No more than twenty students at a time."

When I choke, he adds, "This is an elite establishment, Brynn. I am very selective when it comes to the student body."

And I'm not in yet.

I take a deep breath. He must want me to prove myself. "My grades are good. Really good." It hits me that my math final will be starting soon, and that I'll be missing it, and failing the class.

Will he still let me in if I can't pass remedial math? "I actually have a final today, but I'll find a way to make it up. I'm a hard worker, and I learn fast. If you give me a chance, I swear . . ."

He holds up a hand to stop me.

"Brynn, I think you're under the wrong impression why it is you're here."

The breath deflates from my lungs. I passed the hazing test. Why bring me out just to tell me I'm not getting an interview?

"Why am I here?"

He leans back in his seat, hands resting on the black folder sitting in the center of his desk.

"Because you're special."

A lump forms in my throat, because there's something about the way he says it that makes this feel more fact than compliment.

"Excellent grades, despite significant barriers to success. Honors lists and academic achievements since elementary school. I did a bit of research after my staff processed your scholarship application."

It takes me a moment to realize what he's talking about. The counselor at Jarvis helped me find it last Christmas—a general scholarship for college. He had told me the odds weren't good of getting it since I was a junior, and hadn't done any legal extracurricular activities, but I applied anyhow. I never heard back.

"You got my name from a scholarship application." A sudden sickness boils in my stomach. Caleb *was* following me. Our crossing paths in Uptown, and on the train, and at the Sycamore library wasn't "fate," as he'd said. It was planned. Odin already knew who I was. I was Caleb's mark, just like Grayson was mine.

"I appreciated your essay on breaking through the glass walls," says Dr. Odin. "I, too, dream of breaking through such walls. Of a different, safer world, without corruption."

I catch myself before I laugh. This guy's never seen the kind of walls I have—the ones that lock you in a neighborhood where your dad was shot, in a school where the classes you need to get out aren't even offered, in a house with a guy who solves problems with his fists.

"No offense, but you don't look like you're hurting for much."

His eyes flash with steel.

"Don't let appearances fool you, Brynn. We are all hurting."

He says it in a quiet, low voice, but somehow it has the same effect as a person shouting at the top of their lungs. My breath catches, and then heaves out. I shouldn't have said that. I was distracted by the fact that Caleb conned me.

He set the bait, and reeled me in.

I'm kind of impressed. I can usually smell a scam a mile away.

"Can you keep a secret?" Dr. Odin asks. "Everything said in this office remains confidential."

It's one of the things I'm good at, but that doesn't make me eager to agree.

"All right."

He nods.

"This is a place for important people, and I take great pride in helping them realize their full potentials. But my students are extraordinary before they ever reach me."

I'm not really sure where he's going with this, but I don't have a good feeling about it.

"Being a part of a program like this requires a certain level of discretion. I need to know that you can keep what happens here to yourself, for the sake of your peers and for our continued success."

That bad feeling is now a stage five alarm blaring in my brain.

"What exactly happens here?" I ask.

"Learning," he says. "Growing. Camaraderie. Success."

"You sound like a pamphlet."

"I believe in our cause wholeheartedly." His chin lifts as I soak in the fancy art and antique furniture. "Speak your mind, it's all right."

"I know criminals who believe in their causes, too," I say.

"I bet you do." He looks at me as if to say, *like you.* "Fortunately, and sometimes unfortunately, legality is subjective. There's a moral code that goes much deeper than any law. The starving child who steals bread to survive, is he wrong? The man who kills his wife's murderer, does he not have that right?"

I don't exactly love him talking about murdering people in my entrance interview, but I get his point. Just because it's illegal, doesn't always make it bad.

He leans closer toward me. "The girl who steals money for college, should she be faulted for trying to better herself?"

"What are you . . ." The first time I saw Caleb was in the arts building in Uptown. He must have seen me with the ballerinas. He must have called Odin and reported what I'd done.

And yet, I'm still here, which means I haven't been disqualified yet.

I rub my damp palms on my thighs. "I mean, if people want to give cash to a stranger, that stranger technically didn't break the law."

The director smiles. "There's a gray area between right and wrong. You're here because you see that. Not everyone does."

"Okay."

His face grows somber. "There's also a gray area between what's right and what's legal, I'm afraid. Laws are made by people with money and power. Sometimes creating a safer world means removing those who pretend to protect it. Politicians, for instance, who care more about the cash in their pockets than the people they've sworn to represent."

The pieces are starting to fit together, though the edges are still unclear.

"Sounds like a job for the cops."

"And it would be, if the police were not friendly with the politicians."

Corruption, he said earlier. Maybe he does know a thing or two about it.

"So you take down the bad guys?" I try to picture him in spandex and a cape, and it's not a pretty image.

"I collect secrets. Secrets which the students at my school gather for me."

I stare at him, and then look around for a hidden camera.

"Is this real right now?" I ask. "Are you messing with me?"

He shakes his head.

I wait.

He waits.

"What kind of secrets?" I finally ask.

"Any kind, as long as they matter."

"And what makes a secret matter?"

"What someone is willing to do to keep it hidden, I suppose."

"What do you do with them?"

"That depends. A secret, in the right hands, has a great amount of power." He smiles at my expression. "I don't mean to scare you. I only use this information to help people who need it."

Which sounds like a really pretty way of saying *blackmail.*

Paranoia creeps up my back, making my skin prickle. Is he trying to trap me with this? Get me to do something illegal? I can't think of why he would want to—I don't know him—but his request is far from ordinary and a million miles away from the interview questions I was expecting.

"I'm listening," I say.

Dr. Odin looks pleased.

"If you accept your position here, you'll be asked to gather some information for me. To help me air some dirty laundry, so to speak. Your job, Brynn, is to be my eyes and ears."

"Sure, no problem." I hope he catches the sarcasm, because I'm laying it on pretty heavy. "How am I supposed to do that exactly?"

"The same way you did what you did last night at the party. By reading a situation and making friends."

I wait a beat. "You know about last night."

"Of course. I hear you put on quite the show."

I'm glad Caleb told him I passed their test, but it stings a little, too—a tiny echo of Marcus spying on me for Pete. I thought the party was a game put together by the students, a way to pick an applicant who was fun, and up for a challenge. I didn't think the director would be in on it.

What exactly does Dr. Odin get out of playing matchmaker with a bunch of teenagers?

"Think of your position as detective work," Dr. Odin continues. "As an after-school job."

You can work off enrollment costs. It's what I do.

"People sell bad pizza as an after-school job," I say. "They wash dishes, or, or . . ."

Dr. Odin chuckles, raising a hand to stop me.

"If you're concerned about getting in trouble, you don't need to be. You'll be protected. No one will ever know what you're doing as long as you don't tell them. We go to great lengths to protect the privacy of our students."

"Of course you do," I manage. "And if I get you something useful?"

"You'll be afforded a scholarship to attend the university of your choice."

I gape at him. Charlotte alluded to this at the tracks, but hearing it from the director makes it feel a lot more real.

"So who is it?" I ask. "Who's this person with all the secrets?"

Dr. Odin chuckles. "I appreciate your enthusiasm, but there are many problems in this city, and many people who cause them. You will have lots of opportunities to use your skills, but first we'll need to develop them. Start small."

"How?" I don't want to sound too eager, but not every day do people put a college scholarship on the bartering table.

Dr. Odin's grin widens. "Well, for instance, I might ask you to see what kind of information you can find online about Grayson Sterling."

It takes a beat for this to sink in. He's trading a scholarship for a few minutes poking around online? It can't be that easy.

"What do you want me to find out?"

"Anything you can," Dr. Odin says with a small shrug. "We'll touch base after you do some research. I find the more I know about someone, the better I'm able to gain their trust."

Fair enough. I'm still sitting here.

What he's asking is becoming a little clearer. This isn't just about online research or trading numbers with some spoiled politician's kid. He wants me to build trust with Grayson.

He wants me to get some secrets.

"And then?" I ask.

"And then we'll take the next step."

The challenge warms my veins. If I got Grayson to give me his number, I can get him to give me a lot more.

"We'll work with you on everything you'll be asked to do outside the classroom," the director says with a reassuring nod. "More importantly, at Vale Hall you'll be given a top-notch education. Tuition, room and board, and classes will be paid for. Medical needs will be covered. A stipend will be given for other living expenses—clothing, haircuts, transportation, whatever you need."

I make a sound halfway between a choke and a gag.

"You're talented, Brynn, and you'll fit in here well. I want you to join us."

A second passes. Then another. I sit a little straighter. No one's ever wanted me anywhere. No one's ever picked me out because I was special, or good at anything.

But I am good at something, and Dr. Odin is offering me a place here, and a possible scholarship to college, because of it.

"Do I need to sign something?" I ask. "Does my mom? I'm not eighteen."

He pushes the folder beneath his fingertips in my direction.

"Mr. Moore spoke to her this morning and explained that you had been accepted into school here."

With fumbling fingers, I take the folder and open it. Inside is a packet of printed papers with a fancy V logo at the top. I scan to the bottom. My mom's curly script is above the line *PARENT OR GUARDIAN*. *Allie Hilder*. It doesn't look forged.

You're taking her now? Just like that?

She knew I'd been accepted. She knew even when I didn't.

It's like I've swallowed splinters, and not just because she let me go. Because I didn't tell her any of this. She had to hear it from someone else. I thought I'd have more time.

But maybe this is the way it happens. One day you just leave. You don't talk about it, or think about it. You just go.

"I'm told she was surprised, but quite proud," he says. "You can check in with her later, if you like. We'll see to it that you get a phone. If you brought one, just give it to Mr. Moore. He'll have the data transferred to the new model."

"I didn't bring one."

The lie slips out as easily as if I rehearsed it. I don't know why I say it; my phone is right there in my back pocket, hidden beneath my baggy shirt, and if he searches me he'll know that I'm lying. But my phone, even if it's prepaid and I only have a few numbers in it, feels like my only connection to home. For some stupid reason, I don't want to give it up.

"Fine," he says. "When you speak to her, I'll ask that you don't tell her the details of what we've discussed."

My head is spinning. This is everything I've wanted. *Everything.* I'll still have to work to earn my keep, but that's nothing new.

"If you agree, you can begin here immediately. Ms. Maddox has already taken the liberty of preparing your room. And if I'm cor-rect, the upper classmen have Vocational Development in a few minutes. You're welcome to join them. Jump in, as they say."

"Okay." As I say the word something changes inside me, cuts the last rope holding me back. I want to scream. I want to jump on his fancy desk and dance.

Goodbye Jarvis High. I'm going to Vale Hall.

"A word of caution," Dr. Odin says.

I sober immediately, waiting for the catch.

"If I find out the truth of what you're doing here is exposed, this all goes away. You'll be asked to leave, no questions asked."

I force my shoulders back. "I won't tell anyone."

His smile is like a lion's: wide, and dangerous.

"You're going to love it here, Brynn," he says. "I promise."

CHAPTER 11

Ms. Maddox is round and wrinkled, and probably close to five hundred years old. She doesn't speak, according to Dr. Odin, but I'm not sure if that's because she can't, or she just won't for some reason. All I know is she walks slower than anyone I've ever met in my life, shuffling across the catwalk while gripping the bannister in her left hand. Honestly, I'm shocked she made it up the stairs.

Since she's not much for conversation, I try to make my own assessment of the place. The second floor looks to be mostly bedrooms—at least, that's what I'm gathering. All the doors to all the rooms are shut. I wonder if Caleb or the others are behind any of them, if they can hear my shoes squeaking over the shiny marble floor. If they do, they don't come out.

Finally, she opens a door near the end of the hall. I'm not sure what I expect, but as I step inside it's definitely not this.

A giant four-poster bed sits against the far wall. The window is draped with gold and lace. A desk sits close to the door, a closed silver laptop atop it. Books are stacked neatly beside it.

"Holy Jesus," I say. This isn't your typical dorm. This room is fit for royalty.

Ms. Maddox crosses herself with a scowl.

"Sorry," I mutter.

She warms at this, and reaches for my hand. Her grip is warm and soft, and when she squeezes I feel everything beneath my collarbones go hot. I clear my throat.

She leads me forward, over the plush beige carpet, and I see that the room is L-shaped. Around the corner an oval, wood-framed mirror stands beside a closet. Both doors are open, and inside there is a neat row of clothing on hangers.

"Oh," I say, suddenly realizing what's happened. "Sorry. This must be someone else's room." That explains the laptop.

She shakes her head and pulls me closer to the closet, reaches in, and takes down a hanger. A white shirt with a black raven in flight hangs on the hook. She holds it up to my chest.

It's the right size.

"These are for me?"

She nods and smiles, then replaces the shirt. I gape at the other clothes. Jeans. T-shirts. Sweatshirts. Even a dress.

I have zero words for this.

She takes me next to the bathroom, where there's a bathtub big enough for a horse, and a shower with glass doors. The mirror over the white stone sink is spotless and stretches the length of the counter. A toothbrush, still in its packaging, sits in perfect alignment with a hairbrush, a blow dryer, and a flat iron. There are shampoos and soaps already on the counter, and to the side, neatly arranged, are compacts of makeup with fancy looking brands I've never heard of.

"All of this is mine?" I step forward, opening a box of eye shadow with a pallet of colors ranging from dark gray to copper. The hollowed-out drug store eye shadow on my dresser at home doesn't hold a candle to this.

Ms. Maddox, still holding my hand, gives it another squeeze.

This is crazy.

Any time, someone's going to pop out and tell me this is a mistake.

Not Ms. Maddox, though, because she's not saying much of anything.

Finally releasing my hand, she opens a small door opposite the sink, where a stack of white, fluffy towels sits.

I don't know why it's the towels that break me, but they do. I begin to laugh, and soon tears are streaming out my eyes. Nothing about this is funny, but I can't get myself together. I feel like something inside of me is exploding, and I can't hold it in.

Ms. Maddox gives me an odd look, pats my shoulder, and then heads back to the main room.

I look at myself in the mirror, seeing my ragged clothes, and messed up hair, and crazy eyes, and stop laughing all at once.

I'm out of Devon Park.

I'm going to finish high school at Vale Hall.

No more living with Mom.

I see her face when I look at myself. Her eyebrows. Her nose. Her mouth. And I can't figure out why I was laughing because now I can barely breathe.

A dozen questions fire through my mind—what the rules are here, and where do I get food, and what my class schedule will be. I don't even know what I'm supposed to be taking, or where to go to meet my teachers, or if I can leave to see my mom on the weekends.

Vocational Development starts in a few minutes, I remember, and my shoulders bunch together. All my life I've prided myself on being one step ahead of the game, but now I can't keep up.

Pulling away from the mirror, I follow Ms. Maddox, who stops straightening the already straight sage-green comforter on the giant bed to point to the nightstand, where a sleek new cell phone sits, plugged by a charging cord into the wall.

This is my new phone, I guess. And the bed I will sleep in tonight. It's not exactly a lumpy twin mattress with a holey blanket. I'm in some alternate reality—the same things are here, they're just so much better.

She straightens and taps the watch on her wrist. Time for class.

"Can I have a minute?" I ask her, voice tight. "I'll meet you downstairs?"

She gives an understanding nod, and when the door closes softly behind her, I'm alone, standing in a strange, beautiful room, assigned to me by a rich vigilante who'll send me to college if I, of all things, keep conning.

Either this isn't real, or I'm the luckiest person alive.

I fish my cell out of my pocket, but I don't want to use it. I stuff it in the back of the nightstand drawer along with the cash and Caleb's note, and pick up the new phone, already feeling more elite.

I dial Mom's cell phone number. It rings only once.

"Hello?"

Pete.

If there's one way to cast shade over this bright opportunity, it's talking to him.

"It's Brynn. I need to talk to Mom."

"She's busy," he says bluntly. "Where are you? Whose number is this?"

"A friend's," I say, not wanting him to call me back. I should have used my old phone. "Tell her it's important."

"Where are you?" he asks again. Even the sound of his voice makes me sick to my stomach. "We had a deal. I need you to start tonight."

It hits me like a brick to the head. If I wasn't here right now, I'd be there, getting ready to sell drugs.

He doesn't seem to know I'm gone. Mom must not have told him.

I take a deep breath. He's going to figure out I'm not coming home soon enough.

"I can't." A trickle of adrenaline spreads through my veins. "Not tonight. Not ever, actually."

He's quiet. On nervous legs, I rise, and open the curtains over the window beside the bed. The view takes me off guard—the property seems to stretch on for miles. There's grass, and gardens, and trees. Snaking walking paths that back up against the woods, fading in the distance.

The adrenaline pumps through my blood, giving me a rush. The distance makes this easier—that, or this cush bed and fancy phone. Either way, standing up to Pete is better than any high his drugs can possibly provide.

"What's gotten into you?" His voice is cold as ice.

"I'm moving up in the world, Pete."

Half a dozen insults flash through my mind, but I don't want him turning on Mom because of something I've done, so I wrap it up.

"Tell Mom I'll call back soon." I hang up.

And then I toss the phone on the bed and do a little victory dance.

VOCATIONAL DEVELOPMENT IS held in a classroom on the main floor, though it looks about as much like a classroom as this mansion looks like a school. There are antique tables and plush velvet couches rather than desks and cracked, plastic bucket chairs. The windows are closed, covered by heavy drapes, and a movie's playing on a screen the size of a small car that's mounted to the wall. Beside it sits Moore, who glances up from his laptop as I waffle over the threshold.

"Have a seat, Brynn," he tells me. I'm grateful the lights are off so I don't have to make too much of a scene walking around the room. I have no idea what to expect from my first class here. At Jarvis, Vocational Skills is where you learn how to be an electrician or a plumber, but something tells me they learn different kinds of trades here.

"Hey," whispers a boy on a nearby couch, patting the empty cushion beside him. He was at the train tracks last night—the one in the plaid shorts and button-up shirt. *Henry.*

He looks nice enough.

As I move toward him, I count the heads in the room. Caleb's presence on the couch to the left reminds me of how I got tricked into following him, and my stomach gives a quick flutter of nerves. Charlotte and Sam are sitting on the opposite end. At the table in front of them sit three girls—I can only see their backs. They're whispering to each other. Call it intuition, but I bet it's about me.

Are all these students bringing back secrets for Dr. Odin? We're like a secret society. A vigilante CIA.

An old movie plays on the screen—at least I didn't walk in in the middle of a lecture. Though I missed the beginning, the plot is easy enough to pull together. A guy has just convinced some poor dope to carry five grand across town for him, and to avoid getting mugged, he has to hide the cash inside a handkerchief alongside his wallet, which is filled with his own money. Thinking he's made an easy five grand, the dope runs for it, only to discover he's been tricked. The hanky's not filled with cash, it's filled with tissue. Surprise bonus? His wallet's also gone.

When it's over, the lights come back on, and I'm surprised to see people shuffling their laptops and papers around. I wonder if I was wrong to assume this was a time filler—they could be studying the actors, or cinematography or something. I wish I'd brought a notepad, just to have something to do with my hands.

"What did we see here?" As Moore closes his laptop, the screen behind him goes dark, and whispering fills the room. Henry writes something down in what looks like a journal bearing the words *Vale Hall Academy, Vincit Omnia Veritas* on the front. I remember seeing that phrase etched in the stone in Dr. Odin's office. It must be their motto.

"The pigeon drop," says Caleb.

I'm not sure what he means, but it reminds me of how Pete and Eddie call the people they rip off "pigeons," meaning they aren't that bright.

"Good," says Moore, walking my way with a stapled bunch of papers. I take them as he hands them to me, reading *Vale Hall,* and the same inscription over the top that Henry has on his journal— *Vincit Omnia Veritas.*

Below it are the words: *Vocational Development Syllabus.*

I know the word, though I've never had my assignments compiled in a list at Jarvis. This feels fancy—the pressure is on. My eyes journey down the dates and tasks on the page, and I find this week's module entitled, *Classic Methodologies.*

"The mark—in this case we'll call him the *pigeon*—agrees to help someone in need, thinking that if he does, he'll walk away with money," says Moore, heading back to the front of the class. "Obviously, it doesn't pay off, as you saw in this clip."

I almost laugh. This cannot possibly be what it looks like.

Classic Methodologies, I read again.

"What's going on?" I whisper to Henry.

"Job training," he answers, and in his smile, I see truth.

Vocational Development teaches scamming.

This is a school for con artists.

A laugh bubbles up my throat. Dr. Odin said he'd work with me on my after-school job, but I didn't think that meant the classes would be like *this.*

Moore shoots a narrowed glance our way, and Henry sinks in the cushions.

"Everyone wants a shot at more cash," Moore says, and I stare at him like he's a whole new person, not the same stiff security guard that drove me here. "The pigeon drop, like most of the techniques in this class, relies on our sense of greed."

"It relies on an antiquated sense of ignorance." My gaze shoots to a girl in the front row, who's examining the ends of her dark hair. "Nobody in this day and age would fall for something like this. The play's over before it even starts."

"That's defeatist, Geri," says Henry.

"It's a lot like your last date," Geri answers, and I bristle when Henry starts to nervously rake his fingers through his blond hair. "The pigeon drop won't work."

"Not with wads of tissue and a handkerchief," I mutter.

Everyone turns to stare at me as if I spoke straight into a microphone. Now that I've got a clear view of the girl in the front row, I recognize her from the train yard. She was the one who asked how I got invited, and if I could believe Damien Fontego was there. *Geri,* Henry called her. I'd thought she was my competition, but I didn't see her at Grayson's party. Clearly she's already a student here, so maybe I got it wrong.

Or maybe she was messing with me, just like Caleb.

"See?" Geri finally says, her cheeks sucked in like she's eaten something bitter. "Even the new girl agrees with me."

Definitely messing with me. The we're-in-this-together vibe has vacated the building.

"She has a name," says Caleb. My gaze flicks his way, but he's staring ahead, arms crossed over his chest.

"Yeah, but that's a lot to remember," says Charlotte.

"Baby steps," agrees Sam.

"Enough already," groans Moore, thumb pressed between his brows. "I take it you've got a less *antiquated* plan, Brynn?"

My cheeks burn. Swallowing the knot in my throat, I sit up on the cushions, wishing I hadn't said anything.

"No," I say. "I mean, maybe."

Moore blinks in slow motion, which I take to mean he does not find my answer suitable. When I look over, Caleb's looking my way. Not at my face, but my hands, and suddenly I'm not sure what to do with them. I pick at a jagged end of my thumbnail.

Geri gives a loud sigh and turns back around.

I can't believe I'm going to say this. I'm getting arrested, that's all there is to it. I remind myself that this is why I'm here. That Dr. Odin said I was protected. That Geri was just talking about why this scam wouldn't work, like it was a math problem rather than illegal activity, and Caleb was the one who recognized it from the film clip in the first place.

I take a deep breath, gripping the syllabus in my hands.

"I once made two hundred bucks off a dog collar," I say, remembering the rich, married prick I'd watched proposition my mom at the Gridiron, then stiff her on a tip when she said no. "I told this guy there was a necklace that the pawn shop down the street was selling for two hundred and fifty dollars, but I'd just seen the same one online going for over two thousand, and I wanted to snag it before the shop realized they'd underpriced it."

Geri scoffs.

I lean forward in my seat, glaring at her perfectly layered hair. It's on now.

"I showed him my fifty, and said if he fronted me the difference, we could sell it online and split the proceeds, half and half."

"No way he went for it," says Geri, but when she turns she's considerably less smug than two minutes ago. The girls beside her are whispering to each other, and glancing her way, as if expecting her to get this under control.

"He spotted me two hundred. I bought a dog collar for a buck and gave it to him to sell online. He walked away thinking he screwed me."

Geri snorts. "That's luck."

"It's psychology, actually, Ms. Allen."

We all turn to find Dr. Odin standing in the door of the room, loosening the baby-blue silk tie around his throat. Everyone sits a little straighter. Everyone but me, who sinks in her chair and cringes. I didn't know the director was here, listening.

"We all want to be a part of something," says Dr. Odin. "Excitement is chemical. The promise of a payout releases dopamine in our brains, which makes us feel good. Sharing a secret with another person triggers a hormone called oxytocin, specifically designed for bonding. Our brains are designed to build relationships. Smart people know this. They capitalize on it."

People like us. People who go to scamming school.

Dr. O nods at me. "Well done, Brynn."

And then he leaves.

Henry bites his lip, stifling his laughter. I'm not sure if I'm supposed to take a bow or hide under my table. At my old school, attention, even good attention, was an invitation for trouble.

In front of me, Geri's facing forward, perfectly still. I can practically see the steam coming out of her ears.

"That's it for today," says Moore, cuing everyone to pack up their belongings. "Remember we have a field trip Tuesday. Geri still leads the class in points for the quarter, which means she's close to winning the much-coveted platinum pig." I look around for some idea of what this is as her friends cheer, but see nothing platinum or piglike. "Henry's at the back of the pack."

"But still feeling strong, Coach," Henry calls.

"Don't call me that," Moore responds. "Have a good lunch. Brynn, I'll catch up with you tomorrow for your tour."

"Okay." A new rush of nerves takes me over as I prepare for the dreaded lunchtime cool-kids-table hierarchy. Will Henry invite me to sit with him? Will Caleb or Charlotte or Sam? Something tells me I'm saved from an invite from Geri and her two friends, though I wish Dr. Odin hadn't stepped in when he did. I can fight my own battles, and I don't need to start here with the reputation that I'm a teacher's pet.

My stomach grumbles, but not from hunger.

Henry doesn't say anything, though, and before I can ask what he's doing, he's joined Charlotte and Sam, who corral him quickly toward the door.

"Well look who made the varsity team," says Geri behind me, in a way that sounds more like, *thanks for vomiting on my favorite shirt*. She's wearing workout clothes, though her makeup doesn't look like she's done much sweating. "I guess you weren't too busy to talk today, were you?"

Echoes of her *Okay* at the train yard when I went to confront Caleb press through the walls of my memory. I didn't mean to ditch her, but clearly she's holding a grudge.

Making her look bad in class probably didn't help.

Whispers of *Bloody Brynn* echo from my memories as her friends, also in workout attire, flank her on either side. I don't want to make enemies here.

"I'm sure I have a lot to learn," I say, gaze flicking between them. "Got any pointers?"

Geri huffs out a laugh, then takes a step forward, into my personal space. This close, I can see the tired shadows beneath her eyes that her makeup doesn't cover.

"If you do actually manage to get a job on the outside"—she holds a finger up in front of my face, and I fight the urge to slap it away— "don't blow cover." The second finger pops up. "Don't take risks." The third finger rises. "Don't make friends. Otherwise we're all screwed."

With that, she departs, passing Caleb by the door. He acknowledges her with a dip of his chin, but no smile.

So much for not making enemies.

Caleb's the only one left in the room. Exhaling hard, I head toward him, trying to put Geri's warning aside so I can sort out whether or not I'm irritated at him. He tricked me into following him yesterday—I was so convinced he was on my tail, I tracked him straight into a deserted train yard. But I've got to hand it to him. He was so subtle, I never considered that I was doing exactly what he wanted.

Welcome to the school for con artists.

He's wearing jeans and a casual baby blue shirt, a little wrinkled and rolled up to the elbows, and when his gaze turns my direction it triggers an internal shift, another wave of unsteadiness. Caleb is clean cut—all long limbs and sexy glasses. At my old school a guy like him and a girl like me never would have crossed paths.

"Well, she's friendly," I say, nodding to the door Geri just breezed out of.

"She's going through some stuff." He doesn't add any more, which makes me wonder if he has something to do with that.

As he holds open the door for me, an invisible shield rises up between us. He's not only vague, he hasn't been honest with me. Every meeting and conversation we've had has been orchestrated by someone else. For all I know, he only waited for me right now because the director told him to.

He pulls the strap of his backpack higher on one shoulder. "How did it go with Dr. O?"

Odin, he must mean. I make a mental note to call him that so I don't look stupid.

"He gave me a room upstairs, so I guess pretty good."

His jaw twitches at my tone.

"Nice," he says.

This is awkward—the last time I saw him we were pressed together, dancing for a crowd of people. Now it's clear we were both acting. This is the real us—two people grasping at conversation, unsure where the other stands.

"So what's this platinum pig all about?"

Amusement flickers across Caleb's face. "Petal is given to the student who has the most points at the end of the quarter in conning class. She's very special."

Conning class must be Vocational Development. I add the term to the Vale Hall file building in my brain.

I snort. "She's not an actual pig."

"She's so much more than an actual pig. Just ask Charlotte. Petal's currently residing in her room."

I take that to mean she is not an actual pig.

He leads the way out the door, and I follow, my stiff gait loosening with each step. We come to the kind of kitchen that could appear on a cooking channel, with a mile of white cabinets and every stainless-steel appliance ever made.

There's a bunch of people talking beside the giant center island—not just the kids from my last class, but at least ten more. A girl laughs. Her high voice makes it easy to pick her out of the group—blond hair, tiny build. She's wearing white shorts and a red tank top.

Dollface.

I look up then at the boy who's making her laugh, and recognize him, too. The guy with the muscles I last saw at the party.

They're all here. The girl with the shampoo hair who made a pass at Grayson at the party. A couple others as well. Seeing the other recruits makes me feel minutely better—at least I'm not the only new kid—but I don't know why they're here if they lost. As far as I know, Dollface and the others didn't finish the assignment with Grayson.

And I doubt they met with Dr. O before I did, given I got here before nine in the morning.

"No, she's here. *Now*," Charlotte hisses. When Dollface points my direction, Charlotte spins toward us. Her yellow summer dress cuts high on her thighs as she gives an overly enthusiastic wave.

Everyone goes silent, and then looks everywhere *but* my direction.

My stomach drops.

"You remember Charlotte," says Caleb, scratching the back of his neck.

Dollface has stopped laughing. Sam grabs Henry's arm and pulls him in the opposite direction, toward the open door that leads outside. Both of them are avoiding my gaze.

They're leaving.

Caleb scowls. "Henry and Sam, they . . . have some stuff to work on. For class."

"Right."

Charlotte whispers to Dollface, who cringes and checks something on her phone.

"That's Lila," says Caleb. "She's a junior here."

A junior. The girl I thought was my competition to get in is already enrolled.

My face turns stoplight red.

Geri, Caleb—they weren't the only ones playing me at the track. These people are already students. Everyone was pretending *but me.*

"Wow," I manage.

It stings. I hate that five minutes ago I was hoping Henry would sit by me at lunch. I hate that Caleb clears his throat when he sees my face. I hate that I can't fake normal, or force myself to blend in when that's literally the only reason I've been invited to go to school here.

From the group comes whispering, and I hear Geri's amused snicker.

I stare down at my worn Converse. There were other shoes in the new closet, but I needed something that was mine.

"So you're all pals." I'm unable to hide the tightness in my voice. "That's nice."

"Brynn . . ."

"Am I the only new person?"

He gives a reluctant nod.

"What about that actor—Damien Fontego? Did he actually go here?"

"Yes," Caleb says quickly, then winces. "It was thought by some that he might impress you."

He did, which makes me feel like even more of an idiot. The show at the train yard was all for me. Everything was staged.

The worst part is, I don't even have a right to be mad, because the trade-off is more than worth it. If I play my cards right, I won't just go to school here, I'll get a scholarship to college.

Don't make friends. I shouldn't have been so quick to dismiss Geri's advice.

"Caleb, I need to talk to you." Charlotte calls him from just outside the back door, as if she didn't see me standing right beside him.

"I'll see you around," I say, stepping back. They've got their little club, that's fine. I've been on the outside all my life—first as the girl whose dad got killed at the mini-mart, then as Bloody Brynn. I'm no stranger to being alone.

"Wait," he says, but I'm already heading toward the stairs. By the time I hit the hallway to my room, I've made a pact with myself. I'm going to get through Vale Hall. I'm going to do whatever I have to, keep my head down, just like at Jarvis.

I survived Devon Park. This'll be cake.

CHAPTER 12

Later, after I've explored every inch of my room, showered, and paged through the books on my desk, I crack open my fancy new laptop and use the codes left on fancy Vale Hall letterhead beside it to log into the secure server.

It turns out I have an email account already set up, and a message waiting from a Brigit Shrewsbury telling me to settle in, and that we'll discuss my class schedule tomorrow.

I'm about as settled as I'm going to get thanks to the welcoming committee downstairs, so with nothing else on today's agenda, I open the Internet and type *Grayson Sterling* into the search bar.

Dr. O wants me to do some online research? Perfect. There's no time like the present.

Tapping my teeth together, I scan through the hits that come up. Either there aren't that many Grayson Sterlings in the world, or he's the most popular, because the first eight sites all connect to him. The first two are *Tribune* stories about bills his dad has voted on, the next an announcement about some fundraiser in a few weeks at the Rosalind Hotel.

A little farther down I find a *Pop Store* article entitled, "Political Parenting Gone Wrong." I click on the link.

The screen is filled by the image of a guy with a twisting snake tattoo across his flat right pec. His skin is pale, his jeans low enough on his hips to make me seriously question if he's going commando. His dark brown hair is tousled, but it's impossible to tell if this is the Grayson I met last night because his face is hidden by both hands, which are flipping off the camera. The caption beneath reads: *Grayson Sterling, Daddy's Little Angel.*

I can't help but smirk, remembering how he folded a hundred-dollar bill into a paper airplane and sent it flying. Adding *issues with authority* beside *spoiled brat* to my Grayson file, I read the short article below.

Sources confirm Grayson Sterling, son of Senator Matthew Sterling, has been arrested for crashing into a parked police cruiser in West Chesterfield, a northern suburb of Sikawa City, Thursday night. Despite his offense and multiple witness accounts, the younger Sterling walked free from the local police station later that night, accompanied by the family lawyer. This is his third arrest in the calendar year, and his fourth to date involving substance intoxication. Yet, despite his age and obvious crimes, seventeen-year-old Grayson continues to evade the legal system, leading concerned citizens to question if Senator Sterling, the sweetheart of Sikawa City, is as squeaky clean as he would have people believe.

"Doubtful," I say aloud. The cleaner someone looks, the more dirt they're usually hiding.

Grayson has a history of run-ins with the cops, and connections powerful enough to clear his record—all good information to pass on to Dr. O. I look for other details that might come in use—social media pages, or school-related stories, but nothing else comes up. He must have his personal information locked up tight.

Instead, my search leads me to the senator's website. It's straightforward enough. Matthew's picture fills the right side of the screen, directly above a button to donate funds to his campaign.

There are lots of photos of the senator with the chief of police. Bet that helps when his son gets arrested.

I lean back in my chair, thinking of this security guard Pete had a deal with in White Bank. The guy worked the nightshift at the Wednesday Pharmaceuticals warehouse, where he'd let Pete in to take a stash of pills to sell in exchange for a cut of the profits. Pete valued this mutually beneficial relationship more than any other.

I can't help thinking Matthew Sterling must have a similar relationship with the police chief. Some kind of agreement. You scratch my back, I'll scratch yours.

The knock at the door makes me jump. The clock at the bottom of the screen says it's just after seven thirty. I'd lost track of the time.

Closing the laptop, I hesitate before rising to answer the door, the kitchen incident still fresh in my mind. I have to answer, though; it could be Ms. Maddox or Moore.

It's Caleb.

He's standing alone, in the same jeans and rumpled blue shirt as before, his hands shoved in his pockets. Dark pieces of hair hang down over the sides of his glasses and frame his wary gaze.

He's wearing Converse shoes—black, like mine, and folded down at the tops. The white rubber ends are scuffed. I didn't notice if he had those on before.

"Nice Chucks." I'm unable to hide the suspicion in my tone.

"Dinner's usually at six in the dining room," he says.

At the mention of food, my stomach clenches. I'm starving; I haven't eaten anything today beside the chocolate bars someone left in the desk drawer.

"I don't know if anyone told you that," he adds quietly.

No one did, and that hurts, even if I didn't give them a chance because I've been hiding in here.

"I'll add it to my calendar," I say.

"Breakfast starts at seven," he says, "but it's on your own. The staff puts out food in the kitchen. Cereal, or waffles, or whatever.

Someone's usually making eggs. And you're always welcome to whatever's in the fridge if you're hungry."

"All right."

"If you have questions about anything, you can ask me. Or any of us. We're not all that bad."

I snort.

"I mean, besides staging a recruitment rally at a deserted train yard and possibly not being completely welcoming earlier today, what have we really done?"

My lips turn up, just the smallest bit. "You tricked me into following you."

"I'm still going with fate on that one. You have no idea how many times I walked by trying to get your attention."

My grin gets a tiny bit bigger. "You spied on me." Dr. O knew about the ticket con with the ballerinas, information I'm sure he got from Caleb.

Caleb pushes the bridge of his glasses up his nose. "You haven't exactly been up-front, either."

"How have I—"

"The licorice incident? You could have given me a head's up." His dark eyes are gleaming.

"You didn't seem too upset at the time."

He gives a short laugh, but his smile fades, and so does mine.

"I'm sorry," he says. "I know it's a lot to take in."

He sounds honest, and my throat gets a little tight.

"It's okay," I tell him, and it kind of is.

A long moment passes.

"Well," he says. "Goodnight."

Maybe it's just because I've been alone all day, but I suddenly wish this conversation wasn't over so quickly.

"Goodnight," I say, masking my disappointment.

I step back and start to close the door.

"Are you hungry?" The words are fast, the question spilling out of him as he leans into the narrowing gap between the door and the wall.

I stop.

"I was just going to go make a sandwich." He juts a thumb in the direction of the stairs.

It occurs to me he might be saying this for my benefit—he probably ate with the rest of the group an hour ago—but I don't challenge him on it.

The hallway behind him is quiet.

"Where is everyone?" Call me a coward, but I'm still not up for facing the crowd.

"Out."

I wonder why he stayed behind. If it was just to talk to me. If Odin asked him to do it.

If he feels bad for me after what happened in the kitchen earlier.

Right now, I don't really care. It's my first night in a mansion, I miss my mom, I don't even have my own pajamas or toothbrush, and my seventeenth birthday begins in less than five hours. I don't really want to be alone.

"I could eat a sandwich." Tentatively, I step outside the room and close the door behind me.

His smile is brief and warm, and it helps to settle my nerves a little.

"This one's Charlotte," he says, tapping the unmarked door beside mine as we pass. "Lila's over there. Michone and Paz are at the end of the hall. Geri, Alice, and Beth are on that side. Beatrix is in Europe for an internship, but she'll be back in a few weeks. Ella and Dev just graduated."

All the names are overwhelming, but I try to commit them to memory.

"Who had my room before me?" I ask.

"Margot. She finished the program."

The dip in his voice makes me think he misses her. Maybe they were friends. Maybe they were more than friends.

I don't really care right now.

He keeps walking. "The guys are on the third floor." He points beside the last room to another staircase that heads to an upper level. "Sam, Henry, and I are going into senior studies. Joel's a junior. You saw him at the train tracks." He winces a little, and I'm reminded again of all the things everyone knew but me. "There are a few more underclassmen."

I shake it off. "Any other celebrities I should know about?"

He smirks. "Damien wasn't a celebrity until he got that internship on Broadway. He was an absolutely normal, not Hulkishly muscled, senior named Damien Farnell my freshman year."

I try to imagine a skinny, less-tan Damien cruising around these halls, books in hand, but can't.

But then again, I never would have pictured him at a train yard in the middle of the night, either.

"Dr. O told me only twenty people can go here at a time."

"Eighteen right now, counting you," says Caleb. "He's rich, but not that rich. Maintaining this place isn't cheap."

"There were clothes in my closet when I got here. And a laptop. And a cell phone."

"Exactly."

"Are they really mine to use?"

"They're really yours to keep." As we reach the stairs he takes the lead, and I follow him down.

"That's way too big of a gift." It doesn't feel right, accepting things like this. Where I'm from, people only give you stuff when they want something in return.

Which he does. He wants secrets.

"Think of it as investing in our futures," Caleb says.

We reach the kitchen, and he heads straight to the fridge. There he pulls out two kinds of bread, mayo, mustard, and a stack of sandwich meats.

"What sounds good?" he asks.

"Anything." There's so much food. At my house, we're usually lucky to end up with plastic packs of bologna. "All of it?"

He smirks and pulls two plates from the cabinet. "Cheese?"

"Of course."

"Lettuce and tomato?"

"Obviously."

"Pickles?"

"Let's not get crazy."

I reach for the bread.

"Have a seat," he says, stopping me with a bump of his elbow to my arm. "I got this."

I sit in a stool on the other side of the island, nerves dancing behind my sternum. It's strange to be alone with him without one or both of us working some angle. I kind of wish I could summon that girl who asked him to dance. Even the house feels too quiet; I keep looking over my shoulder, expecting someone to come striding up.

"So what else do I need to know?" I ask.

He stacks two pieces of what looks like sourdough onto both plates, and then ties off the package.

"Classes are in the mornings at ten. Each year has its own instructor. We have Ms. Shrewsbury. She's . . ."

"The shrew?" I finish, realizing the person who sent me the email about my schedule and the teacher they were talking about at the tracks last night must be one in the same.

He grins, and because I don't want to get caught in that grin again, I look down at his hands as he slices tomatoes on a cutting board. He has clean, blunt nails. Long fingers. The way they move is competent and graceful.

Maybe I should focus on the cheese. There's nothing graceful about cheese.

"So you do have regular classes? Not just Vocational Development?"

"Unfortunately. We go Saturdays and year-round since most of us work during the week."

A bolt of nerves zings up my spine at the mention of a job, and the potential that everyone here is doing some kind of blackmail reconnaissance for Dr. O.

"It's a little different than what you're probably used to," Caleb goes on. "Current events, history, literature, even math and science are all taught in one class." He lays the tomatoes on top of a generous heap of turkey and ham and moves to the lettuce. "Music is Monday and Thursday afternoons, language is on the other days— Shrew will connect you to someone in-country for live video chat instruction."

My brows lift.

"Like someone in Colombia if I want to speak Spanish?" I know none of my dad's language, and since he was the only one who immigrated to the US, his family was never around to teach me after he died.

"Or someone in Japan if you want to learn Japanese."

"Or someone underwater if I want to learn dolphin?"

"Or," he says, tipping the knife my way, "someone in Middle Earth if you want to learn elvish."

"Wow," I say. "You're a huge nerd. I had no idea."

It kind of makes him even better.

His warm laugh softens some of my frayed edges. He's comfortable here, and it loosens some of the knots in my muscles.

I take one of the finished sandwiches he passes my way and dive in, finding it even better than it looks.

"If this doesn't work out for you, you should seriously consider a job in the sandwich industry." I wipe the corner of my mouth with the tip of my finger. His eyes dart to my lips and then away, and I feel a blush creep up my neck.

"I'll keep that in mind." He takes the stool next to me and holds up his sandwich. Tentatively, I tap mine against his, like we're toasting with the fancy glasses the kids used at Grayson's party.

"Congratulations, Bloody Brynn. You're a Vale Hall Raven now."

My throat locks up as I try to swallow.

I set my sandwich down on the plate, remembering the laughter in the gym that day, the burning in my eyes when that stupid speaker's nose cracked against my forehead. I remember the tampons, taped to my locker in tribute to the name, and the jeers from the other kids on the bus. I must have been an idiot to think that wouldn't have followed me here.

"Why'd you say that? Who told you to say that?" My voice is hard enough to make his brows shoot up. I should have stayed in my room.

He lowers his sandwich, brows pinching together.

"I heard your friends say it on the train yesterday. I'm sorry, I thought—"

"They're not my friends," I snap.

The scene replays in my head. Marcus, Jesse, and Terrance stopping me on the red line. Me, trying to hide that I'd been in Uptown. Caleb, sitting in the back of the car, writing in that book.

I grimace at the memory of Marcus's voice saying *Bloody Brynn*. I force a breath. "I mean, one of them kind of is. It's complicated."

"Oh." He looks down at his plate. "I get it."

"Not like that," I say quickly. "Marcus and I used to date. We don't anymore."

"No?"

It's an invitation to elaborate, and though we're kind of on a shaky limb in the old trust tree, I take it.

"This may be a huge surprise to you, but I'm kind of a loner."

It comes out more serious than I intended. I'm not sure if I expect him to laugh or say something sarcastic, but he only nods, like he understands, and though this is a level deeper than I was aiming, I go on.

"My dad died when I was little. He was shot, actually, which didn't exactly make me the most popular girl at school." I pick at the crust of the bread, remembering how kids I knew weren't allowed to come over to play anymore, and how I was the only girl in my class not invited to Melanie Lu's birthday party. I can still feel the sting of their whispers.

"I'm sorry," says Caleb. He's turned toward me on his stool, sandwich forgotten.

"It was a long time ago," I say, even though sometimes it doesn't feel like it. "Then my freshman year this guest speaker tripped on his microphone cord and plowed straight into me. Broke his nose on my forehead. Blood everywhere—Bloody Brynn—you get the idea. Since I was already the resident leper, no one felt especially sorry for me."

He stares at me for a beat. Then barks out a laugh.

"Are you serious?" He looks vaguely horrified now.

"Would I make something like that up?"

"I thought it was some kind of British thing. *Bloody Brynn*," he says in a terrible accent. "Or maybe that it was your Fight Club name or something."

"Both of those things would have been much cooler," I agree.

"I never would have said it if I'd known."

He seems sorry, and actually offended on my behalf, which is both strange and sort of settling at the same time. So settling that the name doesn't even seem that terrible anymore. My stomach's calm enough that I can take another bite.

Maybe Caleb's all right after all.

"We have to change your luck," he says, nodding, as if I'm the one who suggested it.

"Tell me about it."

He rises, grabs my hand, and pulls me upright. Before I know it, he's pulling me toward the door that leads outside.

"Where are we going?" I ask.

"You'll see."

"We can't just leave . . ." I stare back longingly at the last un-eaten quarter of my sandwich.

"We have to. This is important."

I laugh a little, letting him keep his hand wrapped around mine. A warmth streaks up my arm from where we touch. Excitement bubbles in my chest, overcoming my wariness.

Caleb's stride is fast, and I jog to keep up. Soon, we're out the back door, and moving past the pool—a glowing blue rectangle in the fading light. The night air is warm, and it smells like chlorine and fresh-cut grass. He releases my hand when we get to the gate on the far end, and a bigger part of me than I care to admit is sorry about this.

"Where are we going?" I ask again.

"To see Barry."

"Who is Barry?" Nerves shimmer through me at the thought of another person joining us.

"You'll find out soon enough."

A stone path leads alongside an enormous grassy field, spotted with trees and park benches. The lights from the house guide our way, but the shadows stretch longer the farther we go, and my eyes begin to adjust to the growing dark.

"I was cleaning boats on the river when I heard about this place." His voice is a little lower, and he kicks a rock along the path in front of us. "I didn't think it was real."

"Is it?" I ask, knowing exactly what he means. "Does Dr. O really do all this vigilante stuff?"

Caleb watches our feet as we walk. "Did you hear about that priest in White Bank who was giving drugs to all the altar boys?"

I shake my head.

"Crack in exchange for certain *favors*." Caleb's voice tightens over the word, his implication making me cringe. "The police had tried to bust him for a while, but no one agreed to testify. So, Dr. O sent someone to sell him drugs. The whole interaction just happened to be recorded."

I stop, looking up at Caleb. "The priest went to jail."

"That's right."

"And the person who sold him drugs?"

"Now has a scholarship to NYU, courtesy of our honorable director."

I picture the NYU shirt I saw last night at the train tracks.

"Sam."

He nods.

I cringe. "Did he actually . . ."

"No," says Caleb quickly. "Dr. O puts our safety first, always."

That's a relief.

We begin walking again. I blow out a breath, still unable to believe that Dr. O actually does the things he claimed to do. That everyone here has some sort of assignment. That somewhere like NYU is actually on the table for someone like me.

I'm just about to ask what Caleb's assignment is when he holds out a hand, pointing ahead to where a hedge has risen from the shadows, taller than I am and thick as a wall. The path cuts through a gap in the center, and as we continue on, the sight steals my breath.

The gardens, because surely that's where we must be, are a wild tangle of flowers and vines, trees and white marble sculptures of birds and angels. A pond appears to my left, and in the glow of small glass lanterns a school of koi fish makes slow, lazy circles. Flowing from the pond is a stream, and when we reach the arch of the small wooden bridge climbing over it, a lawn opens before us, dotted with fireflies.

"Brynn," says Caleb. "It's time to change your luck."

CHAPTER 13

his is Barry?" I ask.

We're standing on the grass in front of a bronze statue of a fat, smiling, cross-legged-sitting man that I'd always assumed was Buddha.

"Charlotte named him," says Caleb. "She prefers Barry."

I hardly know Charlotte, but I can picture her doing this.

"You have to rub his belly," says Caleb. "It's good luck."

"He's not going to bite me or something, is he?"

"That would be an awful trick, Barry," says Caleb, giving the statue a stern look.

I rub a circle around his smooth stomach.

"I already feel luckier," I say flatly.

"I knew it." Caleb bumps me again with his shoulder, and this time, I bump him back.

He smiles a little, and I do, too.

Wandering across the grass, he stops at a bench and sits down. After a quick check of his cell phone and what looks like a text, he tucks it back in his pocket and pats the seat beside him.

Something tells me to keep my guard up, because being around anyone shouldn't be as easy as this feels now, but I fight it. For one night I just want to live inside a single moment, without the past biting my heels, or the future pushing me down.

"I can't believe this is happening." I glance back toward the house. You can't see the roof from here, but the glow from the lights paints the sky gray over the hedge wall. "Are you ever scared all this is going to disappear? You'll wake up one morning back in your old bed, and all this will just be some insane dream?"

His heel begins tapping; a flutter of movement then a sudden halt. "You won't have to go back, Brynn."

This quiet affirmation pierces through my shield, and my next breath is quaking in my chest. I try my best to hide it, to keep myself steady, but I know he sees.

I will not cry for the life behind me. I will not.

But everything I had yesterday, that I *knew* yesterday, is gone. I'm not the smooth girl who asked him to dance. Not Bloody Brynn. I'm not protected by Pete's reputation. I'm not even pretty Allie Hilder's daughter here. I am a blank slate, and I'm petrified, because without the battle I have to fight every day, I don't know who I am.

"Tell me this isn't crazy," I say.

"I can't."

Instead, he tells me about blueberry pancakes for breakfast on Saturdays, and field trips they've been on—not just to the zoo or museum, but on airplanes, once even to the Smithsonian in Washington, DC. He tells me stories about the others—Henry's botched project on medieval armor that involved welding all the spoons in the kitchen together. Sam's list of college acceptances. How Charlotte nearly caught Geri in points for conning class by selling pretend Girl Scout cookies outside a supermarket in Maryville.

He moves when he speaks—a subtle but constant motion. His shoulders rise, his hands circle, his body leans in and away to accent his words. He doesn't grow still until he asks a question, and then he's intent in his listening, angling his head toward me, soaking up every word.

We talk, and laugh, and when he grows quiet and looks up at the stars I realize how much time must have passed since we came outside.

"Why are you being nice to me?" Asking the question out loud turns my skin to glass, enabling him to see all my secrets, but I push on anyway. "If it's because Dr. O told you to, you can save it. I'm fine."

He leans forward, elbows on his knees, his back sloping down to his belt. "Maybe I thought you could use a friend."

"That sounds like something people say when they find a stray puppy."

"It isn't what Dr. O said when he found me." He grins, but I don't get the sense he's joking. It makes me wonder how he got here, how this group was really put together.

"So we're friends, then."

He seems to ponder this for a while, then lifts his arm in front of him and closes his hand in a loose fist.

Reaching for my wrist with his other hand, he pulls it toward him, and maybe it's this night, or the garden, or my own newfound good luck, because the way his thumb brushes over my thin skin makes my pulse go haywire and my skin warm.

He opens his hand and a firefly crawls onto my thumb, lighting neon yellow and buzzing its fragile wings.

Caleb doesn't say anything, and I don't, either. His fingers are cupped around mine; his body is leaning my direction. We hold perfectly still, watching the firefly crawl into the palm of my hand.

I become aware of my breathing, and his breathing, and all the places his skin touches mine. Of the tickle of the small insect's legs, and the chirp of the crickets around us.

"I'm glad you're here," Caleb says.

My heart trips over itself, and I smile up at him.

Then his phone buzzes in his pocket, shattering the moment. As the firefly launches into the night, Caleb pulls away. With a frown, he scratches the back of his neck.

"Come on. It's late." He doesn't check the message.

Instead, he helps me up, and we walk back to the house.

"IS EVERYONE STILL out?" Just a few lights are on inside now, and the main floor is silent.

"It seems so." Something's changed since we were outside. He doesn't meet my gaze when he talks, and he slouches a little more. It makes me nervous. Maybe I misread things outside. Maybe this whole night was encouraged by Dr. O after all.

He pauses by the back door. "Before we go upstairs, there's one other thing you should see."

Leading me around the back of the kitchen, we enter the dining hall, a long room with an enormous oak table and an honest-to-God chandelier hanging from the ceiling. The lights are low as we make our way to the far end of the room, where a carpeted stairway leads down to a dark basement. I hesitate as he motions for me to go first.

"Is this the part where you show me your collection of dead cats?" I ask warily.

He snorts.

"Just when things were going so well." I take the lead, since he seems unwilling to do so, and descend into the shadows.

"Where's the light switch?" I ask when we reach the bottom. My hand trails along the smooth wall trying to find it.

"It's ahead. Keep going."

A chill creeps over my arms as the hall opens to a larger room. I can't see anything, but the temperature grows cooler, and the wall beneath my fingertips disappears.

And then I hear movement, and whispered voices, and my stomach twists because I know exactly what's happening. The scene may be different, but the story is the same. I stop and turn back to face him. His eyes are nothing more than a glint of light through his glasses, but I stare up at them anyway. Heat fills my chest as my nails dig into my palms.

"I'm actually pretty tired." I try to move past him, but he holds out an arm. His hand touches my stomach, a blind reach in the dark, and then jerks back quickly.

"Wait," he says.

"Was this part of your plan? Get me outside so your friends could set up an ambush?" I push past him. "So much for starting over."

Bloody Brynn. He probably only asked me about that so he could use it against me.

"*Wait.*" This time he blocks my way. "Anytime, Charlotte," he calls, and the heat expands in my lungs, ripping up my throat.

I want to go back to my room.

I want . . .

The lights flip on, blinding me momentarily, while behind me several voices ring out, "Surprise!"

I'm still facing Caleb, whose mouth is now lifted in an apologetic grin. We're standing close—too close. My hands are on his chest, poised to push him out of my way.

"Surprise," he says quietly, for only me to hear.

I don't want to turn around—I hate surprises and I have no idea what I'm going to see—but at this point I don't have much choice. I pull back from Caleb, arms dropping to my sides, and turn to find Charlotte, barefoot, in the same dress as earlier, wearing a crooked red pointed party hat on her head.

Her eyes flick between us, and maybe it's just that I'm on edge, but it's almost like she's not pleased with what she finds. The look is washed away by a nervous smile.

"Happy Birthday?" Behind her stands Sam and Dollface—
Lila—and Joel in his muscle shirt. Henry is standing on a chair in
the center of the room, draped in party streamers.

It's my birthday. Well, almost—at midnight it will be. I'll be seventeen years old.

This is a party. For me.

"Oh," I manage.

"Told you she'd think we were going to murder her," says Sam.
"You know she's Southside, right?"

My smile catches me off guard, and I hide it behind my hand.

"It's a surprise party," argues Charlotte. "Who doesn't love surprise parties?"

"I love them!" shouts Henry.

"See?" says Charlotte.

Caleb, now beside me, motions me inside with a tilt of his head.
"It'll be fun. I promise."

Fun. I know the concept, but haven't exactly had a lot of time
for it recently. Or ever.

I take one step, then another, and when I'm close enough it seems
to release Charlotte from her stance, and she bounds toward me.
She's holding what looks like a Hawaiian lei made of construction
paper in her hands. With a huge smile, she hangs it around my
neck.

"Welcome to the pit," she says. "Sorry about the weirdness earlier. We didn't think you were coming until tomorrow and none of
the party prep was done."

I half laugh.

"I'm hugging you now," she says. "Don't knife me, okay?"

Now I more than half laugh. She hugs me, and it's the kind of
hug someone gives you when they've known you a long time.
"Happy Birthday, Brynn. Welcome to the greatest school on Earth."

"Thanks," I say.

Sam leans in and kisses me on the cheek. I blush a little harder and glance to Charlotte. She only laughs, and snaps her fingers twice. "Music, Henry!"

A moment later speakers begin to play some strange pop song I've never heard on the radio. With Charlotte's arm threaded through mine, she introduces me to Lila, who hugs me as well and asks if I like chocolate cake because that's what they made, then Paz, who still looks like she should be in a shampoo commercial even in her pajamas. Alice and Beth, both juniors, seem nice enough with Geri gone, though they mostly keep to themselves.

Geri, I'm told, is working.

A sophomore named Michone introduces herself, then cocks a hip and tells me I don't have first dibs on cereal just because I'm a senior.

Charlotte corrects her, but she only lifts a brow, and says, "Yeah, we'll see."

"Nice job with the licorice." Paz gives me a high five. "No one's ever played Caleb before."

"No one played Caleb," calls Caleb. "That's not what happened."

Paz and Michone give him a look that says otherwise.

I giggle. Actually giggle.

Then Henry has his arm over my shoulder and is leading me around the giant room. There are couches and plush chairs arranged in front of a giant television mounted on the wall, bean bags on the floor in the far corner by arcade games. A bar along the back wall is covered in bowls of snack food, and to its right sits a piano and a drum set, and two guitars on stands.

Red and yellow streamers hang from the high corners alongside painted signs that say *Happy Birthday Brynn!* I can't really look at any of them without getting choked up. I haven't had a birthday party since before my dad was shot, and those I only remember from pictures.

"We're here basically every night," says Henry. "Ms. Maddox

always makes sure there's snacks and sodas in the fridge, but if you want something special, she'll make sure you have it."

I nod, unable to speak.

"I have the high score on Pac-Man," he continues, pointing toward an old arcade game. "Caleb likes to pretend that he lets me win, but don't believe him. He's a filthy liar."

"I suck at Pac-Man," I tell him. "No threat to that high score on this end."

This seems to please him. He leans closer. "You look like you're going to cry."

And I sort of hate him right then, because he's exactly right.

Tears stream from my eyes, and though I cover my face it doesn't matter, because they just keep coming. Everything inside that's been simmering since Pete took my college money has finally boiled over, and I can't keep it all in. These people actually like me. I'm set up in a mansion north of the city. This will be the first birthday I've ever had that my mom won't make me cupcakes.

And then Henry's hugging me, and we're swaying back and forth, and he's singing "It's my party and I'll cry if I want to," and somehow I'm laughing, too. My emotions are a broken stoplight—stop, go, stop, go—and I can barely hold myself together.

I've never had this problem before.

"We need cake!" he shouts. "Stat!"

"On it!" Charlotte hollers, and over Henry's shoulder, I see her sprinting toward the bar like the house is on fire. It might as well be the funniest thing I've ever seen because I crack up, and Henry joins me.

They light candles on a huge chocolate cake and sing "Happy Birthday." While we eat, Sam plays the guitar and Charlotte sings. She's got the kind of voice that belongs on the radio, and when Henry joins in with the harmony, my jaw hits the floor.

"Play with us," Charlotte calls to Caleb, but he glances at me and then shakes his head.

"Come on," Henry says. "Caleb's our resident Mozart." I look to the piano, and then to Caleb, who's standing on the edge of the circle that's gathered, hands in his pockets.

"Another time," he says, and even though I want him to play, too, I don't want to embarrass him.

So we make our way over to the TV and play some monster car video game they all love called Road Rules. I crash off the path instantly, but Charlotte insists I keep trying, and after two more pieces of cake I finish in sixth place—out of six.

They all cheer for me.

All but Caleb, who smiles my way, and when no one else is looking, mouths, *Told you*.

I don't want this night ever to end. My bones don't feel so heavy. My brain isn't already planning out two steps ahead. The fact that this will still be here tomorrow blows my mind.

We hang out until almost four in the morning, and then trudge upstairs together, disappearing into our respective rooms. I crash on the giant bed, sinking into the comforter, and replay every part of the party in my head, over and over again, so I have it forever committed to memory.

The last thought I have is of Barry Buddha and my sudden good luck, and when I sleep, I dream of fireflies.

CHAPTER 14

"Rise and shine, my celebrity friend!"

I blink, then scramble up, the construction paper lei crinkling as I grab the covers. I'm at Vale Hall. Someone's in my room. I must not have locked the door.

"Yikes," says Charlotte, eyes widening. "You look . . . really nice."

Her sarcasm does not escape me. She's already in full makeup and is dressed in a green romper with matching flip-flops. Her wavy orange hair floats around her pretty face. Clearly she's already gotten into some caffeine. Or crack.

She closes the door behind her, cell grasped in one hand.

"What time is it?" Grabbing the phone on the nightstand before she can answer, I see that it's 9:14 in the morning.

Charlotte plops down on the side of the bed. "I take it you haven't been online yet." She presses a few buttons on her phone, and then passes it to me.

I take it, rubbing my eyes with one hand. When the screen comes in focus, I shove myself up.

It's a photo on the *Pop Store* website of Grayson. And me.

It must have been taken just before I left the party, because he's leaning close, holding my hand to write his number on my wrist. My face is shadowed by the low light someone's tried to brighten, but my smile is obvious, like I'm enjoying his flirting rather than celebrating the fact that I've just tricked him into asking me out.

"You looked hot," she says.

"What is this?" Shock clears the sleep from my head. I didn't know there'd be pictures of us. I certainly didn't think there'd be pictures of us on a news site, however trashy. *Senator's Son's Flavor of the Week,* the caption says.

"That," she says, "is you earning a scholarship to Dartmouth. Well done, Birthday Girl."

Memories of last night's party come rushing back to me, but they're shadowed by this new information.

Charlotte's right. Dr. O wanted me to dig around online for Grayson, but this is even better. It proves I've already established the trust he was talking about.

I snag the phone from her hand. The article is only a few lines, posted along with other local celebrity sightings. *Senator Sterling's son seen at family function with mystery girl. Will she be the first to tame Grayson's wild side, or just another castoff in his long line of broken hearts?*

"I am *not* his flavor of the week." I point the phone at Charlotte. "Who took this?"

"Doesn't say. Probably some jealous lady-friend posted it and *Pop Store* snagged it from there. Happens all the time."

"It does?"

"Yeah." She waves a hand, showcasing five perfectly manicured fingers. "I've been on there like three times."

"Really?" I wonder if Dr. O's already seen this. Probably not. He doesn't seem like the type to watch trashy daytime TV.

"Really," says Charlotte, examining the picture again. "You did give him a fake name, right? And tell him you were homeschooled by a tutor or something?"

School didn't come up, but I make a note to keep that in mind for the future.

"I told him my name was Sarah."

"Boring." She rolls her eyes. "They all have pretentious names like Acorn or Autumn Moon. You should have gone with something more exciting."

I sigh.

She takes back the phone. "So is he as bad as everyone says?"

"He's got the attention span of a gnat."

"That's not so bad. My last assignment was with a mean girl who only wanted to talk about her nose job."

That sounds like my own personal brand of hell, but I imagine Charlotte's pretty good at the friend act, based on the way she's been with me. She's the kind of person who's comfortable around other girls—who makes them comfortable, too.

I wonder if she's using those skills on me right now.

I pull the covers up to my neck.

"Class starts in less than an hour." Charlotte walks to my mirror, where she twists her hair into a messy bun. "You might want to deal with your face before you get breakfast."

"It's Saturday." The second I say it I remember Caleb telling me they go to school on Saturdays, and through the summer, *since most of us work during the week.*

I'm supposed to meet with Ms. Shrewsbury—the Shrew—to go over my class schedule.

Shooting out of bed, I stumble to the bathroom, and lock the door behind me. When I look at the mirror I see what she must have meant. My cheek is green. Shamrock green. And the crushed construction paper lei beside my jaw is damp with drool.

Gross. I must have laid on it while I slept.

After scrubbing off the mark, I comb my hair, then glance down at the makeup on the counter. Tentatively, I open the eye shadow, finding all different colors, some with more shine. I pick a charcoal and try it out. Then some eyeliner, and a little lip gloss.

My cheeks don't even need blush. I kind of like the girl staring back at me in the mirror.

By the time I'm out of the bathroom, Charlotte's picked out an outfit and laid it on the bed for me—a short, spaghetti-strap dress with black and white stripes. The fact that it looks like it might be my exact size makes me a little uneasy.

"Who picked all these clothes out?" I ask, reaching instead for another T-shirt, this one gray with a raven on the breast pocket.

"I don't know. Dr. O, maybe."

A frown pulls at my face. I don't love the idea of an old man cruising through a women's clothing department picking out outfits for his teenage residents.

"I mean, Ms. Maddox probably," she says with the wave of her hand. "I don't know. It doesn't matter."

But it does kind of matter. Where gifts come from is important. Who you owe is important.

I turn my back, hesitating before I strip off last night's shirt and put on a new one. I've never changed with another girl in the room who wasn't my mom, but Charlotte doesn't even notice. She goes to the vanity beside the closet, rummaging through what looks like a jewelry box, and emerging with some dangly earrings.

"These are all wrong for you," she says. "I'm taking them."

I snort. They're gold and beaded and, she's right, not really my style.

"Thanks." She tucks them into her pocket. "Happy Birthday to me."

She slips another pair into her pocket without asking. Then, after a quick glance over her shoulder, what looks like a necklace. It doesn't bother me—they don't really feel like mine anyway.

I smooth down the school shirt, tracing the black raven and the words *Vincit Omnia Veritas* beneath it with my fingertip.

"What does it mean?" I ask, pointing to the letters.

"Truth conquers all."

I smirk. Of course the motto of a school for liars is about truth.

"Can I . . ." She motions to the clips I've jammed into my hair. When I nod, she takes them out, her fingers gently pulling the strands as she refits two on each side of my head. The short ends stick out a little more, but now like I did it on purpose.

"Thanks," I say quietly.

"Don't mention it."

A wave of nerves crashes over me. Last night went well, but there are a hundred ways things can go wrong today. I don't want to earn more of Geri's wrath by answering another question wrong. Fingers crossed we don't have any other classes together.

It's going to be fine, I tell myself. I'm here for a reason. I have people I know now. The kleptomaniac currently digging through the jewelry box, for one. Henry, Sam, and Caleb, as well.

Have any of them seen the *Pop Store* article?

I grab my brown messenger bag and put a notebook from my desk inside. As I pull my hand out, my knuckles brush against the pack of gum Mom gave me yesterday, and for one dizzying moment I'm back at home, surrounded by sky-blue carpet, the smell of cigarette smoke, and the distant wail of sirens.

Has she told Pete where I am yet? I can't check my old cell with Charlotte standing here, so I don't know if she's tried to call.

"Ready?" Charlotte asks.

I need to look forward, not back.

"Ready."

I don't like not knowing what other supplies—pens, pencils, paper—I'll need, but I shove it down and put on my best game face. This may be Vale Hall, but I grew up in Devon Park. Rule number one: don't show weakness.

Charlotte's already walking out into the hall, and after a deep breath, I follow her into the next room. The outside of the door may be the same plain white as the others on this hall, but the inside is an explosion of color. There are clothes everywhere—hanging on the backs of chairs and over her standing mirror. Twinkle lights stretch between the four posts of her bed. One wall is covered with doodles—flowers and faces and quotes, written right on the paint.

"Wow." Where I'm from they call this kind of thing defacement of private property.

"What do you think?" She holds her arms wide and spins in a circle.

"It looks like a rainbow threw up in here."

She cackles. "You can decorate however you like. Just keep the hallway clean. Ms. Maddox's rules."

I smile at the memory of how the old lady held my hand as she showed me around my new room.

"She seems nice."

"Don't let her fool you," Charlotte whispers. "She doesn't say much, but she hears *everything*." She returns from her closet with a red leather bag and slips her laptop inside. I look down at my messenger bag, noting the ratty strap and the edges where the seam has popped. Next to my new clothes it does look a little worn.

I don't know which looks more natural on me—the bag and my old Chucks, or these designer jeans and my feather-soft shirt. I feel caught somewhere in the middle of fantasy and reality, and more than a little like a fraud.

"Adios, Petal," Charlotte says, drawing my attention to her nightstand, where Petal the Pig sits in a shoe box.

She's literally a piggy bank, spray painted silver.

Somehow, this makes me considerably less nervous.

Charlotte pats Petal's worn head—the pink beneath is peeking through—and then we're off.

"How long have you been here?" I ask as we head toward the stairs.

"Awhile," she says. "Since midway through my sophomore year."

"Wow," I say. "And Sam and Henry?" I hesitate. "Caleb? They've been around a long time, too?"

At Caleb's name, she slows, hugging the strap of her bag against her chest. Her teeth tap together, as if she's not quite sure what to say.

"Look, about him."

I slow, too, but my face is on fire, so I keep my eyes straight ahead. From the way she's tensed up, I'm pretty sure she's about to deliver some bad news.

"I don't know what's going on with you two but be careful with him."

"Nothing's going on." My tone is too defensive. I try to soften it. "We're just friends."

The word reminds me of last night, when he didn't answer after I asked if that's what we were—*friends*. I bite the inside of my cheek.

She snorts. "Uh-huh."

"What?"

"Look, things can be intense here with school and everything." She looks at her nails. "Just be careful. Caleb's a good guy."

I balk. "And I'm the trash from the south side, is that it?"

"No." She grabs my arm before I head for the stairs. "I like you. That's what I'm trying to say. I don't want you to get hurt."

Me to get hurt? Which means that Caleb would be the wild card in this situation. I try to align this Caleb she paints with the boy who put a firefly in my hand, but I can't.

"I'll be fine," I say, confused, mostly because she cares enough to warn me. I don't have a ton of people watching my back.

"I know."

We're on the stairs now, and though a dozen more questions as to why I should be careful of Caleb are popping up in my mind, I don't ask them, because I can hear voices from downstairs. If I can hear them, they can probably hear us.

"Sammy's been here about ten months," she says, picking up the previous thread of our conversation. "Henry came just after me. Caleb's been on the longest. He was fourteen when he got here I think."

I remember him telling me he was a freshman when Damien

Fontego was a senior. I can only imagine what kind of secrets he's gathered in that amount of time.

"Do you ever go home?"

"This *is* home," Charlotte says bluntly. "My country club parents not-so-politely told me I was dead to them, so here we are."

I wonder what a pretty white girl did to get kicked out of the suburbs. My mind returns to the jewelry, now in her pocket. I bet it was theft.

I glance up at the ravens over Dr. O's closed office door as we make our way to the kitchen. Chills crawl over my neck. It's like they're watching me.

"Good morning, Charlotte. Brynn." I turn sharply to see Dr. O coming from the kitchen with a steaming mug of coffee in his hand. His white dress shirt has been crisply pressed, and I can practically see my reflection in the leather shoes that emerge from his beige pants.

"Morning, Dr. O," says Charlotte. "Did you see our girl made the *Pop Store* highlight reel?" She slings an arm around my shoulders.

I wait for his response, suddenly not sure how he'll take it. But his brows arch, and with a free hand he motions for the phone Charlotte's now flashing toward him.

"Quite a mark you seem to have made," Dr. O says, beaming at me.

My cheeks warm. I don't want to look like a suck-up, but if a scholarship's on the line, I'm not wasting a moment.

"I looked up some of the things we talked about."

He laughs. "There's no rush. I'd rather you settle in. Get comfortable."

I shrug. "I found a couple things."

He takes a sip of his coffee. "Well, then." With one hand, he motions toward his office.

With an encouraging wink, Charlotte heads toward the kitchen, while I follow Dr. O beneath the black marble ravens. Taking our same seats as yesterday, I tell him about the *Pop Store* article and the various dropped charges.

"There's a picture I found of his dad and the police chief. They seem close. Maybe the senator's calling in some favors."

I'm not sure if this is the kind of secret I should be looking for. It feels pretty obvious, but Dr. O nods, and writes something down in a leather notebook on his desk.

"Very good," he says. "Anything else?"

"If he has social media pages, they're all locked," I say, wishing now that I'd waited until I had more to report. "Everything else I found has to do with his dad's work."

"His father's a powerful man."

"His son's a spoiled brat," I say.

"Oh?"

I tell Dr. O about the hundred-dollar paper airplane, and how I used that to start my game. His head tilts back as he laughs, and when he smiles at me, I feel like I've just aced a test.

"Very good," he says. "This is exactly what I was looking for. How do you feel about taking things a step further? Making contact? Something simple. A phone call maybe, or some text messages. I don't want you to get into anything too involved, just a brief check-in to maintain the connection."

"Sure," I say. "I can do that."

"Good," he says. "Let me know how that goes. In the meantime, go get some breakfast before Mr. Moore finds you. He had some work to do for me yesterday, but he's planning on completing your orientation this morning."

I stand up, ready for my new assignment. Ready for orientation, and my meeting with the Shrew, and my new classes.

"Well done, Brynn," Dr. O says as I head for the door. "I knew you'd do well here."

I smile all the way to the kitchen.

WHEN I GET there, Ms. Maddox is cooking at the stove and the whole place smells like an IHOP. My mouth begins to water.

"Get something to go." Moore's curt voice behind me has my spine pulling straight. When I turn, I find him striding in from the outside door, wearing a black suit, his sunglasses up on his head.

Charlotte, dropping off an empty cereal bowl in the sink, leans close.

"With Moore, the best plan is to nod and smile."

I nod, but I don't smile. The guy takes serious to the next level; even the smallest grin might overload his circuits. Still, I'm kind of excited to talk to him. The conning class teacher has to be a master of scams. Maybe he's got a few tips for me.

"I'll just take an apple." I grab a red one from the basket on the island.

Moore heads toward the back door. I assume this means I'm to follow him, and after a brief look at Charlotte, I do. On my right, I catch a glimpse of the dining room and my stomach twists when I see the others gathered around the table eating together.

My gaze lands on Caleb just as he does a double take in my direction. He's leaning back in his chair, an empty plate before him on the woven placemat. When I smile, he almost goes tumbling backwards.

"Brynn," barks my tour guide.

I jump and hurry through the door Moore's opened, feeling Caleb's stare warming my back.

Outside, Moore takes off around the pool, and I quicken my pace to keep up.

"By now you've seen the house," he says.

It takes a beat for me to realize this is a question.

"Yes. My room is great. Thanks."

"Thank Ms. Maddox. I'm in charge of the security of his estate, and the safety and discipline of the students." His words are flat, like he's already over this little talk. Most of the cons I know have a certain charisma, but not this guy. He's all business.

He lowers his glasses as we step outside. "That means I'm the one who shows up if there's a problem, and I'm the one who deals with you if you step out of line."

Well. Let's hope I won't have to be dealt with.

"We're walking." He marches outside, pointing down to the aqua water flowing from the rock waterfall as he passes by.

"Pool," he says, as if I'm a toddler and don't know this word. "You don't go in it without informing an adult first."

"Yes, sir." I shove the apple inside my bag and hurry after him.

Instead of heading toward the gardens where I went with Caleb, Moore takes a sharp left, leading me down a stone staircase to another path that circles the building. There, he stops.

"You see the fence?" He points ahead, to where a white picket fence stretches from the front gate past the gardens.

"I see it."

"That fence lines the edge of the property on all sides. You don't leave Vale Hall without telling me where you're going. My number's already programmed into your phone. I prefer text communication."

"I'll bet you do." I can't see him happily taking calls from teenagers all hours of the night. It reminds me that I should find a better hiding place for my old phone, just in case he comes looking.

He lifts his glasses to look me in the eyes, one brow cocked. His voice may lack emotion, but there's a hard intensity in his brown eyes that says not to mess with him.

I give him my biggest, cheek-stretching smile.

He lowers his glasses. "Medical and mental health concerns are managed by private physician. Prescriptions can be arranged if necessary. Any other health supplies you may need," he sighs, making me think he probably means condoms or feminine hygiene, "can be found in the supply closet at the end of your hall."

He returns his glasses to cover his eyes and starts walking again. "If you need a ride somewhere, you have to let me know twenty-four hours in advance. If you need to be picked up, text. Mr. Belk or I will be there as quickly as we can. If you ever feel unsafe, or find yourself in trouble, I'm who you call, not the police."

I figured the cops would be left out of whatever happens here, but I can't help wondering if this is just protocol, or if other students have found themselves in trouble before.

Dr. O puts our safety first, always. That's what Caleb said when he told me about Sam busting the priest. Settled, I follow Moore around the side of the building, to a garage I didn't see yesterday. When he types a code into the small box on the side, the metal door slides open quietly.

A small wince forms in my throat. There are six cars in three lines. A black sedan, a black SUV, Charlotte's Jeep, and three other sports cars that look like they belong on magazines in car repair shops.

"Do you drive?" he asks.

I glance up at him. "Um . . . no."

I regret this answer as he presses a button to lower the garage. "Never mind then."

I stare longingly at the cars until the last possible second, dreams deflating. I should have lied and said yes. Maybe he would have passed over some keys.

He continues on around the front of the house. "There are no weapons on campus. There is no fighting. There are no boys in the girls' hall or girls in the boys' hall. There is no disrespecting your teachers, the staff, or your fellow students. Curfew is at eleven. You're to be in the house by then."

He doesn't specify where in the house, so I imagine the pit must be okay.

"You don't bring anyone not enrolled on campus. If the director approves you to meet with someone, it's done in the community."

"What about my mom?"

"We'll schedule visitation after you're acclimated. To give you time to focus on your assignments."

"Visitation sounds like a prison word, Mr. Moore."

"I take the security here very seriously, Ms. Hilder."

This doesn't exactly set me at ease. I knew there'd be rules, I just didn't expect them to be so strict. Still, I understand why. If word of what people are doing here gets out, Dr. O goes to jail. Probably Moore, too.

Maybe even us.

The risk we're all taking hits me like a punch to the gut. This falls apart and there's no private school, or college scholarship. No fancy rooms upstairs or parties in the pit. This isn't a normal school. If I don't do well here, it's not just a matter of failing a class. My future could be ruined.

But this is nothing new. I took these kinds of risks running cons. I avoided the cops and kept secrets when I had to. The same principles apply here, just on a different—much larger—scale.

I picture Caleb, sitting in the garden telling me about how great this place is. No one would do what we're asked to do if the reward wasn't worth it. No one would be here if Dr. O didn't make good on his promises. He's already given me a room and a phone and a laptop, and I haven't even really done anything yet. That's a bigger chance than anyone's ever taken on me.

Besides, he's actively making the world a better place, like with that priest Caleb was talking about. Dr. O needs my help. No one's ever asked me to do something that important before.

"Anything else?" Moore asks.

Somewhere in the distance, a lawnmower buzzes to life. The air smells sweet, like honeysuckle.

I shake my head.

"Good." With that, he turns, and continues on our tour.

CHAPTER 15

Read the next two chapters quietly. We'll regroup in thirty minutes to review." Before me on the lawn, Ms. Shrewsbury— aka the Shrew—waves an ancient hardback copy of *A Tale of Two Cities* in her wrinkled hand. Though we're outside in the sunshine on picnic-style blankets, she's dressed for December weather. The cloak she wears is draped over her boney frame, and her salt and peppered hair is pulled in a tight braid down her back.

Her sharp gaze locks on the boy sitting in the grass in front of me. "Henry, I expect you to lead the discussion with no less than three thoughtful questions about the French Revolution."

"Of course," says Henry dramatically, but when he turns back my direction his eyes are wide with panic. "It is definitely the worst of times," he whispers, quoting the first line of the book.

I hide my laugh in a cough.

"Ms. Hilder." Shrew snaps my attention back to the front. "A minute please."

I'm guessing this is about my schedule, though her tone makes me feel like I've done something wrong. I rise from the blanket, where I've been sitting cross-legged since Moore delivered me to the rest of the senior class, and approach our teacher.

Charlotte and Sam, sitting beside each other on the right, whisper for me to turn back before it's too late. I hope they're joking. Caleb sits in front of them, but doesn't look up as I pass, even though I'm only five feet away from him. He's hunched over his book, writing something in it with the black pen he holds in his left hand. Clearly he's very invested in this topic.

That, or something's on his mind.

He was there for me last night. Even though I'm new here, and everyone seems to be his friend, I hope he knows I can be there for him, too.

"Welcome to Vale Hall, Ms. Hilder," says the Shrew, in the least welcoming way possible. "I've taken a look at your transcripts. They're pitiful, to say the least."

I clasp my hands together behind my back, taking a quick glance over my shoulder to see if anyone's paying attention. Instead, I catch Sam gaping at the phone hidden in his book, and Charlotte's sly grin in his direction.

"What's wrong with them?" I ask.

"Everything," she says. "Remedial math? Basic English? You didn't even finish your junior classes."

A sudden fear that I'm here too soon, that Dr. O will send me back once he realizes that I left before Jarvis's school year ended, grips my chest.

"That's because I'm here—"

She holds up a hand. "Excuses will get you nowhere. We need to focus on solutions."

I balk.

She retrieves a notebook from the roller bag she's carted down here, then licks her fingers and flips through the pages.

"I've never had a student graduate late, and I don't intend to start now," she says. "It's time for us to play some catch up, my dear. Clear your schedule. This is going to take some work."

She turns the notebook toward me, and there, below my name, is a checklist of assignments that make my stomach sink like a rock.

"This is a lot of reading," I manage. And math. And everything.

"Do you want to go to college or not?"

I stand straighter, taking the notebook. "I'll get it done."

Her mouth quirks in a hint of a smile. "Good. I'll have the materials you need delivered to your room."

"I'M NEVER GETTING all this done," I say aloud three hours later, staring at the stack of books on my desk. More than half of the readings and assignments are online, and I have no idea how to use the tracking system Shrew set up. Overwhelmed is putting it mildly. Totally screwed is closer to the mark.

I'm still staring at my desk when a buzzing pulls me from my thoughts. At first I think it's the vacuum—on the way up I passed Ms. Maddox slowly pushing it down the hall—but as it stops and starts again, I realize it's coming from my nightstand.

Lunging toward the bed, I jerk open the drawer and fumble with my old phone. When I see *MOM* in the caller ID, I flip it open.

"Mom?"

She's already hung up.

I'm just about to call her back when the screen switches, and I see that I've missed several more calls. Three from her, and one from Pete, about an hour ago.

Chills prickle along my skin, as if the temperature of the room has just dropped several degrees.

Something's wrong.

I lift the phone again to dial the number, but stop myself. Mom never calls me this much. Not even when she slipped on the ice last winter and broke her ankle did she light my phone up like this.

I stare at Pete's number.

He's the one who's trying to reach me. He's pissed about our conversation the other day, or maybe he thought I was lying and that I'd really be home by now. He's probably using my mom's phone to trick me into calling.

But I might be wrong.

The knock at the door has me leaping up, a cold sweat on my brow. A moment later, Ms. Maddox inches into the room, vacuum first. I hide the phone in my pocket just in time.

"Sorry, I um . . . I need a minute," I say over the noise. "Can you come back?"

She smiles, and motions for me to continue whatever I was doing.

She hears everything, Charlotte said.

Surely this sweet old lady isn't spying on me.

Not wanting to chance it, I grab my bag and duck out of the room, waving at Lila and Paz as I pass them in the hall.

Everyone is milling around downstairs, and I don't want to rouse suspicion by going outside. When I near the dark stairs leading to the boys' wing, I veer that direction, stopping in the turn halfway up the carpeted corridor to dial a number I haven't dialed in a long time.

"Pick up pick up pick up," I chant as it rings. My gaze keeps roaming toward the lower hall, but though I hear voices no one seems to be coming this way.

"Hello?"

It's just after noon, but Marcus sounds like he's half asleep.

"It's me," I say quietly. "Brynn."

There's a shuffle of fabric, telling me that he was indeed asleep, and then his voice is louder. "Brynn? What's going on?"

"A lot," I tell him. "I need you to do me a favor."

"Hold up," he says. "Are you in jail?"

"*No.* There'd be a message beforehand if I was. *An inmate from the local penitentiary is trying to reach you.*" I don't even know why I'm bothering to explain this to him. "Listen. I don't have much time."

"Yeah," he says, focused now. "What's happened? I heard you went AWOL."

So nice of him to assume I was in jail. "Who'd you hear that from?"

He hesitates. "You know who."

Pete.

My heart is beating a mile a minute. Things are going really well here, and if Dr. O finds out I have another phone, it could ruin everything.

"What'd he tell you?"

"Just that you didn't come home last night. Says he's worried."

I snort.

"Yeah," he agrees.

"Why's he want to talk to me?"

"I don't know," he says. "How am I supposed to know this stuff?"

"Does he have any idea where I am?"

"If he did, he wouldn't ask me about it."

Which means Mom didn't tell him I'm here. The relief is fleeting—it's just a matter of time before he breaks her down. Is he mad because I told him I wouldn't sell his drugs? Or just because he can't control me like everything else in his life?

"Where are you anyway?" he asks.

"Doesn't matter," I say. "Have you been to the house or seen Mom?"

"No."

"Do me a favor and swing by. I missed a bunch of calls from her." I haven't asked anything of Marcus in a long time, and even though I don't completely trust him, I know he wouldn't lie about my mom.

"So call her back." He yawns.

"No." A lump forms in my throat. "It's him calling from her phone. I'm sure of it."

"Why would he do that?"

"I don't know, just do me a favor and check on her okay? Make sure she's all right." My pulse ticks faster. "Be cool about it. Pete can't know I called you."

"Sure, sure."

"I'm serious, Marcus. He knows I'm in contact, he'll bust you up trying to get details."

"You worried about me?" I can picture that cocky smile perfectly, and with it comes a pang of regret. Once that smile actually made me feel better. Now it reminds me how little he takes seriously.

"If you were smart, you'd worry about yourself."

Marcus swears.

"I'm calling you tomorrow," I tell him. "You'll see her by then?"

He pauses. "What are you gonna give me?"

"That isn't funny."

"You're asking me to sneak around behind my boss's back? I gotta get something for this."

"You'll get me not kicking your ass," I say, temper hot. "Don't make me call your mom and tell her you're dealing, because I will."

"Come on, Brynn," he says. "That's messed up."

This whole thing is messed up.

"So you'll do it?"

He mumbles something, then, "Yeah, I'll do it."

"Thanks." We're done, but I don't hang up, because as much of a pain as Marcus is, he's the only connection I have to Mom right now.

"Brynn?"

"What?"

He hesitates. "You all right?"

Homesickness washes over me, cold and suffocating. I hate the weakness it brings. I don't get to miss torn bed sheets and cold chicken wings from stupid Gridiron Sports Bar. I have a brand-new laptop and a closet filled with designer clothes. I have a *future*.

"I'm good."

"Watch your back out there."

I'm just about to tell him I will when a stair above me creaks. "Hey."

I jump, and stuff the phone into my bag. When I turn, Caleb is standing four steps above me. He must have been in his bedroom.

"Hey." My thoughts are flying—did he see the phone? If so, how much did he hear? Will he tell Moore or Dr. O I smuggled in contraband? It's not like I've given away any of Vale Hall's precious secrets.

After a beat, he comes down the rest of the stairs so that we're on level ground. I still need to look up to him, and it makes me aware of how much bigger he is than me. Even though he's lean, his shoulders are broad, drawing back to pull his shirt tight across his chest.

"Were you talking to someone?" he asks.

"Just myself." Here in the stairway. Which is perfectly normal.

He scowls, his chin lifting a tiny bit. Whatever comfort we found last night feels out of reach. I'm jumpy, and he's wary, and it creates a kind of tension between us, as if we're standing on ice that's too thin.

Charlotte's words run through my head: *Be careful with him.*

I wish I knew why.

"What are you doing over here?" he asks.

"I was . . . just coming to say hi." My shoulders rise, drop. I need to go back to the dining hall. To my room. Somewhere. But my feet won't move.

"Oh," he says, brows lifted. "Hi."

"Hi," I say.

One side of Caleb's mouth lifts, and for a flash I see the guy who put a firefly in my hand. Then the moment passes, and even though he's still technically smiling, his guard is up.

"Don't let Moore catch you on our side," he says quietly. "And hide the phone. He likes us to use the ones he can trace."

Of course he does. That's why I was supposed to hand over any phone I brought in. I know it's just for our security, and the security of the program, but I'm unsettled all the same. No one cared where I went or who I called before.

"I'll see you around." He moves past me toward the turn in the stairs. "Heard Ms. Maddox is making tamales for your birthday. Remember, dinner's at six."

Without waiting for a response, he disappears around the bend, leaving me alone in the stairwell.

CHAPTER 16

'm still thinking about that call, and Caleb, and the phone, now hidden on the top shelf of my closet, later that night as I stare at the books on my desk. Something's going on at home, and the not knowing is like a finger prodding a bruise. If Mom's in trouble—if my leaving is the cause of her trouble—I don't know what to do.

Getting out was not supposed to involve getting dragged back in.

My frustration shifts to Caleb, and his strange distance on the stairs. He obviously heard me talking to someone, but even if he disapproved, he doesn't seem like a snitch, despite the fact he barely acknowledged me at dinner.

Leaning forward, I rest my forehead on the desk. There are other things I need to focus on, and since I have no idea where to start with Shrew's assignments, I reach for my shiny new phone.

Make contact, Dr. O said. Maintain the connection.

I transferred Grayson's number from my wrist to the back of Caleb's note from the Heatherwood party, and after retrieving it from my nightstand, I carefully transfer the numbers to the keypad. Then I stare at the screen for a full minute, unsure what to text. If I say the wrong thing, he'll blow me off. If I come on too strong, he'll become suspicious.

I need to keep it simple. Dr. O said he didn't want me to do anything *too involved.*

I review what I've learned about him, both online and at the party. He likes games. He gets bored easily. Money grows on trees to him, and he does whatever he wants without any legal consequences.

I tried to talk to Charlotte at lunch, but even though she led the recruitment efforts at the train yard, she only knows the basics about him.

He's eighteen. He goes to a rich kids' school called Kensington Prep. He lives in Heatherwood with his sister, who's sixteen, and his mom and dad, who are never home. She didn't think he played any sports or was involved in any clubs or other activities.

That was when Geri broke in and told me to do my own research.

I don't care what Caleb says, that girl's got issues.

Setting the phone down, I stretch, and crack my knuckles. For this to work, I'm going to need to be likable, approachable, *trustworthy*. I've got to do something that's going to catch his attention and remind him why he was interested in the first place.

Taking a deep breath, I summon the girl I was at the party and pick up the phone.

Tell me something interesting, I text, then press send.

I set the phone on the desk, then pace around the room. A tight breath siphons from my throat. I've just become that girl who waits for the wrong guy to call her back, unable to think about anything else but him.

Only, not because I like him. Because I need him to like me.

Come on, Grayson.

My phone buzzes. I'm on it in a flash.

I have a 911 Carrera.

I don't even know what that is. Opening my laptop, I run a search.

It's a Porsche. Of course it is.

I wonder if it's too obvious to ask if Daddy bought it with taxpayer money.

Boring. Try again.

I've been to eleven countries.

Hasn't everyone?

There's a break, and I hold the phone with both hands, staring at the screen. It buzzes.

I'm color-blind.

Now we're getting somewhere.

What's that like?

Normal for me, he writes. *I didn't know I couldn't see red until 5th grade.*

That must have been a surprise.

A few moments pass.

It's like finding out nothing is as good as it could be.

Says the guy who has access to everything.

Your turn, he writes.

He must know who this is, otherwise he wouldn't be playing. Still, I can't help wondering if he responds to random people just for fun. I saw him at that party. He was willing to jump ship the second I said I was leaving. He didn't seem particularly attached to anyone.

If I'm going to keep his attention, I need to be unexpected. I have to be different.

And I doubt there's anything as different to a rich kid from Heatherwood than a poor girl from Devon Park.

Biting the inside of my cheek, I consider this. I can't give him too much truth—I don't want to blow my cover—but a little bit of Brynn might actually work here.

I like scary movies, I write.

Which ones?

The old ones. The Exorcist. Pet Sematary.

Me, too.

I bet. He's got no reason to be honest with me. For all he knows, I don't know a thing about him. He could tell me anything.

I could tell him anything, too.

What else do you like? he asks.

I imagine his mind's gone to the gutter, so I keep us afloat.

Christmas trees, I say. *Chicken wings. Cupcakes on my birthday.*

Mom always makes me cupcakes today. I wonder if she had already gotten the mix before she knew I was leaving. The thought kind of bums me out.

When is your birthday?

Today.

I stare at the screen, kicking myself for writing that. I should play it off, pretend this was a joke. That information feels too personal.

How old are you?

I don't respond right away.

He doesn't appear to need an answer. *Now you have to go out with me.*

I lower the phone, tap it against my thigh. This is going well, but I need to keep him on the line a little longer. This is a guy who's used to getting what he wants when he wants it. I need to keep the upper hand. Maintain the connection, but not get too deep.

Another time. I have a ton of homework.

Who does homework on their birthday?

People who have to make up missed classes.

He doesn't respond for over a minute.

Where do you go? Not Kensington Prep.

You asked around about me? How sweet.

That's me, he writes. *Sweet.*

Yeah, I doubt it.

I need to cut this off before he gets too comfortable.

I have to go.

Come on. It's your b-day. I'll get you a drink. Your choice.

I grin. *Not tonight.*

Then soon.

Maybe.

And with that, I shut off my phone, and crack open a book.

CHAPTER 17

Despite Caleb's stories about field trips to places like the Smithsonian, our Vocational Development class loads into the black SUV on Tuesday morning and is taken to a farmers' market along the river. It's a swanky setup, with jewelry booths and artisan chocolates, and is packed with people who walk tiny, groomed dogs on harnesses and carry reusable grocery bags.

And probably a lot of cash, which is what most of these vendors will take.

Not that I need cash anymore.

I grin, thinking about my meeting this morning with Dr. O. He was so impressed when I told him about the texts with Grayson, and the pictures of us both making stupid faces we exchanged last night. *Keep it up,* Dr. O said. By the end of the week he wants me to call Grayson on the phone.

No problem.

"The long con is about rapport," Moore tells us before we get out of the car. I sit up straighter, glancing at Charlotte, who only winks in my direction. "People do things for people they like. You're in the business of telling them what they *want*. Which is what?"

"Whatever *we* want," chimes Geri.

Moore nods.

I can't believe this is my life.

"Selling can be a complicated skill, but it's a necessary one—not just for your assignments, but for everything in life." Moore turns back in the driver's seat to face us. "Walk around, figure out how these vendors work. Look at this guy." He points ahead to a man balancing two flats of strawberries in one arm and a bag in the other as he crosses the street. "You think he needs all that? No. Someone talked him into it."

"I love strawberries," says Henry longingly from the front seat.

Moore freezes him with a look. "We're salesmen today."

"Sales*people*," Geri corrects.

"Thank you, Geri," Moore says flatly. "Each of you is going to have the opportunity to talk someone into buying something they don't need."

"But what if they *do* need it?" Henry asks.

"That's the point, Henry," calls Sam. "You're going to make them think they need it."

"Make them think they need what?" Henry asks.

Moore sighs. "Pair up. I want you to go buy something under five dollars. In twenty minutes we'll meet back here to trade items. Whoever sells their item for the highest price point wins today's challenge." He looks to Sam, sitting on the opposite side of Charlotte. "Partner up with Brynn. Show her the ropes."

Sam gives me a fist bump over Charlotte, who's already assuring everyone she'll be bringing us both down. Her smiles fades when Moore chooses Geri as her partner.

As the rest of the class pairs off, Moore unlocks the doors. "Remember, at any point during today's exercise you sense someone's on to you, drop what you're doing and send me a message. I'll come to you."

"Let's all try to be kind today," Henry says as we step outside. "No buying things that will be impossible to turn around, deal?"

From the way the others laugh, it's clear the competition is on.

· · ·

TWENTY-FIVE MINUTES LATER, Sam and I are cruising through the row of booths with a neon-yellow knit hat, complete with ear flaps. Henry and Caleb found it, and though I'm glad we didn't end up with a box of rotten bananas, like Geri so sweetly gave to them, an ugly winter hat in the dead of summer is going to be a hard sell.

"Maybe we can pawn it off as something else. A designer purse? An egg carrier?"

Sam fiddles with the top button of his plaid shirt, sizing up the crowd. "In what world do people use an egg carrier? And don't say Devon Park, I know for a fact that's not true."

"Is that right? How exactly do you know?"

"I'm your neighbor," he says. "I grew up in the brick end of Amelia."

I glance up at him, surprised. The brick end is on the opposite side of Devon Park, toward White Bank, where all the houses are made of crumbling red brick. That's the rougher end of the township. Marcus doesn't even live that far over, and his place is pretty dicey. It hadn't occurred to me Sam didn't come from money. He's a natural fit at Vale Hall.

I glance from his newsboy cap, over his perfectly shaved jaw, all the way down to his fitted shorts and boat shoes. The preppy nerd look he's rocking doesn't exactly scream Southside.

"NYU's a long way from there."

Dimples form in Sam's cheeks as he grins. "It's an even longer way from juvy."

We take a turn around another row, and I catch a glimpse of Charlotte and Geri arguing over the small patch of wheatgrass we got from the juicing station. Sam winces as Charlotte throws her head back and groans.

"Why'd you get locked up?" I ask.

"I was taking the SAT for people. Hundred bucks a pop. Someone recognized me at a testing site."

That's a risky move. Schools are pretty serious about the rules for standardized testing. Still, I'm impressed. I haven't taken the SATs, but I doubt they're easy. If someone hired Sam to do the job, it must mean he's pretty smart.

"Well aren't you the little felon," I say. "How'd you get out?"

"Moore showed up at the detention center. Said if I was smart enough to pass the SATs, I might be smart enough to pass his test. If I could, he'd get the charges dropped." Sam chuckles dryly. "He's a special guy."

I laugh.

"Figured it was a scam—I know how the system works, people like me don't get a lot of second chances. But I took his test." He shakes his head. "One question. Why'd you do it?"

I look over at him, trying to imagine him doing the things he talked about, but I can't. "Well?"

"In my neighborhood, you use what you've got to get what you need. So happens, I've got a pretty decent brain."

I understand this. Without the ability to read a room, or a mood, or an elevator full of ballerinas, I wouldn't have survived a week in Devon Park.

"My mom's in Bennington," he says. "You heard of it?"

Bennington's a women's prison in the northern part of the state. I know about it because a lady on my street got put away for beating up her kids while she was strung out.

That place is no resort. When that lady came back, she couldn't look anyone in the face for a year.

"Yeah." I twist the knit hat in my hands, thinking of him visiting her in prison. That can't be easy.

"She's the third generation in my family to serve time." He kicks the grass with the toe of his shoe. "Turns out I don't want to be the fourth."

I get it. My parents might not have been in jail, but Devon Park's its own kind of prison, and the odds of breaking out are about as good as winning the lottery, or starring in a movie.

A thought sparks inside of me, and I hold up the hat.

"I think I have an idea."

"EXCUSE ME!" I say, bumping into a woman with stark white hair shaved up the right side of her head. On one arm hangs an empty shopping bag, and in the other hand is a trendy leather clutch. For the last ten minutes, I've been watching her criticize every booth owner for not having a natural whey powder she saw on television.

She doesn't answer, just sighs and steps out of my path.

"Ma'am?" I turn to find a handsome NYU-bound student heading my way.

"Yes?" I say.

"I'm sorry, but are you an actress?" Sam pulls nervously at the brim of his hat. "My friends and I have this bet. I swear I've seen you on that show, *Mission 12*."

The woman is now absently picking up oranges and setting them back down.

I lower my voice, just enough that the woman can still hear. "How much did you bet?"

"I knew it!" Sam throws his arm up in a victorious V. "Can I get a picture with you?"

"Of course! I was actually just at a photo shoot for Pop Store." I pull the hat out of my pocket as he steps beside me and do my best modeling impression. "They had me previewing fall fashions."

"You wore that?" Sam asks.

"I did." I give a little giggle. "Apparently it's going to be everywhere next month."

"It's cute," the woman says.

I laugh again. "I know, right?"

"You're kidding." Sam's eyes go round. "Okay, this is crazy. Can I buy that for my girlfriend?"

I glance down at the hat, then scratch my head.

"I don't know . . ."

"I'll give you thirty bucks." He pulls out his wallet. "She would totally freak out to know you wore it."

A crowd has started to gather around us. A familiar buzz fills my blood.

"It's going to be retailed for over a hundred," I say.

The woman leans closer, narrowing her gaze down at the thick yarn stitching. "I'd give you fifty."

Sam's already digging through his wallet. "Hold on. I have sixty dollars here."

"Caroline?" The screeching voice makes all three of us turn toward the aisle. Who Caroline is, I have no idea, but Geri is standing in the back of the crowd, holding her arms out in my direction. Her smile is as wide as a slice of cantaloupe.

"What is she doing?" I mutter to Sam.

He gives an almost imperceptible shake of his head.

"I thought you were out sick today." Geri rushes toward me, blocking out our mark. Behind her, I see Charlotte, hands on her head.

I'm sorry, she mouths.

"I didn't see you in first period—I thought you might have caught that flu bug you said your mom had. Anyway, we'd better hurry and get back before lunch is over. Don't want Mrs. Boston to write us up for tardiness." Geri grabs my sleeve.

"You're in high school?" asks the woman.

"Um, yeah," says Geri, as if this is obvious.

The woman tilts her head and points my direction. "She's not an actress?"

Sam gives a weak laugh.

"Of course she's not an actress!" Geri jabs me in the side. "I mean, we did *Oklahoma!* at our school for the spring play, but we were both just extras."

The woman scoffs, her face scarlet. She leaves before I can stop her. Before I can fix this.

Geri just outed me. For a spray-painted piggy bank.

I look to Sam, certain she's broken some rule in this exercise, but he's only motioning for us to retreat. Others are watching, and we don't need this kind of attention.

I snag Geri's arm as we hurry away. "What was that? What happened to 'don't blow cover'?"

"You didn't, *Caroline*." Geri bats her eyes, continuing on. "Don't get all huffy. I was just playing with you."

My blood turns to steam. I stomp after her, but when I get to the car, my pace slows. Caleb and Henry are leaning against the back bumper, and the others are already gathered nearby. I don't want them seeing this. I don't want to give Geri the satisfaction of winning.

"How'd you do?" Moore's brows lift as he looks down at the yellow hat in my fist.

I want to tell him what she did. I want to out her, the way she's daring me to with that taunting hair flip she just performed, but my past is too ingrained in my present, and I can't.

I'm not a snitch.

"No luck," I grumble. Beside me, Sam's breath exhales in a hiss. Charlotte stares at the ground.

Caleb's gaze does not leave my face.

"Too bad," says Geri. "We got twenty bucks. That's enough to buy Petal a new pigpen."

No one can top it. Not even Henry, who claims he and Caleb deserve extra credit for the three dollars they earned selling the rotten fruit to a composter.

Moore's quiet hum does not mask his disappointment, and for some reason, I can't help but feeling like I just let him down.

"Geri wins again," he says.

For now.

CHAPTER 18

"You have got to be kidding me."

I drop my messenger bag inside the doorway of my room, staring at the giant words painted on my comforter, which now hangs from my ceiling on the far wall.

Home Sweet Home.

It doesn't stop there.

Not only are my clothes and sheets piled in the shower and soaking wet, but my desk and chair are upside down, my curtains are covered with silly string, and someone's drawn what I guess to be an entire flock of ravens on the left wall.

In red lipstick.

I groan loud enough to shake my bones. My afternoon was a rush of trying to memorize notes and scales in music theory, and Spanish feeling words, and by the time I reached dinner, it was all I could do to not throw meatballs from my spaghetti at Geri and her snickering friends.

Now I see what they thought was so funny.

But as much as I want to call her out, I can't let her see that she got to me. I refuse to let her win.

So I tear down my comforter, grab a towel from the bathroom, and start cleaning the walls. I don't want to leave the mess for Ms. Maddox in case she decides to tell Dr. O and we all get in trouble, but it becomes obvious quickly that my efforts are only staining the walls pink, and my hands bloodred.

"I like what you've done with the place," says Charlotte, appearing in my doorway.

"This is never coming off," I growl, wiping away the sweat as I scrub more pink circles into the wall. I can't stop thinking about Geri laughing at me at dinner, and how she sabotaged the con Sam and I set up at the farmers' market earlier. This girl is going down, one way or another.

Charlotte goes to the bathroom and returns with some makeup removing wipes from under the sink. She kneels beside me, carefully clearing away one of the birds.

Why didn't I think of this?

"I'd say we could return the favor," says Charlotte. "But Geri's got Alice on room watch while she's gone."

I remember Geri leaving after dinner but assumed that was because she didn't want me tearing into her when I'd seen what she'd done.

"Where is she?"

"Henry heard she's undercover at some bar. Probably trying to trick some old guy into buying her drinks or soliciting a minor."

Baiting old men into illegal activity is a terrible assignment—not that I feel sorry for her.

"Is that why she's so nasty?" I ask. "Or is she always this welcoming to the new people?"

Charlotte pauses, one hand still on the wall.

"Do you seriously not know?" she asks.

"Know what?"

She gapes at me, then gives a surprised laugh.

"Before you got here, Grayson Sterling was her assignment."

"Her *what*?"

"You didn't think that act today was all about Petal, did you?"

She glances worriedly at the door, then whispers, "She's just plastic, Brynn."

"Yeah, thanks."

She pulls a wipe out of the container and takes down another bird.

"Geri wasn't making any headway with Grayson, so Dr. O reassigned her a few weeks ago to something less involved. She claimed it was because Grayson didn't have any juicy information she could give Dr. O, but everyone knows it was because he didn't trust her."

It takes a moment to absorb this information. I try to picture Geri texting Grayson, the way I have been this weekend. Sending stupid pictures back and forth. I can't. *She's going through some stuff,* Caleb said before. He wasn't kidding.

"It's put a lot of heat on her," Charlotte adds with a frown. "I think she's afraid of getting kicked out."

My stomach hollows out.

"That happens?"

She gives a small shrug. "It's a job, isn't it? If you don't do your job . . ."

A strained silence makes my skin prickle. If she lost her assignment, she's probably getting desperate, trying to do whatever she can to stay on.

As much as I want to, I can't blame her for that. If this doesn't work out, I don't know what I'll do.

"Why didn't he trust her?"

"Would you?" asks Charlotte, and I kind of get her point. If I were running a bank heist, Geri wouldn't exactly be my first pick for the team. "I'm sure you'll do better."

Moore's words from earlier fill my mind. *The long con is about rapport.*

These exercises with Grayson feel like small steps, but they're

each in place for a reason. Dr. O wants me to build the relationship. He wants secrets—that's what he told me on my first day—
but if I'm going to get that, I'll have to be more than entertaining
over the phone. Grayson will have to think of me as a friend.

I don't have a lot of experience in that arena.

"Do you trust me?" I ask.

Her lips smush to the side. "This feels like a trap."

That was a stupid question. The newness of our friendship—if
that's what it is—becomes crystal clear. "Forget it."

"No," she says, bumping me with her elbow. "I trust you."

But even though I asked the question, I'm hesitant to believe the
answer. What have I done to earn that trust? Nothing.

"Why?" I ask.

"Because you say what you're thinking," she says. "And because
you know when you're lying."

"Everybody knows when they're lying," I say.

"No they don't. Most people convince themselves they're telling the truth to feel better about being scumbags. People like
us, we know the difference."

Like us. Some of the tension pulls from between my shoulders.

"Because we know we're scumbags?"

She flips her hair over her shoulder. "Because we don't pretend
to be angels." She rises. "I'll be right back."

As she disappears out my door, Geri's smug face appears again
in my mind, the dark smudges beneath her eyes revealed through
the thin layer of powder. Was she right? Did Grayson really not
know anything? I wish there was a way to find out everything she
had on him without actually asking.

"Dr. O's positive all these people are hiding things, right?" I ask
when Charlotte returns. "I mean, it's possible some of them haven't
done anything wrong."

She's brought a giant bag of M&M's and sets it on the floor between us.

"He wouldn't send us in if they were squeaky clean."

The words are effortless and reassuring. Dr. O wouldn't take any unnecessary chances.

"Why's he do it all anyway?" I picture our fearless leader with a halo, leading his small army of scumbag teens. "Is he FBI or something? Some secret branch of the cops?"

"He owns businesses," she says with a smirk. "Some companies that make medical supplies, I think." She takes a blue M&M, and then pushes the bag my way.

I take a red one, cracking the candy shell between my teeth.

"But what's he get out of this?"

"I think he'd probably say you don't always have to get a reward to make something worthwhile."

"He *is* rewarding us. Scholarships for spying? A mansion to live in while we buddy up to his marks? Why does someone who has everything take these kinds of risks?"

"Well, I don't know that he has *everything*," she says.

"What does that mean?"

She grabs a handful of M&M's and lays on her side, head propped up on her bent arm. "He's alone, isn't he? He's not married. And he doesn't have any friends unless you count Shrew, who may not even be a mammal. No girlfriends or boyfriends that anyone knows about. I heard his folks died in a car crash when he was a kid or something. We're basically his only family."

The painting of the woman in the white dress in his office comes to mind.

"What about his sister?"

"He doesn't have a sister."

"That big painting hanging on his wall. The woman in the dress. He said that was his sister."

She arches a brow. "Maybe she died with his parents, then. He told me he's got no family left."

It's sad. Even when Mom and I are in opposite corners, we still have each other.

"Stop overthinking," she says. "We've got it good here—mostly." She glances again at the wall.

Maybe she's right. Someone hands me a diamond, and the first thing I do is look for cracks. Why Dr. O's doing this doesn't matter, just that he is, and that miraculously I'm somehow a part of it.

And if Geri doesn't like it, that's her problem.

Charlotte takes another M&M, and then I take one, and it hits me. We're having girl time. We're doing the friend thing.

I take another M&M.

"Why'd your folks kick you out?" I ask.

She lays back, staring at the ceiling, and after a while, I do the same. We're lying just a few feet apart, and maybe it's stupid, but eating M&M's after dark on the floor of my bedroom feels like the kind of thing that only happens in the movies.

"Because I killed a guy."

I very slowly shift to put a few more inches between us.

She cackles, then slaps my arm. "Thanks a lot for the vote of confidence."

I laugh weakly. Of course Charlotte didn't kill someone. But something about this place makes anything seem possible.

"They kicked me out because I'm dramatic," she says.

I rise on my elbow to face her.

"This guy pissed me off, so I lit his family room on fire. I guess it was a little dramatic."

I choke. "You what?"

She points to her hair. "Hell knows no fury like a redhead scorned."

"What'd he do?"

"Lied about me. Said I did some stuff I didn't."

Note to self: stay on Charlotte's good side.

"You see any more earrings you like in my room, you just go ahead and take them."

"Relax. I'm reformed. I'm Matches no more." She holds her hand in a prayer position before her like one vengeful angel.

"Matches?"

"That's what Margot used to call me."

It takes a moment to place the name. "Margot had my room before me."

"Yep." Charlotte's back to chomping on M&M's. "She and Geri were like this." She crosses her first two fingers together.

So Geri lost her assignment, and her best friend.

Okay, I feel a little sorry for her.

"I heard she finished the program."

The chomping stops.

"What?" I roll onto my stomach, facing her.

A scowl creases Charlotte's freckled brow.

"She left the program. She didn't finish it."

"Why?" I ask. Shrew said nobody had failed under her teaching. Did she screw up her assignment, like Geri? Is that why Geri's trying to knock me down—because she's seen firsthand what happens when you don't succeed?

"Just wasn't for her, I guess." Charlotte rolls over, too, knees bent so that her feet are up in the air.

Worry needles me. "She didn't get what Dr. O needed."

"No. It wasn't like that."

I wait as Charlotte sorts through her handful of M&M's, discarding the yellow ones in a pile beside her elbow.

"You're not telling me something," I say.

She inhales. Exhales. "She and Caleb used to be together. They were super close, then . . . I don't know, things kind of fell apart."

The thought of Caleb with someone else makes this chocolate taste not quite as good.

"Fell apart how?"

She looks down at her fingernails, and I suspect she's considering how much to tell me.

"They argued," she says finally. "Then she disappeared."

"Like he offed her?" It's meant as a joke, but neither of us laugh.

"Please," she says. "Like that would fly on his med school applications."

My brows lift. I hadn't heard Caleb wanted to be a doctor. I try to picture him in a white lab coat, but for some reason only see him in his T-shirt and jeans, with ink stains on his long fingers.

"So?" I press.

"He's been here a long time. I told you that. Dr. O listens to him."

It takes a moment to realize what she's telling me.

"He told Dr. O to kick her out of school."

"Maybe," says Charlotte, in a way that tells me this is exactly what she thinks. "She had a month left before graduation when she quit. She said she couldn't do it anymore, but I don't know. I think he was jealous of her assignment. She and the guy got pretty close, I hear."

Maybe he's jealous, but Caleb doesn't seem like the vindictive type. Still, I can't take the chance of getting too close, just in case.

"How do you and Sam do it?" I ask.

"We remember what's real and what's pretend."

She makes it sound easy, but as she frowns down at a yellow M&M, I can't help but think this will be more complicated than she's letting on.

CHAPTER 19

My next two days at Vale Hall are a blur of more work, figuring out where I'm supposed to be when, avoiding Geri and company, and leaving messages for Marcus to call me back on my old phone. Nothing more has come through from Pete or my mom's number, leading me to think things have either blown over, or blown up, and because there's nothing I can do about it here, I distract myself with research about Grayson. Since I don't have access yet to his social media files, I end up spending more time in random searches, and stumble upon some unlocked photos of him on *Pop Store*.

In most of them, he's got that same irritated look on his face that he did at the party when I first saw him. Even in those where he's not annoyed, he's not smiling.

Perhaps he's allergic to happiness.

I stare at the phone on my desk, thinking of Dr. O's new task. Calling Grayson is the next logical step, and we've been texting all week. But I hesitate, thinking of Geri, and how she failed to form a bond with him. I need to play this carefully.

As if on cue, an incoming text makes my phone buzz, and I jump in my seat. It's a picture of a television with the title image of *The Exorcist*.

Taking it as a sign to move forward, I make the call.

Grayson picks up on the first ring.

"The house is empty," he says, and I can hear the smile in his voice.

I'm not a genius, but I think he's suggesting I come over, and we both know where he expects that to lead.

"You'll be all right," I tell him, leaning back in my chair. "But if you see any demons, let me know and I'll call a priest."

"How do you know I'm not already possessed? Maybe you should come over and check me out, just to be sure."

"Tempting. But what if I get possessed? Who calls the priest then?"

"It's a risk we have to take."

"I see your point."

"So you're coming over?"

"Definitely not," I say. "You've clearly already given in to darkness."

"Tease."

I smirk, actually impressed by his nerve.

I want to respond something snarky, but stop myself. He's not wrong, I am teasing him, just on a deeper level than he knows.

For a second, I almost feel bad about it. But then I remember what Charlotte said—Dr. O wouldn't choose these marks if they didn't have something they were hiding.

What secrets do you have, Grayson Sterling?

"Saturday," he says. "River Fest. I'll be in the white tent on the south lawn at eight."

"That's good to know," I say.

No *Want to hang out?* Or *What are you doing this weekend?* Straight to the point. I run a quick search for River Fest on my laptop and find that it's a music festival at the riverside park in Uptown. Immediately my mind turns to logistics: lots of people, lots of opportunity to blend in if things go sour.

Only, this isn't a short con like those I'm used to running. This is about rapport. Building trust, something Geri couldn't do. I need to take my time.

Does Dr. O want me to meet Grayson in person? Nerves shimmer through me at the prospect of seeing Grayson face to face.

"You should . . ." He hesitates, and I can hear the soft groan of a mattress as he moves. Of course he's been lying in bed while we've been talking. "You should come. Hang out with me."

He sounds a little uncertain. I wasn't expecting that from a guy who's used to getting his way.

"I'll think about it," I say.

"Bye, Sarah."

"Bye, Grayson."

I drop the phone in my lap, staring at the website for River Fest, still up on my screen. Dr. O will definitely be pleased with how this went, but a small part of me wishes I didn't have to tell him. That I could somehow get a good secret out of Grayson without leading him on.

But it's business, nothing personal, and I'm not walking away from this without earning everything Dr. O's offered.

I try again to break into my analysis of French current events, but my brain has officially reached its boiling point, so I head down to the kitchen for a snack. Cheers arise from the pit for whoever's winning the driving game, but I don't join them. I grab some cheese and crackers, and head back toward the stairs.

Just as I reach the first step, the front door opens, and Caleb steps inside. He doesn't see me at first, even though I'm not more than ten feet away. He's staring straight ahead, and for a full beat I'm blown away by his fancy suit.

Or more specifically, the way he fills it out.

It's black and simple, fitted around his shoulders and waist and long legs. The collar of his white button-down shirt is open, and his hair gleams a little more than usual, like he's got something in it to make it extra shiny. Absently, he closes the door behind him and turns the lock.

My throat has gone completely dry.

"Hey." I have to say it twice to actually obtain enough volume to be heard. We haven't been alone since that day on the stairs, and though he's been polite to me around the others, he hasn't exactly been overly friendly.

He startles, and his gaze lands on me. For a second, I'm sure something is wrong; there's a glitch in his composure, like he's just witnessed something horrible.

I step down to the floor, the plate still in one hand. "You okay?"

"Yes," he answers too quickly. The moment passes, and he's standing tall again, with only the darkness in his gaze to tell me something's wrong. "You?"

I cock a brow at him. "Where were you?"

"Nowhere. Working." He scratches a hand down the side of his jaw.

Because the double answer isn't suspicious at all.

"Did it go all right?" I'm not even sure what his assignment is.

"Why wouldn't it?"

He shrugs out of his suit coat. Below the crisp white collar his shirt is a little wrinkled. It could have been from the way his coat was resting, or from someone else's hands, and I can't block the sudden image of another girl dancing with him close, like I did at Grayson's party.

"I'm just taking a break if you want to hang out," I offer.

Caleb's chin lifts and his eyes find mine, filled with a thin, unmistakable fear. It charges through me like an electric current, bringing me to the tips of my toes.

And then, in a blink, it's gone.

He heads up the stairs, giving me too much room as he passes.

"I've got to finish the French Revolution paper," he says in a hurry. "Another time, maybe."

"Sure. Great." I sound like an idiot.

He stops.

"Brynn?"

"Yeah?"

He looks back at me over his shoulder, and I'm positive now something is seriously wrong. The urge rises in me to do something, but I don't know what. Is Caleb in danger? Should I get Dr. O or Moore?

The movement of his hand down by his side catches my attention; the tapping of his first two fingers against his thigh. Then his fist bunches, and loosens, and his hand is still.

"Don't get too caught up in a job, all right? It's easy to forget what's real when you're working."

He closes his eyes, and for the briefest moments, laughs. The brokenness of it tightens everything inside me.

"Okay," I tell him, but he's already out of reach, climbing the stairs to the boys' wing.

CHAPTER 20

Friday afternoon we meet for PE in the exercise room, a glass-domed building adjacent to the pool. The treadmills and workout equipment are all pushed against the wall, leaving a large open space for the eight of us enrolled—the five seniors, Lila, Paz, and Joel—to gather.

Not including music, which is currently an independent study until I test out of theory, this is the only class I don't have with Geri, and I'm glad. Ever since the night she trashed my room, I haven't been able to look her in the eye—not because of the damage, but because of her connection to Grayson. Finding out what she knows would be a smart move, but instead she only reminds me of my own possible failure.

I have to do better than she did.

"Partner up for sparring," orders Min Belk, the other security guard. He's bulkier than Moore, and younger, maybe thirty, with a scraggly goatee and black, buzzed hair. For today's special program he's wearing athletic pants and a shirt tight enough to reveal the outline of things I really wish I couldn't see.

For the last half hour, we've been crouched in something called the horse stance, breathing and chain punching. It doesn't look like that much work, but my thighs are on fire and I'm breathing hard.

"I call Brynn!" Henry lunges around Charlotte and Sam toward me, but is blocked by Belk, who points at Joel.

"You go with Joel," he says. "Caleb, show Brynn what to do."

Nerves thread through my tired muscles. At breakfast Caleb rushed in last minute, and in Shrew's morning class he barely participated. As far as I know, he hasn't told anyone why he came in late last night.

He's spooked and no one seems to notice but me.

Either that book is *really* interesting, or he's avoiding me.

Again, I replay his advice not to get caught up with Grayson and wonder if he might have gotten caught up with someone. Part of me wanted to ask Charlotte earlier, but I don't want her thinking I'm not heeding her advice to give him some space. For all I know, this is why she warned me in the first place.

"But I called her," Henry explains, as if this is enough to justify our partnership.

"But Caleb knows what he's doing," responds Belk in the same tone. "When you can get through ten strikes without screaming *hi-ya* and checking yourself out in the mirror, you can train someone."

"Fair enough," says Henry, but his eyes flick to mine and then to the ground, and it feels like I've been the one to turn him down.

As Caleb strides over to stand in front of me, shoulders hunched and hands in his pockets, the urge rises in me to ask again what happened last night. But, like with Grayson, I force myself to slow down. He won't tell me anything if he doesn't trust me.

"So what's first?" I ask, trying to keep things light. "Crouching Tiger or Hidden Dragon?"

His eyes lift to mine. The depth of his gaze is magnified through his glasses, and it takes me off guard.

Around us, the others begin punching and deflecting, moving across the room. Charlotte's giggles fill my ears, followed by Sam's low laughter. We stand motionless in the middle of all of them.

"Caleb?"

He blinks and rolls his shoulders back.

"First you have to find your center," he says. He gets in the same position as earlier and I mirror him, knees slightly bent, elbows locked against my sides, upturned fists ready to rotate and strike.

"Centered," I say, but when he gives my shoulder a little shove, I tip backwards and have to readjust my feet.

"Hey," I grumble.

"Your center." He puts one hand in the middle of his chest, and the other on his stomach. I get back in position, but I don't feel any different—repeating the same word doesn't make me magically understand. I glance at the mirror, and though my knees are softly bent and my arms are right, there's something off.

"You're stronger when you're relaxed," he says.

This helps not at all. In fact, I'm tenser now. He's looking at me, making me aware of my T-shirt, falling off one shoulder, and these stupid yoga pants I found in my closet that are so tight you can see every curve. Of the way my body bends—all wrong—and my muscles, growing tighter by the second. I should be loose, but I can't get there. I've worn this armor all my life.

"Relax," he says quietly. Then, to my surprise, he steps closer and touches me.

One hand on my collarbone. One hand on my belly.

I give a small gasp and watch his Adam's apple bob directly in front of my face. His hands are warm; I can feel them through my shirt. When his thumb moves the tiniest bit at the base of my throat, my skin tingles with goose bumps.

He doesn't move.

My heart is hammering against my ribs. I am too light, too hot.

The only boy who ever touched me like that was Marcus, but even then, even when we went all the way, it was always like we were rushing to finish something. Check off a box. Satisfy curiosities. I'd known him forever, so while the steps were new, he was always familiar.

I never felt with him the newness, the urge to explore, that I do right now.

And then, somehow, I understand. The heat from his hands connects inside me, pulling everything inward while the rest of me unwinds.

Caleb pulls back slowly, and when I look down at his hands I see black ink smudges on his fingers—faded marks that have probably withstood more than a few washes. Then his fists are grasped and he's back in position.

I try to even out my breaths, focusing on that ball of heat he's left within me.

"You don't let go of your center," he says, and maybe I'm making it up, but his voice sounds rougher than before. "You hold it, no matter what."

I don't totally understand the concept, but I know a thing or two about holding onto things. I've had plenty of chances to give up on my dreams, but I didn't.

"All the moves are fluid," he says. "You send energy my way, I send it back to you. Hit me."

It takes me a second to register his last words. *Hit me.*

I try, but his hand slips around my fist and shoves it to the side.

"You throw a punch at me, but I don't absorb it. I push it back your way. Use it against you."

"That's not very nice." My voice sounds far away.

He aims the tiniest smirk down at my hands. "Again."

I strike, and he deflects, simply by pushing my arm to the side. *Pak sao,* he calls it. Such a minimal effort, so contrary to all the fights I've seen. This is quiet and calm, and even though we're sparring, my pulse finds a familiar rhythm.

"Good," he says. "Let's switch."

This time it's him coming at me, and though I'm not as skilled at defense, I get the hang of it. I watch our hands and think of energy traveling back and forth between us. I feel all the places we touch, the hard bones of his wrist and the soft skin beneath. I hear his breath, and mine, and before long I'm aware of nothing else.

"That's a wrap," Belk calls.

I startle, arms dropping to my sides. My hands and wrists are warm and sting a bit from the gentle slap of his hands. Caleb's eyes are on mine, his lips slightly parted, and it might be stupid, but it feels like we were doing something a lot more private than practicing Kung Fu.

He takes a quick step back.

"Wait," I say.

He pauses. I don't want him going cold. I want him to stay here, with me, and for some reason I get the feeling I'm not the only one grasping onto this moment.

"You're good." His mouth curls in a polite, forced kind of smile. I hate it. He's knocking down my walls and using the bricks to build his own.

"Wait." I don't know what else to say.

When I move closer, he leans away, like we're the wrong ends of magnets.

And it stings.

"What happened?" I ask. Right now, whatever's going on with him feels a lot less isolated than last night. Something's wrong, and maybe he can put on a good show for the others, but I see past it.

"Did you see me?" I jolt as Henry slings an arm over my shoulder. "I destroyed Joel."

"You wish," the big guy calls as Caleb turns to get his bag.

"Sore loser." Henry juts a thumb toward his partner. "So are you coming out tonight or what? I'm thinking popcorn and bad movies where things blow up."

I glance again toward Caleb, but only catch sight of his back as he leaves the room. I want to go after him, but I can't do that without cluing Henry in that something's wrong.

"I've got to study." The reminder comes with a small dose of panic. Last night I missed over half the questions on my reading quiz for a book they already read last winter, and I have no idea how to conjugate the Spanish verbs I need to do for homework. I've been here only a few days and I'm already floundering.

"Fine." Henry pouts. We grab our bags and head toward the door. "But tomorrow's River Fest and you're totally coming."

Grayson's call pushes aside all other thoughts. He'll be at River Fest. *8 PM. White tent.*

Geri's failure presses against my chest. I still haven't told Dr. O about my phone call with Grayson.

I cannot fail at this task.

"It's a music festival," Henry says when I don't answer. "Bands, all day. Food trucks. Tons of drunk people to practice cons on. Seriously, you're not missing it."

No, this is one opportunity I cannot miss.

We shake on it, and by the time I'm outside, Caleb's nowhere to be seen.

CHAPTER 21

That night, while three-quarters of the school—Caleb included—is out working or playing, I call Marcus.

Blindly sweeping the top shelf of the closet, my fingers finally brush the edge of a small plastic case. I knock it toward me, catching it against my chest. Even though I'm alone and my door is locked, I scan the room.

No one's here of course, and the silence puts me on edge.

In the closet's shadows, the phone screen glows a dull yellow. I have no missed calls and a quarter of a lit battery. If I'm going to keep this up, I'll need to find a charging cord. I didn't have time to grab the one from home when I left with Moore on Saturday.

Sinking onto the carpeted floor of my closet, I dial Marcus's number.

He picks up on the last ring.

"Who's this?"

"It's me," I whisper. "Who do you think's been calling you?"

He grunts, and in the background I can hear the clicking and high-pitched whine of a video game.

"I've been busy," he says. "My cousins came up from Baltimore."

He's talked about them before. His mom's sister has three kids. *Good people*, he always says.

"That's great. Did you see Mom or not?"

"I saw her."

I wait. "And?"

He hesitates.

Dread, thick as tar, pools inside my lungs. I was right. I *hate* being right sometimes.

"What happened?" I ask.

"She's fine."

"Don't lie to me."

"Why not?" The sudden bite of his tone makes my shoulders bunch. Caleb's words whisper to me from earlier: *You're stronger when you're relaxed.*

I breathe.

"That's your game, isn't it?" he continues. "You lie about where you're going. You lie about who you're with. Where are you, even?"

I can't answer. I close my eyes and see the dark ink smudges on Caleb's fingers.

"Yeah," Marcus says. "That's what I thought. You don't want to hear lies, stop speaking them."

I can't, I want to say. I shouldn't even be talking to him.

"We were supposed to stay friends," he says, bringing a lump to my throat.

That's what we said when we broke up. We were sitting on the front steps, the split between my house and Pete's. We hadn't talked for a week—ever since he told me he was going to start selling. *I gotta do this,* he said, like he didn't have a choice. I told him we were done, but he already knew. Before he left, he said he'd be there for me, always. That I was the best friend he'd ever had.

I said okay just so he'd go. And then I went inside, heartbroken.

"We are friends," I say, the word bitter on my tongue.

"Yeah? You ask for favors but you don't even tell me where you are. You don't come to me when you're in trouble. You threaten to tell my mom I'm working for Pete. You want it straight? This friendship's not doing much for me."

He's not wrong, and the guilt's as sharp as a snakebite.

Something's up. I've known Marcus since the third grade and he's never been this harsh to me. This is a different person than I talked to a few days ago.

In the background, the video game gets louder again. He's shutting me out. He's my only tie to home and he's shutting me out.

Maybe I deserve it.

I've lied to him—by omission, at the very least. I've avoided him since we broke up, keeping my focus on getting out of Devon Park. I've blackmailed him to check on Mom for me, only seeing him as the guy who chose Pete over me, who chose drugs, and Devon Park, over *me*.

"I'll be a better friend. I'll be an *actual* friend," I amend. "I want to tell you more, but I can't. You just have to trust me."

"Trust you?" He laughs, and it hurts. "I may be dumb, but I'm not that dumb."

I stare ahead, a familiar shield leeching from my bones to coat my skin. *You don't need this,* it says. I should hang up the phone, figure out another way to talk to Mom.

But I don't.

"You're not dumb," I say quietly. "You're one of the smartest guys I know."

Sometimes IQ is measured on paper, sometimes by the strength of your backbone. If Marcus wasn't smart, he wouldn't survive the place we call home.

"I'm sorry," I say.

He's quiet for a long time.

"You do it?" he asks.

"Do what?"

He scoffs. "Take his stash."

I pull at a fold in my jeans. "What are you talking about?"

"Someone snatched a crate of Pete's pills from the house the other night. Thought it might have been you. That's why you ran."

Dread pools in my stomach. I know now why Marcus is so angry. He's never like this, and the thought of Pete putting his hands on him turns my hate to poison.

"He rough you up?" I ask.

"He's old," says Marcus. "What can he do to me? Nothing."

The truth lies bare in his answer, and I swear on everything holy in this world that I'm going to stop Pete. Somehow, some way, I'm going to remove each hooked claw he's planted in the people I care about.

"I didn't take anything from him." Not pills. Not the cash he accused me of stealing.

It could have been Eddie, or one of his other dealers. Of course he'd assume it was me.

"Pete's pressing your mom for where you are," he says. "Far as I know, she hasn't given you up."

Cold, jagged fear scrapes down my spine. She's in trouble because of me. Because I left. Because I told Pete I wasn't coming back.

"How bad is it?"

He sighs. "Not too bad."

It should make me feel better—at least she's alive and not in the hospital or something—but it doesn't.

"You coming home?" he asks.

My thumb stops tapping my knee, a move I hadn't even realized I'd been doing. Mom wouldn't want me worrying about her. She'd want me to keep plowing forward.

But she's my mom.

I can't go home; Pete will know. If he's smart, he'll be watching the places she goes, to keep an eye out for me. I can't chance going to her work or meeting her at the grocery store. I can't get to the house—for all I know, he'll have Eddie watching the door.

I can't just leave here, either. Moore will want to know where I'm going, and if he figures out I'm meeting Mom there will be questions. He'll probably think I'm going to tell her about my job with Grayson. I'll be out of here, like Margot.

"Tell Mom to catch the train to Uptown this weekend," I say, remembering what Henry told me. "There's this music thing there. River Fest."

Enough people will be there for me to keep hidden in plain sight. I can check in with Mom, and hang out with Grayson.

Marcus groans. "Rock music. You're joking."

Good. He's heard of it.

"Do you know where it is?"

"The park. That's where it always is."

Riverfront Park runs along Lake Street. The last time I was there was a week ago when I hustled those ballerinas.

"Saturday night, nine o'clock." That should give me enough time to make an appearance with Grayson before I duck out to see her. "She's supposed to be at work then, but tell her to be careful sneaking out, just in case Pete has eyes on her. I'll meet her at the fountain."

Tomorrow suddenly feels so far away. So many things could happen before then. Pete could find out she's coming to meet her. He could follow her. He could hurt her.

"I'll try," Marcus says.

Voices filter down from down the hall, Charlotte's laughter ringing above the others. They're home from their movie. I need to go.

"Marcus?"

"Yeah."

"Thank you."

He's quiet again, and then with a muffled "Mmhm," hangs up.

As the lights on the phone go black I sit in the dark of my closet, stomach churning, hearing Caleb's promise in my head. *You won't have to go back.*

He's right; I won't. I don't need to. Devon Park's followed me straight to Vale Hall.

CHAPTER 22

River Fest is jam-packed with people when we get there at 7:30 PM. Belk takes us in a black SUV and parks in a garage off of Lake Street, offering a not-so-gentle reminder that he'll pick us up at eleven sharp.

The group is supposed to stick together but as soon as Belk pulls away Joel, Paz, and Lila go running off toward the main stage where an electric guitar is currently wailing. Sam and Charlotte say they're going to go practice the pigeon drop by the vendors lining the grass along the lakefront, but since that seems to be code tonight for *make out*, I'm left standing with only Henry and Caleb.

There's still a half hour before I need to go see Grayson, and an hour and a half before Mom is supposed to meet me at the fountain—*if* she comes. More pressure than I'd like is riding on timing tonight, which is why I didn't tell anyone about any of it.

It's not that I'll get in trouble for seeing Grayson—I'm just doing my job—but I can't have anyone watching me, like at the Heatherwood party, when I duck out to meet Mom. If Moore finds out I've contacted her, I'll be done here. Removed from the program, like Margot.

Which means Caleb can't find out, either. If Charlotte's right, and he was the reason behind Margot's expulsion, what's to stop him from reporting me to Dr. O, too?

"So first it's caramel and cheese popcorn," says Henry. "Then

pork tacos at the food trucks. Then deep-dish pizza. Then funnel cakes." He grabs my hand and begins pulling me toward the end of the row of vendors.

"Wait," I say, dragging my feet. I need to ditch these two to pull this plan off. "I want to hear the bands."

"Popcorn takes precedence," he calls over his shoulder.

After dragging me through the crowd, he stops in front of a vendor with a copper and white striped awning. There are barrels of different kinds of popcorn in the metal cart beneath, and my mouth waters as the scent of sugar and butter permeates the air.

"Three larges," orders Henry.

I check the price and move to stop him. Belk gave me a prepaid debit card with the name Sarah Muñoz—the alias I told him I'll give Grayson—before we came, but I feel strange using it, like it's someone else's money. I've never had a card before.

"A small." I'm going to have to do this before I break away if I don't want to raise suspicions. Despite my hunger, nerves have tied my stomach in knots. I check the time on my phone. Only five minutes have passed.

Twenty left before I meet Grayson.

"What are you talking about, '*small*'?" Henry looks offended. He repeats his "three larges" order to the vendor.

"You don't argue with Henry about food." Caleb's lowered to speak directly in my ear, putting us close—closer than we already were because of the crowded line.

"Got it," I say evenly. We are friends, and friends do not get all warm and tingly when other friends whisper in their ears.

He straightens, hands in his pockets, brows drawn together. There are some girls behind us gawking, and when he glances back, they succumb to giggles. His expression doesn't change; he must be used to this.

I check the time again.

"Everything okay?" he asks.

I look up at him and find the same wariness I saw yesterday in the gym—the same concern he's trying to hide behind the olive branch he's now extending my way.

"You tell me," I say, surprised by the ease and immediacy of my words.

I can't tell if my words have wounded him, or if he was already wounded before I spoke. Either way, it needles me. There are layers to him I don't understand, secrets that go deeper than Charlotte's story. I can feel it when we're together. Maybe if they didn't exist I could let it go; write him off as the shallow prick who got his girlfriend expelled because of a bad breakup. But I know what it's like to hide behind a curtain, to keep all your hopes and dreams and pain locked down, and that likeness makes him feel, of all things, *safe*.

Before us, Henry moves to the other side of the cart to pay.

"I wish I could," says Caleb.

The music seems too quiet. The crowd around us stills. Or maybe it's just the genuine intent in his rough voice, imploring me to understand everything he's not saying.

"Popcorn!" Henry is suddenly between us, three paper bags of popcorn, streaked with melted butter, cradled in his arms. He gives one to Caleb, who bends closer to say something in his ear.

Henry nods, the serious expression taking me by surprise.

Caleb turns to me. "I'll see you later."

Taking my wrist, Henry guides me toward the lawn in front of the amphitheater. Caleb goes in the opposite direction, bag of popcorn swinging in his hand as he cuts through the crowd and disappears.

"Where's he going?" I ask.

"He's got some stuff to do."

The vagueness of his answer makes me a little paranoid. Like he doesn't trust me with the truth, or worse, is trying to spare my feelings.

Caleb may be meeting someone, a girlfriend, or his assignment.

"By 'stuff,' I don't suppose you mean 'work,'" I say.

Henry plunks down on an open spot of grass, and reluctantly, I lower to my knees beside him. He smiles expectantly, waiting for me to take a bite, and when I do, he lifts his arms in triumph.

He wasn't lying. The popcorn gets an A+ on the snack scale.

"He's not working," says Henry. "Everything's basically wrapped up with the mayor, and he doesn't have any new assignments yet."

Before us, a guy wails into his mic about some shattered sea of souls, while Henry's head bobs to the beat of the bass drum.

"What?" I'm not sure I heard him right. "The mayor?"

"Ex-mayor soon enough." Henry blinks up at me. "You didn't know? Her daughter, Camille, is Caleb's *special friend*." He air-quotes the words.

The seconds are ticking by, but Henry's words keep me from rising.

"Well, she was," he says. "I doubt she will be much longer."

"What does that mean?" Things might be awkward between Caleb and me, but I don't like the idea of him failing and getting booted out of the program.

Maybe that's why he was so stressed the other night.

Henry leans closer. "Caleb found out her mom was meeting sinister types at their house late at night. He told Moore. Moore camped out across the street and took some pictures of these visitors coming and going. You see where this is going."

Straight to the blackmail bank.

I'm impressed. Caleb must have some serious skill to pull off such a high-profile con. At the same time, the gravity of that job tugs at something inside me. The remembered whisper of shame every time I imagine someone I've tricked finally realizing they've been the target of my manipulation. I have a hard time imagining someone as nice as Caleb destroying another person.

We all do what we have to do, I guess.

"Do you have an assignment?" In my short time at Vale Hall, I've seen almost everyone come and go, but Henry always seems to be around.

"Not one like the rest of you," he says. "I get sent out sometimes, but it's always a one-time thing."

I glance over at his charming smile and perfectly ironed shirt. "What's that mean?"

"Usually he wants me to take something, or plant something."

I can't help it. In a morbid kind of way, I'm fascinated. "Like drugs?"

"No," says Henry, as if I've just spoken blasphemy. "Like documents. Or once, ladies' thong underwear." He wiggles his eyebrows.

"Gross." This level of blackmail is beyond just looking for secrets; Dr. O's creating secrets, too. "He's a puppetmaster."

"Yes," Henry agrees. "Yes, he is."

I bite the inside of my cheek. All this good versus evil stuff feels suddenly subjective. Who am I to say Grayson's a bad guy? I'm not exactly innocent, and neither is Dr. O.

"You ever feel weird about it?" I ask him.

"I'm too shallow for guilt, Brynn."

I elbow him in the side. "I don't believe you."

There's more to Henry than a pretty face. You can feel it when you're around him. He's a swan on the water, graceful and poised, while beneath his legs never stop churning.

It's getting close to eight o'clock. Tension is coiling in my muscles. As much as I want to stay, I need to keep moving.

"I hate to leave you here alone," I say, "but I've got to go do something, too."

"What kind of something?"

I hesitate, but the truth is pressing against my teeth. I don't want to lie to Henry.

"My special friend is here."

He looks all around, as if I mean literally *right here*.

"He's in one of the tents," I say, motioning to the colorful party gazebos erected along the lawn. In the distance, close to the stage but higher on a hill, I see one with a white roof.

"Oh," he says, with such understanding I wish I'd told him sooner. "Need a wing man? Want me to play the part of your devastatingly handsome, jealous boyfriend?"

The image triggers a reminder of what Charlotte said about Caleb, and his jealousy over Margot's mark. It doesn't align with the guy who just said he wished he could tell me what was going on.

Worry needles at the base of my neck, but I smile at Henry, and shake my head.

"I'm good."

"Can I have your popcorn, then?"

I pass it his way.

Five minutes later, I'm scoping out the white tent from a careful distance. The party inside is blocked by a rope partition, and just behind it, security guards stand at intervals. The presence of them makes my nerves multiply, and makes me regret that I didn't tell Dr. O or Moore what I was doing today.

I'm almost relieved when I don't see the senator's son inside, but just as I turn to go, a flash of black catches my eye, a smudge of dark in a sea of khaki and white.

It's Grayson, looking like a hungover movie star—black shirt open one too many buttons down the front, dark sunglasses, slim shorts, and leather shoes. His skin is pale in comparison, his bed-head hair gelled in place. He's talking to another guy, more preppy than Henry, who's waving his hands in circles as he talks, and seems to be laughing at his own jokes.

Grayson could not look less impressed.

I pull out my phone.

Here lies G.S., killed by reckless enthusiasm.

I wait a beat, and when Grayson checks his phone, he smiles.

I smile, too.

As he looks around, I hide behind a group of people, peeking at him between their shoulders.

Where are you? he texts back.

Right behind you.

He checks his phone. Turns. I cackle as he taps a girl in a red dress on the shoulder, only to immediately retract his hand and take a step back.

Cold, I text.

He shakes his head. Steps deeper into the tent.

Colder.

He turns, heads toward the refreshments.

Frigid. You suck at this game.

He steps toward the open front of the tent.

Warmer.

Warmer.

Soon he's standing on the edge, facing the lawn. He walks toward the barrier, and the wicked idea strikes me that I should lead him on a wild-goose chase all over this park. I bet he'd go straight into the mosh pit in front of the stage.

I am a terrible person.

Stepping out, I reveal myself, and a smirk lights his face. He waves me through the line of security guards, and as I pass a series of heavy-duty fans, the rush of air blows up the bottom of my loose tank top, exposing my belly button.

He looks.

The look lingers.

And all I can feel is Caleb's warm hand on my stomach, and the heat that pooled beneath his touch.

I give my head a little shake. I can't think about that now. I probably shouldn't think about it ever.

"I thought you'd never get here," he says.

I check my phone. Seven after eight.

"I like to make an entrance," I say, melting into the role. I'm

Sarah now, and Sarah doesn't get agitated when spoiled boys act like brats. She leans into it.

She takes that energy, and sends it back, just like in Kung Fu.

"You want to get something to drink?" he asks.

It's a polite question, and it throws me a little, because his tone is still cool, and his posture, still hunched. The sunglasses hide his eyes, making him hard to read.

"Definitely," I say. I still have an hour before I have to meet Mom at the fountain. Plenty of time.

He leads me into the tent.

"Nice setup you got here," I say.

There are high, round tables positioned around the tent, covered with hors d'oeuvres—skewered shrimps and cheese plates and fancy baked pretzels. Regret flashes through me as I'm reminded of the popcorn I left on the grass beside Henry.

"It's for donors," Grayson says, not hiding the boredom in his voice. "My family gives money to the city. They always set up some kind of party as a thank you."

"That's nice of them."

"I guess."

He leads me toward a makeshift bar in the back of the tent, where a man in a white apron is pouring sodas into clear plastic cups. Subtly, I scan the groups inside, looking for trouble, looking for Grayson's father, the senator, but finding mostly teenagers, or younger adults.

"I'll have a Coke," I say, and Grayson orders it and then hands it to me.

"So," I say, taking a sip. The bubbles explode on my tongue, cool enough to focus me. "Having fun?"

"Obviously."

He looks out to the stage, where the lead singer is practically making out with the microphone.

"Why are you here then?" I ask.

He seems surprised I've called him on this. "What else is there to do?"

"I don't know. Ski the Alps. Save the whales. Rescue kittens out of trees."

"Saving the whales is tomorrow," he says. "And I've already rescued seven kittens from trees today, so I'm above quota."

"Your dad must be so proud."

He glances at the ground. "Of course he is."

The flatness of his voice suggests otherwise.

So there's tension between the senator and his son. I store that in my mental Grayson file.

"Lucky you," I say, and then throw out a little bait. "My dad doesn't know I'm here. Thinks I'm studying."

He glances over.

"He's way too strict about stuff. I guess your dad's probably the same." I shoot him a sideways glance, trying to read his face.

"My dad could care less what I do, as long as it doesn't make him look bad." His mouth pulls into a tight smile. "Let's pretend I didn't say that."

"Say what?" I cup a hand over my ear. "I didn't hear anything."

The singer ends his song, and the audience explodes in applause and screams.

"Who are you, by the way?" The scowl has returned. "I don't even know your last name."

"Muñoz." I say, giving him the name on my fake debit card. I look over his shoulder to see if anyone's looking at us.

"Where do you live?"

"North of here." Best to be vague; not give him a neighborhood.

"What school do you go to?"

"You're full of questions." I hide the edges of panic in another sip from my drink.

"You're not answering most of them."

I pick a story fast. "I'm homeschooled. I know a girl who knows your sister; she told me about the party."

"Who?"

"You'd be a great cop."

He sticks his hands in his back pockets. "Just wondering how you got to my house that night."

"Why?" I ask. "Think I was there to rob you?"

He looks over, showcasing three separate crinkles between his brows. "Were you?"

Maybe he *is* onto me.

"I don't think you want my real answer," I say.

He scoffs, and I relax a little.

"My mom wanted to know," he says. "Since we're famous and all."

The picture from *Pop Store*. I see it perfectly framed on Charlotte's phone—my victorious smile, him leaning close. Almost like we're both interested.

"Oh yeah," I say slowly.

"I thought you might not want to see me after what it said."

Will she be the first to tame Grayson's wild side, or just another castoff in his long line of broken hearts?

The change in his tone throws me off. He's quieter, each word thin and brittle.

It strikes me that Grayson's life is always like this—that people could post pictures of him at any time. That nothing in his life, not even in his own home, is private.

I would hate that.

"I don't even remember what it said," I lie.

Now he's the one who looks relieved. Maybe it shouldn't surprise me. All around us are clusters of people laughing and flirting and drinking, but not one person has even looked our way since we came into this tent. No one's waved at him, or has asked who I am. Grayson doesn't have a single friend here.

Just like at his party, he's surrounded by people, but alone.

I feel sorry for him.

I set down my drink on the nearest table. "Want to play a game?"

He grins.

"Absolutely."

CHAPTER 23

The game is simple. It's called the color grab—at least that's what Pete used to call it when he first taught me how to pick pockets. He'd plant himself on some bench, and send me out to retrieve something blue, or red, or green. The actual item was always my choice, but if I got caught, it didn't count.

Those summer days, ripping off tourists along the lake, are the only good memories I have of him.

Grayson's a quick study. I tell him to find something green, and he brings back a dollar from the tip jar on the bar. He sends me to find something red, and I stumble into a girl, extracting a pair of red-framed sunglasses from her open purse as I brush her arm and apologize.

I send Grayson back to her with the glasses, and he looks like a hero.

I stick the dollar in the tip jar, and the bartender gives me a wink.

For blue, Grayson surprises me and manages to slide a girl's bracelet right off her wrist while they embrace. I can't see her face, but her dark hair is satin-smooth against the back of her white fitted dress, and she leans into him with a little too much familiarity.

"You cheated." I punch his shoulder playfully when he returns to our base camp at a corner table. "You know her. You told her what you were doing."

"I didn't tell her, I swear." He slips the bracelet into my hand below the table. He's come alive in this game, his whole body warped by giddy excitement.

"Uh-huh." I take the bracelet back toward the girl in the white dress, fully expecting Grayson to stop me and admit his lie, but he stays behind the table, bouncing on the balls of his feet like a kid waiting in line for a roller coaster.

"Excuse me," I say, tapping White Dress on the shoulder. "I think you might have dropped . . ."

She turns, and the rest of my words lodge in my throat.

Geri.

Geri is here. Dressed for the party. Hugging *my mark*—the mark she lost when Dr. O reassigned her. She didn't come with us from school, which means she arranged this on her own. How did she know that Grayson and I were meeting? It doesn't matter. In a snap, my shock boils, and turns to fury. She's here to sabotage me. She's going to blow this, the way she blew my con with Sam at the farmers' market.

"What are you doing?" I mutter, stepping closer.

"He's watching," she sings with a smile. "Oh, is that my bracelet? Should have figured you'd be behind that. After all, you do like taking things that aren't yours, don't you?"

Her jealousy hits me like the snap of a rubber band. She's risking my position at Vale Hall, my *future*, out of spite.

"I didn't choose this," I say. "I didn't take anything from you."

Her eyes harden, and her pink, shimmery lips form a thin, flat line.

"But you did." She holds out her hand for the bracelet. "Think of this as Natural Selection. Survival of the fittest."

Act normal. Grayson is watching.

Unfurling my clenched fist, I reveal the bracelet. I've squeezed it so hard the beads have left red marks on my skin.

She takes it and checks her wrist, as if surprised that it fell off.

Oh, how I want to punch her right in her pretty nose.

"Does he know?" I ask between my teeth. "Did you tell him?"

"Please. I'm not that evil."

I beg to differ.

She snaps the bracelet on and looks back up at me, her face pure innocence.

"Did you need something else?" With a small frown, she looks back to a table beside the bar, then behind her. "Hold on, did you guys take my purse, too?"

I don't stick around long enough to answer. Turning, I head back to Grayson, painting a grin on my face as I try to hide the panic and rage crackling across my nerves. I need to make this about him—to build him up for pulling off the bracelet grab, even if he already knew her. Even if she let it happen. Even if the only reason she came here was to throw me off my game.

I can't believe I ever felt sorry for her. I don't care if she is worried about losing her position at school. She's not taking mine to make herself feel better, or to prove that Grayson's unbreakable.

Survival of the fittest.

Yeah, we'll see about that.

But as I approach Grayson, I can feel the energy leaping off of him. Something's changed, intensified, since I left his side, and it brings on a wave of wariness.

Geri must have told him something. That, or he overheard our conversation.

His hand makes rapid circles, motioning me over. *"Hurry."*

Instead of telling me what's going on, he grabs my hand and drags me out of the tent. Soon, we're passing the fans, stepping over the rope partition into the fringe of the crowd, the chaos of River Fest. Humidity dampens our skin. Hundreds of voices fight to be heard over the drums and screams of the singer.

It's then that I see what's in his other hand. A black bag—a satchel with two straps so you can wear it like a backpack.

Did you take my purse, too?

Please tell me this is not what I think it is.

"Did you say get something black? Because . . ." Apart from the missing shirt, he's transformed into that guy in the picture on *Pop Store*, flipping off the camera.

A cold breath of caution fills my lungs. This isn't a game for Grayson. He isn't doing this for kicks; he needs the rush.

As much as I love the idea of sticking it to Geri, a greater fear consumes me. We left Vale Hall with only student IDs with fake names, and a prepaid debit card. But Geri came separately—what if she drove herself using a real license? What if something in her bag leads him back to Vale Hall?

She knows better.

She wouldn't risk her position just to screw me.

Glancing over my shoulder, I search for Geri and find her alone, on the outskirts of the party, arms folded neatly across her chest.

Smiling, right at me.

"Hold on." I tug on Grayson's arm. "Hold *on*."

He slows, but does not let go of my hand.

"You had her so distracted, she didn't even see." His laugh is manic as he drags me past a row of cones, toward the side of the stage.

My heart is racing now. Geri planned this—she wanted Grayson to take her bag, that's the only reason she would smile that way at me.

"She's going to figure it out," I say, trying to hold to the con. "You don't hit the same person twice, otherwise they'll be on to you."

Ignoring me, he pulls back the leather flap and peers inside.

His eyes go wide. "Oh," he says, and then lets out a holler.

"What is it?" I push his hands aside to see what he's looking at.

Inside the purse is a leather wallet, some makeup, and a Ziploc bag filled with white pills.

Filled to the brim. The plastic seal is practically bursting.

With a hiss, I close the bag back up, looking over my shoulder to make sure no one's seen.

"We have to put this back. *Now*."

"Relax." He grabs the bag away, opening it back up as if he's not exposing something completely illegal, but rather like he's just been given the keys to a new car. "She has no idea it was us."

"*Us*," I repeat, certain now that Geri planned this as a way to screw me over. "There was no *us* about it."

"Don't get boring now. We were just starting to have fun."

Anger bites through my panic. I move close, blocking the bag from view. "Grayson, if we get caught with that, we're busted. You see how much product is in there? That's a one-way ticket to jail."

"Relax," he says again, though he's not smiling anymore. "My dad's got friends in the police."

The *Pop Store* article bursts in my mind—"Political Parenting Gone Wrong." Maybe the senator's status does buy them some forgiveness with the cops, but based on my last conversation with Grayson, his father's good graces may be running thin.

"This isn't a D&D or some backyard brawl," I argue. "This is drugs—a serious amount of drugs. How's it going to affect Daddy's campaign when you get pegged with trafficking?"

He grimaces.

"How do you know all this?"

I know, because I've seen Pete distribute pills to his sellers. He's careful not to give them too much at one time in case they get picked up. Down to the exact number, he knows which class of pharmaceuticals will push a charge from "possession" to "intent to sell." Those aren't slap-on-the-wrist fines, they're felonies.

"I just do, all right?"

A sickness sloshes in my gut. Geri came to this party to bring me down—to make sure I fail where she had failed. There was no other reason for her to be there. Grayson's not even her assignment anymore.

"What are these anyway?" He opens the bag, removing a small handful of pills. "Oxy? Not Adderall." He says this with the familiarity of someone who's had experience in this arena.

But I don't answer, because I'm staring at the pills themselves, and the small W pressed into the white shell.

Someone snatched a crate of his pills from the house the other night. Thought it might have been you.

Marcus's words slam through my head. These cannot be the stolen pills he was talking about.

Geri could not possibly want me out this badly.

And yet, only Wednesday Pharmaceuticals are stamped with a W, and Pete only sells Wednesday Pharmaceuticals.

Did Geri steal those drugs from him? Because of *me*? How would she even know where I live, or what Pete does?

It's a stretch to assume that Geri arranged all this—that she would go this far to see me suffer—but I can't dismiss the tingling at the base of my neck that says all of these things are connected.

"Who is she?" I demand, my voice shaking now.

"Just a girl. She comes to parties sometimes. I didn't know she was into all this."

Because she might not have been before now. This might be something special she pulled together just for today—for *me*.

If this is true, Geri's not just messing with me, not just challenging my position at the school, she's trying to get me arrested.

The weight of these intentions bends my spine, just as it turns my blood to ice.

I've come too far to be screwed by some jealous, conniving pixie.

"Hey!" A male voice booms behind me. "You can't be back here! Bands only!"

Terror trips my pulse, then sends it screaming onward. I didn't even notice where we were when Grayson brought me here.

The thrill surges through his eyes once again, then he swears.

"Give it to me," I hiss. The black leather satchel looks less suspicious over my shoulders than his.

"What are you guys doing back here, huh? What is that you've got?"

"Sorry." I wave without looking back. "We were just leaving."

The man is closer than I thought, and when he grabs my arm, I jerk away from him automatically. He seems to take that as a sign that I'm resisting and wrenches me harder against him.

I glance up at Grayson's face—at the glazed, wild look in his eyes—and fear explodes inside my chest like the burst of a firework.

Before I can stop him, he wheels back, and decks the security guard in the face.

CHAPTER 24

"Stop!" I screech, leaping forward to grab Grayson's arm. There's not much space to move between them, but he still manages to shake me free. A wild smirk lights him up, and sinks my stomach like a stone.

The security guard is gripping his face with both hands. His nose is a bloody mess. He reaches for the radio at his belt.

We need to get out of here. If Grayson gets arrested for fighting, there will be questions—the kind I can't answer, about who I am, about what I'm doing with the senator's son.

About the half pound of Oxy in the satchel on my back.

"Go! *Go!*" I reach for him again, this time shoving him back with all my strength. He's stronger than he looks; I can feel the muscles beneath his shirt flexing, winding up for another strike. That stupid, crazed grin is wiped off his face now, as if he's just realized what he's done.

"Come on!" Hooking his bicep in the crook of my elbow, I try to pull him away. After a moment, his arm drops, and he stumbles after me. We escape past the cones at a run, bumping through the crowd in front of the stage, racing toward the lawn below the donor's tent. We don't stop there—we keep running until we finally reach a long strip of grass and trees beside the fountain. Groups of people are gathered here, talking or eating, but no one seems to recognize Grayson or know what just happened.

"What was that?" I finally release his arm, and he shoves his sunglasses atop his head. There's a smear of red on his right knuckles.

"Did you see that guy?" His moves are jerky, his words sharp. "Some people have zero respect."

"Some people?" I say. "You just hit a security guard!"

He balks, as if shocked that I'm not on his side.

"He grabbed you."

Was this some twisted attempt at chivalry? Did he think he was defending my honor? I shift the bag on my back. It might as well weigh a hundred pounds.

"I had it under control."

His hands slap to his chest. "This isn't my fault."

I've seen more than a few fights in my day, and more than a few people acting tough about it, but this is ridiculous. I never should have played that stupid color game with him. If I'd known he was such a loose cannon, I wouldn't have.

"You've got some serious rage issues," I say.

He falters—a twitch of his shoulders that sets off a shudder that rakes through his whole body. With a sharp swear, he punches his leg with his swollen fist.

"Yeah," he says. "Well, it runs in the family, I guess."

I go still, because even though he's saying it like an excuse, there's more to it. *My dad could care less what I do, as long as it doesn't make him look bad.*

A cool drop of sweat slides down my spine. "What's that supposed to mean?"

"Nothing," he says, the way I've said *nothing* when the school social workers ask me what's going on at home.

The edge curling my own hands into fists drops away suddenly, leaving me off balance. I'm thinking like Brynn, not like Sarah. Grayson's just given me a crucial piece of information, one I need to explore. If his dad's violent, proof of it could be what Dr. O needs, what *I* need to earn my scholarship and to push past any petty revenge scheme Geri's got her heart set on.

But for some reason, I can't make myself ask about it.

It's the drugs, I tell myself. It's like I'm carrying a ticking time bomb. I need to get rid of them. If I could drop this bag and leave, I would, but someone here could see me. Some kid could get ahold of it.

I should throw it back at Geri, tell her that her little plan didn't work, but I don't even want to be caught traveling the length of the park again with it on my back. Security outside the white tent could search me. For all I know, Geri could deny the bag is hers, and put all the blame on me.

This is time I don't have to waste. I'm supposed to meet Mom in a matter of minutes.

"I've got to go." Grayson's stare is fixed on the ground, jaw working back and forth. "I'll take the bag."

"Hold on," I say, trying to regroup—to force Geri out of the equation so I can focus on the con.

He needs to believe I'm on his side. If he takes the drugs and gets caught, he'll be in trouble. He might rat me out, say I was with him. He might refuse to see me again.

This is a hit I need to take.

"I'll take it back to her. Make it look like some kind of mix-up," I say. "She'll never know the difference."

As far as Grayson needs to be concerned.

"Are you okay?" I ask.

His gaze rises and holds mine for one second. Just long enough to hollow me out. The anger is gone now, and what's left is a thin, raw terror, stretching the muscles of his face, and bringing a tremble to his closed fists.

"I have to go," he says again.

He turns and walks quickly away, hands in his pockets, back slumped. I'm torn between chasing after him and looking for Mom.

In the end, I stay, weighed down by the heaviness of his absence, by the guilt and fear that have washed up in his wake.

This all went out of control—or maybe it started that way. Either way, I wish I'd never come to this stupid festival.

Making up my mind to call him and at least leave a message, I reach into my back pocket for my phone, but before I get it, a hand closes around my bicep, the grip tight enough to make me gasp.

"There you are," says Pete, breathing beer and a smug kind of victory right against the side of my face. "Nice to see you, Brynn."

CHAPTER 25

I try to get away. I fight. But Eddie's on my other side, and his arm is a vise around my shoulders. Even as I try to twist free, the crowd seems to close in. No one notices the girl trapped between two men making their way toward Lake Street. My protests are lost in the noise.

Pete is here, and it can't be by accident. The bag burns against my back. He found out Geri took his stash. He tracked her here. Right now, anything seems possible.

He hasn't reached for the satchel, but he isn't stupid. He's not going to air this much product in a crowded place where so many people might see. Against the odds, I cling to the sliver of hope that he doesn't know what I'm carrying.

"Get off me," I say as we pass the fountain. The sun has fallen behind the buildings. It must be close to nine.

Mom should be here.

But she isn't, which means she could have told him I was coming.

Which means he managed to pry the information out of her somehow.

My nails bite into the palms of my hands.

"Where is she?" I demand.

We're headed toward Upper Lake Street, near the edge of the festival. Pete doesn't have a car, so he must be trying to get me on the SCTA. There will be cops there, and I can make a scene; make it impossible for them to hold onto me without people staring.

But if the cops come to my aid, they'll see what I have in my bag.

"You stole from me, not once, but twice, Brynn," he says quietly, and despite the muggy air, a chill rakes my bones. "Did you think I would let that go?"

I don't make it easy, and when I kick Eddie in the knee, he grunts and sidesteps. To keep me from running, Pete tosses me onto a park bench and my hip smacks hard against the wood. My breath comes out in a whoosh.

Before I can scramble up, Eddie sits beside me, that giant, tattooed arm again over my shoulder. He's wearing an undershirt; I can smell his sweat, and it makes my nose crinkle.

"Don't be a pain," he says.

"It's what I do best," I snap back.

"You've been busy." Pete stands in front of me, rocking on his heels. Behind him, people mill around, no one sparing more than a glance in my direction. "Taking my pills is one thing, but this? I got to admit, I always pegged you for the goodie two-shoes. *This* is impressive."

He knows I have the drugs. I am shaking so hard my body will become unhinged.

"Where is my mom?" I keep the words short, so he can't hear them wobble.

"Where is she every night? At work."

I don't believe it. Marcus told her to come. If she knew I needed to see her, she'd make it happen.

Unless . . .

"What'd you do to Marcus?"

Pete chuckles. "I thanked him for his honesty. You know, I'm not all that hard to deal with when you treat me with respect."

A burst of rage has me jolting up, but Eddie shoves me back in the seat.

Marcus told Pete I'd called.

He probably didn't even tell Mom I wanted to see her.

He sold me out. Again. And the worst part is, he didn't have a reason not to. Like he said on the phone, this friendship isn't working out for him.

"We're family, Brynn. You should have told me you had an in with the big boys."

"I don't know—"

He holds up a hand, and I stop. I hate that I stop. I'm out now; he can't control me. Frantically, I search behind him for someone I might recognize. Caleb or Henry or the others, Moore or Belk, even Grayson, but not because I want their help. I don't want them to see this.

"When your mom saw that picture on her little show, I didn't think it could be you. My Brynn plays it straight. She goes to school and gets good grades."

Pop Store. Mom saw the picture of Grayson and me.

"I'm not *your* Brynn."

"But to see you here. With *him*." His laugh is a slick, dangerous taunt. "The senator's kid. You've really hit the jackpot now, haven't you sweetheart?"

I keep my mouth closed now.

He saw me with Grayson.

He saw me, and I don't know what he's going to do with that information, but I have a bad feeling it involves stabbing me in the back.

He shakes his head. "Cons in Uptown—that's what you said, isn't it?" He shakes his head. "I had no idea that pretty face could pull in a catch like this."

I feel sick. Everything I've touched is falling out of reach, like it was all too good to be true.

I want to tell him to go to hell. I want to kick him square between the legs and watch him suffer. But I can't even get up off this bench.

"What do you want?" I ask.

"I want my share."

I'm not sure I heard him right. His share? He doesn't want the pills that are right now two feet away from his greedy little hands?

"It-it's not like that," I stammer.

Eddie's arm tightens. I squirm, but can't break free.

Pete kneels down in front of me. His fist comes to rest on my knee, a light tap, but a threat of so much more. The bag is a lump between my shoulders, and I press it hard against the wooden back of the bench, as if this will somehow keep it hidden.

"Do you know how much those pills you stole were worth?" he asks. "You want to run off and play big girl, that's fine, but you don't disrespect me, or the life I provide you, on your way out the door."

His anger is clear now, and sharp as a blade.

"I want a cut of whatever you've got going with your rich friends. It's the least I deserve for training you."

He doesn't know I have the pills with me.

Everything inside me screams to give him Geri's bag. Maybe it will distract him long enough that I can get away. Maybe he won't come after me anymore.

But if I show him the pills, there's no way he'll believe I didn't steal from him—that I'm not selling his product to Grayson. Even if I get away, he knows who my mark is, and can use that against me.

He could tell Grayson who I really am.

Pete leans closer. "I want eighty percent of your pull by next week, or I tell the Wolves some kid stole my product and is selling on their turf."

I freeze. The Wolves of Hellsgate can't know what I have in Geri's backpack. They won't demand money, like Pete. They'll kill me.

"Brynn! I've been looking everywhere for you!" At that moment, Henry bounds through the crowd, dimples deep from his bright smile and eyes as blue as the afternoon sky. "I told you by the popcorn stand, not over here."

I swallow a quivering breath as he looks from Pete and Eddie, his eyes growing wide.

In that moment, I would give my right arm to have him gone. I don't want him to see them, this part of me. I don't want him to get hurt.

I don't want Pete to tell the Wolves he's involved.

"Well," Henry says, now examining Eddie's biceps. "You are certainly large and intimidating, sir."

And then, as if he couldn't possibly misread a situation more, Henry sits down on the other side of me, opening his half-eaten bag of popcorn.

CHAPTER 26

W ant some?" Henry offers the popcorn first to Eddie and me, then to Pete.

"So you *are* friends." Pete looks pleased with himself.

"Oh sorry," Henry says. "Brynn and I are classmates now. We go to private school up north. Vale Hall, have you heard of it?"

I want to shove the words back in his mouth. Now Pete knows where I'm staying. He knows how to find me.

"Vale Hall," Pete repeats evenly. "Afraid I have not."

"It's kind of a big deal," Henry brags. "Pretty exclusive. I can't imagine what security would do if something happened to one of us."

"Or two of you," says Pete.

"Or two of us," agrees Henry, and now when he looks at Pete, his gaze is unflinching. "So maybe you should leave before they find out."

Pete's sneer turns to a hard chuckle.

"You got some salt, kid."

"Henry." He puts his hand on his chest. "And thanks very much for saying so, sir."

I'm so busy gaping at Henry, I don't see the two men approach behind him.

"Is there a problem here?"

My chin juts up sharply to register the new arrivals. In his sunglasses and gray jacket, Moore looks like a Miami gangster, but Dr. O is dressed in black, as if he's heading to a funeral.

Probably mine.

The urge to laugh and cry rise up simultaneously. Apparently, River Fest is *the* place to be. The only person not here is the one I was supposed to meet—Mom. I guess the silver lining is that I don't have to wait long for Dr. O to figure out Pete is onto me. The director can rip the Band-Aid off right now.

"Well," says Henry. "Don't say I didn't warn you."

"Who are you?" Pete asks Dr. O. Beside him, Moore looks menacing, and when Pete rises from his crouch, he doesn't get too close.

"My apologies," says Dr. O. "I'm their school director. Henry, I'll take it from here."

But though Henry nods, and folds up the top of his popcorn bag, he doesn't stand up. He reaches for my hand, squeezes it, and doesn't let go.

Did he know Dr. O and Moore would be here? He doesn't seem at all surprised to see them. Still, he couldn't have called them at the estate once he saw me with Pete. More than a few minutes are necessary to drive from the northern end of the city.

Dr. O must have already been here, or at least nearby.

"So this is some kind of field trip, is that it?" Pete looks amused.

I pull the straps of the bag tightly around my shoulders. It's like I'm trying to hide a giant pink elephant in the middle of a crowd.

"It's healthy for our students to break from their studies. Makes them more well-rounded individuals," says Dr. O smoothly. "Now, if you could move your arm, sir, Brynn might be a little more comfortable."

Eddie snorts, and looks to Pete. Pete chuckles, but when Moore steps forward, he's silenced, and his face grows hard. I can't see Moore's expression, but it must be pretty scary, because I've never seen anyone intimidate Pete before.

Eddie's arm slips off mine, and Henry and I both jump up. I look from Dr. O to Pete, unsure which side to stand on, or where I belong. I'm caught somewhere in the middle.

Dr. O steps closer to Pete, his shiny black shoes reflecting the lights embedded in the stones around the base of the fountain. The sky is dimming, gray swallowing the last bright streaks of dusk.

"Mr. Walsh, is there something I can help you with?" asks Dr. O.

The surprised tilt of Pete's brows feels like victory, but it's small, and fleeting. Six years I have waited for the moment when someone could put Pete in his place, and now it only comes when I've screwed up.

"I guess Brynn's mentioned me." Pete puffs out his chest.

"She hasn't," Dr. O replies pleasantly. "But I know of you, all the same. As a student at my school, Brynn's safety is my business."

I should run. That's what I should do. Only, I can't move. I'm watching this like it's a car wreck, and I can't look away.

Pete's mouth rounds in offense. "You saying she isn't safe with me?" He motions for me. "Brynn, come here."

I don't move.

The corner of his lip twitches as he turns my way.

"Brynn. Now."

His face is red. I remember how he took my conning money. I remember the pitch of his voice when he yells at my mom.

Under Pete's glare, my fancy clothes grow heavy on my skin. This girl in my shoes feels pretend. Pete and Eddie see the real me. Dr. O, Moore, even Henry, only see what they want to see—what I want them to see. Confidence. Strength. Fearlessness.

But I am not those things.

I've tricked them, the way I trick everyone.

"She's not a dog." Henry's hand has moved to my elbow, but he doesn't hold me back, or pull me away. He's just there beside me. With me.

His blue eyes find mine, and they see past the con, past the façade. And in the space between heartbeats, my feet take root in the ground, my spine straightens, and I'm fused back together, the different parts of me all becoming one. I am Devon Park and Vale Hall. I am lies and truth.

I am better than anything Pete could try to make me.

Dr. O slides in front of me, a wall to block my mom's boyfriend. "If Brynn wants to arrange a visit with you, my staff will put that together. In the meantime, I think it's best for her to be with her classmates and focus on her education."

"It's best for her . . ." Pete laughs. "What are you, her father?"

"Are you?" asks Dr. O.

Pete sobers.

"If that's all," says Dr. O. "It's time for you to leave."

They stand off as the seconds tick by.

"All right," says Pete finally. "All right, so that's how we're playing it." His gaze rises over Dr. O's shoulder to meet mine, the temper I know so well simmering in his stare. His thoughts are clear, even if he doesn't say them out loud. *This isn't over.*

But with Dr. O between us, it feels like it might be.

Gradually Eddie rises, and to my shock he and Pete walk away.

I am shaking from the inside out. My knees are not strong enough to stand. Maybe Henry knows this, because he wraps his arms around my shoulders.

"You all right?"

No. Yes. I have no idea.

No one's ever done for me what they just did. I half expect Henry to rip open his shirt and reveal a giant S on the blue spandex beneath. Sometimes Marcus stuck up for me when we'd hear people say *Bloody Brynn,* but after we broke up, he never stopped them.

It sinks in then that the only reason any of this just happened was because Marcus told Pete where I'd be. I want to hate him, but instead I just feel . . . numb.

Moore and Dr. O exchange a few quick words, and then the

director turns to me. Removing a handkerchief from his pocket, he pats at the sweat on his forehead and offers a tight smile.

My moment of relief is gone. Now it's time to face the music.

"We'll wait for you at the car," Henry says, and he goes with Moore toward a black SUV on the street.

Though we're surrounded by a crowd of people, Dr. O and I might as well be alone in his office.

I force myself to stand straight, but the shame washes over me, thick and potent.

"How did you know I was here?" There are a dozen other things I should say, but this is the first to come out.

He holds out his arm for us to follow Moore and Henry toward the street.

"I was on business nearby. Henry sent a message to Mr. Moore when he saw you'd run into Mr. Walsh."

Was Henry following me? Did he see me with Grayson?

If he did, he could have seen the drugs in the bag over my shoulder.

"Mr. Belk will get the others," says Dr. O. "We've had enough rock music for one night, don't you think?"

Here's the part where he says I'm out, but before he can, I make one last play for my own survival in the program.

"Sir, I didn't know . . . Pete wasn't supposed to be here . . ." I'm screwing this all up. "I'm sorry."

I've stopped walking, and so has he.

"You don't need to apologize for him. I have known men like Pete, and it saddens me that we have that in common." He hesitates, and the breath he takes seems hard earned. With a series of blinks, he inhales, and says, "If he bothers you again, please tell me."

It takes a second for these words to process. He doesn't know I called Marcus. He doesn't know that Pete was here because of something I'd done.

He doesn't know I met Grayson, or that I'm carrying enough drugs to get us all sent to prison.

I should tell him—confess everything. He came here to make sure I wasn't in trouble. He stepped in, risked his program and all the bigger things he's doing, to stand up for me. I owe him the truth.

But the words don't come out. Maybe because I'm scared he won't believe me—he'll think I got the drugs from Pete, not Geri. Maybe because there's a darkness in me, heavy and slick as oil, that wants to make her pay for this.

Maybe because I'll do anything to stay in this program—*anything* if it means not going back to Devon Park—and that doesn't make me any better than her.

"I will," I tell him.

Dr. O reaches for my shoulder and gives it a gentle squeeze. "Brynn, you're not my first student with a troubled past. Nor are you the first young woman I've known to find herself in danger and not tell anyone. We all deal with our demons in different ways."

I swallow.

"Let's go home. I hear Ms. Maddox made my favorite blueberry pie."

I follow him to the car, leaving behind the hordes of people, and the throb of the bass. The smell of popcorn, and a boy who might, under that layer of violence, be hurting.

I get in the car, so that Moore can take us to the place where I sleep in a big bed, with a door I don't even have to lock. Where I can have blueberry pie, and learn Kung Fu, and eat M&M's on the floor of my room with my friends.

Where I will hide the truth, alongside a bag of stolen narcotics.

Home.

CHAPTER 27

I bury the bag of pills in the garden, behind Barry Buddha.

I can't hide it in the room and chance Mrs. Maddox poking around while she's cleaning, or one of the security guards doing a random inspection. It's not like Barry's going to tell on me, but it still feels like a violation of his trust.

Then I place Geri's bag outside her room, with a note that says, *Thanks for letting me borrow this the other day! XOXO, New Girl.*

The days pass in a blur, and I start to find my place in the routine.

We wake up, eat breakfast together, and go to class. We meet for lunch, then break for language or music or PE. I watch Charlotte and the others leave every few days to work on their assignments and lead their pretend lives. Sometimes Caleb's missing, too, but I never see him come or go, and if he does, he doesn't tell me about it.

I study every waking hour.

I text Grayson, but he doesn't respond.

Moore comes to me a few days after the festival to bring me a note. I recognize Mom's handwriting immediately.

Stop worrying. Love you more than ice cream.

It's enough to keep me from thinking too much about Pete, and if he's giving her or Marcus a hard time for what happened with

Dr. O. The thoughts don't disappear completely, though, and every night when I lay in bed, and every morning when I wake up, there's a pit in my stomach.

Beatrix, a junior with a buzzed head and long, willowy limbs, returns on the second week of July, and as a celebration, Ms. Maddox makes her favorite—mac and cheese. While we eat, Bea—as she likes to be called—tells us all of her trip through Europe. How she went to *futbol* games and plays in London after finishing a three-week internship for a marketing company in Paris.

"Speaking four languages was incredibly useful," she says with a deep laugh.

I bet.

As she talks, I feel as though the air is thinning. Yesterday I failed my first test ever—in Spanish—and though Shrew is letting me make it up, there's no way I'm going to pass. A month in at Vale Hall and I'm still behind in everything. I suck at music theory. Every English and history quiz I fumble with, because they all rely on a base of knowledge I don't have, that I didn't learn at Jarvis, which means the questions themselves don't even make sense.

On top of that, Grayson still hasn't called or texted me back, despite several attempts on my end to make contact. And I'm afraid to tell Dr. O any of it in our weekly check-ins, because I'm pretty sure I already dodged a bullet with the whole Pete thing. I don't know how many passes one gets around here, but I get the feeling it's not a lot.

Quietly, I duck out of the dining room, grab the books I already brought from upstairs, and set up shop in the study beside the kitchen. The buzzing of voices nearby is comforting, and if I go to my room, I'll think too much.

Almost an hour passes before the group heads downstairs to the pit. All but Caleb, who appears at the edge of the couch, a book in hand.

"Seriously?" I mutter under my breath. It has to be against the law in at least forty-eight states for someone to look that good in sweatpants and a white V-neck T-shirt.

"Hey," he says.

"Hey," I respond brilliantly. Before I drool or do something just as classy, I divert my eyes to his feet, and find he's wearing ridiculous fuzzy bunny slippers.

I can't help smiling. "Nice kicks."

He glances down at them. "They're from Henry. Obviously."

"Obviously."

"You mind?" He motions to the cushioned chair across from me. The windows beside the pool are all open, bringing in the scent of jasmine and chlorine.

We haven't been alone since River Fest, when he disappeared after he said he wished he could talk to me. Since then he's been nothing but nice, but when he's around I think about that night in the garden, and even if it's stupid, I miss hanging out with him.

When I shake my head, he sits down, leaning into the pillows, long legs bent before him. I focus on my book and reread the same sentence four times before he says, "I'm sorry about what happened at River Fest."

I flinch in response to the clutch of panic in my chest, and my gaze shoots up to find him already looking at me, shoving at the glasses that have slipped down his nose.

He can't know about the drugs; Geri wouldn't have told anyone, and I'm pretty sure Henry didn't see anything. Guilt chases my fear away. No one knows that I'm the cause of what happened— that Pete was only there because I'd called Marcus. Dr. O's been nothing but good to me, and I lied, right to his face.

"Henry told me about your stepdad," Caleb says.

I slouch in relief, but my face flushes all the same. Of course my stupid move would become school gossip.

"Not stepdad," I correct. "Mom's loser boyfriend."

"Mom's loser boyfriend," he amends. "I wish . . ." His cheeks take on the faintest tint. "I wish I'd been there."

It's not his job to look out for me, and it prickles my pride that he sees me as helpless, even if I was in over my head.

"I don't need a knight in shining armor," I tell him.

"I didn't say you did," he says. "But I would've stood with you, even so."

Our gazes hold, just for a second, and something inside me softens, and stretches, and warms. I like the me I see reflected back in his eyes. I like that he pays me respect, and in exchange, I give him honesty.

I just like being around him.

Then he looks down at his book again, scribbling right on the pages, unaware of the way my lungs feel like they're swelling inside my chest.

I should be reading up on Supreme Court cases for an essay I need to write for Shrew, but I can't stop stealing glances at his fixed brows and his messy hair, and the way his hand moves over the page. I should ask about his assignment, and where he went that day at River Fest, but I don't want to think about him and his *special friend*. Whatever he's got going with the mayor's daughter can stay outside Vale Hall's walls right now.

"What do you write in there?" I ask him.

He closes the book with the pen inside.

"Just some thoughts. If I'm distracting you, I can go."

He is distracting, but not in the way he thinks.

"No." I drop my chin. "I think too much alone."

About Pete. And Marcus. And Geri. And my mom.

About how Grayson is ignoring me.

"It gets easier," Caleb says.

I manage a weak laugh.

After a moment, he stands and moves over to the couch, which I've effectively covered with books and notes and my open laptop. He manages to pick his way through enough of it to sit beside me.

The cushions compress beneath his weight. The back of his hand brushes my bare knee, turned out because I'm sitting cross-legged. And just like that, my pulse is flying.

"How can I help?"

I almost tell him not to worry about it, but that's the old Brynn talking. The new me doesn't need to keep track of favors, or who owes who.

"I don't know. The Supreme Court paper? Spanish verb conjugations? If you have a *Chemistry for Morons* book available, I wouldn't turn it down." I rub my eyes, blotting out the world.

"Well aren't you two just the cutest."

I open my eyes to see Geri, standing with Beth just behind us. Bea's party seems to be moving to the pool; some of the others head through the patio door outside.

"Looks like Caleb's found a new couchmate." She tilts her head, her dark hair cascading over one shoulder. I'm surprised to see her—she's been leaving for work at seven every night for the past two weeks.

"*Geri,*" warns Caleb on a heavy sigh.

"What? I know how partial you are to this loveseat, Caleb. This was your and Margot's special spot, wasn't it?"

The lines in Caleb's neck go taut.

In a rush, I'm reminded what Charlotte said about them—how Caleb got jealous and had Margot kicked out of school. Wariness raises a wall between us, even if I don't completely believe it. It doesn't matter if Caleb has an ex-girlfriend, but I do have to be careful if he's got an in with the director. I need to be on my best behavior.

Which means no jumping over the back of this couch and pummeling Geri, however much I want to.

My anger over what she did with the drugs hasn't waned—the

heat is just beneath my collar, and my grip tightens around the edges of my book. She's been avoiding me since River Fest, probably pouting because I'm still here, and waiting for just the right moment to humiliate me again.

I'm so sick of her games, but I'm not going to give her another chance to rattle my cage.

I put on my you-don't-bother-me smile.

"Did you get your bag back?"

Her mouth tightens. "I did."

"I hope you don't mind. It was a little heavy, so I took out some of the things you'd left inside."

Her gaze narrows to slits. "Don't worry about it. They were yours anyway."

If I had any doubt she stole the pills from Pete, it's gone now. This girl is pure evil. She has no idea what Pete's capable of—what he will do now that he thinks I've robbed him.

Thoughts of the Wolves of Hellsgate make me shiver.

I'm safe here. But Mom is not, and neither is Marcus. Pete will use whatever resources he has to make me suffer if this gets out.

"I don't think so," I say evenly.

"Then what did you do with them?"

"Hm." I tap a finger on my chin. "Didn't I return them with the bag?"

"I don't think so."

Caleb and Beth's stares bounce between us.

"Oh well," I say. "I'm sure they'll turn up. Probably when you least expect it. That's what always happens to me."

I don't know what I'm going to do with those pills yet, but from the way her jaw is grinding back and forth, I can tell I've hit the mark.

The threat of danger is so often worse than danger itself.

"I don't mean to be rude, but Caleb was just giving me a tour of his favorite couch, so . . ."

Geri gives a forced laugh, and stomps off in the direction of the stairs, Beth trailing after her.

"Um." Caleb stares after Geri with a scowl. He's obviously uncomfortable, no doubt because of the mention of Margot, but I'm not worried about that, or what happened between them, or even Geri's stupid pills.

I've shown her she can't break me, and it feels good.

"You don't have much experience with bullies, I take it," I tell him with a smile. "Here's the trick: they send energy your way, you send it back."

He grins.

"Sounds like really solid advice."

"A smart guy passed that along. Although turns out he had kind of a couch fetish, so I'm not sure how much stock I should put in anything he says."

He laughs, and the temperature in the room goes up ten full degrees.

I lift up Shrew's binder of death, still filled with five pages of uncompleted assignments. "I'll help you with the Tulsa Bag Switch if you can figure out this Supreme Court paper."

Despite me being the only one to successfully complete a Tulsa Bag Switch during our last conning class exercise, Geri still leads the upperclassmen in overall points for the challenge. Because I'm late to the game, I can't even win in my best subject.

Caleb glances down at the open notepad I've set in my lap. "We did that paper last year. I've still got my old stuff. You know what, though?" He pulls out his phone. "Hold on a second."

It takes more like a minute, but soon Sam and Henry appear from the pit. I look for Charlotte, too, but remember she's out at a party with her pretend friends.

"I was winning Road Racers," says Henry, even as Sam shakes his head to say this isn't true. "What's so important?"

"Brynn needs help with Shrew's massive checklist." Caleb's cringing down at the binder of assignments Shrew put together.

"Been there." Henry stretches out on the rug like a kid making snow angels. "I nearly quit my first month."

"You did?"

He lifts his head. "About thirty times."

"Your schedule was nothing," Sam says. "Try transferring from a public school in Amelia."

"Hello." I point to myself. "Devon Park over here."

Sam winces. "Good luck."

"She's doing the Supreme Court thing," Caleb says.

Sam cracks his knuckles, then squeezes in between Caleb and me. "Lucky for you, I have personal, in-depth experience with the justice system. Let's do this."

IT TURNS OUT Charlotte is the master of all things science, and after she gets home from her party, she helps catch me up on homework and quizzes. Shrew's tests are online, and over the next two days I ace three of them in a row. The seniors help me celebrate that night with Kung Fu movies and popcorn in the pit—the best parts are when Caleb and Henry reenact the fight scenes, complete with terrible, dubbed-over dialog.

Caleb remembers basically everything he's ever read, and after class the next Monday we go down to the garden, where he quizzes me on a series of short stories about the Revolutionary War. I try to convince him to take off an article of clothing every time I get a question right, but he only laughs like it's a joke.

Which it is. Kind of.

And then before I know it, we're loading into the SUV again, and Moore's driving us to a quaint, outdoor shopping area in Uptown alongside the river for another conning class field trip. Before we even leave the car, I'm wishing I'd played sick, because the last time I was in the area, so were Pete and Eddie. But as we pile out, Caleb takes a place at my side.

"Lightning doesn't strike the same place twice," he tells me as if reading my mind.

"That's not true," I say. "Lightning actually strikes the same place over and over again because it hates me."

"Your science is a little questionable. What exactly is Charlotte teaching you?"

I shove him in the chest.

His hand covers mine as he rocks back, and maybe I'm reading too much into it, but his fingers linger a second longer than they need to.

"Meet me back here in three hours," Moore announces. "You know the rules."

We're collecting pledges today for a philanthropy organization—an actual charity supported by Dr. O that provides at-risk schools with computers. We're all wearing matching shirts—bright yellow—that say *Equal Start,* the name of the program, and carrying around clipboards and buckets for donations.

The goal of today's activity is to practice our sales pitch—whatever gets someone to hand over the cash—as a building block for our long con assignments.

Of course, it would be more lucrative if we made up the charity and pocketed the proceeds, but that's not really the point.

I'm matched with Henry, Charlotte with Sam, and Caleb with Geri before I stop listening to the other pairings. This is good, I tell myself. Geri hasn't tried anything confrontational since I put her in her place about the drugs, but if she tries to sabotage me again, Caleb will stop her.

Still, jealousy prickles across my ribs. As much as I like Henry, I wish I was matched with Caleb today. He's been lingering on the edge of my thoughts since that night in the study, and the more I try not to think about him, the more I do.

As we break into pairs and scatter around the mall, I can't help being a little jumpy, and exposed. I have to remind myself that Pete and Eddie don't know we're here, and neither does Marcus. This is a huge city, and I'm a needle in a haystack.

Beside me, Henry sighs. "I could really use a win today."

He's last in points for class, and I get the feeling it's been that way for a while.

"Me, too," I say, gaze narrowing on Geri as she approaches her first mark, near a kids' play area. She's all smiles now, and maybe it's an act, but she doesn't seem too concerned about her missing drugs.

She's probably trying to get under my skin.

For the next twenty minutes, Henry and I talk to different shoppers, claiming everything from our poor orphan backgrounds to Henry's inability to read. Driven by a desire to knock Geri down a peg, I throw in all my tricks, showing Henry you can still be yourself while telling the lie. This seems to trigger a switch inside him, and soon he's raking in the dough. He even convinces one rich old man to fork over forty dollars after a sob story about *Equal Start* laptops being sent to kids who have rare blood diseases like him.

We stop to count our earnings in front of a cooking store—the fancy kind where they call pots and pans *cookware* and people spontaneously orgasm over piecrust mixes.

"Twenty bucks says I can walk out of there with an eight-inch skillet," says Henry, staring through the window like a puppy waiting for adoption.

I smirk. "Forty if you can get the clerk to gift wrap it for you first."

He thinks about this a moment, then paints a flustered expression on his face. "I can't find my receipt anywhere. Oh my God, my mom is going to *kill me*. Like *dead*. My aunt's getting married this afternoon, and they were supposed to be delivered yesterday . . ."

I bury my face in my shoulder, stifling a giggle.

"I've created a monster," I say. "To think, just hours ago you were only a sweet little thief."

He bites his top lip, then pulls me closer.

"I have a hypothetical for you."

"All right."

"Let's say you know this ridiculously handsome guy, who's also very sweet, and generous, and smart."

"And modest," I add.

"Very, *very* modest," he says. "And let's say that he took something that may have affected his beautiful princess friend, who is also very smart, and kind, and forgiving . . ."

"Uh-huh."

He looks to the ground, kicking at the pavement with the toe of his shoe.

"Which is unusual for him, of course, because he has rules about taking things from his friends, but he really wanted to help her out because she seemed to have gotten herself in some trouble."

I'm getting a bad idea now of where this is heading. "Henry. Just say it."

His cheeks puff out as he exhales.

"I may or may not have dug up your bag of drugs and planted it on Grayson Sterling."

CHAPTER 28

"You *what?*"

My vision doubles, then slides back into place. Henry's grabbing at the front of his perfect hair, pulling it forward over his forehead. The bucket of donations swings as my hands jerk up to grab his shirt.

"You didn't have a purse when we got there, and then after I saw you with Pete and his goon . . ." Henry's expression turns pained. "I thought maybe they put you up to selling those pills for them."

A pressured laugh escapes my lips, dying as soon as it comes.

"You're serious."

"There're *so* many pills in that bag," he says, imploring me to understand. "I didn't want you to get in trouble."

He hugs the clipboard against his chest like a shield.

Usually he wants me to take something, or plant something. This is exactly what Henry's specialty is.

"Does Dr. O know? Moore? What happened with Grayson?" I drop the bucket, the change inside rattling against the plastic, and reach for my phone in my pocket. Grayson hasn't responded to me since River Fest. Is it because his dad found out about the drugs Henry planted on him?

It runs in the family, Grayson told me when I said he had rage problems.

Is he safe?

"Of course Dr. O and Moore don't know," Henry says miserably. "That's why I took it—so you wouldn't get busted. I was trying to help you."

"You're some help!" I shout, and he looks over my shoulders, reminding me we're in public, that anyone might hear.

I don't care.

If Grayson found those drugs, he's going to think I did it. I told him I'd take care of them; he probably thinks I set him up, which means my rapport is ruined. Which means I'm done, just like Geri wanted.

Henry's staring at his shoes. "I don't want you to get kicked out. If Pete gave you those drugs, or if they were yours . . ." His chin lifts, and he meets my eye. "If you're in trouble, you can tell us."

But how can I, when Geri's the reason I'm screwed?

"What exactly did you do?" I want him to give me every detail, just in case there's some microscopic chance I can salvage this.

"I put the bag in an air vent in his bedroom."

"How did you even get in his house?"

"His mom had a fundraising dinner two nights ago. I snuck in with the catering staff."

How he can pull off a heist like that and not destroy everyone in conning class points is beyond me.

"Did anyone see you?"

He shakes his head.

"Does Grayson know?"

"No." He steps closer, reaching for my shoulder. "See? I thought you could use this, you know? You can be the one to find his drugs— you can expose the senator's son for being a dealer. Dr. O would eat that up. You'd be done with this assignment, and Pete would think you're busted, so you wouldn't have to worry about him anymore."

Henry's right.

He actually pulled this off.

A part of me is tempted to hug him right now. To follow through on this insane plan that's just fallen into my lap. But the problem is that Pete didn't give me those drugs—Geri did, and as much as I want a scholarship, and to finish out high school at Vale Hall, Grayson didn't do anything wrong.

I'd be framing an innocent guy, and not just in a small-con, earn-a-few-bucks kind of way.

I'd be putting him in danger with his potentially violent father.

This lie would hurt him, possibly send him to jail. His father's career could be ruined, and maybe that's Dr. O's goal anyway, but there has to be some real reason behind it, otherwise I'm just a con.

Otherwise I'm just like Pete.

"I can't," I say.

Henry slumps. His hand drops from my shoulder. "Why?"

"I just can't."

He pulls at his hair again. "Caleb said to leave it alone. I should've listened. I'm sorry."

My blood runs cold.

"Caleb knows about this."

"No." Henry winces. "I just told him I was worried about you after River Fest. That Pete and Eddie showed up and were acting like jerks."

Caleb's words from the other night filter through my frantic thoughts: *I would've stood with you.*

"You can't tell him," Henry says. "Please don't tell him."

"Why?" I ask, recalling what Charlotte told me about Margot getting kicked out. "Because he'll tell Dr. O?"

Caleb's smart. If he does know what Henry knows, it adds another layer to the situation.

"Dr. O?" Henry shakes his head quickly. "He wouldn't do that."

"Then why?"

"Because he likes you," says Henry as if this is obvious, but even as I warm I can't focus on the words. "Caleb's like the big brother of our effed-up family. When I first got here, I couldn't sleep. Caleb let me stay with him. When Sam got drunk on our trip to DC, Caleb kept it under wraps. He tried to help Margot, too, but she was too far gone."

"What's that mean?"

His gaze flicks over my shoulder to where Caleb and Geri are still standing, then to the ground. "She let it slip who she was on assignment. Dr. O sent her packing after that. He erased all records she was ever here. Had Moore delete her alias online. It was like she didn't exist."

A shiver works down the length of my spine. Is Charlotte's version of the story right, or is Henry's? It doesn't matter. Either way, I need to get those pills back before Grayson or anyone else finds out about them.

Grayson's safety might depend on it.

My future at Vale Hall does, too.

I walk away, leaving Henry standing in the shadow of the cooking store—a clipboard hanging in one hand, and a bucket of money at his feet—and call Grayson.

My hands are shaking as it rings. *Come on, Grayson. Pick up.*

He answers. And he must see my number, which means he doesn't hate me. All is not lost yet.

"I want to hang out," I say.

"Well, that's direct."

"Soon."

He's quiet a moment.

"Yeah, okay. Come over tonight at seven. My parents will be gone."

With that, I fake an excited goodbye, and shove the phone back into my pocket.

CALEB FINDS ME on the stone steps in front of the river, watching the riverboats and the kayaking tours pass by, listening to the cars on the metal bridge a couple blocks down. The air has the tiniest bite to it, a promise that fall is right around the corner, and there's not a single cloud in the blue sky.

I'm going to get those drugs back tonight, before Grayson finds them, and then I'm going to throw them away.

"Hey," says Caleb, and despite the worry gnawing my ribs, I hear Henry's voice.

He likes you.

The words cling to me, making me aware of the way the clothes slide over my skin, and my breathing, and the ink stains on his fingers as he taps them against his thigh.

"Henry said you might need some company."

The tension between my shoulder blades ratchets tighter.

Caleb comes beside me, leaning against the railing over the river. We still have an hour before Moore comes, but I needed a break to sort things out.

"Oh?" My gaze gets stuck on the bottom corner of his lip, between his teeth.

I look away.

"Actually he said, *I totally blew it with Brynn, she hates me, you have to fix this.* And then he offered to give me the high score on Pac-Man if I smoothed things over."

"I knew you had ulterior motives."

"It *is* Pac-Man."

My head hangs forward as I grip the railing. As much of a predicament as Henry's put me in, I don't hate him. He stood by me when Pete showed up at River Fest. In his own way, he's trying to be a good friend.

I guess.

"He tell you what happened?" My eyes flick in his direction, trying to read what Caleb will do with this information.

"Henry has his faults, but spreading other people's business is not one of them."

He likes you.

Guess that one slipped past Henry's moral code.

"Are you all right?" The genuine way he says it makes me want to confess everything, from my calls to Marcus to Geri's bag of drugs.

"I'd be better if you distracted me." I need to get to Grayson's to fix this, but it's still early afternoon, and I'm not even sure if he's home. Breaking in before we hang out tonight defeats the purpose. I just have to wait it out.

"Your hair looks good like that," he says.

Even though I'm sure this is part of the distraction I just ordered, I touch my hair self-consciously. I've gone with a messy ponytail today. Not all the pieces stay back because it's still too short; dark strands curl around my ears and frame my face. Some of them brush my neck, which heats as Caleb's gaze drift there.

He likes you.

"*You* look good, I mean. All of you. Not just the hair." He clears his throat.

Despite my predicament, a glow begins to pulse inside me. I like the way he trips over the words.

I wonder if he does the same when he's working with the mayor's daughter.

"I didn't mean you had to flirt with me."

"What if I wanted to?" he says, and over the worry, and the frustration, and the fear that I'm riding the line of getting kicked out of school, is the hope that this is true.

"Would that be okay?" His grin fades, and he swallows, reminding me that I like a boy whose job is to make other girls like him.

From the look on his face, it seems he might be thinking the same thing.

I look across the river and point to a black glass skyscraper on the opposite bank.

"I don't know if you know this, but you can see that building all the way in Devon Park on a clear day. When you're on the train platform the tip of it sticks out above the rest of the city. It's like a hundred stories or something."

I close my eyes. Smooth transition, Brynn. No way he feels awkward now.

"A hundred and ten." He wrings his hands together. "It's United Tower. Finished in 1973. It was the tallest building in the world until 1998."

I snort. "You just made that up."

He shakes his head. "The structural engineer built these giant tubes that stop at the fifty-fifth, sixty-sixth, and ninetieth floors to help support its massive height and weight in the wind."

He's serious.

"Now you're just showing off."

The tilt of his lips is reluctant, but I'll take it.

"My dad used to take me on this architecture cruise the first Sunday every month before . . ." He hesitates, and thin shadows form beneath his eyes. "Before I got a job working on one. You can only hear the same speech so many times before you know it by heart."

This feels important somehow—a glimpse into Caleb's past that up until now he's been so elusive about.

"What else you got?" I ask.

He points upriver, past the nearest bridge, to a pair of stone buildings, connected by a sky bridge near the top. A tower stabs into the sky on the left wing, marked by a clock that must be twenty feet in diameter.

"The Spearmint Building. Designed after a cathedral in Spain and finished in 1921. The outside is made from terra-cotta, six different shades that get lighter at the top, so it looks brighter the closer it gets to the sky."

Okay, now that's impressive.

I point to another building across the river. The old newspaper factory. I've spent a lot of time admiring it waiting for the Lake Street train to come.

"The Times Tower, built in 1922."

"I like the flying buttresses," I say. "I always thought it looked like the love child of a skyscraper and an old church."

He nods rapidly, as if he agrees. "There are a hundred and fifty stone pieces in the base that come from different structures around the world. The Alamo, and the Taj Mahal. Even the Great Wall of China."

I'm grinning at him.

He looks a little embarrassed.

I tilt my head toward the path alongside the river, and we begin to walk.

Caleb knows every building we pass.

He points out old factories and stores, skyscrapers and apartment complexes. He tells me about the different materials used in each building, and how each era is represented by its own unique style.

The farther we go, the faster he talks. He moves his hands to point out new things and describe different shapes. After half a dozen more sites, I realize this isn't just bonus knowledge from some job or weekend trip with his dad. He's into this, and as I listen, I can't help but be, too.

Holy cow, I like this guy. Like, *really* like him.

As we emerge on the sidewalk from under another bridge, he points above to the pink balcony reaching out over the river walk.

"That's the Rosalind Hotel. First site in Uptown to be put on the National Historic Registry." The name takes a moment to place and brings a flash of the *Pop Store* article on Grayson's family. His dad has a fundraiser coming up here sometime soon.

I shake the Sterlings from my head.

"Caleb."

"Yeah?" He stops when he sees I've stopped. His smile fades a little when he looks at me. "I'm talking too much. Is it time to go?"

"*Caleb.*" I am one hundred percent nerves—the good kind, like I just drank a fizzy soda and can still feel the bubbles in my belly. A reckless bravery courses through me, and before the rational side of my brain kicks in, I grab his shirt and say, "Come here."

Dragging him closer, I rise up on my tiptoes and kiss him, right on the mouth. He smiles against my lips, and I'm smiling, too, and for a moment I think we're both going to laugh. Then he tilts his head and kisses me—really kisses me. Slow and soft and warm. His ink-stained fingers cup my cheeks, thumbs grazing my skin. I sigh, and my eyes drift closed, and I don't care that there are people walking by. Let them look. For one minute, Brynn Hilder isn't afraid of anything.

My hands clasp around his back. We move closer, and hold tighter. Then there are only his lips, and the rasp of his teeth, and the gentle feel of his tongue.

Kissing him makes me feel like stars must, just before they burst. Because right now I am the brightest version of myself that I have ever been.

I'm so focused on our kiss, and the pounding of my own heart, that I don't see the two men standing behind him until it's too late.

CHAPTER 29

Don't let us interrupt."

Caleb and I break apart like the wrong ends of a magnet, my elation crashing before I siphon in my next breath. The speaker has a low, gritty voice, and is built like a brick, with broad shoulders, thick legs, and a ruddy tint to his face. He must be hot in those dark jeans and black T-shirt, because sweat glistens on his forehead.

"Ryan Ikeda," says his friend, who is taller, with oily hair, and has his hands tucked into the front pocket of his sweatshirt. There's no reason for him to be wearing such warm-weather clothes on a day like today. My guess is that he has a weapon stashed inside.

Carefully, I take a step back. I should be relieved that they've mixed up Caleb with this Ryan person, but a quick glance to Caleb's face takes me by surprise. He's someone else now. His head tilts in curiosity. His eyes go sharp. There's a coolness to him that carves away the secrets, that crushes his depth and vulnerability.

If not for his hand, gripping mine hard enough to bruise, I wouldn't recognize him.

"That's me," he says. Even his voice is wrong.

And then I get it.

These men are somehow connected with Caleb's assignment. Ryan Ikeda must be his alias with the mayor's daughter.

He's just been caught cheating on his *special friend*, with me.

"We need to talk," says the brick man.

I don't like this—this guy says "talk" like some people say "break." But when Caleb's hand slides out of mine, and he whispers, "Tell Moore I'll be back later," what choice do I have but to back away? If I out Caleb on assignment, his position at Vale Hall is jeopardized. The work he's already done with the mayor's daughter is rendered useless.

He won't get a ticket to college, and become a doctor, like Charlotte said.

"Sure. All right," Caleb tells them. I can't tell if he's wary or worried or perfectly comfortable. This Ryan persona is a stone wall.

I'm still standing beside him, ready to fight, or run, or who knows what else, when he glances over at me. His brows arch in surprise, as if he didn't expect I'd still be here, but in that moment, I see through the act. The truth is there in his dark eyes—the silent plea to *go*.

And so I do.

I walk back to the car alone, and when Moore does a head count, I tell him Caleb's working and will come home later. But I keep my phone in my hand the whole ride home just in case he calls, and my stomach twists a little more with each minute he doesn't.

AFTER EXPLAINING TO a very intrigued Dr. O that Grayson's invited me over, I'm given a rundown of safety protocol, and instructions to poke around about the Sterling family.

I agree, even though Dr. O doesn't know that I already have a hunch his dad's dangerous.

Moore drops me off in Heatherwood at seven, reminding me he'll be parked down the street for when I'm ready for pickup. The driveway he backs out of looks longer without all the cars that were parked here before. Their absence makes the boxy house feel giant and more angular.

I check my phone again, but there are no messages from Caleb. Instead, there's a picture from Henry of the saddest puppy in the world, with the caption: *Actual photo of your loyal and dedicated friend, Henry.*

I fight the automatic grin, and tuck my fear over Caleb away. He has his job, I have mine. He's smart, and even if those guys are trouble, he'll figure out a way to get out of it.

Telling myself this makes me feel zero percent better about leaving him.

I shove the phone into my messenger bag and ring the doorbell.

Focus, I tell myself. It's just like the old days. Get what I need, and get out.

Grayson answers after the second press of the bell, short hair gelled up. His salmon, collared shirt is only half tucked in. There's a beer in his hand with a fancy label I don't recognize, and as I'm standing on the woven mat, he takes a swig.

I'm *so* impressed.

"What's up?" he says.

"Not much."

He stands back and lets me in, and my chest gets tight—not like it does when I'm with Caleb, but in a nervous, uncomfortable kind of way. The two of them are so different, and not just in looks. If Caleb is a flame, burning hot and steady, Grayson is razor blades, and gasoline.

There's music on downstairs, but no one is around. Without the people, the living room seems enormous and sterile. A vast waste-land of white carpet and Pottery Barn vomit. Even the books on the glass end tables seem staged, like they're not actually meant to be read.

I need to get into his bedroom and find the air vent. That's where Henry said he stashed the pills.

"You want something to drink?" Grayson asks. He's different from the last time I saw him. The door that cracked open after he hit that security guard has been slammed shut, and I'm left again with the cold, cocky son of Senator Sterling.

He hasn't mentioned the pills, so maybe Henry's right and I'm in the clear. For now.

"Water," I say.

"Really?"

"So this is what the old folks mean about peer pressure."

He doesn't appear to get my joke.

"Water's good," I say, following him into the kitchen. He pulls a glass out of one of the white cabinets and fills it at the fridge. After handing it to me, he seems not to know what to do with his beer, and scowls at the label.

"Want a tour?" he asks.

"Sure."

His tour guide skills could rival Moore's. He shows me the living room, and the dining room, and the back porch, which admittedly has a killer view of the woods below. His commentary is not exactly award-winning.

Then he brings me downstairs, where I can't help thinking about dancing with Caleb, sliding licorice in his back pocket. Is he back at school or still with those guys? Who were they, anyway? Friends of the mayor's daughter? Her bodyguards? Though they didn't act outright hostile, they were clearly used to the intimidation game.

When I confessed the weirdness of the situation to Moore on the ride here, he didn't seem too worried. I tell myself that's because there's no reason to worry, and not because Caleb, or any of us, are expendable.

"Where's your family tonight?" My gaze moves from the TV on the wall to the couch Grayson sat on when we first met.

"Does it matter? We've got three hours."

My muscles between my shoulder blades lace together. I'm not an idiot—I know what this looks like. Me calling him to come over, following through even when he told me the house will be empty.

Suddenly I don't want to be down here, alone with him. I'll figure out another way to get the drugs once he's distracted.

"Let's go back upstairs," I suggest, not so gently. "We can watch a movie or something."

"There's a TV in my room." He keeps walking down the hall-way. I follow, biting the inside of my cheek.

Everything in his bedroom is a little too neat, and the whole place smells vaguely of cologne. Framed pictures are situated gallery-style on the wall above his desk—one of him and his father at a car race standing beside a man in a yellow driver's suit, another of the two of them on some chartered boat, where Grayson is holding either a giant tuna or a small shark by the tail. They're both laughing.

Every picture on this wall makes it seem as though they actually like each other.

"You and the old man have had some good times," I comment, looking for the air vent.

"I guess." He takes another drink.

"What's that mean?"

"Means why are we in my bedroom talking about my dad?"

I roll my eyes, then motion to the treadmill on the far side of his room, walking over to get a better look at the floorboards. There aren't any vents near the ceiling, either.

"You run?"

He nods and tilts the bottle back again. "Every day."

"Whoa," I say. "You like it?"

His brows flatten and pull down. "Does anyone?"

"Then why do you do it?"

"I used to be a chubby kid."

I laugh. "So?"

He sits on the edge of his bed, where a navy blue comforter has been folded down. "So the campaign advisor recommended I get a treadmill, and now I'm not."

I stare at him.

"You're kidding, right?"

He shrugs again and looks down at the bottle. I follow his gaze and see the vent—the only one apparent in this room, beside his nightstand.

Next to his bed.

"Want to watch a scary movie?" His voice is flat. I can't tell if he's trying to be cool, or if he's bored, or if he's actually nervous and trying to hide it.

"Sure." I optimistically hope he means for us to go back to the main room, but instead he takes the remote on his nightstand and fires up the flat screen on the entertainment center across from the bed.

I could go to the bed. Snuggle up with him while the movie plays. Hold onto him and pretend to be scared. Sooner or later he'll get up to get another drink, or go to the bathroom, and then I can pop the metal grate off the vent, grab the pills and shove them into my bag, and Grayson will be none the wiser.

But how far would things go before that happened?

My mom's voice rings through my head: *Don't put yourself in situations you can't get out of, Brynn.*

Still, I don't want to make him suspicious. This isn't just about the pills, it's about the job. I've led him to believe I like him. If I change now, I chance blowing the strides we've already made.

I sit on the corner of the bed.

The movie comes on. Cue classical violin music and images of a gray, winter woods. This could be any of half a dozen horror movies I've seen.

"Come over here," he says, setting down his drink and sliding back on the bed. He props himself up on the mountain of pillows, creating a place for my body in the nook of his arm. Maybe I'm psychic, because I'm slammed with a sudden image of the future—him on his side, me on my back, his hands roaming, my eyes pinched closed.

I never imagined doing something like this with someone I didn't really care about.

Does he care about me? He doesn't even know the me I'm pretending to be that well.

I wonder if Geri's been in this room, and how far Caleb went with the mayor's daughter. For all I know, this is an expectation of the job. If students are willing to steal and plant drugs on each other in the name of competition, what else will we have to do?

My skin is too hot. My pulse, too fast.

I don't want to do this.

"Let's go upstairs," I tell Grayson again, feeling the pills slipping through my fingers along with whatever thin connection we've formed. "I'm hungry."

"We can order something later."

"That was actually my nice way of saying no."

For a second, he honestly looks confused. Then his neck turns red, along with the bottom of his jaw.

"You called me," he says. "You're the one who initiated this."

"I've been trying to talk to you since you walked out on me in River Fest."

He scoffs. "Seriously? You didn't come over tonight just to talk."

"Okay," I say, because he's right, even if he doesn't know what he's right about. "So I changed my mind."

"You changed your mind."

"That's what I said." I stand up. He keeps this up, he's going to witness Devon Park in full effect.

"Wow," he says. "You *are* a tease."

My gaze turns to slits. "Want to see if I'm teasing when I kick you in the crotch?"

His eyes widen.

"Who taught you how to talk to girls? I'm surprised you don't have a permanent slap mark across your face."

"I don't have too many complaints."

"Well aren't you lucky."

He scoffs. "Apparently not tonight." He swings his legs over the side of the bed, face now glowing. "I'll see you around, I guess."

He won't look at me.

"Are you kidding me?" I ask. "You want me to leave because I won't sleep with you?"

If things were different, I might punch him. As it is, he seems to take my words like a beating. He rounds over his knees, mouth pulled into a tight line.

Oh no. Mark or not, he does not get to play the injured party when a girl doesn't do what he wants.

"Do you have any friends who are girls?"

"Of course I do." Which sounds a whole lot like, *What are you talking about?*

It honestly hasn't occurred to him that I might want to hang out with him for any other reason, which is obnoxious in one way, and sad in another.

And awful, too, because it's not like I'm really here for the most genuine reason.

"That explains some things." My temper cools, one slow degree at a time.

"Friends are overrated," he says. "Girls. Guys. All of them."

I chew on this a moment, then round the corner of the bed to sit beside him—not too close, though. I look again at the pictures on his wall. He looks happy in these old photos, but that easy smile is long gone. He's alone now, either by choice or because of some other reason, and I can't burn whatever relationship we have.

"We'll see, won't we?"

He looks skeptical. "We're friends."

"Sure."

"Friends with benefits?"

"Don't push it."

He snorts. "What do you want to do?"

"We could actually *watch* the movie."

A wince creases his face. "I hate horror movies. I only said I liked them because you did."

It reminds me of a dozen things I've said just to make him like me. How odd this friendship is.

"Why didn't you text me back after River Fest?" I ask.

He shrugs.

"Thought I messed things up, I guess." He grabs his beer and begins pulling at the label. "What'd you do with the pills?"

His words remind me why I'm really here, and my heel gives a fluttering tap on the floor.

"I gave them back to your friend."

"Oh," he says. And then, softer, "Thank you."

"No problem."

Then we sit on opposites sides of his bed, and watch the movie.

CHAPTER 30

Grayson seems all too happy not to focus on the strangers in black masks on the screen, standing outside the family's windows. Instead, he tells me about his sister's upcoming trip to Italy, and how his parents secretly take separate vacations.

"Why do they do that?" I ask.

"To recharge for the next round of pretending they like each other."

Fair enough. It has to be hard to be in the spotlight all the time. "What's your dad like?"

Grayson stiffens. On the TV, the girl screams and runs upstairs. Why, in horror movies, they always run upstairs, I'll never know.

"He's all right, I guess."

We're broaching on dangerous territory here; I can feel it in the way he stiffens and begins picking at his fingernails.

"Is he good at his job?"

"He was reelected last term."

"Ever do anything shady?"

He gives me an odd look.

"You know politicians," I say. "They're always getting into trouble."

"Not my dad," says Grayson.

I tap my teeth together, tempted to push harder, but afraid of crossing a line that shuts him down.

"At the River Fest you mentioned something about rage."

He doesn't answer right away.

"I shouldn't have said that," he says. "I was just fired up."

The bulge of his jaw tells me he's lying.

"My mom lived with a guy who had rage," I say. "He used to take it out on us." It's too close to the truth for comfort.

"Your dad?"

"No," I say. "Someone else."

"What happened to him?"

"Nothing. I left."

"You're lucky," he says, as if he doesn't have a sports car, and a yacht, and his own fancy private school.

He's surrounded by a barrage of things, and none of them make him happy, or safe.

He's right. I am lucky.

A nauseating, unsteady feeling, like car sickness, begins to make my stomach turn. I think this is the kind of thing Dr. O wants to know about, the kind of thing he may be able to use. But violence is personal, and despicable, and shaming, and the thought of sharing this with anyone else feels wrong.

"You ever think about leaving?" I ask.

He stares blankly at the TV, where some dude is getting repeatedly stabbed.

"Things used to be better," he says.

I follow his gaze to the wall with the pictures. All the father-son adventures they went on. There isn't a single picture of his mom or even his sister.

"What happened?"

He's quiet for a long time, and when he finally speaks, the words are bitter, pulled through the cage of his teeth.

"Susan Griffin happened."

I want to ask him who that is, but there's a noise upstairs, like the mechanical growl of a garage door opening. Grayson's head tilts to the side. "That's probably my sister. I'll be right back."

The mission, temporarily set aside, springs back to the forefront of my thoughts.

Now is my chance to get the pills.

I listen to his steps to make sure he doesn't double back, repeating the name in my head. *Susan Griffin*. I wonder if I should know her—if she's the daughter of someone important that Grayson's dad didn't like, or the wife of someone important that his dad liked a little too much.

I'll look her up later. As the stairs creak, I lunge off the bed, snatching my messenger bag in one hand as I reach for the silver grate of the air vent. Breath held, I listen for any sound upstairs, and pull back the metal, revealing a wide tube disappearing into darkness.

I don't see a bag.

Sweat dewing on my forehead, I reach into the darkness, feeling nothing. Did Henry get the wrong room? Is there another vent in here I missed? I can hear voices upstairs now; I don't have much time. Edging on panic, I lay on the floor, flat on my stomach, reaching my entire arm down the shaft.

My fingertips brush against something firm and plastic.

The sealed ridge of the bag.

The floor begins to creak. Upstairs voices raise. Is he yelling for me? Is he fighting with his sister?

Pinching the thin plastic between my thumb and forefinger, I drag the bag out, wincing as it scrapes against the vent. Finally, it's free, and I jam it into my messenger bag, pulling the leather flap over the top.

I am about to return to sit on the bed when I hear the crash upstairs.

My heart stutters, then speeds on in double time. I replace the grate over the vent, then head for the door, bag over one shoulder, one hand inside on my phone just in case I need to call Moore.

With light steps, I hurry to the stairs, careful not to make a sound as I climb each step to the main floor.

Two men speak in raised voices.

"Let it go already," Grayson says.

"Ungrateful little bastard," says the other. His voice is older, unfamiliar.

"Grayson?" One hand is still on my phone as my line of sight rises above the white carpet of the living room.

The crash must have come from the kitchen; a quick scan of the living room reveals nothing out of order.

"Who is that?" The older man's voice comes from that direction, low and hard as steel.

I grip the pills in the bag against my side. Speaking up was a bad idea.

"Just a girl from school," says Grayson quickly. "No one you know."

He sounds defensive and unsettled, and his choice to lie about who I am adds a layer of wariness to my anxiety.

Another spell of silence, and as I climb to the top step, a man appears at the back of the kitchen, beside the glass-topped dining room table.

He looks like Grayson, but more polished. A collection of hard edges and rigid lines, offset by white, gleaming teeth and a smile as smooth as butter. His eyebrows are perfectly shaped. His cheeks have a slight sheen to them. His dark hair is speckled with gray, though not a strand is out of place.

I would not trust him if my life depended on it.

"Hello," he says. "I wasn't aware anyone else was here."

"Surprise," I say.

Grayson emerges from the kitchen, a shadow behind his father. I have never seen him look as uncertain as he does right now.

"Yes, it is, considering my son told me he was ill, and that's why he couldn't make tonight's dinner. Unfortunately for all of us, it was cancelled at the last minute."

Grayson's head drops.

"I heard something break," I say. "Is everything all right?"

I stare at the senator. His glare tightens, and for a moment, all that polish disappears, and he's cold, and severe.

In his suit and loose, red tie, he may look nothing like Pete, but I've seen that expression dozens of times. It triggers a learned reaction in my body. A readiness. A tensing of every muscle.

"A glass slipped out of my hands. These clumsy fingers." The senator looks down at them with a hardened smile.

"Right," I say.

"Sarah was just leaving," says Grayson.

I don't move, despite this clear dismissal. This place is a bomb, ready to blow. I can't help thinking I'm the only reason it isn't already up in flames.

"I was," I say, because Grayson's gaze is pleading. "Grayson, you coming? You can drive that fancy car of yours."

His father gives a snort. "That's an awfully brave offer."

If this is a joke, I don't think it's funny.

"I'm actually pretty tired," Grayson says.

I almost say that he didn't seem pretty tired five minutes ago, but I'm fairly sure that won't come out right.

"Come on," I say. "It's not even nine yet."

"I don't feel like it, all right?" His cold tone brings a flush to my cheeks, and reminds me, in a punch, of leaving Caleb with those guys earlier today.

Matthew Sterling gives me a brief, but victorious, smile.

"I'll walk you out," he says, as if the door isn't visible twenty feet away.

I grip the bag tighter against my side.

"Did you drive?" he asks when we're out on the front steps. He's frowning at the empty concrete pad and the yellow light pooling from the front gate. "I didn't see a car when I came home."

"I'm down the street." I look around his side, but Grayson's out of sight now, maybe back in the kitchen.

"Ah." The senator gives a knowing hum. "In case you needed to sneak out? I was young once, I remember how this goes."

He acts so high and mighty with all his fake nostalgia.

"What's your name?" he asks as I turn to leave.

"Sarah," I say.

He closes the door behind us, and we're alone.

Wariness slides through me. I have to be careful here. I can't say something that's going to give Grayson problems with his father when I go.

"How long have you known my son, Sarah?"

"We go to school together," I say. "A couple years, I guess."

"He hasn't spoken of you before."

"Well," I say, acting mildly offended. "Maybe he doesn't tell you everything."

Sterling's gaze narrows on me. "Or maybe he doesn't tell *you* everything."

I'm not sure what that's supposed to mean.

"My son is a troubled young man. Please keep that in mind."

I nod, even though he's speaking in opposites. If Grayson's troubled, it's only because this guy has a chokehold on him. This whole conversation gives me the creeps, puts my threat meter on red alert.

But it's hard to leave, because if I go, there are no witnesses to stop Matthew from roughing up his son.

"Have a good night," says the senator.

It will only make things worse if I stay. That's the way it worked with Pete. You give people the idea something's wrong, and he gets embarrassed. The cure for embarrassment? Making sure it doesn't happen again.

The senator watches me as I make my way down the driveway. He doesn't go inside until I pass through the open mechanical gate and turn down the sidewalk. As soon as I'm out of sight, I lean against the high stone wall and gulp down breaths of night air.

I don't know what's going on in that house, but whatever it is has Grayson seriously spooked.

Phone in hand, I text him to call me later, but there's no response, so I dial Moore's number for a pickup.

He's already down the street, ready to take me and my felony quantity of illegal drugs back to the estate.

CHAPTER 31

I don't tell Moore about what happened, or about the woman Grayson mentioned, and when I get back to Vale Hall, Dr. O has already left for his small cottage at the far end of the property. If I wanted, I could have the staff contact him, but I don't.

I go to my room, consider flushing the pills, but imagine them clogging the toilet and overflowing the bathroom. Instead, I rinse out two bottles of shampoo, dry the insides with my hair dryer, and empty the pills into them. Then I hide them in the back of the bathroom vanity, behind some cleaning products and containers of scented body wash.

Then I do three things.

I text Caleb: *Are you back?*

I send Henry a photo of a very vicious looking housecat with the caption: *Me.*

And I open my laptop and type *Susan Griffin* into the search bar.

A dozen hits come up on the first page. Everything from employment links to social media pages. Pictures of women—blond hair, black hair, light skin, dark skin—fill the images page. I don't know who I'm looking for, or why.

On the fourth or fifth page, my eyes stop on a *Pop Store* link entitled "Dead Artist's Family Paying Big for Dirt on Politician."

It's dated three years ago, and like most of their stories, is only a paragraph.

Family members are searching for information regarding the
death of thirty-eight-year-old artist Susan Griffin, and are looking to Sikawa City's favorite family-first politician for answers.
Susan, best known for her historic murals within the Town Hall
building, was found by highway patrol in her car on Route 17
Saturday morning, after colliding, headfirst, into a tree. This
comes just two weeks after our very own Scandal Alert source
caught her leaving a high-end bed and breakfast north of
the city with State Representative, Matthew Sterling. Though
the US Senate hopeful adamantly denied the affair, many have
begun to question his sterling reputation. Was Ms. Griffin
interfering with his run for Washington? The family is offering a
$10,000 reward for information. *Pop Store* will match that price
for exclusive leads.

I read the article again, then sit back in my chair. The facts connect, awareness like a cool breath raising the fine hair on my arms.

Susan Griffin had an affair with Grayson's dad.

She was killed in a car wreck.

Grayson is clearly afraid of his father, and a temper runs in the
family.

It doesn't take a genius to put it together.

In a frenzy, I lean forward and type *Matthew Sterling Susan Griffin*
in the search bar. Only information on the senator comes up. I try
senator and *artist* and *Sikawa City*, but there's nothing significant.
The City Hall website boasts her impressive murals of the city's
skyline, but offers little more than her name and that she was born
and raised locally—there isn't even a picture.

Somehow *Pop Store* is the only site that reported her death.

And ninety percent of what *Pop Store* reports is pure gossip.

This is the kind of thing Dr. O's looking for, but what good is
this secret without proof? Caleb saw meetings at the mayor's house

taking place. All I have is a random *Pop Store* article, a hunch that the senator's violent, and a name. Susan Griffin.

Dr. O can't do anything with that.

After ten minutes of debating, I go get Charlotte.

"Whoa," she says after I explain what's happened. "You think Grayson's dad killed her?"

I'm pacing in front of where she sits on the end of my bed, biting my nails.

"I don't know."

"That's huge. Did Grayson tell you anything else?"

"No. We got interrupted."

By his father, who likes to break things and scare the hell out of him. That part is too personal to share.

I reach for my phone in my back pocket, but Grayson hasn't texted back, and neither has Caleb. I wish either of them would, even if just to tell me to leave them alone. At least then I'd know they were all right.

"You've got to press him," says Charlotte. "Oh man. If he knows, you've got this in the bag. Hello scholarship."

I imagine Dr. O pulling me into his office. Telling me I've done a great job. That Matthew Sterling will be getting locked up and I should start filling out college applications.

But the excitement is interrupted by the look on Grayson's face when he told me to leave, and a vision of what the senator might do if he finds out I'm snooping around.

If he did kill someone and get away with it, I'm dealing with one manipulative bastard.

"What if Grayson gets in trouble for telling me something he shouldn't?"

At the chill in my voice, her gaze lifts from the fingernails she's examining to my face.

"What if he does?"

"He could be living with a killer, Charlotte."

"Not to sound like an ice queen, but that's his problem." She rises. "It's not like you've overheard his dad plotting out his son's untimely demise. Your job isn't to arrest him; your job is to deliver information to Dr. O. He's the one who makes the call." She explains this slowly, as if I might be too dense to understand.

I turn away.

"You know the reason we're so good?" she asks. "Why there's twenty of us here and not a hundred? Because we can turn it off. Don't feel, and you won't fail."

Her voice is softer now, but a dull knife still does the job when it's jabbed into your chest.

I've run cons since I was twelve; I know how to play the game and get out. But I've never been in this deep before.

"I'm just trying not to get myself killed before graduation," I say. She sighs.

"Look. It's messed up, I know, but did you really think you were going to get a full-ride scholarship if the job wasn't a little bit dirty?"

"This is more than a little bit dirty."

"You don't know for sure. Not yet anyway. And seriously, Dr. O would never let you get hurt. The stuff I faced at home? Way worse than anything that's come up since I've been here."

This is hard to believe. We're all playing with fire right now, and each day that passes, the flames just get bigger.

"The country club was a real war zone, huh?" I sit beside her on the bed, rubbing at the lines between my eyebrows with my thumb. The urge rises in me to tell her about the pills, but if I'm caught, she'd be in just as much trouble for secret keeping. It's not worth risking her future, too.

She pulls at the curls in her hair, and something about her hunched posture and the hollow look in her eyes tears me up.

"Sorry," I say. "I didn't mean anything by it."

She nods. "I know."

Her hand presses absently to her throat, as if trying to stop the words.

"There was this guy before I came here—a friend of my parents. We talked a lot. He always asked what I was doing at school or what songs we were doing in choir. He had us over to his house a lot for cookouts or football games."

My insides begin to twist, a slow, uncomfortable pressure.

"Sometimes he paid me to housesit when he went out of town. We lived just down the street."

Lines form between her brows.

"Sometimes when I went to housesit, he'd still be there."

I don't move. If I do, I might hit something. What she's telling me isn't a total shock—girls get cornered by older guys a lot in Devon Park—but I'm sick on her behalf, all the same.

Maybe this is what friendship is—hurting with another person's pain. I sit beside her, unsure if I should touch her or give her space.

"Did you tell anyone?"

"Not for a while," she says. "Then he asked me to housesit again, and I said no, and my mom got mad about it, saying I was a spoiled brat and that I needed to help our friends when they asked."

She laughs suddenly, a tired sound that ends in a groan, then covers her face with her hands.

"She didn't believe me when I told her. My dad, either."

"You lit his house on fire." The memory comes with a huff of breath.

She nods, letting her hands drop to her lap.

"Dr. O took care of it. He put that guy in jail. My own parents wouldn't even do that."

A quiet rush of pride fills me. Dr. O did good by Charlotte. He's done good by me. He's looked out for all of us.

"Wow," I say.

"Wow is right." She's paler than before. Her gaze bounces around the room, sticking on nothing. After a moment, she clears her throat and rises.

"Charlotte . . ."

She holds up a hand.

"I didn't tell you for pity."

I nod, swallowing to steady my voice. "I know you've got a lot of friends, but if you get in trouble, I've got your back."

She meets my gaze, and there's gratitude and loyalty reflected in her green eyes.

"Don't feel, don't fail," she says, heading toward the door.

"Right."

On the bed, my phone buzzes. My heart lurches when I see Caleb's name.

In the pit. Come alone.

Despite everything, warmth tingles in my chest. My lips remember the pressure of his, my waist, the warmth of his hand.

Time to find out where the hell Caleb's been.

CHAPTER 32

Cutting through the shadows, I pass the dining room table and pad softly down the carpeted stairs to the basement. The lights are off, like they were the night of my birthday party, and the same reluctance slows my steps as I enter the room.

Why is Caleb hiding in the dark? If this is a trap, if Geri somehow got his phone and is pranking me, she's going to reach the end of my good graces.

"Hello?" My fingers sweep blindly for the light switch. I brace for another surprise as I flick it on, but the room is empty.

"Turn it off!" Caleb's strained voice comes from the couch on the left side of the room that faces the TV.

Flipping the switch back down, I rush toward him, bumping into the end table as I round the side of the sofa.

"What is it?" I sit on the edge of the cushion and reach forward into the black until my hand finds his shoulder.

He jerks away.

"Caleb?"

"Hey . . ." He gives a quiet cough, stunted by a tight groan. His breathing is too shallow. "Did anyone follow you?"

"No. Why? What's going on?"

"You didn't tell anyone I was back?"

"You just texted me two minutes ago."

He's quiet. I can't make out his face in the dark.

I twist away, fumbling for the small lamp on the end table.

"Brynn—"

The dim, yellow glow washes over us, and brings a gasp to my throat.

Caleb's lip is cracked, his chin smeared with dried blood. His glasses are broken on the side; one thin, plastic arm emerges from his clasped hands on his lap. An inch-long cut on his jaw is raised and looks to be in serious need of some stitches. He prods at it gently with his fingertips when my roaming stare locks on the wound.

"I was hoping you could grab me a Band-Aid." His mouth twitches at the corner.

"A *Band-Aid*? Caleb, I'm pretty sure you need an ambulance."

"Come on," he says. "It's not that bad."

He won't look at me, even when I crane my head to meet his gaze.

"What the hell happened?"

He sighs, a sound thinned by agony. "Work."

My fingers drum on my thighs. It's hard to look at him like this, to see him in pain. I want to make it stop. I want to make the people who did this to him suffer.

I've weathered Pete's anger long enough that to know in times like this, you can't do either.

"What hurts?" I ask.

His gaze flicks my way. "My face. My ribs. A little of everything."

He could have a concussion. Are his eyes dilated? It's hard to tell. I reach for the bottom of his shirt. He flinches, and when I meet his gaze, he holds his breath and gives a curt nod.

Slowly, I pull up his T-shirt, stifling another gasp. His stomach muscles are pulled taut, and his skin is a collage of bruises—angry red, brown, and purple. It's possible his ribs are broken. The scrape wrapped around his right side is pink and angry.

I have to be calm. I must stop shaking.

"Caleb, we need to go to the hospital."

"We can't." He brushes the shirt back down, staring at me with a wild look in his eyes. "No one can know, Brynn."

"But Moore . . ."

"Not Moore. Not Dr. O. Not Belk. Not *anyone*."

"I don't understand. They're supposed to help us."

"Please," he says, and it breaks something inside of me. "Please don't say anything."

I grip my knees to stop my hands from trembling. Hiding this is wrong—Caleb needs medical attention. But I know this game; I've played it with Mom when Pete's gotten rough. Doctors ask questions we can't answer. They draw attention we can't risk. With Caleb, they'll need adult permission to treat him, which we don't have.

There's a reason Henry isn't down here now, or Sam, or Charlotte. Caleb called me.

With this, Caleb trusts *me*.

"I'm going to get some bandages," I tell him. "I'll be back in a minute."

At the dip of his head, I sprint up the stairs, all the way to the supply closet in the girls' wing. It's late, and though no one's in the hallway, I can hear Paz's radio, and Bea talking to someone in her room. Geri's door is closest, but when I listen I hear nothing inside. She's either sleeping or pulling another late night on the job.

Easing open the closet door, I grab the first aid kit and a couple towels. I charge back down the steps. On my way through the kitchen, I snag a bottle of water and fill a cup with ice, then return to the pit.

Caleb's exactly where I left him, sitting rigidly, staring at nothing.

I wrap some ice in a towel and pass it his way. He presses the cool pack against his lip while I twist the top off a small bottle of peroxide and drench a cotton ball. He watches my hands like I'm holding a prison shiv.

"Ready?" I ask.

He takes off his glasses, gathering the pieces on his denim-clad thigh.

"Brynn," he says quietly.

The silence between us is weighted with shame. He says nothing else, leaving only his uneven breath and the too-bright images in my mind of a beatdown that never should have happened.

"It's all right," I say. For him. For me.

I will not let him down.

When the soaked cotton touches the cut on his jaw, he flinches only the slightest bit, training his eyes ahead on the black television. The white ball is quickly stained copper by his blood, and I discard it on the floor for another, cleaning the wound with steady hands. There are some butterfly bandages in the first aid kit, and I use those to close the wound as best I can, trying not to think of hours before when I touched this face for a very different reason.

I hand him the bottle of water, and he tips it back, hissing as liquid touches his split lip. He reaches again for the ice.

"How did you get back?" I whisper.

"I walked from the train station." The towel against his lips muffles his words a little.

"Caleb, that's got to be five miles."

"Please," he says. "Only like four and a half."

"Ha." My head falls into my hands. "Those guys did this, didn't they? Who are they?"

"They're nobody." His words are edged with sandpaper.

I shake my head. "You don't get to pull me down here and then pretend nothing's wrong."

"It's nothing you need to worry about."

"Why? You think I can't handle it? You think this is the first time I've patched someone up? I've got news for you, Caleb—"

"I don't want you to get hurt." He's facing me now, eyes not quite aligning with my gaze. He looks young without his glasses. Lost and unfocused. "Believe me, Brynn. They will hurt you."

Icy fingers crawl down my spine. I grab for his glasses, steadying myself with the task of fastening them back together with medical tape from the first aid kit.

He sighs, leaning back against the cushions.

"My assignment was with the mayor's daughter. Camille."

His *special friend,* according to Henry. "I heard you busted her mom for meeting with sinister types."

As soon as it's out of my mouth, I know. The men who did this are the people Caleb exposed.

My hands still on his glasses.

"I saw Camille a couple weeks ago," he says. "She knew what I'd done. Not the details. Not everything. But that I was somehow the reason her mom was being investigated."

"The night you came in late," I say, remembering his wariness and distraction. "You were in a suit." I hand him his glasses, which now sit a little crooked on his face.

"It was an event at the museum. I went to check in with her. Make sure she was okay. The press has been roasting her mom since the news broke."

His head hangs forward, the genuine concern for his assignment bleeding through. A tiny prick of jealousy is overridden by understanding. Did I not feel the same in Grayson's house earlier tonight?

These are our jobs, but not all of it is pretend.

I shift, so that I'm sitting closer, my knee bent beside his thigh. "How did she know?"

"I have no idea. I was careful. Brynn, I was *meticulous.*"

"She told her mom?"

"Worse. She said she'd tell the Wolves—the club her mom had made deals with. She said I'd better watch my back." He exhales, one hand pressing against the side of his rib cage.

I picture the Brick Man and his oily-haired friend from earlier today, and the sheer gravity of it all presses me back into the cushions.

Caleb's mark knows what he did.

Caleb's twisted up with the Wolves of Hellsgate motorcycle club.

He scratches a hand through his black hair. "Maybe I deserve it, I don't know."

"You're just doing your job."

"I ruined her life. And her mom and dad's. Even if the mayor somehow avoids prison, Camille will never get away from this."

It would be that way for Grayson, too. If I find proof the senator killed Susan Griffin, Grayson's life may not get better. The media is already on him all the time. They would never give him peace.

But his dad might be a killer, and that cover-up is worse than anything I could do.

"This is happening because the mayor screwed up," I say. "What was she doing with the Wolves, anyway?"

"They gave her campaign money when she was running. From what I could hear, that came with a price. She's been looking the other way while they've brought drugs and guns and whatever else into the city the last few years."

"And now the Wolves are pissed because the deal's off."

"No more drugs, no more guns. The highways are all being watched as part of the investigation."

"And they know you're the reason why."

"I didn't confirm it, but yes."

This is impossible. This cannot be happening.

But the bruises on Caleb's body say differently.

"How are you still alive?" I ask, thinking of that man they hung from the bridge a few months ago. "These are the *Wolves* we're talking about."

"I told them I'd fix it."

"How?"

"I have no idea. But I have three days to figure it out."

CHAPTER 33

"You have to tell someone." I know Caleb doesn't want to go to the ER, but this is deeper than I thought. He's involved with the Wolves. He's got seventy-two hours to reverse the mayor's investigation.

If he can't—and he can't—they'll take this beating to the next step.

"Moore or Dr. O. *Someone*. Caleb, this is insane. You have to leave the city."

"I can't."

"You have to."

"I *can't*."

"Why?" My voice cracks across the room. Fear heats my veins, swelling inside me with every rapid breath. I thought Geri was the worst thing that could happen on a job. This is a million times worse.

"They'll kick me out. I'll be gone. I've seen it happen."

"With Margot?" The mention of his ex-girlfriend stutters our momentum.

"Yes." He presses the heels of his hands against his forehead. "I need this."

"You don't." I grab his wrist, pulling it until he looks at me. "This is your life we're talking about. What does some stupid school matter?"

"This stupid school means more to my family than you under-stand." He peels back my fingers. "I told you I'll be fine."

He's closing off again. I'm losing him, and I can't—he has to understand how important this is. His parents can deal with a little disappointment if it means he stays alive.

"What are you going to do?"

"I'll figure it out. I don't know. I just need some time."

Time is something he doesn't have. He has no clue what he's doing. He probably made this promise just to get away. I get that, I would have done the same, but now he has to make a plan.

He's screwing his thumb into his temple, his lips pulled in a tight line.

I doubt he has a plan for the next five minutes, much less the next week.

"Come on," I say, putting away the contents of the first aid kit. "You're coming to my room."

He glances my direction.

"You can't stay here," I huff, standing up. "And you shouldn't be alone in case you have a concussion or something. You can crash in my room until we come up with a plan. If anyone asks where you are, I'll just tell them you've got the flu."

The ice-filled towel drops into his lap.

"Thanks," he says.

He tries to get up, but needs help, and as soon as he stands his shoulders hunch, and he grips his elbows. Slowly, stiffly, we head toward the stairs. His legs seem to be fine, but every move jostles his wounds, and by the time we reach the kitchen his eyes are bleary and his jaw is locked in a grimace.

This is nothing compared to what they will do next. The Wolves are lethal, and afraid of nothing. Pete's careful never to sell in their territories for fear of retaliation. If word ever got back that he'd crossed lines, the Wolves would tear him apart.

What has Caleb done? What mess has Dr. O sent him into?

Will he not tell the director about the Wolves because this out-come was a calculated risk? It can't be. Dr. O looks out for us. He helped Charlotte when not even her own parents would. He stood up to Pete for me.

But what happens if Grayson learns the truth of what I'm doing? Dark images fill my mind of a different night, where Caleb's the one patching me up.

Would Grayson do that if I find the proof to expose his father?

I can't think of that now. I have to help Caleb figure out a way out of this.

Even if that means telling Dr. O behind his back.

A soft squeak of shoes on the tile in the foyer halts my thought, and I pull Caleb down behind the kitchen island. His breath comes out in a strained push, his hand squeezing my forearm as we both listen.

The light switches on, and Caleb and I both duck lower. Steady, slow footsteps cross the carpet in the living room, and then pause.

We hold our breath.

Is it Moore or Belk? One of the other students? I chance a quick peek around the side of the island and see a long eggplant skirt through the legs of one of the stools.

Ms. Maddox.

What is she doing up right now? She normally goes to bed in her room upstairs just after dinner.

She hears everything, Charlotte said.

I meet Caleb's gaze, find a new fear reflected back at me. His lips are pulled in a thin line.

Keep going, I will Ms. Maddox.

She moves a stool beneath the lip on the opposite side of the island, only a few feet away. I slide closer to Caleb, until we're pressed against each other, my shoulder to his chest, my hip against his thigh.

The light turns off. The footsteps recede, and climb the stairs.

We wait until the house is silent before rising.

Ms. Maddox's room is on the opposite wing, across from the girls' hall, but the stairway is the same. We hurry up it, Caleb's scowl tightening with each step. I keep the lookout for anyone in the hallways, but Ms. Maddox is gone, and at this late hour even Paz's radio is silent. The floor creaks as we pass Charlotte's door, and we both freeze and wince at the sound. Then I hurriedly usher him into my room, locking the door behind him.

Once inside, he straightens, looking around the space I haven't yet decorated. He seems uncertain what to do with his hands and shoves them in his pockets. In the light, I can see the dark droplets of blood on his bright *Equal Start* shirt.

The last time he was in this room was probably with Margot.

Bringing him was definitely not my best idea.

"Sit down," I tell him, a little gruffly. He makes it to the bed and sits on the foot, hunching over his knees.

There's a bottle of Tylenol in my vanity, but that's not even going to take the edge off. With a muttered curse, I hurry into the bathroom, grabbing one of the shampoo bottles from the back of the cabinet beneath the sink and removing a single white pill. I hold it in my hand, the small W gleaming up at me in the overhead lights.

Looks like I'm moving Pete's product after all.

Back in the bedroom, I hand it to Caleb.

"What is this?"

"Doesn't matter," I say, swallowing my irritation. "It'll help."

He's in enough pain that he doesn't argue. He takes the pill, and I hunt through my closet looking for something that will fit him. All I can find is the fuzzy white bathrobe, which I shove in his direction.

"You've got blood on your shirt."

He frowns down at his chest, and then gives the bathrobe a wary look.

"Right," he says.

But he can't take the shirt off himself. He reaches for the hem, and tries to drag it up, but grunts when he can't lift his arms above shoulder height.

"Here." I step in to help him, my fingers brushing against his stomach and side as I lift the fabric. His sharp intake of breath makes me pause, and something shifts between us. The air thins, and warms. The inside of my knee presses against the outside of his. My fingertips still lie in the ridges of his stomach.

His gaze is on my lips; his hands cup my elbows.

I inch closer, pulled by some magnet inside him. His fingertips skim the backs of my arms, making my whole body electric, lightning encased in bone. The wanting in his dark eyes makes it hard to think.

I focus on his mouth, and the cut on his lip, and it shakes some sense into me.

He is hurt.

"Sorry," I mutter, gathering his shirt in my hands.

He releases me slowly, as if thawing.

"This isn't how I imagined it would go," he says quietly.

"You didn't imagine me taking off your clothes in my bedroom?" I try to make my voice light, but the words spill out too fast. I cringe as I slip the shirt carefully over his head.

"No, that part's about right." A grin whispers over his lips.

I try not to stare at his chest when I hand him the bathrobe, but it's impossible. Even with the bruises and scrape, he's built like an underwear model. My fingers itch with the urge to touch him again, to feel the soft warmth of his skin and the muscles that flex beneath. My mouth is too dry to swallow.

This kind of wanting is new, and it leaves me unsteady.

I'm relieved when he puts the bathrobe on and ties the knot around his waist. He toes off his shoes and smiles, and then blinks slowly.

"What'd you give me again?"

"You don't want to know. Get some sleep."

"I . . ." He looks back at the pillows, as if confused. "I should sleep on the floor."

Every part of me warms.

"You don't have to."

His throat works to swallow. "I do if it makes you feel better."

"It doesn't," I say.

I help him lay back, and turn off the light.

By the time I get back, his eyes are half closed. I take off his glasses and set them on my nightstand.

"Come lay with me," he says, and every squeak of the bed as I crawl up from the bottom sparks a new cascade of nerves through my body. But Caleb is still, and finally comfortable.

I don't get too close, but his hand finds mine in the dark, fingers curling over my palm in a way that makes my breath catch. This is the second time today I've been on a bed with a boy, but this feels so much different than it did with Grayson. Right, even if the reasons he's here are dead wrong.

"Thank you," he whispers.

And then his breathing slows, and he's asleep.

For a long time, I lie there, unable to move, anchored by his fingers woven through mine. My thoughts won't quiet, turning from the Wolves, to Camille, telling Caleb to watch his back, to Grayson, and his dad, and Susan Griffin, and the pills in the shampoo bottles beneath my sink. Louder and louder and louder my thoughts grow, screaming in my ears for answers I don't have.

Getting out of Devon Park was supposed to make everything easier, but everything's just become more twisted.

I slip off the bed, and tiptoe into the closet, reaching for my old phone to dial the number to Gridiron Sports Bar.

It takes two hand-offs, and me telling the manager it's an emergency, before I hear, "This is Allie."

Mom's voice brings an immediate clench in my chest, and I'm eight years old all over again, afraid of the thunder rattling the windows.

I half close the closet door with my toes.

"Hey, Mom."

She's quiet a moment, and in the background, I can hear the clang of pots and pans and a man's voice shouting "Order up!" She must be in the kitchen.

"You all right?" she asks. "What's wrong? What happened?"

Where do I even start?

"I'm okay." I keep my voice to a whisper, though I doubt Caleb's waking up any time soon. "Just checking in, I guess. I haven't heard from you in a while."

She groans.

"I've been training this new hire. Kid can hack the CIA on a phone but can't work a basic cash register."

I smile a little.

"How's that fancy school?"

"It's good."

"You making friends?"

I picture Charlotte. Henry. Sam. Caleb, lying bruised and bloodied in my bed.

"Yeah."

"Okay, hold on. Were you on *Pop Store*? I saw this picture of Senator Sterling's son and this girl that looked exactly like you. It was the craziest thing."

That stupid photo from Grayson's party makes me cringe. Pete had seen it on the *Pop Store* website, of course Mom would have, too.

"Not me," I say, though it's hardly worth denying now.

"Too bad. Thought you might be famous for a second."

I can hear her smile, and I squeeze my knees tighter against my chest.

"Mom, is Pete giving you a hard time?"

"Don't you worry about Pete."

The answer is immediate, as if she was expecting it. From the way she's blocking, I'm guessing she doesn't know he's found me.

"Maybe I should come back. You and me could go somewhere." Get far away from Pete and Dr. O and these crazy assignments. For one glimmering second it seems completely possible, even if we've never been able to do it before.

I press my forehead to my knees.

"Your dad used to say that. Let's go somewhere, you and me." Another voice shouts in the background. "He used to ride the bus to Amelia for night classes after his shift at Jay's—was taking this GED prep course when he died. He always said he wanted to get out of Devon Park. He did, I guess." Her voice gets thick, and she coughs to clear her throat.

I didn't know he was going to school. She never talked much about him. I never even met his parents—Mom said she called them when he died, but they didn't have the money to fly up from Colombia for the funeral.

"He'd be proud of you," she says.

Now my throat's closing up, too.

"You can't come back, honey."

I pinch my eyes shut.

"When you left . . ." She pauses and lowers her voice. "The day you left, I felt like I breathed for the first time in seventeen years." More clanging in the background. "I'm not a babysitter, give me a sec!" She sighs. "This kid is going to be the death of me, I swear."

"Mom?"

"If you stayed here, you know what would happen?"

"What?"

"This," she says, as if she's pointing to something. "Honey, you would have turned into me."

Tears squeeze out of the corners of my eyes.

"How come you stay?" I ask.

I lean out of the closet, staring at the shadowed figure on the bed. Caleb needs to leave, to hide. He's not safe here.

"I don't know," Mom says after a long moment. "Don't like the idea of quitting, maybe. That, or I'm too stupid to walk away."

It feels like the most honest thing she's ever said to me.

"We don't all get this kind of shot, Brynn. Don't ruin it because you're scared. Whatever's got you rattled, work it out, and don't be foolish enough to look back."

"Okay," I manage.

"I've got to go. I love you more than doughnuts."

She hangs up before I can come up with a response, and I grip the phone and swallow until the tears stop burning my eyes.

Then I lay back in bed beside Caleb, facing him with my knees curled against my chest, trying not to tremble. I listen to his steady breaths until mine match, and drift into a restless sleep, only to be woken by the buzz of my new cell phone, just before five in the morning.

It's a message from Grayson.

4 PM, Pier 19 on the lakefront.

We need to talk.

CHAPTER 34

The next morning, Belk summons me to Dr. O's office after breakfast. Even though I'm told there's nothing wrong, I'm positive this has something to do with Caleb. Ms. Maddox saw us last night, or someone caught him sneaking out of my room early this morning after Grayson's text.

As much as I value Caleb's trust, maybe this is for the best. Dr. O has to help him now.

Tension stiffens my gait as I walk beneath the watchful glares of the marble ravens, past the portrait of the woman wearing the white gown. The chair is still in front of Dr. O's desk, and I take it while he finishes typing something on his laptop.

When he closes it, he smiles at me, and I mirror his expression, deflecting my own churning thoughts.

"Brynn, I'm glad to see you. How are you?"

I force my heels to stop bouncing against the rug.

"Fine?"

He tilts his head. "Is something the matter?"

The question doesn't feel like a trap, but it must be. Why else am I here?

"No," I say.

He rises and walks around the desk, then sits on the edge of it in front of me, no barrier between us.

Here's the part where he asks me about Caleb. I can feel the confession right on the tip of my tongue, the guilt stretching the gaps between my ribs. I don't want to betray Caleb, but I don't want him to get even more hurt.

"You have a meeting with Grayson at the park today, do you not?"

Dr. O's question catches me off guard. *We need to talk,* Grayson's last text said, and his name brings a new wave of apprehension.

"Yes." I just cleared it with Moore this morning. I'm meeting him at the car at three.

"How has it been going since your last meet-up at his house?"

This must be a test. He's going to want to know what I've learned so far, or what strategies I'm using from class. I'm sweating now. If he doesn't think I've done enough, I could be reassigned like Geri.

Stop. Breathe.

"We've talked," I lie. "I'm still trying to get to know him. Build up the trust, you know?"

He appraises me with a cool stare.

"I know the stress you must be under. I've felt it myself."

I don't want to seem disrespectful, but I'm sure everything about my expression is screaming *yeah right.* Quickly, I lower my gaze to the twisting vines and flowers on the rug below our feet.

"My parents died when I was twenty-two, did you know that?" When I shake my head, he continues. "My father left my sister and me with this house, but considerable amounts of debt."

I remember how Charlotte suspected his sister had died. *He's alone, isn't he?*

"Wasn't he a politician?" A congressman, I thought Dr. O had said.

"Yes, but not a particularly honorable one, nor a very kind man." A muscle in his jaw ticks, and I'm reminded of how he said he'd dealt with men like Pete before. "I didn't realize until he died how questionable some of the deals he made were. My sister and I had to be resourceful to stay afloat. You are not the first, I'm afraid, to play these kinds of games."

I picture Dr. O in my place, befriending people to learn their secrets. He must have been good at it. I trusted him almost immediately.

"I understand how corrupt some people can be," he goes on. "And how important they are to keep managed. If someone doesn't rein them in, they hurt people. Like my sister."

He's looking over my shoulder, to the painting on the wall behind me. The woman in the white dress. I follow his gaze, studying the narrow bones of her wrists and the shadowed divots above her collarbone.

My eyes drop to the lower right corner of the painting, where the letters S. G. are slashed in black paint.

"Susan was a talented artist," he says. "That's a self-portrait she did based off a picture I took on her birthday several years ago. She's used our mother's maiden name for her work."

My head swivels back his direction, but his eyes remain on the painting.

S. G. Susan Griffin.

Dr. O's sister.

"We track your Internet browsing history," he explains. "It's a safety measure—I'm sorry for the violation of your privacy. Analytics sends me an alert when certain key phrases are used in searches."

Like his sister's name.

The *Pop Store* article flashes before my vision—the affair with Matthew Sterling and the car crash. The reporter had speculated the senator's involvement. For a moment, all I can do is stare at the director—the man who took me out of Devon Park. Who stood up to Pete. Who protected Charlotte when her own parents wouldn't.

He sent me to befriend the son of a man who might be involved with his sister's death.

He targeted Grayson from the beginning—before Charlotte mentioned his name at the train tracks. He made my assignment seem like a game—every text, picture, and call bringing me closer to learning some mysterious secret. But he knew the secret he wanted me to find the whole time.

I am torn between running, raging, and hiding. He's tracking my Internet use. Caleb said they're tracking our phones. If Ms. Maddox really is listening in like Charlotte mentioned, what doesn't Dr. O know?

"I take it this means Grayson's mentioned Susan," he says.

The floor feels like it's tilting beneath my feet. This was supposed to be about making the city a less corrupt place, not about personal vendettas.

"He mentioned her," I manage. "He said she came between him and his dad. That's all I know."

Dr. O's gaze turns down to the floor, and for a moment he seems lost in his own thoughts. "Susan met Matthew Sterling at a fundraiser a few years ago—they were auctioning off one of her paintings. All her life she'd said she wouldn't fall for a man like our father." He shakes his head. "When she figured out he had no intentions of divorcing his wife, she broke it off."

I can't believe what he's telling me. I had to search the Internet for clues about her. Go to Grayson's house, pretend to be his friend. I had to connect the dots, while he knew all along where I would eventually end up.

"She was on her way home from meeting him when she lost control of her car. Her death was labeled an accident almost immediately, despite swerve and brake marks on the road, and another car's black paint on her front wheel well. The police never looked at Matthew Sterling as a suspect, despite my insistence."

Because the senator and the police chief are friends—I saw the pictures of them together online. If Sterling wanted this to go away, he knew the right people to make that happen.

Unable to sit any longer, I rise, arms crossing over my chest.

"Did the senator kill her?"

"I have my theories."

"You have *theories*?" I say, a little louder, shocked that he wouldn't tell me this.

"If he did this to Susan, he made bribes and misused his authority with the police, and the news, and everyone else involved. Her death could have been unrelated. A horrible accident, as the police reported. I need the unbiased truth."

"Which you wanted me to get from his son."

"That's right."

He pulled me out of a snake pit just to throw me to the wolves.

A hard breath pushes out between my teeth. I thought Dr. O was better than this—better than Pete. He told me I was special. But no, I'm still the same girl, just in better clothes. Trusted only because of what I can do for someone else.

"What happens if the senator decides I'm getting too close?" My voice wavers. Caleb's desire to keep the Wolves' involvement a secret is becoming more understandable by the second. Maybe Dr. O can protect us, but the extent to which we need that protection is what's really scary.

"My security officers are always watching you," says Dr. O, brows furrowed. "Mr. Moore is always aware of your whereabouts. If you ever feel unsafe . . ."

I can't listen to this. Of course I feel unsafe. He's put me in a very *unsafe* position.

"And if it all turns out it really was a big accident?" I ask. "Will I be reassigned like Geri or cut loose like Margot?"

Dr. O's eyes take on a hard gleam. Pushing off the desk, he comes close, one hand on my shoulder.

"This job is personal to me, Brynn. Know I would not have given you this assignment if I wasn't absolutely sure of Sterling's guilt, and of your abilities."

It's meant to be a compliment, but the fact of the matter is he suspects a man killed his sister, and he's looking at me to find the evidence. He didn't even answer what happens if I can't get it.

"One day this will be behind us, and I'll be writing a check for your college tuition." He smiles, but the steel is still in his eyes. What he's not saying is crystal clear: *If you fail, this all goes away.*

I'm overthinking this. Dr. O isn't the bad guy here; Grayson's dad is. The motorcycle club is. But the lines aren't as clear as they should be. I'm stuck in the gray area, the space between right and wrong, unsure which way to lean.

Dr. O gave me a home—a future I'd never have otherwise. He stood up to Pete, and maybe that doesn't matter to anyone else, but it does to me.

If this is the price of admission, what choice do I have but to pay?

"Grayson's scared of his dad," I tell Dr. O. "If I could convince him he'd be safe, he might tell me more."

"I can help him." A fierce edge, like I heard at River Fest when he confronted Pete, sharpens his words. "If you bring him to me, I can protect him from his father."

I rise to leave, thinking of Caleb, alone and recovering in his room, and wondering if this is true.

Before I make it to the door, Dr. O calls my name.

"One more thing," he says, and I turn to find him back behind his desk, opening his laptop.

"No boys are to be in your room, understand?"

Surprise heats my cheeks. He *does* know. One of the girls could

have seen Caleb leave this morning, but the hall was quiet—
everyone was asleep.

Ms. Maddox.

There's no point denying it; that will only make it worse.

"I understand," I say.

He nods. "Good luck today. We'll talk when you get back."

CHAPTER 35

Twenty minutes later, I'm standing on enemy territory, fist poised an inch away from a white, wooden door.

I knock twice. Three times. I wait, and when I hear a groan from within to "go away," I knock knock knock KNOCK KNOCK . . .

Finally, Geri comes to the door.

I woke her up, and I take what little pleasure I can in that. She's wearing black-striped silk pajamas, and not a speck of makeup.

Good. I've caught her with her shield down.

"Good morning, sunshine," I say, and then I push past, into her room.

"Hey—"

"We need to talk." I take in the posters on her walls. A few bands I've heard of, and to my great irritation, one of the same exact Wonder Woman print I had at home above her desk. I turn my back to it. "No games. No Natural Selection crap. No pathetic attempts to get me thrown in jail."

She crosses her arms over her chest. "I wouldn't call it pathetic."

"I'm still here, aren't I?"

The shadows beneath her eyes darken as she tightens her glare. "I had a late night, so why don't you just get on with it."

"Great." I roll my shoulders back, surprised at how much taller I am than her—a few inches at least. She's smaller, too, and in nothing but her PJ's, she looks like a normal teenager rather than the spawn of Satan.

Her shoulders cave in a little—do they always do that?—and she's squeezing her biceps hard enough for her fingers to leave white prints. I've caught her by surprise, that's all it is. Once she rises, she'll drink her daily dose of evil juice and be back to her bitter self.

"You hate me," I say, "And I get that's because you lost your assignment, and you're a big baby who needs to cut people down to build herself up, but I have a new strategy for you."

"Yeah, what's that?"

"It's a crazy concept." I pace to her nightstand and then back. "But if you give it a try, you might like it. It's called . . ."

She groans. "Yes? The suspense is killing me."

"Not being a mean girl."

She looks at her nails. "No. I can't. I love it too much."

"I know," I say. "But here's the deal. You stole drugs, then planted them on me to get me kicked out of school. And as I have those drugs, and could potentially re-plant them on you to have you arrested for trafficking, you should probably cease and desist, and do what I want."

Her sigh is long and dramatic.

"Everyone knows your stepdad's a drug dealer. Dr. O's never going to believe your innocence over mine."

"Who is everyone?" I ask, refusing to be rattled.

"Just the director. And security. And all the students at this school." When I cock my head to the side, she smirks. "Please. You think we didn't know exactly who you were when Caleb dragged you to the tracks that night? Have you seriously paid zero attention in Vocational Development? It's called research, you should try it out sometime."

So what if everyone knows where I came from? I'm here now, and that's what matters. But the idea that Dr. O would believe her over me throws me off track, even if I know he trusts me more. That's why I'm assigned to his sister's case.

"That's why I'm here," I say, planting my hands on my hips. "Act tough all you want, but I know you're scared, otherwise you wouldn't be messing with me. So here's what I'm going to do."

I reach my hand toward her.

"I'm no threat to you," I say. "What's in the past, is in the past."

She eyes my hand like I'm holding roadkill. "How big of you."

"And in exchange," I roll on, "I want everything you've got on Grayson Sterling."

She laughs, but the laugh dies, and she's left looking like she's just taken a bite of a lemon.

She stares at me, and I stare back, and finally, she says, "*You* want *my* intel. I think that's called cheating."

"I think it's called working together," I say, my own defenses growing thin. "I've pulled a lot off on my own, but this is bigger."

Our standoff is interrupted by Paz's radio, next door. The bass thumps through the wall.

"Help me." My hand is obviously not going to get the shake I was going for, so I drop it. "This isn't about some stupid platinum pig. This is a real job we're talking about, with real consequences."

Grayson wants to talk today, but I'm not sure if it's about what happened with his father the last time I was at his house, or Susan, or something else. I need to be as prepared as possible.

"Petal isn't stupid," she says quietly.

I groan.

"I don't know much," Geri concedes. "He's a loner. No close friends. No dates that lasted more than a day. He doesn't like sports. He doesn't play chess. He drinks like a fish and takes whatever pills he can find, and generally just hates life."

"Why?" I press.

"Because that's the burden of privilege? How do I know? He was over me the second the lights came back on."

In a blink, I'm back in Grayson's room, sitting on the edge of his bed, the shock and irritation raising the color in his cheeks when he realizes I'm not there for a hookup.

Like Geri was.

Just a girl he'd seen at parties—that was how Grayson had described her after he snagged her bag at River Fest. I would've guessed he didn't even know her name.

She seems smaller than she was even a few minutes ago, her arms wrapped lower, around her stomach, and the lines tight outside her eyes. She's hurt by what happened, and I'm sickened by this strange, sudden power I hold. Now I'm the one who has her backed into a corner; I'm the mean girl—no better than the jerks who called me Bloody Brynn.

Don't make friends, she'd told me my first day. Was she talking about Grayson?

"Did Dr. O . . ." I don't even want to ask if he condoned this—if he encouraged it.

"No." She steps forward. "And you're not going to say anything to him about it, either."

"I won't." Part of me wants to ask what her new assignment is, but pity drives me back on course. "You didn't hear anything about Susan Griffin?"

"Who is that? One of his girlfriends?"

"No one," I say quickly. "Forget it."

I'm not sure where this puts us. We're not friends now, but not enemies, either. This new ground can't be working for her, either, because she keeps glancing at the door, so I mutter a quick "Thanks."

"Brynn," she says as I'm turning to go.

I pause.

"He's hiding something. No one's that cold unless they've got something big behind the curtain."

I look at her one more time, black pajamas and messy hair, the misery of her confession too hard to hide without her makeup and fancy clothes.

"Thanks," I say, and head to my room to get ready to meet Grayson.

A FEW HOURS later, Moore pulls onto the highway, heading south toward the lake. I bite my nails, staring out the window, thinking of Geri and Caleb and Susan Griffin, and what I'm going to say to Grayson today.

Beneath the car, the wheels rotate on the asphalt. Two guys are arguing about baseball on the radio. The afternoon sun is covered by a thin layer of clouds, painting the sky white. In an hour it could clear up, or it could be pouring, but for now the weather remains indecisive.

"Why do you do this?" I ask Moore. He can't like taking teenagers to fake dates.

He doesn't answer.

"Is it the money?" I bet Dr. O pays him a chunk of change to keep his mouth shut about what really happens at Vale Hall.

Brake lights flash before us, and he slows to a crawl. The clock on the dash says 3:25 PM, but traffic in the city sucks, no matter the time.

He's silent long enough to assure me my question will go unanswered.

"My aunt brought me up in an apartment off Seventh and Crawford," he says. "She taught me to run scams outside the Bingo hall two blocks over."

I jolt at Moore's sudden disclosure. Seventh and Crawford is in Devon Park, near Gridiron.

"The army was my way out. They told me I could actually do something worthwhile with my life." We merge onto another freeway and begin to pass signs for the lakefront. "What they should've said is, you'll change, but nothing here will. Makes you wonder what the point of it all is. Thoughts like that can swallow you, you're not careful."

He flicks the turn signal and changes lanes.

"Odin found me after I got out. He gave me this job, said it was a chance to clean things up. I'd defended us from the outside, now I could do it from the inside."

I see Matthew Sterling, standing in the doorway of his kitchen while his son cowers behind him. Even if this is all some twisted revenge plot to bring Susan's killer to justice, getting him out of office is the right thing. If he's capable of running some woman off the road and covering it up, what else has he done?

"So no," he says, "it's not because of the money."

"But it kind of helps, doesn't it?"

He snorts, but this bridge between us only reminds me of Caleb, recovering in his room under the guise of the flu, and how I can't tell Moore because he'll tell Dr. O, and if Dr. O knows Caleb's cover's been blown, he might get kicked out.

"Don't make the mistake of thinking you're out of Devon Park just because you're out of Devon Park," he says quietly, as we pull off the freeway into a parking lot near the piers. "These people play for keeps."

I'm more surprised by this than him telling me about his past. It's like some kind of secret, and judging by the way he isn't looking at me, I'm not sure I'm supposed to acknowledge it at all.

As he pulls up to the curb, he tells me he'll wait, but this is more public than Grayson's house, and I don't know how long I'll be. I tell him I'll text when I'm ready to be picked up.

I don't falter as I get out of the car. I'm here for a reason, and it's not just to get a scholarship, or because I owe the school director. It's because Grayson's dad might just be the worst kind of person, and if he is, I might be the only one who can expose him.

CHAPTER 36

The pier in the summer is always brimming with people, and today is no exception. There's an art show going on in the park that lines the docks, and the stalls are filled with everything from jewelry to photographs to paintings.

I make my way toward the water, the sky above turning more gray than white as I step onto the wooden plank walkway in front of pier eight. Blocking my way right is a street performer, a man painted silver, head-to-toe, who's dancing the robot. The techno music from his stereo blasts into me as I pass, and soon I'm standing beneath the wooden arch painted *Pier 19*.

Like many of the piers beyond it, this one is private, blocked by a partition, and two security guards wearing khaki pants and clever polo shirts with anchors on the breast pocket. One holds a tablet, and as I approach, asks my name.

"Sarah Muñoz," I say, using the one Grayson knows. A slow trickle of adrenaline makes my pulse quicken.

"Go ahead," the guard says after a moment, and I saunter past in my wedge heels and blue knit dress, blowing out a tight breath only once I'm out of earshot.

The wooden planks give a little beneath my step, but they're newly finished with a deep brown paint, and the railings on either side don't have a speck of bird crap on them. Twenty yards away, a gazebo stretches over the lake, lifted on the scaffolding over the gray-green water below. I expected some kind of party, otherwise he could have called me to talk, but I'm uneasy to see only a handful of people gathered at the end of the walkway.

Grayson, wearing black pants and a steel-gray collared shirt, has broken from the group and is striding toward me. There's a nervous energy about him that immediately puts me on edge, a tension clipping each step. His gaze shifts over me, never staying still.

"You came," he says, stopping before me.

"I was invited, wasn't I?"

Below us, the waves lap against the wooden support beams.

"What's going on?" In times like this it's best just to get to the point. "You said we needed to talk. Is it your dad? He give you a hard time after I left?"

Grayson doesn't answer. Taking a chance, I reach for his arm, but he jerks back.

"You want to hear something wild?" he asks.

My hand falls slowly to my side. "Sure."

"I don't think Sarah Muñoz is a real person."

This is not good.

"I thought it was weird that you weren't online, but then I ran you through our background check system. There are plenty of Sarahs, but you're not one of them."

I trip up, but only for a second.

"Why would you do that?" I ask.

"Who's Brynn Hilder?" Now his gaze holds mine, and doesn't waver.

I say nothing, but it's hard after this punch to the gut. I want to crumble. I want to run.

I can do neither. Denying it will only make this worse.

"How'd you hear that name?" I ask, Geri's voice in my head. *Don't blow cover.*

"So it's true?"

I expect his anger, but all I feel is his hurt, and disappointment, and that gives me the tiniest shred of hope. He wants to believe I'm on his side. I need to prove that I am.

"I looked for Brynn Hilder, too, but there's nothing. Not even a school ID."

That's because Dr. O had our identities wiped off the Internet when we came to the school. Moore told us that once before a conning class field trip. It helps us avoid situations like this.

"Who told you that name?" I ask again.

"Nobody." He looks away. "It doesn't matter."

"It does to me."

"Why? You're the one lying about who you are. Why does anybody owe you anything?"

His voice is sharp, and when I jerk back he looks behind him to see if anyone at the gazebo has heard. No one seems to notice.

"You're a con artist?" he asks.

Geri. Had she already driven the nail into the coffin before I walked into her room this morning? Panic traces down my limbs as I grasp for a possible way out of this.

"I . . ."

"Were you trying to steal something? Isn't that what con artists do?"

"No." It's too late for me to deny everything; he knows too much. "I mean, they do, but I never wanted to steal anything."

"So what do you want?"

"Nothing," I say. "I didn't think . . ."

He waits, and now the anger comes, turning his knuckles white as he grips the railing.

"I didn't think you'd talk to me if you knew who I was."

He scoffs.

The words rip out of me, water through a broken dam. "I'm not like you. I didn't grow up like you. I'm the kind of person people like you don't look twice at."

"People like me?" he says. "Stupid people, you mean? People who don't see people like you coming?"

"That's not what I meant."

"Who *are* you?" he asks, though I don't think he's looking for an answer.

"I'm Southside, okay? Is that what you want to hear? If I would've told you that from the beginning, one of those rich kids at your party probably would have called the cops." My voice breaks. I can't lose this. I can't lose him. Too much is riding on it—not just my scholarship, but the safety of the others at Vale Hall. If Grayson knows who I am and what I'm doing, he could tell the police. They'd investigate Dr. O. We would all be busted.

The first drops of rain begin to fall, like spots of ink on his crisp, gray shirt.

"You should leave," he says, without looking over. His voice vibrates a little, like he's not fully in control.

"Grayson."

"Leave," he says between his teeth.

This is it. I'm hanging from a cliff, one last finger on the edge.

"What happened with Susan Griffin?"

The lines around his eyes tighten with anger and regret. "Nothing."

"I know she was killed in a car crash."

His face visibly pales. It's like his soul has stepped away from his body and left only a shell of a boy behind.

"Did your dad have something to do with it? Is that why things changed between you?"

"Shut up," he snaps, glancing behind him. "Shut *up*."

"If you tell me, I can help you." Dr. O will make good on his promise, I believe that, even if he didn't tell me the whole truth about this assignment.

I close the space between us, grasping Grayson's forearms. A rain drop slides from his hairline down his forehead. He doesn't even blink.

"Are you with the cops? The press?" He takes a step back, shaking his head. His wrists slide through my grip. "I knew it."

"No. I'm not. I'm just a friend."

"*My* friend?" He chokes on bitter laughter. "You're just like him." *Him.* His father.

"Don't come near me again. People that mess with my family don't get away with it."

The threat is as sharp as a slap. He has the ability to hurt me, maybe have me run off the road like Susan, maybe worse. Does he know people in gangs like the Wolves, like Caleb's mark? Will they come after me next? Right now, anything seems possible.

"*Go,*" he growls.

I am a grenade and he is the pin. I will incinerate if he sets me free.

He waits for me to stumble back a step, then turn, and flee into the fair. Even after I cross the line into the park, I can still feel his eyes on my back. I know he's watching, maybe just to see me burn.

CHAPTER 37

I run until my lungs are on fire, until the sky breaks open in a full downpour. As the vendors scurry to cover their wares with tarps, I collapse on my knees beneath an oak tree, the sides of my head gripped in the vise of my hands as I try to contain the chaos in my mind.

Grayson Sterling knows who I am, and that I was here to con him. My cover is blown, and if I try to get close again, Grayson will find a way to hurt me.

I should call Moore. Tell Dr. O. But all I can think of is Caleb, bruised and bloodied, pleading with me not to turn him in. *I need this,* he'd said, and I get it, I can't go back to Devon Park, to Pete, after finally getting out. But how long can we hide, or pretend nothing is wrong, before our mistakes catch up with us?

I'm kneeling between Piers 22 and 23, hidden from the walkway by a park bench and an overflowing trash can. I can see through the rungs of the seat, all the way to where Grayson and the others still mingle beneath the gazebo at the end of the dock. They're all wearing light colors—white or cream or baby blue. All except him. He's harder to spot in gray and black. He blends with the darkening sky, and the deep stain of the wood.

He knows my name.

A sickness sloshes inside me, hot like acid, scratching at the base of my throat. Geri did this, or maybe Pete. I reach for the hate, pulling it around me like a blanket, but it's thin and shredded by fear.

I don't know what to do.

Retrieving the phone from my bag, I huddle over the screen, swiping through until I see a picture of Caleb's face—he's smiling, pointing ahead at a building near the river. Only yesterday I took this picture, but it feels like weeks ago.

Before I can think too much about it, I've pressed call on his number, and am listening to the ringing of the phone. I'm not sure what I'm going to say, but he trusted me when he needed help, and now I need him, too.

"Hey," he answers, voice rough.

My forehead presses against my knee.

"Brynn?" he says after a moment. "Are you there?"

"Yeah," I say.

A pause.

"Where are you?"

"At the piers."

I hear the rustling of blankets, and then his voice is louder, closer to the phone.

"Are you all right?"

I close my eyes.

"No."

A beat passes.

"Is it . . ." Another rustling noise, and he's alert, urgency pressing through the line. "Is it the guys from yesterday?"

"No. No, it's not that."

"Okay. Hold on. I'm coming to you, okay? Can you tell me exactly where you are?"

His concern makes me feel infinitely worse.

I tell him I'm near the parking lot. When he asks what happened, I can't get the words out. "That's okay," he says. "Get somewhere safe."

On his end, a car door slams. I listen to the rain, punctuated by the sound of his voice. Is he driving? I didn't even know he could.

"I'll be there soon. Keep talking. Stay on the line."

My gaze focuses on a dark figure moving down Pier 19.

Grayson.

He's hunched against the rain, no umbrella to shield him. Every few steps he jogs a little ways, though I can't tell if he's in a hurry, or if he's just trying not to get too wet.

"Brynn?" Caleb asks.

"I've got to go." I hang up.

Grabbing my bag as I rise, I track Grayson as he heads into the park, through the stalls. Before he disappears from view, I'm hurrying toward him, trying not to lose him in the thinning crowds.

Hope sears through me, ripping through the dark inside. This is my second chance, a shot to clear things up. I have to make him understand that I can help him.

Cutting through a stall of knit caps and scarves, I burst out into a new aisle, searching for Grayson. The rain is starting to come down harder; big drops that soak my hair and my dress and run down my face. Finally, I catch sight of him at the end of the row, heading toward the parking lot.

I run then, full out, to where the path leads through a cluster of trees. Just past the curtain of leaves, I slam on my brakes, seeing that Grayson has stopped to talk to someone. A guy with a baggy shirt, stained deep red from the rain. The flat rim of his ball cap is pulled down over his eyes.

They talk for less than thirty seconds, and then Grayson leaves, heading toward a private lot set aside in the parking area. The other guy watches him go, and when his chin lifts I catch a glimpse of his face.

And I turn to ice.

Two choices: go after Grayson, or go after Marcus.

My feet make the decision for me, and soon I'm barreling toward my ex-boyfriend as he heads toward the street. He recognizes me the second before we collide, eyes white-ringed, and mouth spewing three full curses as I shove him back.

"Easy, Brynn," he says, catching himself before he falls.

"It was you." I've lost all sight of Grayson. He's gone, and maybe that's for the best. "You had to tell him my name, didn't you? Pete put you up to it? Or was it all your idea?"

Marcus glances up, as if looking for answers, then back to me.

"Not my fault Sterling was looking to score."

"And you just happened to be there selling."

Marcus adjusts his hat, hiding his eyes.

"So what?" I ask. "You just show up one day, offering up your stupid pills, and happen to drop that I'm not who he thinks I am?"

"Something like that."

My nails dig into the heels of my hands. It had to be him, not Geri. The one guy from home who actually meant something.

"I had a good thing going and you blew it," I hiss. "You ruined it for me."

"*I* blew it?" he tosses back, stepping up. "You were out, Brynn. You should've kept going. Some of us still got to live in the real world. Far as I'm concerned, this is just me getting mine."

"This is Wolves territory!" I shout.

"That didn't matter to you, did it?"

He's listening to Pete, not to himself. If he thought about this, thought about *me*, he'd know I'd never do something so risky.

"You're better than this," I tell him quietly.

"Am I?" His tough exterior is stripped back, and it's just a matter of time before he breaks. "I'm not cut out for prep school, Brynn. I don't get a posse of rich pals. I've got to think about my future, too, you know?"

"Your *future*?" I throw back. "This future selling pills and running stupid errands for Pete goes two ways. Either you're in jail, or you're dead. That's it."

"Least I'll be out then. Like you, right?"

I know he's mad, that these are just words, but they hit like a freight train. These aren't his only options. There are so many places he could go, so many things he could do. I'm trying to fix the gaping holes in my life, and he's just tearing his bigger.

I deflate. And he deflates. Tears are streaming down my cheeks, blending with the rain.

He swears and gives my shoulder a light shove.

"Don't do that," he says. "Come on now. You know the rules."

Stay tough. Never show weakness.

"There are no rules," I say.

A pained look comes over his face, and despite everything, I get it. Those stupid rules are all you've got in Devon Park. Without them, you're lost.

"You know I didn't have a choice. He said I had to."

He couldn't say no to Pete. As much as I hate it, I get it. In Devon Park, Pete's a king, and you don't say no to a king.

"Your mom's okay," he adds. "I saw her yesterday at Gridiron. She's been working doubles. Keeping busy."

He checked in on her, and that means something, even if it shouldn't.

"Better than her being home, I guess," I say.

Over the rain I hear the slam of a car door, and footsteps slapping against the wet cement.

"Brynn?"

It's Caleb, one arm still tight against his side, the marks on his face shadowed by a ball cap with a black raven. He doesn't slow as he approaches; he comes to stand beside me, ready for whatever Marcus might throw his way.

"You've just got them lining up, don't you?" chuckles Marcus.

I wither a little.

"Who are you?" Caleb may be beat to hell, but he's ready for a fight, and that breaks me even more.

Marcus ignores him. "You made Pete look like a fool at River Fest. He doesn't forget stuff like that."

I can't even look at him.

"Come on," Caleb says to me, though he's still watching Marcus.

I start to go, but Marcus moves closer, making me halt.

"Don't make him send me after you next." It isn't a threat, but the opposite. He's begging me not to put him in this position. To leave town. To disappear.

Then he walks away.

CHAPTER 38

The next minutes are a blur. I'm watching Marcus's back as he disappears into the sheets of rain, and then Caleb's before me, his hands on my shoulders. He's saying something about going, and we do. I'm in the Jeep, and he's driving fast, and he keeps squeezing my hand and saying my name like I might try to tuck and roll.

Each memory, each thought, twists an invisible noose tighter around my neck. Pete. Marcus. Grayson. Dr. O. The senator. Susan Griffin.

I don't know what to do.

I don't know what the next step should be.

And then we've pulled over, and the rain is loud against the metal roof of the car. Caleb turns me toward him, and my face is in his hands, and he's telling me to slow down, to look at him, to breathe.

Breathe.

I crumble forward into his arms, crying big ugly tears, but as he holds me against his bruised chest I hear the thunder of his heart, and it steadies me.

And then I tell him everything.

About how I called Marcus to check on my mom, and how she was supposed to come to River Fest. About Pete, and about Dr. O's sister, and how Marcus told Grayson who I was.

I tell him how I miss Mom, and how mad I am at her, because she could do so much *more*, but she's scared. I tell him how I'm scared, too, because what if I'm no better? What if failing this assignment means a lifetime of jobs like Gridiron, surrounded by people like Pete? What kind of daughter thinks that way about their Mom?

He runs his hands up and down my back, and it drags me to a place where I'm safe. Where there is nothing but the rise and fall of his chest, and the rain, pounding against the metal roof of the car.

He takes my hand, and weaves his fingers between mine, and when I finally find the courage to look him in the face, I go still.

He is real, when everything else feels false. His cockeyed hat, his smudged, taped-up glasses. He sees my wounds, even if no one else can. His eyes say what his voice doesn't: *I know.* I feel it when his thumb grazes my jaw, and he brushes the rain-wet hair from my forehead.

I know.

Charlotte told me to be careful with him, but careful isn't an op tion. Careful is a luxury you have when your baseline isn't chaos. When every decision isn't determined by a calculated risk. In lives like ours, you grasp onto those who understand you, or you face every obstacle alone.

With Caleb, I am too far gone for careful.

His eyes roam over my face, dropping to my mouth, making me aware of my lips, and his, and the cadence of our breath. He leans closer, and so do I. His hands are gentle on my jaw, and as his fingers weave through my hair, I slide off his hat and grip his forearms, holding him close, feeling his pulse on the underside of his wrists. He smells like rain, and boy, and my heart is a hammer, striking my ribs.

"Is this okay?" he asks, searching my face for an answer. I

almost laugh, because *yes*, this is exactly what I want. But when I remember Grayson's expectations when I went to his house, I'm grateful.

"Yes," I say.

He doesn't kiss me. He gives a small smile, and then tilts his head and presses his lips to the base of my neck where it meets my shoulder, in the hollow place above my collarbone.

My breath comes out in a shudder.

His jaw has the finest layer of scruff, and the brush of it against my cheek makes my skin even more sensitive. I turn into him, closing my eyes, giving into the softness of his mouth, and his cool, wet hair, and his hot breath as his lips press higher, beneath my ear.

My blood turns to steam, weightless and scalding. My body moves closer, and I gasp as his fingers trail over my shoulder, down my bare arm, and then up my wrist. He moves my hand to his chest, and I feel the way the thin, damp fabric sticks to his hot skin, and how the planes of his body are as hard and angular as his high cheekbones and his jaw.

His hands find my back again, but when they drag down my spine, it isn't with the same comforting intent as before. There's a pressure to his touch, and it burns through my muscles, making me arch closer, bringing a pull low in my belly, like hot taffy. His hand traces around my hip and over the side of my thigh, hooking beneath my knee to drag me closer. Everywhere he touches, there are sparks. A wake of heat that trails behind his fingertips. The car's center console is in the way, and I'm half tempted to crawl over it because I want to be closer. I want his arms all the way around me. I want his chest against mine, and his back beneath my hands.

He seems to sense it, because his hands have grown heavier, and his breath, quicker. He holds onto me like I might slip away if he doesn't. His mouth runs over the shell of my ear, and the tiniest noise slips from my lips.

He turns his face to me, his forehead pressed to mine, his glasses perfectly crooked. I lean closer, *closer*, until I can feel the barest touch of our lips.

It's not a kiss, but somehow it's more.

And then, very slowly, he pulls back.

His hands loosen their grip on my leg and my hair. When we separate, it feels like something is tearing between us, even if he keeps my hands curled in his against his chest.

I don't understand what's just happened. Why he pressed the pause button. Is he hurt? Is he afraid I'm hurt?

"I'm okay," I tell him.

"Yeah," he says. "You're not, though."

He takes a deep breath while I wait for an explanation.

"I don't want to be that guy." He squeezes my hands a little harder.

I hunch back in my seat, torn between finding this kind of chivalry touching or despicable.

"Were you?" I ask. "Being that guy, I mean."

His head snaps my direction. "No."

"Well, there you go."

He shakes his head and laughs, but it ends in a sigh. For a long moment we stare at the front windshield, watching the rain. We're parked off the street somewhere in the city. Through the cascading water I can make out the red outline of a stop sign.

"Henry says you like me," I say.

In slow motion, he tips forward, until his forehead comes to rest on the steering wheel.

"Henry's the worst," he groans.

I smile. "Is it true?"

"Yes." He turns his head to face me. "But sometimes I wish it wasn't."

His honesty, even after everything that's happened today, is disarming.

"Why?"

"Because this thing we do . . . it's complicated."

"Which part?" I pull my heels onto the edge of the seat, hugging my knees. "Owing a motorcycle club, or working with potential murderers, or just generally pretending to be someone else?" My mind shoots to Geri, to her confession about Grayson, and the car seems to get smaller.

"Sometimes the pretend part becomes real," he says, and I'm not the jealous type, but these words are like a needle straight to my heart.

"You and the mayor's daughter?" I don't want to know, but I do.

He stiffens, brow furrowed. "I was thinking more of you and the senator's son."

"Me and Grayson?" I give a half laugh. "There's nothing going on with me and Grayson."

"You sure?" His expression is guarded, hard to read.

I want to assure him I am, but the words don't come as easily as they should. I don't like Grayson, not like that, but it's not as simple as saying I care what happens to him. He's smug, and impulsive, and lashes out when he's backed into a corner, but he's my responsibility. My *job*.

At least, he was.

And now I'm remembering what Henry told me about Margot, how she blew her cover, and Caleb's concern starts to make a lot more sense.

"It was complicated with Margot, wasn't it?"

He settles back in his seat again, one hand hanging loosely on the wheel. "It was very complicated with Margot."

"What happened?"

He takes a breath, then tilts his head back. "We were together for a while. Then she started working with this guy . . . Things changed after that."

"How?"

"She and her mark got . . . close. We'd made a deal not to let it get too far on assignment. It didn't work out that way." He glances in the rearview mirror. "She chose him. She told him everything."

It's easy to forget what's real when you're working, he said to me that night on the stairs.

The rest of the story grinds into place.

"You told Dr. O."

"I tried to get her out of it, but he gave me an ultimatum. The truth about what she'd done, or my expulsion." He looks at me, almost daring me to look away, and I'm reminded of Geri telling me this was survival of the fittest, and Charlotte, warning me to be careful.

My fingers rise to the kiss, still seared on my neck.

Dr. O put Caleb in a hard position, but even so, I can't help the pinch of disappointment. Would he have told Dr. O about Margot had she not betrayed him? I trusted Caleb with everything I've done. If things turn bad with us, will I be the next on the chopping block?

"He kicked her out," I say. *He erased all records she was ever here. Had Moore delete her alias online. It was like she didn't exist.*

"I know how I look," he says. "But before you judge me, there's something I want to show you."

When I nod, he says, "Turn off your phone. The tracking app won't work if it's off."

I turn off my phone, and he turns the key in the ignition.

CHAPTER 39

W hat's in White Bank?" I ask, picturing the last stop at the bottom of the SCTA map as we turn off the freeway. The first time I saw Caleb he was heading this way on the train. That seems a long time ago now.

"You'll see."

This part of town is dingy, the streets dotted with packs of people loitering outside drug stores, churches, and food banks. All of them stare at us as we drive past, putting me on edge. This welcome back to the south side is all I'm going to get.

After a few turns, he pulls into a fenced lot. There's a gate, but it's open right now. The building before us is sandstone, splashed with orange rust. *Wellspring Assisted Living* is painted on the sign over the double glass door entryway.

Without a word, we get out.

In the distance, a siren wails, cuing a bend in my spine and a tightness in my jaw. The front door squeaks as Caleb pushes it inward, and a broad woman in pink scrubs looks up from behind the check-in desk. She's got an irritable kind of gaze, and a nail file in her right hand.

"Caleb," she says.

"Hey Patricia," he answers.

I quickly take in my surroundings: grungy linoleum floors;

seascape prints on the peach-painted walls. The air smells like cleaning products and old people.

We head down the hallway to the left.

There aren't that many rooms in this building, and before I know it, I'm standing before a closed door, perfectly aware that I'm being scrutinized by an old man in a wheelchair against the side of the hall.

Caleb gives me an apologetic look, then pushes inside. A curtain, arced around the door, impedes my view of the room, and he pulls it back to reveal a Japanese woman about my mom's age, with black hair cut to a bob around her chin.

"You're here . . . oh." Her smile melts at once as she registers the wounds on Caleb's face. "What happened?"

"Nothing," he says. "An accident in woodshop. It's not a big deal."

From the way her mouth pinches at the corners, I doubt she believes him, but she doesn't argue. Instead, she turns to me, fixing the upturned sleeve of her white blouse. "I'm sorry. Are you from the billing department?"

I glance down at my blue knit dress, and then to Caleb's casual clothes. We don't exactly look like a package deal.

"She's with me," Caleb says, and the woman glances between us in surprise.

From inside the room comes the steady beep of a machine, and the whoosh of breath like Darth Vader makes in the old Star Wars movies. Two boys sit quietly in chairs on the opposite side of a hospital bed where someone's legs tent the white sheet. One boy is reading, the other drawing. At least they were. Now they're staring at me.

"I didn't know . . ." The woman touches her hair, then brushes off the front of her shirt, though it looks clean enough. She's wearing jean shorts that are a little out of style and thick-strapped sandals. "I didn't know you were bringing a friend," she finishes.

The sign on the dry-erase board over a small table says *MATSUKI* and lists various times and medications.

"Brynn, this is my mom, Maiko," says Caleb. "Mom, Brynn."

Caleb's brought me to see his family.

Unsure what else to do, I reach out my hand. She takes it in both of hers, smiling warmly.

"You're friends from school?" She looks hopeful.

"Yes," I say, glancing to Caleb.

"Are you hungry?"

"I . . ."

"Mom," Caleb starts. She looks up at him, and when he finally sighs she leads me to the circular table, surrounded by two orange plastic chairs.

"I have crackers and soup," she says. "And *omusubi*. That's my husband's favorite."

I glance over to Caleb, unsure if my presence here is really okay.

"It's rice and *nori*," he says, as if this is the answer I was looking for. "Seaweed wrap," he clarifies.

I take one of the seats. Now that I'm clear of the curtain, I can see who's lying in the bed and I bite the inside of my cheek.

An oxygen tube rests beneath the patient's nose, and a large plastic hose has been taped to his mouth. The right side of his jaw and eye are a twisted knot of pink scars, too old to be covered, but too new to blend with the rest of his face. His eyes are closed, and glossy, as if someone's put Vaseline beneath them, and his neck is surrounded by metal plates and screws, holding his head in place.

He is thin, the bones of his bare shoulders protruding above the white sheet neatly tucked beneath his arms.

I am almost certain this is Caleb's father.

Maiko's brows have drawn together at my response, and I wish I could take it back. I didn't know his father was in this condition. I should have waited in the car.

But Caleb brought me here for a reason, and I can't help thinking it's the same reason he called me when he was hurt.

Because he trusts me.

"What would you like?" Maiko asks, and because I don't want to make things worse, I sit, and try to smile.

"I like rice," I say like an idiot.

She beams, and it's Caleb's smile. I can't look away—kindness radiates off of her, and even with his father lying beside us, there's nowhere else I'd rather be.

Maiko motions for Caleb to sit beside me, worry knotting her brows as her gaze slides over his face again. He shakes his head and pulls the seat back for her. After a moment, she takes it, and I don't miss the fleeting wince as she settles into the chair. Opening the Tupperware she brought, she places a triangle of rice, wrapped around the bottom by a strip of dark-green paper, on a napkin before me.

"Those are my brothers," Caleb says, fingers tapping on the back of his mom's chair. "Jonathan and Christopher."

They take this as a cue to get up from their seats and come over.

"Hey," says Jonathan, who must be twelve or thirteen. He's marked his place in a worn paperback of *The Two Towers* with his thumb.

"Nice book," I tell him.

Caleb's lips tilt up, but the strain in his gaze doesn't go away.

"Yeah, it's okay," Jonathan says, in a way that means it's probably his favorite book in the entire world. His ears go pink as he combs his short hair forward with his fingers.

"Are you Caleb's girlfriend?" asks the younger boy—Christopher—who's closer to eight. "He never talks about you."

"Christopher," hisses their mother, which is enough to make the boy's head droop. She gives me a pained look. "I'm sorry about that."

"It's fine," I say, though I'm not exactly sure how to answer. "We're just friends."

Jonathan makes a noise that signifies he knows better, and Caleb smacks him on the head.

"Ow," he whines. "What was that for?"

"Be polite," he says.

I nibble the corner of the rice, avoiding the seaweed part. I've never had *nori* before, and I'm not totally positive it isn't just for decoration.

"Are you studying to be a doctor, too?" asks Maiko. She looks up at Caleb proudly. "Caleb's going to be spinal surgeon."

I glance again at the man in the bed, wondering what happened to him. Saddened, that this must be the reason behind Caleb's future in medical school.

"I don't really know what I want to do yet," I admit. I've always had a goal of getting out, but I never set my sights on what I was trying to get to. All of the possibilities feel like pennies dropped down one of those giant funnels at the mall. If I leave Vale Hall now, I'll have nothing.

"I'm going to be a scientist," Christopher announces. "I'm good at science."

I'm reminded of Charlotte's chemistry lessons, and set down my *omusubi*.

"That's cool," I say. "I made a volcano for my sixth-grade science fair project. White vinegar and baking soda, you ever do that?"

"No," he says, leaving his paper and crayon stub forgotten on the table. "Mom, do we have white vinegar and baking soda?"

She nods. "I think so."

"Those fizz when you combine them," says Jonathan. "You'd probably need food dye or something to make it look like lava."

"Yeah," I say. "You going to be a scientist, too?"

"No. I'll probably just play bass for a metal band or something."

Now I grin, even though Maiko is frowning. Caleb cracks up behind her.

"If it pays for college, I'll consider it," she says tightly. "Now if you wanted to play piano, like Caleb . . ."

"Then I'd be the favorite?" asks Jonathan.

"You wish," says Caleb. Jonathan goes to shove him, but Caleb dodges and drags him into a headlock, ruffling his hair, blinking back the pain as an elbow connects to his side. Christopher hoots out a laugh as their shoes squeak across the linoleum.

"Boys," Maiko says with a wince. She doesn't have to be embarrassed. Seeing Caleb like this with his family feels right. "Your father's resting."

They stop suddenly, and Caleb hunches, shoving his hands in his pockets.

"How long has he been in here?" I hope they don't think it's rude that I ask. I take another bite of rice, this one bigger. It's warm and salty and helps to settle the churning in my stomach.

"Two years in October," Maiko says, which seems like a long time to be in a place like this, until she adds, "Two years before that in the spine center at Mercy." I picture the hospital downtown with the cross on the side that glows blue at night.

Behind Maiko, Caleb pulls Jonathan back and passes him a fold of cash from his pocket. Jonathan quickly tucks it away. The transaction is seamless; it's clear they've done this before.

"Mom, we need to get back," Caleb says.

"Of course." She stands, again with a tiny flash of a pain across her face, and wraps up two *omusubi* in a napkin. "You have a lot of work to do." Her hand reaches up for his cheek, and even though the touch is small, it's clear she loves him. "Be careful in *woodshop*, okay?"

I miss my mom more than ever right then.

"And study hard," she says. "Your dad and I are so proud of you."

He gives her a small smile.

When I stand, Maiko reaches again for both my hands. "I'm glad to meet you. I'm so glad."

"Mom," Caleb says, glancing to the side.

"See ya," says Christopher. "Nice meeting you."

What a gentleman. "You, too," I say.

"If you ever need some dirt on my brother, I'm your man," says Jonathan.

I laugh. "Expect my call."

Now he's blushing. "Yeah. Cool. Or you could come over." He grins. "I could show you the teddy bear Caleb slept with until he was ten."

"That's adorable," I say as Caleb's gaze shoots daggers at his brother.

"If we don't go soon, I'm going to sell Jonathan at the pier for fish bait," Caleb informs me.

"Caleb," Maiko warns.

He doesn't hug or kiss his mom or siblings, but before we leave he gently touches his father's hand. I barely hear him say, "Bye, Dad."

His father doesn't move.

A minute later we're in the hallway, heading toward the exit. He waves to Patricia, and she waves back without looking up. *I'm sorry*, I want to say. *I had no idea*. His stride is so fast I can barely keep up.

When we're back in the car, he exhales, then squeezes the steering wheel so hard his knuckles turn white. A moment later he releases his grip and clears his throat.

"My dad designed buildings," Caleb says. "One day at one of his sites he stepped on a faulty board and fell through two stories of scaffolding."

He's staring at the rundown building in front of us, not offering a single glance my way.

"The first surgery kept him breathing. The second and the third did nothing. How you saw him, that's how he'll be the rest of his life. My mom hopes for the best, but she knows it's not going to change."

"I'm sorry," I say.

His hands fall into his lap.

"We used to live in Uptown. After my dad got hurt, we had to leave. My mom and brothers live in White Bank now. It's closer to her work. She used to teach music lessons." I'm reminded of how his brother wanted to play bass, and how Caleb plays piano, though I've never seen it. He clears his throat. "Now she's with a cleaning service."

No wonder they live in White Bank. A lady on my street had a sister in a place like Wellspring after she had a stroke. Always said they'd be homeless if the government wasn't putting her up.

"She works all the time," he says. "While I live in a mansion."

I remember the money he passed his younger brother behind their mom's back. He must be helping them out.

"It's not as if you're staying there rent free," I say.

The words hang in the air between us. I've crossed a line. I'm about to take it back when he says, "He pays for the hospital room, Brynn."

It takes until Caleb turns on the car and pulls out of the lot for me to grasp his meaning.

"Dr. O covers your dad's care."

This stupid school means more to my family than you understand. I thought he meant that his parents would be disappointed. I didn't realize his dad's care depended on the work he does for Dr. O.

Charlotte told me once that the director had his fingers in different businesses. *Some companies that make medical supplies,* she'd said. Or programs that provide them, like Wellspring.

My head tips forward. I reach for his arm without thinking, knowing now why he can't go to Dr. O about the Wolves. Why he's so afraid of losing Vale Hall. Why, when it came down to Margot or him, he couldn't lie.

If I find out the truth of what you're doing here is exposed, this all goes away.

All of it. Not just Caleb's ticket to med school, but the care his father needs to stay alive.

"It's not the nicest place, but it's close enough to the bus line that she can bring my brothers here after school."

The shame is thick in his voice, and I'm angry on his behalf, for this impossible situation he's stuck in.

"This is where you went during River Fest, isn't it?" I ask.

"Family days are scheduled twice a year. Visits are allowed every other month. That's a long time when . . . you know."

When your dad is in the hospital.

I can't believe they don't make arrangements for him. Surely they'd allow him more time if they knew what his family was going through.

Visitation will be arranged, Moore said when I first got to Vale Hall. Maybe they do know, but they don't want him distracted.

Caleb's gaze flicks my way. "Look. Henry knows, but no one's been here . . ."

But me.

"I won't say anything."

I swallow, suddenly finding my throat tight. The weight of this honor is not lost on me, and neither is his diligence in keeping this secret. Caleb's been here a long time; surely someone would have asked about his family by now. He must have been extremely careful not to let this information out.

My mind turns to his assignment with the mayor's daughter. How did she find out what he had done? Caleb's too vigilant to slip up on a job. Did someone sabotage him, the way Marcus and Pete did me?

Geri. She was Margot's best friend according to Charlotte. If

Geri thought, like Charlotte, that Caleb had gotten Margot kicked out because he was jealous, she might have struck out against him.

"Insurance dropped us after the last surgery," he says, interrupting my thought spiral. "Mom put the house up to pay the bills. When Vale Hall came along, it was the only shot we had." He exhales hard, and then grabs my hand like it's a lifeline. "I will never stop regretting what happened with Margot. But I can't lose this."

He owes Dr. O, just like I do, and Charlotte does, and Moore does. And even if there's some greater purpose behind what we're doing, we still don't have a choice in the matter.

To save ourselves we need to play the game. All of us, even Grayson hiding under his father's roof, even Marcus, peddling Pete's drugs. We become what others want in order to get the results we need.

Which is how I failed with Grayson. When Marcus told him who I really was, I ceased to provide what he craved.

Safety.

You are in the business of telling people what they want.

A thought kindles in my head, a tiny spark that grows and grows, until my blood is pure fire.

"Caleb," I say. "I think I know how to get us both out of this."

CHAPTER 40

The next morning at 7:00 AM, Caleb and I stand outside a dingy bar called Fritz's in East River, the cool air prickling my skin, the weight of our intentions like lead in my bones. I grip the strap of my messenger bag, replaying the plan in my head.

This will work.

This must work.

"You don't have to do this," he tells me, for the tenth time since yesterday.

His tongue darts out over the cut on his bottom lip, now mostly healed. The wound on his jaw looks better, and the swelling is down, but the bruise is a gruesome kaleidoscope of purples and browns. Had Belk seen it when I told him we were heading out before class, there would have been questions. As it was, Caleb had already snuck down to the garage, and was waiting in the Jeep outside while I got us permission to practice cons at a restaurant across town.

Practice something, Belk had muttered, giving me an I'm-too-old-for-this look. Word must have gotten around that Caleb was in my room, or that I came home late with him, rather than Moore, yesterday.

"It has to come from someone else," I tell Caleb. "They're on to you. They have no idea who I am."

"I'd like it to stay that way."

He's staring at the wooden door, scowling at the scratchy yellow words *Open: when I say so. Close: when I kick you out.*

"If we do this, there's no undoing it," he says.

"I know."

You don't cut a deal with the Wolves hoping it works out for the best. You prepare, then you commit, and if things don't go the way you planned, you run for the hills and pray they don't find you.

I force my shoulders back. What we do now will bring me one step closer to getting Pete out of my way for good, and to fixing things with Grayson.

Phase one: make a deal.

"Dr. O's not going to be happy if he finds out," says Caleb.

"He won't."

Adrenaline drips steadily into my veins.

"I'm impressed with the potential you see in us," Caleb says grimly. "If I forget to tell you later, thank you."

He knocks on the door.

Just when I think he's been misinformed about the twenty-four-hour availability of the Wolves at Fritz's, a woman answers. She's in her forties, with dyed red hair and a flannel shirt.

"Yeah?"

"We're looking for Trace," says Caleb. Beside me, he's transformed into the boy I met at the river. His shoulders are back, his gaze hard.

"Trace?" she asks, a smile turning her lips. "I don't know who you are, kid, but unless you got a cut with a wolf on the back, you ain't seeing nobody."

"Tell him Ryan's here to see him. He said to come by anytime."

Her lips flatten into a thin line. Without a grunt, she pulls open the door, and leads us into a small restaurant, a bar covering the entire right wall. The air is warm, and smells like cigarettes and syrup.

"Stay here," she barks, then heads through the door into a back room, leaving us in silence.

Caleb said the men who'd come for him would be here waiting for his solution to their problem. If they had to find him, there would be consequences.

Specifically, pieces of him in the river, so small not even the fish could find them.

The sweet air turns my stomach.

A minute later, the woman is back in the doorway, eyeing the front as she waves us forward. We follow her into a kitchen, where a wall of heat is combatted by three rotating fans on the metal counters. Different machines around us whir or beep. The stove is stained with permanent splatters.

The burly man from the river sits at a small table, wearing jeans and a black leather coat that hangs over his too-tight T-shirt. Though the back is mostly hidden by the chair, I catch a flash of the words *Wolves of Hellsgate* patched around a sneering canine.

Fear slices through me, but I will not give into it. This is a dangerous man, and the only way to beat him is to be smarter.

"Ryan Ikeda," says Trace, sizing me up with a shark's smile while I scan him for a gun or a visible knife, and find none. "You're early. I like that."

"No point in delaying," says Caleb.

"Good." Trace takes a sip of coffee, and then sets the small cup beside a plate of eggs on the table. He passes the woman with the red hair an expectant look, and she responds with a grunt of annoyance, then steps forward.

"Arms up," she tells Caleb. He complies, and she pats him down. Chest. Belt. Legs. Ankles.

She turns to me.

"No wallets?" asks Trace as the woman's fingers slide over my arms and legs. "No phones?"

We left them in the car, parked a block over in front of a restaurant. Caleb said Trace would take them from us—apparently he's paranoid about recording devices, go figure—and if we kept turning them off any time we were together it would raise suspicion back at Vale Hall.

But now we have no way to call for help if we need it.

The woman rifles through my bag, but finds nothing of note. When there's another knock on the front door, she tosses it back to Trace. "We're popular this morning. Don't make a mess in my kitchen."

He chuckles as she disappears back into the front of the bar.

"You brought your friend," says Trace.

"Not really a friend," Caleb tells him, and when I scoff, he winces. "More like a colleague."

"Yeah? How's that?"

"She can fix your problem," says Caleb. "She's good at getting things people want."

Trace's head turns to the side.

"And what is it that I want, little girl?"

He wants my fear. He wants to belittle me, to reassert that he's the king in this room.

So I let him think he is.

"Ryan tells me you've had some trouble getting product into the city recently," I say, tucking my hair behind my ears nervously.

Trace takes another sip. He's giving me the cool stare now, the same I've seen Pete use more than once when a transaction has gone wrong.

"Ryan talks a lot to people he shouldn't," says Trace.

Caleb shifts.

"He says you want drugs. I have drugs."

"Yeah? What kind of *drugs*," he chuckles at the word, like I'm some kid holding a handful of jelly beans, "do you have?"

Beside me, Caleb stiffens, and I clasp and unclasp my hands.

Voices filter through from the front. The woman who works here, and a man. Someone who will hear us shout for help, if we need it.

Unless he's another Wolf, in which case, we're dead anyway.

"Pills," I say. "Any kind you want."

Trace takes another sip.

"And is there a price on these pills?"

"Well, yeah." I fix the bag's strap on my shoulder. "Nothing's free, right?"

He laughs. "You're a funny girl."

I paint myself offended. "Look, if you don't want to make a deal . . ."

"I'm not interested in a few bottles of your brother's ADHD medicine or your mom's antidepressants. Ryan's given you the wrong idea."

I reach into the bag and pull out a bottle of shampoo.

"I use a different brand," he says when I set it on the table beside his eggs and quickly step back.

"Open it."

He does, and sees the pills. With an arch of his brows, he tilts the bottle, the little Ws winking up at me as he dumps some out on the table.

"Well, well." He lifts one and bites off the corner.

He nods, impressed, like someone who didn't expect the cookie he tasted to be quite so good.

"Your colleague is very surprising," he tells Caleb, then turns to me. "Where did you get all these?"

"Nowhere," I say.

He smiles again, then stands. I shuffle back, not even as part of the act. As I bump into the counter, two pans hanging from a rack clang together.

"Give me your bag, little girl."

I hold it tighter against me—I can't show all my cards at once, otherwise he'll know I'm faking. The fans whir, but don't cut the heat. This space is too close. We should have told him we wanted to talk outside, in public.

He holds out his hand. "Now, or you won't leave nearly as pretty."

"Give it to him," hisses Caleb.

I pass it over, pulse thumping in my ears. Inside the bag, Trace finds the other bottle, and a wallet filled with cash Caleb and I just pulled from an ATM. Our payment for Caleb's life.

Trace pockets the bills and sets the bottle beside the first, on the table.

"Very interesting," he says.

"You keep those drugs, and . . . and Ryan goes free," I stammer. "You forget you ever saw him."

Trace laughs. "So *this* is the cost of freedom. Hate to put a price tag on it, but you're not worth much, are you Ryan?"

I freeze. Caleb glances at me. *I told you,* his look says.

Trace reaches for a fork on the table and rolls it between his flat hands.

"I'm paying her . . . I'm giving her a ton of money for all that," argues Caleb, losing his lines.

"Money doesn't fix everything," says Trace, still moving the fork between his hands. He faces Caleb, a flat look in his eyes, and I flash to that man, hanging upside down from the bridge a few months ago. "You've done something very bad. And if you think a few pills . . ."

"It's a ton of pills," says Caleb. He'd choked when I showed him just how many. He couldn't believe what Geri had done. *I never thought she'd do something like this,* he'd said.

"Do you know how much that's worth?" My palms begin to sweat. "Those go for six, eight dollars a*piece* on the street."

"I'm well aware of the worth," says Trace. "And it does not nearly equal what you've cost us."

He jumps at Caleb then, and in a second, has his forearm locked around Caleb's throat. Caleb is taller, and can reverse the move—

I've seen him do it in our sparring practices. But he doesn't. He goes still.

That's when I see the fork that Trace has pressed against his temple.

"Okay." My hands are raised. "Okay, you want more. I get that. I can get more."

Trace's cold, amused eyes turn to me. The plan Caleb and I talked through all night is slipping through my fingers.

"How much more?"

I glance to Caleb, heart pounding. The points of the fork are pressed against his skin, making tiny red divots.

"As much as you want."

Caleb grunts in pain.

"Stop!" I shout. "Whatever you want, I'll get it."

This is a promise I can't keep, but Caleb's life is on the line, and I will promise anything I have to.

"I want everything," says Trace. "I want your supplier."

"Okay." The answer is automatic. *I'll give you anything, just let him go.*

"What are you doing?" Caleb hisses, still clinging to a script that just went out the window. The soles of his Chucks squeak against the linoleum floor as Trace jerks him tighter.

"Stop!" I shout.

Trace does. He leans his head against Caleb's. He drags the fork down the side of Caleb's face, to just beneath his chin. One thrust up, and it's impaled in Caleb's throat.

"Tell me who's in charge, little girl."

Caleb meets my stare. *"Don't."*

Tears burn the corners of my eyes.

I cannot watch him die.

Trace sighs. "Camille was so upset that you betrayed her, Ryan. When she found me, she said she didn't care what we did with you. Does that bother you?"

Caleb's jaw clenches.

I should scream. Even if it is another Wolf out front, the distraction could give us time. But what if Trace hurts Caleb in retaliation? If I call for help, he could be dead before I find aid.

"Why did you rat out her mother? Were you trying to do the right thing? Or was it the thrill you might get caught?" Trace readjusts his grip on Caleb's throat, and he gasps, cheeks staining red.

I reach toward them, but jolt back as Trace digs the fork into Caleb's throat.

The Wolf looks at me as he whispers his next words: "Did you not think we'd find you?"

"This isn't his fault!" Fear rips the words right out of me. "Someone hired him to watch the mayor. It wasn't even his idea!"

There it is. The truth is out, ringing off the metal pots and pans.

Caleb sags in Trace's grip, and for a moment, there is only the sound of the whirring fans, and the buzzing in my ears.

Defeat slumps my shoulders. "Let him go. I'll tell you anything you want."

"Very good." Finally, Trace lowers the fork. "Now we're getting somewhere."

THIRTY MINUTES LATER, Caleb and I climb into the Jeep, trembling from the inside out. We close the doors, and he hits the lock button. Then he hits it again, just to be sure.

"And that," I say, voice unsteady, "is how you properly execute a pigeon drop."

The glow starts at the deepest, darkest part of me, warming all the cold spaces until a grin finally tilts my numb lips.

Trace thinks he's getting the better end of the deal, but from where I'm sitting, it looks a whole lot like we won.

For now.

Caleb scrubs his hands through his hair, and grins back.

"Did I almost get shanked with a fork back there?" he asks.

"Occupational hazards."

The wheels are in motion. This is only just beginning.

I reach under my seat for my old phone, the one I brought from home.

"Phase two," I say, dialing the number as Caleb begins to drive.

Marcus answers on the third ring.

"It's me," I say. "Get someplace you can talk. I've got a deal for you."

CHAPTER 41

I return to my regularly scheduled program back at Vale Hall. After Caleb drops me off, I tell Moore he's following up with his assignment, comforting the mayor's daughter, then rush to Shrew's class to review our French Revolution tests. At lunch, Charlotte and Henry serenade me with songs from *Les Mis*, and my afternoon is spent beside Sam, video chatting our conjugations of *ir* to our Spanish professor in Mexico City.

It's almost as if I didn't spend the morning begging a gang member not to ram a fork through Caleb's jugular.

Suspicions begin to run high when Caleb returns before dinner and rushes to his room with another supposed bout of the flu. Charlotte claims she saw him nearly barf on the stairs. Henry is convinced Caleb's contracted West Nile Virus and his room should be quarantined. Geri gives me the you're-not-fooling-anyone look as she leaves for her assignment, but I can't even muster an eye roll in response. We're on strange ground since our talk yesterday in her room, but even if we've cleared the air, she still planted drugs on me, and might have exposed Caleb's purpose to the mayor's daughter.

I can't trust her.

I duck into my room as soon as I can, but don't touch my homework. At least twenty times I start to text Caleb, but delete my words before I hit send. We can't risk our messages being read.

Dr. O cannot know what we've done yet. Not until all the pieces are in place.

The night drags on forever. My thoughts move from Caleb, to Pete, to Grayson. I keep seeing his face, warped with fear and betrayal when he learned my name. He's terrified that I'm on to whatever has happened with Susan Griffin. What will his father do if he finds out? Will Grayson be hurt? Will I?

Finally, Paz's thumping radio turns off, and our hall is silent.

Barefoot, in only boxer shorts and my sleep shirt, I leave my room, phone in hand, and tiptoe down the dark hallway toward the stairway that leads up to the boys' wing. My eyes stay peeled for sneaky Ms. Maddox. Downstairs, Belk is banging around in the kitchen, and I hurry faster, just in case he comes up for a hall check.

This is a bad idea. I don't even know which room is Caleb's. Still, I don't slow down. I need him to tell me the rest of his day went as planned.

Luckily, the first door on the right is open, and when I pass, I look inside and see Henry in the glow of his nightstand light, wearing some basketball shorts and an undershirt as he plays some handheld video game on his bed.

He glances up at me and blinks in surprise, then scrambles up and comes to the door.

"You okay?"

I nod. "Where's Caleb?"

The change happens quickly, like a cloud passing over the sun. He's sweet, happy Henry, and then fine lines form around his mouth and his eyes, and his brows furrow in worry.

"Next door." When I go to pass, he reaches for my wrist. "Is he all right?"

I glance down the hall. The lights are off, and there's no movement, just the quiet sounds of piano music coming from Caleb's room. Whatever station he's listening to is a lot milder than Paz's hip-hop.

"Yeah." For now.

The music sooths my nerves, despite Henry's questions. The gentle melody reaches deep inside me, to a place my fear can't touch.

"I know he's not sick."

My gaze finds Henry's, shadowed with the dim light behind him.

"You're taking care of him?"

I nod. He blows out a tense breath.

"We're all covering as best we can, but pretty soon Moore or Belk is going to want to see him."

Henry's words wrap around my chest, and squeeze. Caleb's friends don't even know what's wrong, but they're protecting him all the same.

"I know."

His head drops, hair falling in a curtain over his forehead.

"I'm sorry about the pills."

I haven't fully forgiven him, or maybe I just took a step back in trust. Either way, this cracks my resolve.

"I just wanted to help," he says. "I like having you here."

"I kind of like being here." Minus the whole Dr. O sending us into political warfare thing.

When he lifts his head, he's grinning, and I get the sense he's waiting for me to say more.

"You're forgiven, okay? Don't do it again."

His smile widens. He holds out his arms. "Now's the part where we hug."

"Yeah right."

But we hug anyway. My chin on his shoulder. His arms crossed around my back. I'm not much of a hugger, but I know skill when I see it. Henry's mastered the art of the embrace.

When I can finally detach him, I tiptoe down to the next room, and raise my hand to knock, pausing as the music softens, and picks up in speed. Stops, then continues.

It hits me then that this isn't coming through any speakers. This is real music, pulled from an actual instrument, and it is as impressive as it is heart-wrenching. A whisper through the cracks in the door.

I listen a moment longer, then turn the knob, beckoned by the song. Not until I'm fully inside the room, staring at Caleb's back as he sits at a piano against the far wall, do I remember to breathe.

His posture is perfect, his head tilted forward the slightest bit. As I watch, his hands move gracefully up and down the keyboard. He doesn't even seem to look at what's he's doing. His fingers know the song by heart.

Breath held, I listen, marveling at his skill, moved by how each note pulls at something deep inside me. My father, and the lamp of the cow jumping over the moon. Mom telling me how he tried to get out of Devon Park, telling me to make it work here. Moore's story about how the things behind you don't change. Goose bumps rise on my skin, and I rub at them absently.

And then Caleb stops.

I don't move.

I know the second he registers I'm here, because he scratches the back of his neck.

"Can't sleep?"

"That was incredible."

He spins to face me, then jolts up, grabbing the side of his ribs with a wince. As he straightens, I soak in the sight of him. A white V-neck T-shirt shows the rise of his collarbones. Gray pajama pants are tied low on his hips. His feet are bare.

My mouth is dry.

"I thought you were Henry. He . . ." Caleb clears his throat. "He doesn't always sleep the best."

I wish I knew why. Whatever the reason, I'm glad he has Caleb.

I lock the door behind me. He watches, his jaw turning faintly pink, a color that cues a brush of feathers within my ribs.

Caleb's room is a different shape than mine. The carpet is still beige, and the walls are still cream colored, but the bed is to the left, and the black piano sits in front of a three-part window that looks out toward the pool and the gym. Where my closet would be is his desk, and his laptop sits atop it next to a neat pile of books.

"Did you talk to him?" I ask, the moment soured by Pete's face in my mind.

He nods. "It went just like you said."

"He'll be there?"

"Tomorrow," Caleb says. "Two fifteen."

Phase Three of our plan to save Caleb's life, and my future, is in motion. Now I need Marcus to do his part with Grayson so we can move to Phase Four: removing Pete from my life for good.

It's time to deal with my demons, like Dr. O said.

Then it's Phase Five: Susan Griffin.

Technically, I don't need to stay, but I don't want to go. The room now seems bigger without the music to fill the space, and it seems to take more steps to reach Caleb than it should.

"So, is there anything you're not good at?" I ask.

"Math." He smiles awkwardly, but it fades as fast as it comes. "And basically anything computer related. I missed those classes in Asian training."

"But you're a good driver. There's that at least."

He smirks. "You can't make the jokes. Only I can make the jokes."

I smirk, too.

He moves to the side of the bench and pats the space beside him. When I sit, there's a mixture of calm and excitement that clashes inside me, a rush that only comes in the quiet moments between the chaos.

There's no music on the stand above the keyboard, just his copy of *A Tale of Two Cities*, the one I always see him taking notes in. As I set my phone and the envelope of cash beside it, I can't see it and not think of the way he bites his upper lip when he's writing, or the lines that crease his forehead in concentration.

I scoot a little closer. "Teach me something."

After a moment, he wipes his palms on his thighs, and places his hand lightly on the keys. In a matter of seconds, he's worked through the opening of "Twinkle, Twinkle Little Star."

"Slow down," I tell him, finding the same starting note an octave higher. He presses down on a key, and I follow his lead.

"Not so hard," he says. "Press the key, don't punch it, Devon Park."

With a smirk, I touch the key as gently as possible, then pull my hand back with a flourish of spirit fingers. "Better?"

He snorts, then reaches for my left hand with his right, clasping it, so my palm is against his knuckles. My pulse stutters at the contact, and my cheeks warm, even though no one is here to see.

No one's ever held my hand before.

He turns our hands so that mine is piggybacking his, so that each finger overlaps one of his, and then quietly begins to play.

The way he touches the instrument is soft, almost delicate, and now it's my whole body heating because I can feel the strength in his fingers as they move over the keys, and I know if he touched me, it would be like this.

He plays a melody I don't recognize, but with the movement of my hand over his, it's almost like I'm doing it.

"This is clearly my calling," I say, voice unsteady.

A hint of a smile brushes his lips as he brings in his other hand.

"This is how my mom taught me."

The image of a young boy, sitting on his mom's lap, playing piano, softens the ragged version of my own youth.

"Is that why you don't play much?" I ask. "Because of your mom?"

His fingers slow. He doesn't look up, and that's all the answer I need. I should say something that makes him feel better, but the break in his composure reminds me of everything else going on.

"It's how I met Camille," he says without looking up. "Her mom was looking for someone to give her lessons."

An image takes root in my brain, spreading its cold tendrils. Caleb sitting beside the mayor's daughter. Laying her fingers on his. Teaching her, the way his mom taught him.

My hand slips off his, weaving with my other in my lap.

Complicated. He was right about that.

"I should get back." I rise, and round the bench.

"Wait."

He stands, too, and then we're facing each other in the dim light of his bedroom, the tangle of my thoughts giving way to the stutter of my heart as his hand slowly finds my waist.

"Stay," he says, and pulls me closer.

CHAPTER 42

I don't want to leave. Based on the slow arc his thumb is making over my side, he must be thinking the same thing.

If things go poorly tomorrow, this might be our last night together.

My fingers lift and skim the bandage on his jaw. For a moment, he doesn't move, just watches me. Then his eyes close, and he turns into my hand, his breath hot on my palm. He kisses me there, and then on the inside of my wrist, and when I gasp, his eyes open and flash to mine.

There is wanting in his gaze. Wanting, and hesitation, a combination so familiar it echoes in my chest.

My hand slides back into his hair and grasps the silky strands at the base of his skull. Pulling him down, I rise on my toes, and press my lips softly to his. I don't want to hurt his injuries, but I need him to know that I feel it, too. All the need. All the fear.

His answer is the tilt of his mouth, the parting of his lips, and then there's only the warm, wet feel of his kiss, and his soft shirt, bunched in my fist. His fingers spanning over my waist, pulling me closer, and the tiny sigh that slips from my throat.

My hands slide over his chest and shoulders, and then to his back, reveling in the way he curves around me. His arms pull me closer, and the heat of his skin through our thin shirts turns me to fire. His heavy hand slides down my side and then pauses beneath my arm, right where my bra should rest, and it's almost as though he's just figured out I'm not wearing one, because his eyes open, and his kiss breaks away. There is a question in his dark stare, in his wanting fingertips. And an answer as I press my forehead against the side of his neck.

Our shoulders rise and fall, our breath synchronized.

His thumb, very slowly, skims the outside of my breast.

And it feels sort of incredible.

Then my lips and teeth are on his collar, and my hands slide up the back of his shirt. Every move is dictated by some deeper force inside me yelling *more,* and I don't care if I'm doing this right or if there even is a right way, because trust is bleeding into like, and like is blending with something raw, and consuming, and I know if I stop to think about it, I'll freak out.

With a persistent push, I lead him backwards, and when he collides with the bed he sits suddenly. He looks up, the intensity in his eyes sharpened, mirroring every ragged edge within me. My legs are between his thighs, and his hands climb over my hips, to the waistband of my shorts. I am breathing hard, gripping his shoulders as his fingers sear my skin.

He lifts the hem of my shirt and kisses my stomach, and my waist, and I am burning, pure flames, every muscle tensing in response.

"This okay?" His words are muffled against my skin.

Yes, I think. *Yes.* But I realize he's not going any further unless I say it out loud, so I force the word out. "Yes."

He pulls me onto his lap, my knees bracketing his hips, and we're kissing again, separated only by the layers of our clothes. I'm aware of everywhere he touches me, every place his body is pressed against mine. And we kiss, and kiss some more, and then his shirt comes off over his head, and I can barely swallow because Caleb shirtless is perfect. His bronze chest is a landscape of muscle and bruise and sharp lines. His tapered waist is defined by the swell and dip of his abdominals, and cut by the thinnest line of dark hair that drops beneath his belly button to the low waistband of his pants.

He watches my face, reading my reaction, always careful not to go too far. And it's that look that yanks me to a sudden realization of where this is going, and what I'm feeling, and suddenly, all I can think about is this psychology experiment Moore told us about in conning class. The rickety bridge trial or something, where people crossed either a creaky, rope bridge or a sturdy bridge, and then had to rate the attractiveness of the scientist at the end. People always thought the scientist was hotter after the rickety bridge because they were sweating, and happy, and hopped up on adrenaline—exactly how they'd feel if they were getting it on. Their responses to the bridge crisscrossed with their view of the scientist, and their brains screamed *attraction*, when really there might not have been any, and what if that's happening now? What if the Wolves, and Vale Hall, and everything going down tomorrow has got us so jacked up we're not really feeling all the things we think we're feeling?

Because what I'm feeling is *a lot*.

And if this isn't real, and we keep going down this road, losing him will hurt a million times more than losing Marcus.

"Hey," he whispers, brushing my hair out of my eyes. "Where'd you go?"

I go to kiss him again, to block out the noise in my stupid brain, but he pulls back the slightest bit, holding my face in his hands so he can meet my gaze.

"What if this is just a rickety bridge?" I ask.

Confusion pulls at his brows, then relaxes into understanding.

"It's not." His lips quirk at the corner. "Unless you mean that I look better beat up, in which case, yes, there's a good chance this is nothing but a rickety bridge."

He smooths down my rumpled shirt, and I know it's stupid to be disappointed that the moment's gone when I'm the reason behind it, but I am.

"I like you," he says quietly.

"Why?"

His hands drop to my knees. "Why do I like you?"

He seems confused, as if this is a strange thing to ask, but I know me, and I know I'm not easy to get along with. I'm harsh, overly truthful at the wrong times, and I don't know how to flirt when it's not part of some act. Besides lying, I'm not even particularly good at anything.

"Why are you saying it?" I shift off his lap, and then I'm standing, hugging my elbows, feeling like something's going to crack open and spill inside me if I don't hold myself together. "We're con artists. We say things to make people believe whatever we want. We get rewarded for it."

I've stung him. I can see it in his face. He stands, reaching for his shirt. He winces as he shoves it over his head, but I don't help him. I can't let go of my own elbows.

"We're not con artists all the time," he says.

He goes to the piano and grabs the book on the music stand, and just when I'm positive I've really screwed this up, he thrusts it toward me.

I don't understand, but I take it anyway.

"Open it."

I do, starting at the beginning, and flipping through the pages. His writing starts appearing at chapter three—the notes I always see him taking during class, or while we're all studying.

Only they aren't notes at all. They're sketches.

They're drawings of buildings. Houses along the bottom margin, skyscrapers along the side. I turn a few more pages and there's more—a meticulously detailed building that looks like Mercy hospital, complete with the large cross on the side. Each window is perfectly symmetrical, penned with a steady hand.

There's a parking garage on the next page, and then more towers. All different kinds of towers. Ones like those we saw in Uptown.

Others like I've never seen before. Some of them look realistic, some like they belong in the distant future.

It's as if I've opened his private journal, and I know I should close it, but I can't. He doesn't stop me, either. I hear him shift beside me. Hear his breathing change.

"These are really good."

His fingers drum a cadence on his thighs.

"I'm serious. These could be blueprints or something. You could do this for real."

"It's not exactly part of the game plan."

"What game plan? You could be an architect. Build things, like your dad . . ." I fade off as his gaze falls. "That's why it's not part of the plan, isn't it? Because he got hurt."

Now he's the one crossing his arms. "I'm going to med school after my undergrad. Then I'll be a surgeon, and I can fix people like him."

His eyes don't change, don't light up the way they did on the river when he pointed out all the different buildings.

Caleb lets Henry come in here when he can't sleep. He tried to help Margot, even if it didn't work out. He's always taking care of others, even his own family.

"Is that what you want? To be a surgeon?" It's what his mom wants. *Dr. Matsuki.*

"I want things to stop breaking." His words feel like a confession.

"Then build an unbreakable tower," I say. "Put four hundred tubes in it that go to every floor so that the wind can't knock it down. Make it out of solid steel."

He stares at me, mouth open slightly.

It wrecks me, that look. It's like I'm holding his most precious secrets in the palm of my hand.

Exactly the way he has held mine.

"Turn the page," he says, voice rough.

I look down and do as he says, finding a Victorian-style house.

"Keep going."

I flip through more, and more, and stop on page one hundred and fourteen. In the top left corner is a girl—the first person I've seen in this collection of drawings. From the shoulders up, it shows her neck, and her face, turned away.

The ends of her wavy hair brush her collarbones.

Her throat is long and graceful.

I blow out a shaking breath.

It's like looking in a mirror, only one that's been distorted to show only your best qualities.

In this tiny picture, I am beautiful.

"The next page," he says.

I flip to the next, and find the bare bones of the sketch, as if it's been deconstructed. You can still make out my face and hair through the thin page, but the lines are more geometrical, less soft. I can still point out the exact place he kissed.

"The next." His voice is a strained whisper.

On the following page the lines of my neck and shoulders, and the angle of my jaw have been used to create another image. The base of a building, stretching off the top of the page. The slope of my neck has been changed to the smooth, curved siding, and my hair is the splash of a fountain. My throat is a column, and my jaw, a subtly tilting roof.

"I could draw a whole city after you," he says. "It would be strong and beautiful, and it would never break."

I hold the book, open, against my chest.

He takes a step closer. "Lying is something we do, not something we are."

I am still. Unable to move. Unable to breathe as his hand lifts, and his fingers trace the side of my neck.

"When I tell you something, I mean it."

I feel his words like a hammer to my bones.

It's then that my phone begins to buzz on the piano.

I hear it from far away, as if I'm underwater. His chin lifts, and only then do I find the strength to break from this spell he's put me under. Tearing away, I snatch it off the nightstand, catching it on the last ring.

"Hey," I answer, voice shaking. Caleb's eyes are on me—I can feel them warm my back.

"You were right," says Marcus. "Your boy fell for it."

It takes a second to return to where we left off.

"Tomorrow, 2:00 PM?" I ask.

"Rosalind Hotel," he finishes. "He's dying to hear what new info I've got on you. Man, you got under his skin bad."

Still clutching the book against my chest with one hand, I glance over my shoulder at Caleb. He sits on the side of his bed, elbows on his knees.

"You'll bring the stuff?" Marcus asks.

I picture the pills, currently in Trace's possession.

"Yep."

In exchange for Pete's missing stash, Marcus came through. He called Grayson and offered him more information on me, which he'll deliver in a meet-up I will just so happen to attend.

Marcus isn't going to like that I'm not coming through on the deal, but it's for the best.

Phase Three is complete.

"This is crazy, you know that, right?" Marcus asks.

"Crazy's my specialty," I tell him, then hang up the phone.

"Well?" asks Caleb.

There are things I need to say to him; ways I want to kiss him. A million things I want us to do, but in order for that to be possible, we need to make it through the next twenty-four hours.

So I step forward and tuck this Brynn he's found deep inside, until she can be with him again.

Then I do the one thing I swore I'd never do.

I call the cops.

CHAPTER 43

The Rosalind Hotel should be the scene of a black-and-white movie. It's shorter than a lot of the other buildings around, and older, stuck in a different era, with bellmen wearing funny caps and coats with tails, and limos pulling to the curb of the circular drive. A sign boasting the name in glowing lightbulbs hangs above a white overhang at the valet, and flowers overlap from giant blue vases on either side of the glass doors.

Moore sits in the driver's seat of the SUV, navigating our way past the other cars to an open spot beyond the entrance. He's wearing a black suit and crisp white shirt, fancy attire for a glorified chaperone. It occurs to me that he's dressed this way just in case he needs to come in after me, and even if that's the last thing I need, I'm comforted by the gesture.

"I'll be waiting right here," he says, before I can tell him I'll call him later to pick me up. "Keep your phone on this time."

While I'm inside working, he'll be tracking my every move. I have no doubt he'll be keeping a close eye on me after I gave him the slip at the pier.

I swallow down the nerves creeping up my throat. There's so much riding on this—my spot at Vale Hall, the deal with Marcus. Caleb and Grayson's safety. I have one shot to make this work, and if I blow it, all of us are screwed.

Moore waves away a doorman that approaches as I fix my lip gloss in the visor mirror, forcing a steady hand. When I'm done, I tuck it into my tiny purse—one that I borrowed from Charlotte's room—beside my cell phone with the GPS tracking app, almost three hundred dollars cash from Grayson's party and the ballerinas, and a bus ticket I bought this morning online.

Because Moore thinks I'm here as Grayson's date, I'm dressed for the fundraiser in a modest black sleeveless dress and high heels. Gabrielle wore something similar in the senator's family pictures on his website.

I get out of the car, hearing the tires roll over the pavement behind me as Moore pulls into an open space in front of the valet. On my short walk to the building, my teeth are set, my shoulders back. I wobble a little on these ridiculous heels. People are looking— *they know. They see right through me.* A cold sweat dews on my hairline. I grip my purse and force my chin up.

I've got this.

The layout of the hotel is exactly as Caleb described it. Reception is to the left, the bar to the right. Straight ahead through a bank of elevators is an open hall, lit by a decadent chandelier, and filled with men and women dressed to the nines. The room smells floral, and there's a sign propped up on a tripod directly in front of me that says *James. R. Waterford Foundation Event, Third Floor, Ballroom IV.*

I pick up my pace.

Beside the elevators stands a guy in a black suit that hugs his long, lean body. At the sight of him, my mouth goes dry, just as my heart doubles in tempo. He looks down at his phone, adjusting his broken glasses absently in one hand, barely acknowledging me as I approach.

I slow only enough to pass him my phone, which he tucks in his pocket, and to take his and drop it into my purse.

"Moore's parked out front," I say.

"Be careful," Caleb warns, and then he's gone, heading into one of the open elevators while I duck into a crowd.

I don't look back until I've entered a restaurant and walked straight back to the patio exit. Moore's following my phone's movement in Caleb's pocket, straight up to the fundraiser. I'll be back inside before he has a chance to get suspicious. He won't even know I slipped out.

Pushing through the patio doors, I follow the signs and the twisting stone path to the pool. My feet move as fast as I can in these heels, jogging every few steps to get there faster. Soon enough, the blue water appears in the landscaped jungle, a simple rectangle, continued by bright pink tiles.

A wrought-iron fence surrounds the area, and to the left of the gate is a set of stairs leading to a back entrance of the hotel.

Marcus sits on the bottom step, eating a cheeseburger in yellow paper and dressed like his mom's just dragged him to church. When he sees me, he stands, folds the uneaten half in the wrapper, and shoves it into his pocket.

"Hey," he says.

His button-down shirt is a little too big. His pants a little too short. But man, he looks nice. Grown up.

Judging by the way he's checking out my dress, he's thinking the same about me.

"Hey."

Things have changed between us, and as much as I need for this to be a cool, smooth, business transaction, I ache for the carefree boy who used to greet me with that easy grin.

"You got it?" He doesn't look exactly at me.

I nod, but when I pull out the fold of cash, he stares at it, and then swears.

It's time for Phase Four: remove Pete from the picture, and if possible, save Marcus in the process.

"No," he says when he sees the cash. Two-hundred and eighty

dollars doesn't look like much. "Uh-uh. This isn't the deal. You can't change the deal."

"The drugs are gone," I say. "It's this or nothing."

His eyes go wide. He whispers my name. "What are you doing?" he breathes.

"I've got a new deal."

He sinks onto the bottom step.

"Pete's the worst person I know," I say.

"And?"

"And you're not."

He glances to the side. "Spare me the lecture, Brynn. I don't have time."

"Just listen. You keep this up, you'll move on up the ranks. He might have you beating up people who come up short, like he does Eddie. Or stealing the pills from that warehouse yourself. Either way, if you stay clear of the cops, one day you're going to be him."

He pulls at a string on the knee of his worn slacks.

"You're going to be that guy we hate," I say. "People are going to be scared of you. They're only going to be your friend because of what you can give them."

In the distance, I hear the chimes from the Methodist church by the river.

Two o'clock.

Caleb should be in position now.

Grayson will be here any second.

I step closer to Marcus. "You're smart, so you'll move up fast. One day, you'll realize you can't cover all the territory you need to, so you'll hire some kid like you. You'll yank him out of school, and you'll tell him he can make some cash. He'll hate you, but he'll do it because he thinks he has to."

"Maybe he does have to."

"Or maybe he doesn't," I say as the bells go silent. "I've got almost three hundred dollars and a bus ticket to Baltimore."

Marcus's eyes flick to mine, dark and wary.

"You've got cousins there, don't you? Your mom's people?"

He rises, gives me a curt nod.

"Go," I say. "Here's your shot to get out."

His stare is unamused. He's waiting for me to laugh, to tell him this is a prank.

"It's not much, but it'll get you there," I tell him. "Or give the money to Pete and tell him it's all I got from selling his stash. Your choice."

Stepping back, he bumps into the metal bannister, and leans against it as if he's supporting the whole stairway.

I've put him in a bad position, I get that. If he takes this back to Pete, Pete will blame him for my error. He'll accuse Marcus of lying, of helping me, maybe. Worst case, Pete will punish him. Best case, Marcus will never be trusted again.

Or, he can take my deal, and start over.

"My mom," he says after a minute.

"Call her when you get there." I'm pleading now. "Tell her you got in some trouble and had to clear out for a while. She'll understand."

He rubs a hand over his mouth.

"I know," I say, voice breaking. "I know it's hard, but you're better than Pete."

He shoves off the bannister, moving toward me. I think he's going to take the money, but instead his arms come around my back, squeezing me close, smelling like he always did, like Old Spice and home.

"I'm sorry," he whispers. "For all of it."

My elbows are pinned at my sides, but I rest my chin on his shoulder. There's no anger between us now. No Pete. No lies or drugs. No Bloody Brynns. We're both putting Devon Park behind us.

"Go," I say.

He takes a step back.

"Give me your phone," I say. "Pete won't be able to call you that way."

He hesitates, then fishes it out of his pocket and sets it in my hand. He's fidgeting, unable to hold still. In all my life, I've never seen him look like he does right now: disbelieving, hopeful, and scared half to death.

"You got this," I tell him, remembering that day on the stairs outside my house, when he said I was the best friend he'd ever had.

He nods once, and then huffs out a breath.

"Baltimore," he says, and then he tilts his head back and whoops, the sound so loud it echoes off the stone stairs and tears a sob from my throat.

I give him the ticket, and the cash, and I swear I'm shaking apart from the inside out because he *does* have this. He deserves this. He is bright-eyed and ready.

"Go," I say again.

He hesitates at the pool gate, then blows a kiss back at me.

"I'll see you, Brynn."

I hope not.

Then he's gone, taking a big part of my history with him. Taking away the crutch of Devon Park from my life.

I gulp a shaking breath, then another, and soon I'm steadied.

Then, using Marcus's phone, I call Pete.

CHAPTER 44

Pete answers right away, his slick voice hardening my joy.

"Listen up," I tell him. "You and Marcus are done."

"Brynn," he says as I check outside to see if anyone's coming toward the pool. "What a surprise. I was just talking about you."

My ankle wobbles on one stupid high heel.

"I met your boyfriend yesterday."

"I'm sure you did."

"No, really. Tall. Asian. Pretty nice scrape on his jaw, definitely your type."

My hand tightens around the phone. A family's just come to the pool—two toddlers and their dads, one of whom is loaded up with water wings and floaties. I keep hidden behind the elephant-ear leaves of a giant emerald plant.

"Want to know what he said?"

"Nope."

But I don't hang up. My bones feel like they're shaking, plucked like guitar strings. It's after 2:00. Pete should be in Uptown by now.

"Sure you do," Pete says. "He really likes you, this one. Came to my place while we were setting up and told me you got yourself into a real mess." He gives a disgusted laugh, and I can see the way he shakes his head when he's disappointed. "You steal my product, then turn around and sell it to the Wolves? You've got some nerve, sweetheart."

I cringe at the name.

"I don't know what you're talking about." My voice is laced with panic.

"Supposed to seal the deal tomorrow, right? Can only imagine the kinds of strings you had to pull to set that gig up." He almost sounds proud. "Hope you don't mind, Ryan was able to bump that meeting up to today."

"He *what?*"

"Don't be too mad. He did it out of love."

He did it because that was our plan all along. Once Trace saw the volume of pills I'd brought to the bakery, I knew he'd want more. He needed to feel like he bullied the truth out of us, so we let it happen, but in the end, it shook out just as Caleb and I anticipated.

We told Trace I sold drugs for Pete Walsh, and if the Wolves wanted more, they needed to meet with my boss the next day, at 2:15 PM. He'd be at the spot on the river walk where Caleb and I first kissed—right beneath the Rosalind Hotel balcony.

After Caleb dropped me off, he went to Devon Park, where he begged Pete to help me. I'd gotten in too deep with the wrong people—the Wolves of Hellsgate were going to kill me if I couldn't come up with more pills, fast. Since their previous pipeline had closed on account of the mayor's investigation, they were looking for a new supplier, and willing to pay a generous price.

Be it the dopamine and oxytocin, or just good old-fashioned greed, there was no way Pete was turning down that opportunity.

"No," I say, making my voice tight. "No, you can't talk to them. This is my—"

"This wasn't your anything. You lost dibs the minute you stole from me under my roof."

"It's not even your roof!" Even now he has a way of pressing my buttons.

He takes a long drag from his cigarette. From the background comes the honk of horns, and a familiar man's voice, telling him, *It's time.*

He's brought Eddie.

If this goes right, I will kill three birds with one stone today.

"Here they are," Pete says. "Right on time."

"No. Please Pete. This was my score. I'll split it with you."

I whimper even while I'm grinning. He'll be approaching the Wolves now, waiting on the walkway on the other side of the hotel. They'll be a swagger to his step. He thinks he's holding all the cards.

But I'm the dealer.

Pete has messed with my life long enough. He's hurt Mom too many times. He thinks he's so big and bad? Wait until he tries to tell the most dangerous motorcycle club in the city he expects a fair cut of the drug business they're about to take over.

Pete grunts, "You tell Dr. Wednesday, he wants a layer of separation between himself and the Wolves, he doesn't use a teenage girl. He uses me."

Dr. Wednesday?

"You're dipping a little too much into your stash. You're not even making sense anymore." I check the time on Caleb's phone in my purse. 2:06. Grayson will be here any second. I check the walkway to the pool again, but no movement yet.

Come on, Grayson.

Pete groans. "You think I'm stupid, don't you? You think I don't know he brought you in to sell his product out the back door?"

I go still, dread cooling in my veins.

"What kind of cut is Odin giving you?" Pete pries. "What's the high and mighty doctor give his students to sell his pills?"

Dr. O is this Dr. Wednesday he's going on about?

"He doesn't give us anything."

Besides a house to live in, and food to eat, and the best education money can buy. My shoulders slump.

Pete barks out a laugh. "I know you're not that stupid. I raised you better."

"You didn't raise me at all," I snap, but doubt is sanding down the edges of my resolve. "You're confused. The director's not some drug dealer."

He owns businesses, Charlotte told me. *Some companies that make medical supplies, I think.*

No. Dr. O owns programs like Wellspring, where Caleb's dad is. Not giant pharmaceutical companies. Pete thinks the meeting I set up with the Wolves is on Dr. O's orders, some backdoor plan of the director's to sell his pills illegally. Why would he do that if he owns Wednesday? It's not like he's hurting for money.

"Call it what you want. David Odin owns Wednesday, and now you live with him, and just so happen to be selling his product on the street. That's some coincidence, Brynn." Pete adjusts the phone against his cheek, and it scrapes against his stubble. "Kind of makes one wonder how he found you in the first place."

He got my name off a scholarship application. A general form I filled out last Christmas. Just like the ten thousand other kids in Sikawa Public School System . . .

What are the chances that Dr. O pulled my application out of the haystack when a man living in my house was stealing from him?

I know of you, all the same. Isn't that what Dr. O told Pete when he confronted him at River Fest? I just assumed it was a vague, allseeing threat, but Dr. O vetted me before bringing me into his school of secrets. He knew about Pete—Geri said they all did. It wouldn't take much digging to find out where he gets his stash—the little W is right there on every pill.

I shake my head, trying to clear it.

Pete's wrong, I'm not selling drugs for Dr. O, but that doesn't mean Dr. O isn't using me for other purposes, or lying about how he found me.

It wouldn't be the first details the director has forgotten to mention.

It doesn't matter. Pete's trying to get in my head, and I have too much riding on this plan to let it fall apart now.

"Tell Dr. Wednesday I'll be in touch," says Pete. "Right now, I've got to get to a meeting."

My hands are shaking. No, Caleb's phone, on vibrate, is ringing in my hand. He's probably calling to say Pete's not there yet.

A dial tone fills my ear. Pete's hung up.

Distraction or not, Phase Four is complete.

CHAPTER 45

Two minutes later, Grayson comes striding down the path in a navy suit and royal-blue shirt, a prince in this garden of emerald and chlorine.

When he turns at the bench, his gaze starts on the ground, at the shattered phone, and then moves up my bare legs to my dress, narrowing as it reaches my face. In this suit, he looks older, and sharper, and despite our last encounter, I'm relieved to see him in one piece.

"What the hell?" he says.

Before he can bolt, I jump in his way. Our arms brush, and he jerks back, as if I've shocked him.

"I just want to talk," I say, shoving Pete, and Dr. O, and any connection they might have, to the back of my mind. The wheels are already rolling; if I falter now, I chance ruining everything.

It's time for Phase Five: Susan Griffin.

"You set this up?" he demands.

"That's right."

"That guy . . ."

"You won't be seeing Marcus anymore," I say. "He's out of the business."

"Who *are* you?" He says it like a curse, the words edged with frustration. His hands are open before him. It's not the first time he's asked this question.

"My name's Brynn," I say. "I'm from Devon Park, and I used to con people to get money for college."

This level of honesty catches him off guard. Again, he tries to move past me, but I stand in his way. When he bumps against the bannister, he automatically looks down at his suit jacket and wipes the dust off his sleeve.

"I'm not with the cops, and I wasn't hired by any reporters," I tell him quickly. "I was sent by someone to find some things out about your family—things like what happened with Susan Griffin. And if he finds out that I'm telling you this, I'm done, I'm on the streets. I can't even go back to Devon Park."

Grayson rocks on his toes, then heels, back and forth as if he can't hold still. I understand the feeling. Truth is a risk, but it's the only card I have left to play.

"Then why are you telling me?" Grayson says finally.

"Because I want you to know you can trust me," I say. "If you tell me what happened with Susan, I can help you."

That same pale, desperate look comes over him. He shoves his hands in the pockets of his pressed slacks.

"No one can help me."

I step forward. "I can."

"You're a liar," he says, not as an accusation but a fact, and he's not wrong.

"I'm someone with secrets," I say. "Like you. Not everything was a lie, Grayson. I like horror movies. I think your car is ridiculous." I move closer. "I've lived with a guy who scared me."

His gaze lands on mine, checking for confirmation.

"Who is this person you work for?" His tone is wary and thin, but the fact that he's even asking sparks hope inside me. He hasn't walked away yet.

"He . . ." I hesitate, Pete's accusation about Dr. O using me jutting up in my mind. "He's not with the police. He runs his own show." When Grayson scoffs, I step closer. "He gave me a shot when I had no options left. He can do the same for you."

I wait now, my future at his mercy. Images whip through my mind. Ice cream in the pit with Charlotte. Sammy's NYU T-shirt and Henry's hugs. Caleb's fingers gently pressing mine into the piano keys.

I don't want to lose any of it, which means asking Grayson to trust me. Dr. O may not have told me about Susan, but he wasn't lying when he said he'd help.

He was there for me when Pete showed at River Fest. He was there for Charlotte and Caleb's dad.

He will be there for Grayson.

"My dad will kill me if I tell anyone," Grayson finally says, and any whisper of doubt left that Susan's death was an accident, unrelated to the Sterlings, disappears.

"This guy—my boss—he protected me. He can protect you."

"You don't get it." Grayson's voice is sharp enough to make me jump. The echo reverberates off the stone steps, and automatically, my gaze shoots behind him, through the foliage, to where the kids are shrieking in the pool. "I went to the cops. My dad's friends with the chief. He paid off reporters to keep it out of the news. He made the whole thing disappear. Even if I tell you, no one will ever believe me. He could kill me and get away with it."

A cold hand of dread caresses my spine.

"I believe you," I say.

He huffs out a breath and hugs himself, as if he might unravel if he doesn't physically hold himself together.

"Grayson," I say after a moment. "You know my secret. You don't have to be alone with yours."

He looks up at me, caution softening his features.

"You're not lying?" he asks. "This isn't some con?"

"I swear it's not," I say.

He considers this a moment, then nods. He looks sick—pale, with a sheen of sweat across his forehead.

"Not here," he says, glancing back at the hotel. "I don't want to talk about this here."

"Then let's go somewhere." Caleb still has my phone, and should be at the fundraiser, on the balcony that overlooks the river, where Pete and the motorcycle club are meeting. Moore won't know if we take a walk.

Grayson nods, then pulls his keys from his jacket pocket. "All right."

This is happening. He's going to tell me what happened to Susan Griffin. I'll have the information Dr. O needs to solve his sister's murder. Even if the director's intent isn't the purest, he'll definitely help Grayson now, if just to spite the senator.

My mind turns to Caleb. I will him all the good luck I can spare.

"Let's go," I tell Grayson.

He nods, as if trying to convince himself of something, and then leads me back into the lobby, through to the second floor, to a deserted corner where a black Porsche 911 Carrera is parked.

"Can't trust valet not to dent your mirrors," he says. "Those people drive like maniacs."

I open the door and slide into the front seat.

I'LL SAY THIS about the Porsche. It's *fast*.

He pulls out of the parking garage onto Third Street and takes a series of turns before getting on the highway. I don't even have time to look for Moore, or make sure he doesn't see me. Once Grayson's on the open road, he guns it, zipping in and out of traffic like the cops are on our tails.

"Where are we going?" I call over the growl of the engine. The soft leather seat vibrates beneath me, and I pull my seatbelt a little tighter as he tailgates a minivan, then lays on the horn until it swerves into the slow lane.

"It's not far from here."

"What isn't?"

"The place where it happened."

Sickness pools in my stomach.

"Where Susan died?"

He looks over, nods anxiously. Sweat has darkened the collar of his blue dress shirt. He reaches for his tie and pulls the knot from side to side to loosen it, then flicks open the top button of his shirt with one hand.

"You have to see it to understand," he says. "It doesn't make sense unless you see it."

Why? I want to ask. *Why do we have to go there? Why do I need to see it?* But what comes out of my mouth is, "You were there?"

"Of course I was there."

Now that he's telling me, he's holding nothing back.

Now that he's telling me, I'm not sure I want to hear.

"Was it an accident?" I ask, trying to be calm. "Or did he do it on purpose?"

"My dad?" He doesn't use his turn signal as he cuts across two lanes of traffic. "You don't get it."

"What don't I get?" I ask.

I look up at the green reflective exit sign just as he takes an off-ramp toward Route 17.

And that slow stroke of dread becomes a fist around my throat, squeezing tighter and tighter.

"He didn't hit that woman," Grayson says. "I did."

CHAPTER 46

The breath rips from his throat in a hard shudder. The promises I made to help him flash through my head. He hit a woman with a car. He killed someone. Dr. O got Charlotte out of jail time for lighting a guy's house on fire, but this is on a whole different level.

"I'd just gotten my license," Grayson explains as we pass beneath oak trees lining the quaint shops on either side of the road. "I had a different car. A Lincoln Navigator." He laughs a little manically. "My mom made me get it. She said it would be safer."

I can't wrap my mind around it. He did it. Not Senator Sterling. Grayson hit Susan Griffin. I didn't realize how sure I was that his father killed her until this moment.

He changes gears, and the engine roars again. Bursting from the town center, we emerge on a double lane road that curves slightly to the right. There is not another single car around.

We pass a road sign that says *Route 17*. Beneath it are the letters *Slow Around Bend*.

I have a bad feeling where this is going.

Subtly, I slip my hand into my bag, wrapping my fingers around Caleb's cell phone. Sliding my thumb across the screen, I glance down and press the message button.

Switching phones was a stupid idea. Leaving the hotel was even worse. No one has any idea where we are, or where we're going. Moore can't track me now that I need it.

"My dad told me I couldn't tell anyone," Grayson says, voice pressured now. He has a hard time catching his breath. "He said I had to keep it a secret. He was running for senator then. Still just a state representative. The media blows this kind of thing way out of proportion. You've seen the pictures online."

"It's crazy," I say, trying to keep him talking. Hand still in my bag, I fumble over the keys, looking for the letter B.

Brynn is the only B name listed. My face comes up on the screen. A picture Caleb took of me at my birthday party playing Road Racers.

911, I type into the message box.

He glances over. "It wasn't my fault."

"No. Of course not," I say, the way I used to agree with Pete when he was agitated, just so things didn't escalate.

"It's not like I wanted to hit her. I was just trying to get her to slow down. She wouldn't pull over, so I tried to get in front of her, and look. See? Look right there." He points to the curve in the road ahead—a sharp right turn. With the backdrop of trees, it appears almost as if the road stops completely. I imagine it's even more treacherous in the dark.

"I see."

My brain frantically flies through my options. I could open the door and jump out, but he's going too fast. I can't call someone without him noticing, and if he gets mad, I'm not sure what he'll do. He slows just a little, then swerves into the oncoming traffic lane. I drop the phone in my bag.

"Grayson," I warn, gripping the seat again. It's impossible to see if there are cars coming from the opposite direction. One could be just around the corner. "I get it, okay? Go back to your lane."

"I came over here to wave her down, but she sped up. I didn't see the turn until it was too late. Look up. See? No streetlights? How can you have a corner this sharp with no streetlights?"

"Go back to your lane."

"I barely grazed her, but she ran straight off the road into those trees." He points to a wooded area ten feet away. Old trees, with trunks thick enough to stop cars.

"Hands on the wheel," I snap.

He swerves back, and the breath tumbles from my lungs.

"Yeah." He frowns. "Right. Here we are."

At the tightest bend in the road, he pulls off the asphalt. The path is overgrown with grass and weeds, and the car bumps over the uneven gravel before it comes to a stop in front of a large oak.

I don't let go of the seat. I don't get out of the car. I don't even unbuckle my seatbelt.

"Is this where . . ." I'm not a coward, but I can't find the words to say it out loud.

He nods, then shuts off the engine.

I picture it then. Him driving around this corner, speeding, shifting gears, waving down a woman too freaked out to stop. He wouldn't have seen the turn until it was too late, and before he crashed, he must have hit her, and sent her careening into this tree.

"Grayson, why were you following her?"

My voice sounds hollow in the quiet.

He looks over, brows pinching together. "I just wanted to talk to her."

Inhaling sharply, I scan the car for something I can use to defend myself. I long for my old knife—Moore took it from me when I first came to Vale Hall.

I grab my shoe, aiming the pointed heel his direction. Not my first choice, but better than nothing.

"Is that . . ." His eyes widen, as if I'm the one acting crazy. As if I'm the one who might hurt *him*. I should get out of the car now.

Run. But the look on his face says he doesn't understand what I'm doing, or why I'm freaking out.

I hesitate, one hand wrapped the sole of my shoe. The other on the door handle.

"I just wanted to show you," he says. "You had to see it, right? You believe me that it wasn't my fault?"

My son is a troubled young man. The senator's words haunt me now, a reminder that maybe I got this all wrong. Matthew wasn't the one I should have been worried about.

Glancing back, I see the sign for Route 17, fifteen yards away. The birds are singing outside. In the distance, I can hear a car's engine, but it's hard to tell if it's on Route 17, or back at the previous intersection.

Slowly, I lower the shoe, but I don't let it go.

"What happened?" I say.

He takes a deep breath, as if he's about to jump into a freezing lake.

Then he tells me.

The first time he'd seen his father with Susan Griffin had been at a fundraising event in the city. He'd known something was off by the way his father touched her when he spoke. A few weeks later, he caught them again, this time in their own house while he was supposed to be shopping with his mom and sister. His father tried to play it off, but Grayson had already seen them together. It was too late.

When Grayson threatened to tell his mom what he'd seen, his dad hit him. He couldn't have this getting out with the upcoming election for senator. Grayson agreed to keep his mouth closed, but only if his father ended the affair.

He did not.

His father started meeting her at restaurants, and hotels, and bed and breakfasts. Whenever he'd announce he had another "meeting," Grayson became angrier, until he realized the only way to stop the relationship and save his mother the humiliation was to confront Susan himself.

He followed her from an event one night at a gallery in Uptown, but was unable to reach her before she got to the car. So he followed her.

And then he hit her.

Panicked, he ran to her window to see if she was okay, and when she didn't move, he drove straight home to tell his father.

"He said he'd take care of it," Grayson says. "He came back an hour later, and said we were never to speak of what had happened. He'd talked to the police and sorted it all out." Grayson stares down at the keys in his lap. "He had the Navigator sold the next day and bought me the Porsche. Like some kind of reward, or . . . or reminder to shut up.

"I couldn't stop thinking about her, though," he says, voice cracking. "That sound her car made when it hit the tree. I tried to talk to him about it, but he wouldn't listen. I went to the police—I told them I had proof I did it, and they called in the police chief, but he sent me home in a patrol car. Dad and I fought that night."

I stare forward at the tree. He stares down at the keys.

"He told me he'd kill me if I ever told another person. If anyone knew what I'd done, I'd be tried for vehicular manslaughter. He'd lose his job. No one trusts a senator who raises a murderer."

The phrase sounds parroted, like something he was told. He suddenly looks out the windshield, teeth bared, like he believes it, too.

Pity is a hot, sharp jab to my side. "What proof did you have for the cops?"

He scratches his hair forward. "Her phone fell out of her car. I don't know why I picked it up. Freaked out, I guess."

"Where is it?"

"I brought it back here after the cops turned me away. It's in a bag, in that tree." He points ahead to the oak, to a hole in the knotted wood, blackened, and guarded by spider webs. "At least it was. I didn't know what else to do with it."

My churning stomach settles. My muscles go still. Clarity, cool and liquid, fills my mind.

If Dr. O had that phone, he could prove Grayson was here the night Susan died. He could prove the senator covered up her murder. He would have everything he wanted.

And Grayson would go to jail.

I look over at him, wrung out and weak, sweat glistening in his hair.

I thought I could con him, but I was wrong.

I thought I could help him, but I'm not sure I can.

In the end, all I can do is be his friend.

"I wish I could take that night back," he says, and then he crumples forward, hiding his face in his hands.

For minutes we sit like that, my hand tentatively resting between his quaking shoulders. The car silent, with only the sound of the birds filtering in from outside.

I know what I have to do.

It's wrong, but I say the words anyway.

"Grayson, you need to go."

His head snaps up at me.

"What?"

"You need to get out of here. You said you wanted to leave, you should leave."

I didn't anticipate saying that twice today, or ever.

"You said—"

"I know," I tell him. "I thought I could, but if you stay, you're going to jail."

Dr. O wants vengeance for his sister's death, and even if he's after Matthew Sterling, Grayson won't walk away from that. This secret that could destroy his father—the cover-up of a woman's death—destroys Grayson as well.

Maybe he deserves it. Maybe he should be punished for what he did.

Maybe he already has been.

I don't know.

I don't know.

"If you leave the phone, the man I work for will have the proof you were there that night. He'll put your father in jail. If you stay, you'll be used against him."

"He'll kill me."

I believe him.

Grayson squeezes the steering wheel. He picks up his keys from his lap, then stops.

In a rush, he gets out of the car and marches toward the tree. Using a stick to swipe away the cobwebs, he reaches into a gnarled hole in the trunk, and removes a dirty plastic bag. I get out of the car and rush toward him.

A small black phone sits in the bottom. It's an old model, like the kind I had before I came here.

He shoves the bag toward me.

I take it, heart pounding.

The key to Grayson's freedom weighs barely a pound.

And then, like a fire's lit under his heels, he stumbles back to his car, throws my purse out the window, and fishtails onto Route 17. The tires squeal as he tears off down the road.

Numb, I press a few buttons on the phone through the plastic bag, careful not to get my fingerprints on it. The screen doesn't light up. The battery must be dead.

What have I done?

"Brynn?"

I startle at the sound of my name, and turn to find Caleb running from the black car parked ten yards back.

"Brynn!"

In a matter of seconds, I'm in his arms. He holds onto me like a tornado might rip us apart, and I squeeze him back, clutching the phone against his back, wishing he would never let go.

"You all right?" he asks. "Where is he? What happened?"

"He's gone," I say.

Caleb sets me down, and blows out a breath, clearly pleased I'm not murdered in the ditch.

"What did I tell you about your phone?" Moore approaches behind Caleb, and I don't miss the dark gleam of a gun in his hand as he tucks it into the back of his waistband. Without thinking, I hide Susan's phone in Caleb's pocket. He doesn't even flinch.

"I need to talk to the director," I say.

Moore assesses me for a long moment, then nods, and motions us back to his car.

CHAPTER 47

This time, when I go to Dr. O's office, I don't sit in the chair across from his desk. We stand and face each other, as equals.

Moore has filled him in on what he knows—how Grayson convinced me to leave the fundraiser with a promise of what happened to Susan, and then ditched me at the crash site. Neither of them know about Grayson's involvement in Susan's death, nor do they know about her phone, currently in the leather bag over my shoulder.

And they won't, until I get some answers of my own.

"Did he tell you what happened?" Dr. O is fidgeting with the crisp lapels of his suit jacket, a hard, eager glint in his eyes. "Did he give you anything before he took off?"

Somewhere in the back of my mind, I wonder what the price of my deceit will be. Reassignment? Expulsion? The gift of a future comes at a hefty cost.

"Grayson told me everything," I say.

Dr. O's hands fall to his sides. "Brynn, now would be a good time—"

"How did you find me?" It takes everything I have to look him in the eye as I say this. Inside, I am wilting, using every bit of strength not to run back to my room, and curl up in my giant bed, so I can spend one more night pretending this isn't what it is.

A giant con.

"I'm afraid I don't understand," he says.

"Was it through a scholarship application? Or does it have something to do with Pete Walsh stealing drugs from Wednesday Pharmaceuticals?"

His parted lips close in a thin line. There is no denial, no reassurance that this is false. He deliberately misled me, and even if I should have expected it from the director of a school for con artists, it stings.

Stupid chemicals, telling my brain I was wanted. That I was part of something important—a piece of this strange, too-good-to-be-true family. He's had me wrapped around his finger since Caleb led me to that train yard in Sycamore.

I shove my hands in the pockets of my jeans—my old jeans, that I changed into upstairs, when I was searching online for the owner of Wednesday Pharmaceuticals.

It's buried deep, but Pete was right. Beneath the lists of managers and board members, affiliates and local distributors, is majority owner, David Odin, PhD.

"Does it matter?" The portrait of Susan Griffin is framed in his shadow, her back slender and fragile.

"Where you come from matters."

"More or less than where you're going?"

It's a challenge, a reminder that he holds my future in the palm of his hand, but I refuse to back down.

"Pete was stealing from you. Why didn't you stop him? Why bring me here? If you think you could use me as collateral—that I can control him—you're wrong. He doesn't listen to anything I say."

"To the contrary," says Dr. O, head tilting forward. "He seems to listen very closely to what you say."

My thoughts stutter at his implication. If he knows Caleb and I sent Pete to meet with the Wolves, he'll know what happened with the mayor's daughter, which means Caleb's position here is at risk, and his dad is in danger of losing his bed at Wellspring.

I hold the bag tightly against my chest, feeling the lump of Susan Griffin's cell phone tucked deep inside.

"That was very clever of you and Caleb," Dr. O says quietly. "Pitting Mr. Walsh against Trace Benson. You've exceeded my expectations. Pete and his friend Eddie are in the county jail right now, did you know? Held on charges of collusion with an illegal motorcycle club."

My muscles jolt in tandem, a silent, screaming joy loosing inside me. My mind echoes with the practiced words Caleb told the police last night.

I was at this bar, Fritz's, on the East Side looking for my dad, and heard these guys inside talking about meeting some guy named Pete at the river. I think it might have been about drugs. I think . . . I think they might be going to kill him or something.

It's worked. Pete's in jail, and tied up with the Wolves, which means he'll be put away for a long time. The man who took my money, and kept my mom and me on eggshells for years, is gone.

But the fact that Dr. O knows means Caleb's in trouble, and I'm in deeper than I thought.

You've exceeded my expectations.

"You used me to get him arrested," I realize, finally registering the pride that lifts his face. "You wanted me to get rid of him for you."

His silence is all the answer I need.

"This was a game to you. *My life* is a game to you."

"That's not true."

"Tell me how it isn't," I throw back.

"Your safety is a priority to me."

My laugh is a cold, bitter sound.

"Brynn," he says, his tone dangerously reassuring. "I told you when you first came here that you were special. I may choose not to disclose everything, but I do not lie."

"Why would you have to? Everyone else does it for you."

He grunts, as if I've struck him, and when he moves to the side I'm left facing Susan's portrait. Turning away, I find Dr. O sitting in a velvet chair in front of the fireplace. He reaches into his pocket, removing his phone to type a quick message, before motioning to the seat across from him.

"Sit down, and I'll tell you what you want to know."

I don't want to sit down. I don't want to have this biting need to believe whatever he says. He isn't here to rescue me. I'm nothing but a pawn to him.

I sit anyway.

"I learned of the breach at Wednesday nine months ago," he says. "We'd had issues with theft for years, but couldn't pinpoint the source until a guard forgot to turn off the security tape when he met a *friend* in the warehouse. Pete Walsh."

I cross my arms over my chest.

"It should have been a simple matter," Dr. O continues. "Have someone contact the authorities, and fire the guard. But I wanted to see how much damage had been done by Mr. Walsh—the pills he was taking are highly addictive, as you know, and I didn't need the press investigating any foul play that might damage the reputation of my companies. So I asked Mr. Moore to look into the matter. He found you."

Nine months ago, I was going to Jarvis, saving money from small cons for college, and trying not to piss off Pete. That seems forever ago now.

"Mr. Moore told me you had a certain skill set I would appreciate. While I researched your life on paper—yes, I did find your scholarship application—I sent a student to do some reconnaissance, to see if you were Vale Hall material."

"Caleb."

"That's right." Dr. O leans closer, hands on his thighs. "That's how you came to be here. Unfortunately, it complicated some things. I couldn't let Mr. Walsh continue to sell pharmacy-grade opiates around the city, but I also couldn't chance police involvement that would lead to you, and in turn, our work here."

I'm having an out-of-body experience. It's like watching a movie of your life—you're the star, but you now know what everyone else is thinking, too.

"Because of this complication, I assigned one of my students to manage the situation while you adjusted to life at Vale Hall."

I think of Caleb, waiting for me after conning class, making me a sandwich my first night on campus. Would he ever have talked to me if our relationship wasn't completely rigged?

There's a soft knock at the door, and Dr. O stands.

"Come in," he calls.

Geri is framed in the threshold, wearing jean shorts and a fitted yellow T-shirt with a logo across the right breast pocket. At the sight of her, I'm boiling. I'm just starting to get answers and she has to interrupt.

"Over here, dear," says Dr. O.

I don't understand what's happening until Geri takes her place beside the director and is close enough that I can see the words *Gridiron Sports Bar* printed on her shirt.

"Hold on," I say.

"Cat's out of the bag, huh?" says Geri, in a light tone I've never heard her use before. "Geez. That took long enough."

Dr. O places a hand on her shoulder. "While you were working on Grayson, Geri was working on you."

I choke.

"Sorry about the drugs," she says. "I was positive we were both going to jail for that one."

"That says Gridiron," I say, pointing at her like a fool. "As in, the place where my mom works." My blood is heating; I can feel the flush creeping up my neck.

"Have a seat, Geri." Dr. O gives her the chair, and then sits on the edge of the fireplace in front of us. "I asked Geri to take some of Mr. Walsh's pills from his house, and then to make it look like you'd stolen them."

I gape at him, her shirt shoved to the back of my mind. "Are you insane?"

He holds up a hand, even while Geri nods *yes.*

"It was necessary to bait Pete. To give him a reason to turn on you, so that you would have a reason to turn on him."

I already had a reason—I had years of reasons. But I wouldn't have done anything to him if he hadn't ordered Marcus to tell Grayson who I was. I would have left him in the past, to sell his drugs. To tear down my mom, piece by piece.

My head hangs forward. I press my fingertips against my closed eyelids, and see the bag of little white pills, and Geri waving smugly from the tent at River Fest.

Dr. O's words from our first meeting in this office echo in my mind. *I take great pride in helping them* realize their full potential.

He set me up to go after Pete. He knew, if given the opportunity, I would deal with my demons.

"Grayson could have been arrested," I say. "He could have taken them. Overdosed."

"You never would have let that happen. Grayson dies or goes to jail, and you don't have much of a job here anymore." Geri waves a hand, like this is obvious. "Anyway, I knew you'd take the pills when you saw the W."

This must be how Grayson felt when he found out I was a con. I don't even recognize this girl before me.

"Geri met Camille when she worked with Grayson last year," says Dr. O. "They ran in the same circles and became friends. Confidants, even."

At the mention of the mayor's daughter, I'm back on edge, images of Caleb's bruises storming through my mind.

A moment later, I realize what he's saying.

"You told Camille about Caleb."

I feel like the wind's been knocked out of me. If I could breathe, I'd stand up and punch her.

"He could have been killed," I growl. "He could have died. We *both* could have died!"

Dr. O slides closer, but I'm standing now, backing away from him. How could he do this? He betrayed one of his own students.

"You were watched the entire time," says Dr. O. "Mr. Belk was with Caleb the night he was attacked. He interrupted before it could go too far."

"You mean before they shot him? Before they cut him up and fed him to the fishes? Wow, you really are a hero."

Dr. O's face hardens.

"Mr. Moore followed you into that bar—*Fritz's*. He was there the entire time."

I remember the bell ringing with a new customer. Even if that was Moore, Trace had a fork to Caleb's throat. Two seconds too late, and Caleb would have been bleeding out on the tiles.

"It was a risk, yes. But this is why I choose my students so carefully," says Dr. O. "I knew you could handle it."

I don't know whether to laugh or scream.

"Why did you expose him? It goes against the entire purpose of the assignment."

"The mayor's investigation will take her out of office," says Dr. O. "The mere suggestion that she's taken money from a group like the Wolves will ruin her, even in a city like this. But it's hard to nail down a group that powerful. They own politicians and members of the police. The men the mayor was caught meeting with are already free. It was just a matter of time before they reopened their operations."

And Caleb and I stopped them, for now, using Pete.

We solved two of Dr. O's problems, because we thought they were ours.

"How could you possibly know we would do what we did?"

"I didn't. Had you not, I would have been forced to take other measures."

I can't even imagine what he's thinking, and he must sense this, because he adds, with dangerous precision, "I prefer to see justice done, but there are other ways to eradicate danger."

His cold fury takes me by surprise and punches me with a new fear.

Is he a vigilante, or a hitman?

I point to Geri's shirt, unable to take my eyes off Dr. O. "Why is she wearing that?"

"I work there," says Geri, with a little wince. "Your mom's been showing me the ropes. Food service is way harder than it looks."

I've been training this new hire, Mom told me on the phone. *Kid can hack the CIA on a phone but can't work a basic cash register.*

I lunge closer, grabbing the collar of her shirt.

"You stay away from my mom."

"Easy," says Dr. O, removing my grasp. "I've asked Geri to keep her busy, away from her boyfriend and the house where he keeps his drugs. Your mother and Geri have been working long hours together. If anything were to have gone wrong, I would have been notified immediately."

I don't like this—I should have known what was happening with my own family—but knowing she's been looked out for while I was gone makes my anger falter.

Dr. O raises his hands, like I'm a skittish horse that needs to be calmed. "Brynn, I know this is a lot to take in, but look at all you've done in such a short time. Pete Walsh won't peddle his drugs anymore. Members of the Wolves of Hellsgate were caught by the police. You've already changed the city for the better."

My shoulders drop an inch.

I should leave. I should walk out of here and never come back. Dr. O is dangerous, and possibly insane. He's playing with us in some master game of chess that might mean our lives if we lose.

But where would I go? Back to Devon Park? To Jarvis High? I can't leave Caleb, or Charlotte, or Henry, or Sam. They are indebted to Dr. O, and if they leave there will be consequences.

If I leave, I will have nothing.

Nothing but the knowledge that I could have done something big with my life, and I chose not to.

Dr. O's hand finds my bicep and squeezes just a little. With a nod to Geri, she takes her leave, and the director and I are alone again.

"I'm sorry I didn't tell you sooner," he says. "But you have earned my respect and my gratitude, and I swear to you, I will make good on the promises I made when you came here, regardless of how things turn out with Grayson Sterling."

With all he knows, I can't believe he hasn't discerned the truth about his sister yet.

"I'm proud of you," he says.

I look up at him, and I want to tell him he can save it, I don't need these shallow words. But there's apology in his eyes, and truth in his tone, and it makes me realize that it doesn't matter if this is a con or not. He is my boss, just like Pete said, and these risks will have their payout.

Trust is mine to keep, and mine to give, and with Dr. O, I must be vigilant.

I open my messenger bag, and remove the phone, still wrapped in plastic. When he takes it, a small frown pulls at his lips.

"That belonged to Susan," I tell him.

As tears fill his eyes, we sit. I tell him what Grayson did, and that the senator covered it up, and how, in the end, it didn't matter what promises I made, Grayson was too afraid of his father to accept my offer of help. He left me on the side of the road and ran.

I don't expect we'll ever hear from him again.

With a quiet, "Thank you," I'm excused. Dr. O remains in a chair in front of the fireplace, staring at his sister's picture on the wall, unmoving.

As I leave, I pass the stone tablet in the corner.

Vincit Omnia Veritas.

Truth conquers all.

CHAPTER 48

A week later I'm sitting on a park bench in front of Barry Buddha, listening to the crickets sing their night song. The air smells like jasmine, and wet earth, and as my bare feet prod through the grass beside my worn-out Chucks, I contemplate how much this summer has changed my luck.

I live and go to school in a mansion.

Pete is gone, and my mom is safe.

I have real friends for the first time in my life.

And next year, assuming I don't bomb my SATs, I'm going to college.

But these things have not come without a price. I will stay at Vale Hall, and I will do what I must, but my eyes are open now. I will work, but I won't be used.

My phone sits in my lap, lit up by a picture of a boy with a red, flat-brimmed hat pulled low over his eyes. He's grinning and pointing to a road sign that says *City of Baltimore*.

Marcus made it out, and as I grin back at his picture, I remember that stupid motivational speaker that crashed into me all those years ago, turning me into Bloody Brynn.

If you want something bad enough, find a way to make it happen.

Marcus and I, Caleb, Charlotte and Henry and Sam—we're finding a way. We're leaving behind the past.

Bloody Brynn is no more. The new me is stronger, and ready for anything.

"There you are."

I turn to see Caleb, striding down the walkway beside the koi pond. In jeans and a simple black T-shirt, he makes my heart stutter, and when he shoves those glasses up on the bridge of his nose I swear my entire body heats ten degrees.

"Barry and I were having a chat," I say, closing the picture and tucking the phone into my pocket.

"He tell you anything good?"

Caleb sits beside me, his knee brushing my knee, his hand unfurling, palm up on his thigh. I place mine within it, and he weaves our fingers together.

I have not told him I let Grayson go. The words sit on the tip of my tongue whenever he's around, and yet I can't find the right time, or maybe the courage, to speak them.

"He's keeping secrets tonight." I nod to the statue's round, golden belly, and wish, wherever Grayson's ended up, he's found some luck.

"That's not very nice, Barry," says Caleb.

I smile.

"You okay?" he asks.

It's an easy question, the kind that requires only an automatic answer. *Sure. Yep. I'm good.* But I can't lie to Caleb, and even if I tried, he would know.

What we did was risky. Trace could have killed him. The Wolves could have come for us. Pete and Eddie could have failed to show at the meeting or realized what we had planned with the police and gotten away, only to lie in wait until I was close enough to strike.

Grayson could have kept the truth about Susan Griffin a secret, or run us both into a tree.

A hundred things could have gone wrong.

But they didn't.

"I don't know," I say. "Are you?"

He settles back in his seat, a small frown playing on his lips. "I'm glad it's over."

But his words weigh heavily, because this is not over. We owe debts, and as long as we live under Dr. O's roof, we will be expected to pay.

"Not everyone gets this kind of shot." I think of Mom's words over the phone. *Whatever's got you rattled, work it out, and don't be foolish enough to look back.*

"No they don't," he says, but the reverence in his eyes make me think he isn't talking about school, but about me. About being *with* me.

A kind of peace settles over me as he brushes his thumb over mine. The risks here may be high, but the reward is life-changing, and whatever I do, I won't be alone. I'll have Caleb and my friends beside me.

"So," Caleb says slowly. "Ms. Maddox made strawberry pie for the party."

I grin. "Petal the platinum pig party pie?"

He chuckles. "Geri insisted we be on time."

She's been strutting around for two days, ever since Moore announced that she clinched the winning spot for this quarter's Vocational Development class competition.

She deserves it. The girl's got skills.

"I guess we should go," I say.

Caleb's smile beckons my own. "Well it's only eight twenty-five, so including travel time, that leaves us a minute and thirty-four seconds to do with what we will."

I don't let another second pass. I grab his face in my hands, and kiss him, letting his laughter calm my fear and guilt, and take me away from everything that happened last week. I kiss him until his laughter stops, and he's the one kissing me. Until the world shifts, and my back is no longer pressed against the hard wood of the bench, but the soft grass of the garden. Until the stars are reflected as tiny white dots in the frames of his glasses, and his soft hair brushes my cheek.

We are ten minutes late, excluding travel time.

ACKNOWLEDGMENTS

Thank you, reader, for taking this wild ride with me. Ever since I first heard the myth of Valhalla—where Odin, god of gods, sends his Valkyries to collect the souls of fallen soldiers to fight in the final battle of Ragnarok—I have wanted to write this story. Of course, I didn't know Brynhildr would be a con artist, or Valhalla would be an exclusive private school where the director sends his students out to gather secrets, not souls, but that's how it all shook out. Welcome to my brain. I hope you've enjoyed your visit.

This book has been a big change for me, and I couldn't have done any of it without a team of really supportive people guiding me, cheering for me, and working diligently behind the scenes.

Joanna, if you hadn't believed I was capable of writing something new and different, Brynn and Caleb would not exist. Thank you for pushing me, for helping me find my voice, and for the countless other things you do, both as my agent and my friend.

Mel, seven books in and you keep making me better (how dare you). Thanks for pushing me, and warning me when it's time to start coping with baked goods (aka preparing for an edit letter). Mostly, thanks for taking the time to know me well enough to say exactly what I need to hear to pull my stories together.

My Tor Teen Team (say that ten times fast!) is incredible. Alexis, thank you for everything you do to support me and my books. You're the best publicist ever. Zohra, you have been such a huge help during this process. Seth, my covers always rock. And of course, my publisher Kathleen—if not for you, my dreams would still be locked in my laptop. I am so grateful for you all.

My friends are the absolute best. Katie, I don't know what I'd do without you. Sara, you are a rare and wonderful friend. Mindee, thanks for keeping my head on straight. Deanna, I depend on you more than you know. Lindsay, you will always be my sister. Thank you to Jaime and Erin and Meg and Kass and all the book friends, librarians, teachers, and booksellers—your support will never be forgotten. And of course, all my jazzerfriends—my books, and my mental health, depend on you.

My family is my rock. My mom and dad taught me to believe in the power of stories, and fed me lots of *omusubi* as a kid, and for both I am eternally grateful. Steve, Elizabeth, Lindsay, and Lisa, you are the best cheerleaders. And last but not least, Jason and Ren—the good things in life are so much better because I get to share them with you. I love you both.